RUTHLESS RULER
The Institute
Book 3

A.K. ROSE

Copyright © 2021 by A.K. Rose

All rights reserved.

No part of this book may be reproduced in any form or by any electronic or mechanical means, including information storage and retrieval systems, without written permission from the author, except for the use of brief quotations in a book review.

Cover Design by Covers and Cupcakes

This book has been previously released as Bruno's Devotion - Cosa Nostra Series and Valachi novella, First Sons Series.

ONE

Bruno

14 YEARS OLD...

"I DON'T TRUST THEM." My father clenched his fist and lifted his head, seeking out his brother. "Not one goddamn bit."

"Neither do I." The low murmur came from the shadows before my uncle stepped closer, then leaned down. "Which is why we need to do this. We don't want to be the only ones standing there with blood on our hands."

I stared at Cillian as I sat in the corner of the room, taking in the splash of silver amongst the black hair at his temple and his big tattooed hands gripping my father's desk.

My father and his four brothers were adopted. The differences between them were vast; Cillian was taller and leaner than Dad, who carried a few extra pounds of muscle.

But they were the same where it mattered. Both carried the cross on their skin, as well as around their necks, a remnant of being raised in a Catholic orphanage before being adopted. And both had a dangerous intensity. One that didn't come from blood, but had been honed by ruthless violence. Violence they'd brought with them from Ireland. Only, Cillian used that intensity to instill fear, and my father, he'd used it to make money.

A lot of money...

He was always pushing us. Driving the Bernardi name harder, faster, expanding more into Ikon City than ever before with guns and mercenaries. And that meant dealing with other families of the Commission, other families who still saw us as outsiders.

As far as I could tell, that's what this *problem* stemmed from.

A betrayal. One we couldn't prove...*yet.*

"The Valachis have as much to lose as we do in this. It was *Michele's* ally who betrayed us. *His* fucking friend who told us he'd get us the kind of connections we wanted, then stabbed us in the goddamn back," my uncle urged, his tone turning deep and dangerous. "So we use them. We use them and we make it so they can *never* use us."

"This cannot be tied to us," my father growled, then glanced my way as I sat in the corner of the room, my focus seemingly directed at my phone. "This entire *fucking* mess."

"And it won't," Cillian muttered, and pushed off the desk, combing his hand through his hair. "I'll make sure of it. Make the call, Adrian. Play nice, and set up the meet for tonight."

"Tonight," my father repeated, then lifted his head and licked his lips.

He thought I wasn't listening, but I was. I could hear the turmoil in this decision. And I *knew* the kind of shit something like this could create. Dad worked hard, spending days and some nights talking with contacts, playing nice. And when playing nice didn't work, then Cillian would step in. I glanced across the room to where Jannick sat sideways on the sofa with his earbuds in his ears as he watched something on his tablet, his lips curled in a smirk before he chuckled.

He didn't give a shit about business, until the mention of '*business*' made the bitches he ran with drop to their knees. He was all talk, my cousin, all sex, cars, and thick wads of money he flashed around everywhere. He was only interested when it suited him...and right now, it didn't suit him.

"Jan," my uncle called.

But Jannick wasn't listening, or if he was, he didn't care. He just laughed, laughing while the room filled with dark, dangerous tension.

"*Jannick!*" my uncle snapped, drawing my cousin's attention.

"*What?*" Jannick yanked his earbuds free, a flash of annoyance crossing his face.

He was three years older than me. Three years that Dad said was barely recognizable. But I saw it. I saw it in the way his face had grown harder and sharper in the last year, his jaw casting shadows across his throat that hadn't been there before. And I felt it in the strength of his blows when we were '*just playing*'. But we were never just playing.

There was always a battle.

Always a fight.

Always him being the eldest son of my father's brother. He said he was in line for the throne. From where I stood, the throne was bloody game anyway. One cousin didn't want to deal with the business, the other was tired of all the blood. It was a brutal game being a Bernardi, and there was no luck of the Irish here.

Everything we had we fought for, *and killed for*.

I winced and settled my gaze on Dad's face as he rose from his seat, snatched his cellphone from the desk, and strode from the study, casting a disgusted look at Jannick as he left.

"Get those goddamn earbuds off your head before I rip them off," my uncle warned as he slowly glanced over his shoulder. "You wanted to be part of this *business,* then *be* fucking part of it, like Bruno's part of it."

My cousin cut me a menacing glare. "Bruno sucks fucking cock," he muttered under his breath.

Anger cut through me, burning and searing. He wouldn't dare say that in front of my father. My uncle whirled on him and strode toward him. I caught Jannick's flinch as his father ripped the tablet from his hand and hurled it across the room like a damn frisbee until it smashed against the wall with a *crack!*

Hate moved through my cousin's eyes as his lips curled in a sneer.

There was a savagery in him, one that carved deeper than it did for the rest of us.

But it was there, seething just under the surface.

I saw it in the way he hurt the girls he slept with, saw it staring back at me when he watched me from across the room. There was something cracked in Jannick. It was more than just being a hothead, and dangerous. Those traits were bad enough. One belonged in this family, but the other didn't.

No, the other would get us killed.

Even I knew that.

Seconds passed as Jannick's eyes shone with patricide. I could see it all, the fury, the blood, the sick hunger. My uncle saw it too, but there was no fucking way he was backing down. Bernardis didn't back down from anyone...*especially family.*

"Apologize," my uncle growled.

Jannick just stared up at him, hate sparkling in his eyes as he sneered. "I'm sorry."

"Not to me...to Bruno."

Jannick threw that savagery toward me and I fought the urge to flinch. "Fuck that," he muttered.

Whack! My uncle backhanded him across the face.

Jannick flew backwards over the sofa arm with the force of the blow and sprawled on the wooden floor. Heavy steps beat like my heart as my uncle strode forward to stand over him. *"Apologize!"*

There was blood at the corner of Jannick's mouth. The bright red smear was mostly gone with a lick as Jannick pushed himself upwards and cut a glance toward me. Only this time, that hate had moved deeper, twinkling in his eyes as he said the words. *"I'm. Sorry."*

"It's fine," I answered. "Don't mean nothin' anyway."

"Anything," my uncle corrected coldly as he straightened, glaring down at Jannick before he turned and cast a careful glance my way. "It doesn't mean 'anything'."

The study door opened and Dad walked in, his dark eyes dull and distant. I saw where Jannick got that rage from now, the river running deep through our line. "It's done," he said to Cillian. "He's meeting us at Townsen's in an hour."

"Then I'll call the Valachis," my uncle declared. "And after tonight, this all goes away."

All what *went away?*

I still couldn't understand what they were dealing with. The Valachis name had come up more than once. I knew they were another family in the Commission, knew that neither my dad, nor my uncle trusted them.

"Bruno," Dad called, drawing my gaze. "Go home with Connor."

I gave a sigh, palmed off to the goddamn nanny *again*. Who gave a shit if he carried a gun?

"Let him come," Cillian disagreed, watching me carefully. "He can sit with Jannick."

It was the first time I'd been allowed to come to a *'meeting'*, the first time I'd been allowed to be anything but a shadow in the damn corner. They didn't see me as the heir, I knew that. That was all Jannick.

Jannick this and Jannick that. Made me fucking sick of hearing it.

That's what three years got you...it got you *my* goddamn seat on the Commission.

It should be me. I wanted to lead, and I didn't want to murder half of Ikon to do it, not like Jannick.

I stared at him as he pushed to stand. No, he wanted to murder the whole world.

"You want to come?" Dad glanced from the blood on Jannick's mouth to find my gaze. "This isn't playtime, Bruno."

Jannick sniggered and muttered, "Playtime," under his breath.

It was my turn to glare at him, before I turned to Dad and said, "It's about time you noticed me here."

From the corner of my eye, I caught my uncle's smirk. "About fucking time, indeed. Better watch out, Jannick. Young Bruno here is about to steal your thunder."

Dad just held my gaze as my spine straightened. It *was* about time, about time he noticed me listening, time he saw me looking when he made the calls and shook hands with '*contacts*'. It was about time he noticed how I wasn't out fucking whores and flashing money. I was *here*, watching him, learning what it took to become a Bernardi living in Ikon City, a city that'd one day belong to *me*.

"Fine," Dad sighed, holding my gaze. "I guess the time *has* come."

"The Valachis..." Cillian began.

"I'll call them now," Dad interrupted. "It'll be interesting to see if he even turns up."

I waited while Dad made another call, this time in front of us. He kept the conversation brief and courteous. "We want an end to this issue. That end comes tonight," he said, staring out of the window at the setting sun.

The man on the other end of the line said something, something that made my father slowly nod and answer. "Then I'm glad we're in agreement. I'll text you the time. I trust you know the way."

He waited for a second before hanging up the phone, then turned to Cillian. "It's done."

"Now we wait," my uncle grumbled.

Dad just nodded. "Now we wait."

TOWNSEN'S WAS a gentlemen's club. Hidden in the upper-class area of Ikon, it was the kind of place we didn't go to. It was the kind of club that ushered high-priced hookers in through the back door, then turned a blind eye to the shit that happened in there with them. Disgusting shit Jannick had been talking about for the last fucking hour as we sat there. Last year he'd seen some hooker squat over this old dude in a ten-thousand-dollar suit and piss all over him.

Sounded fucking disgusting.

But then, what the hell did I know? I was still beating off to Erica Hawkins' Facebook picture from last year. The one I quickly saved to my phone as soon as she posted it, before she could take it down. The one where she laughed and jumped for joy at the beach in her bathing suit, with one fucking nipple peeking out.

"Those women like it, squatting, showing their pussy to everyone in the room. I wanted her to do it to me..." he muttered.

I tried not to let him see how much that shit disturbed me and scanned the shadows of cats as they prowled the garbage cans that sat outside in the alley. From the back seat of the Audi with the black-tinted windows, Townsen's didn't look like much at all. I sighed and tried my best to ignore the cocky bullshit that oozed from Jannick's lips.

"If I had a bitch like that, I'd beat her," he growled, and cupped his cock.

"For someone who gets a lot of pussy, you sure do talk about hurting them a lot." I stared at the back door of the club as shadows shifted inside.

"That's *why* I get a lot of pussy, you pissant," Jannick snapped, lashing out to punch me in the shoulder. "'Cause I fuck them like I *want* to hurt them."

Pain flared with the blow, but I didn't move, watching as the back door opened and Dad stepped out. He was laughing, shaking his head, and pointed to the car where we waited. Two more shadows followed. I knew my uncle instantly, knew the way he walked, with his hands shoved into his pockets, his head bowed as he strode with long, commanding strides.

I shifted in the seat, pushing up as they disappeared for a moment. Was that the guy who'd betrayed us? Was Dad going to threaten him? Pay him off? *And where the hell was that guy, Valachi?*

They stepped out of the dark alley as headlights flared behind us, blinding me from the rear-view mirror...until the lights died. Through our cracked open window, voices slipped in, Dad's and another's. Moonlight barely reached them as the stopped just at the edge of sight.

I don't know why, but I reached up and switched off the interior lights in the car.

"What the fuck are you doing?" Jannick growled, his focus shifting to me.

But I was already moving, already yanking the handle and opening the door as the first blow came.

Someone moved, it could've been Dad, or Cillian. But the guy stumbled backwards, stepping into the moonlight as I climbed out of the car.

"Get the fuck back in the car," Jannick hissed behind me.

But I couldn't, because I understood now, understood all too clearly. Panic raced through me as Dad took a step forward, cocked his arm back, and drove it into the guy's stomach. I stared as the guy dropped to his knees and clutched his stomach. The sickening wheeze reached me as I stood beside the car.

"You should've kept your damn mouth shut, Harrison," Dad snarled. "You go to the fucking FBI about us?"

"No," the guy whimpered, gripping his side and lifting his head to look my dad in the eye. "There's been some kind of mistake."

Cilllian just strode forward and drove his knee into the guy's face.

The *crack* was sickening as he flew backwards and his head hit the ground hard. For a second, he didn't move. Only then did I realize the car behind us hadn't moved. The engine was idling and white smoke drifted from the exhaust, but no one had stepped out of the car.

A low moan echoed through the alley.

The guy Dad called Harrison rolled on the filthy ground.

"You talked to the fucking DEA," Dad growled and flicked open a knife. "Now they have an open file with my fucking name on it."

I froze at the sight of that knife.

Unable to breathe.

Unable to run.

My pulse was thundering, filling my head with the deafening roar as behind us, the rear door of the black car opened. The man moved like midnight, soundlessly, carefully. His black coat practically skimmed the ground as he strode from the car and headed toward my father.

"Fucking hell," Jannick muttered behind me. "That's Michele Valachi."

Michele Valachi.

The way Jannick said his name sounded like he idolized the man. But that man...that was not a man to idolize. He stalked forward, cautiously circling the man on the ground like a wolf flanks his prey.

"You talked about us," Valachi accused. His voice was low, rumbling. "You fucking talked after I called you an ally and vouched for you myself to the Bernardis? What position do you think that puts me in?"

"No." The tortured gasp tore through the night. "It wasn't like that. They forced me."

"Forced you?" Valachi's savage growl seemed to resound like thunder.

The answer was a moan as Harrison tried to push up from the ground. Until Cillian strode forward and drove his boot into the guy's middle, lifting him from his hands and knees to crash back face-down on the ground. This time he curled onto his side.

"You disgust me," Valachi growled, then stepped forward. "I would spit on you if it wouldn't leave my fucking DNA all over this filthy place."

I swallowed hard as revulsion swelled inside me, and I scanned the alley, searching for any movement that wasn't a cat. I'd seen Dad give someone a beatdown before, seen the kinds of injuries a fist to the jaw left behind. I'd seen cracked and broken teeth, swollen noses, even bloodshot eyes…but this…this was no beatdown.

My father opened his palm. The silver of the blade glinted in the glow of the moon as Valachi took the blade. "But know this…you will die in this filthy fucking alley. You'll die like the dog you are. And your family will know all your dirty secrets. I'll ruin you… and I'll enjoy it."

"No," Harrison pleaded, lifting his hand in surrender.

But there was no surrendering…not then.

My father and my uncle closed in. But Valachi had the key…he stepped close and leaned down. The drag of his hand across the man's throat made something inside me clench. Jannick stiffened at the sight. His eyes went wide as Valachi lifted the bloody blade and plunged it down deep into the man's chest before wrenching the blade free.

Hard breaths consumed him as he lifted his gaze to my father and handed back the blade. A nod, and my father stepped forward. *No!* I wanted to scream. But I knew it was too late…it was all too late as Dad slashed and stabbed, then handed the knife to Cillian.

By the time they were done, the heavy tang of blood drifted toward me on the night breeze. The three men stood over the body, then slowly stepped away.

Valachi moved fast, stepping close to my father and fisting the front of his shirt. "Now are you satisfied?"

But my father just met the infernal man's gaze and never flinched. Valachi might be cruel and cunning, but there was something about the Irish, some savage part of our nature that blood and death didn't appease.

Valachi said something low and savage, a spitting of words I couldn't quite hear, and pointed to the body.

Dad didn't shake his head, just answered. I tilted my head, desperate to hear the low, muffled words they were saying.

I caught the flinch from my uncle before he jerked his ruthless gaze to Dad. "Adrian..."

"It's that or mistrust," Dad answered. *Those words I heard.* That or mistrust...what the hell did that mean?

Cillian shifted his gaze to us. Only now did he see us standing outside the open door of the car. Jannick flinched as Cillian's gaze settled on him.

"What the fuck?" my cousin muttered. "What the fuck are they saying?"

Then finally, my uncle nodded.

The faint sound of sirens came in the distance, just snatches on the breeze.

But it was enough to make the three men step backward. Valachi glanced at the knife in Cillian's hand and muttered. "Then it's done. The Valachis and the Bernardis will be aligned. I'll be in touch with the details."

"What the fuck does that mean?" Jannick growled as Valachi strode toward his idling car. "What details?"

I just shook my head.

Aligned.

The word resounded...not comforting in the least.

I glanced toward the dead man.

The man who'd talked.

The man who'd betrayed.

And I shuddered.

TWO

Bruno

I said nothing as Dad strode toward me, just stared at body in the alley while Jannick climbed into the car and waited. The dead dude's legs stuck out in the moonlight, his feet splayed wide. The shine of his shoes reflecting the glow. I couldn't look away, helplessly seized by that glint as the dark pool of black grew wider underneath him.

He was dead...*dead*.

Beaten, stabbed. All done by my family. My family and a man who walked like he owned the night.

But why?

"Get in the car, Bruno," Dad growled as he skirted the front of the Audi and climbed into the driver's seat.

The engine started as Cillian cut across the alley, a savage glint like stars in his eyes as the doors of the car behind us opened and closed, before the sleek black limousine pulled away.

Cillian just climbed in our car as that black beast slowly rolled past. But I couldn't move. Frozen. Scared. The blinding headlights left a white washed-out haze as the car rolled past.

I saw myself in the gleaming paintwork, saw a kid in the glass.

A scared, pathetic fucking *kid*.

"*Bruno*," Dad growled, snapping me from the trance.

I swallowed, climbed in, and yanked the door closed.

"Seatbelt," Dad snapped. "The last fucking thing I need is to do fifteen fucking years for murder because my kid couldn't buckle up."

Fifteen years in prison.

I yanked the webbing across me and snapped the buckle tight as we moved, following the limousine out of the alley and across the street. But the limousine turned right, and we turned left. Dad watched the rear-view mirror as he drove and the needle on the speedometer never once went above twenty-five.

We sat in silence.

Chilling silence.

I shivered, unable to get warm, as Dad slowly drove us home. But he didn't slow at the house, just kept driving to the warehouse where he spent most of the damn time and pulled up alongside Cillian's dark gray Chrysler.

Cillian reached around and handed Jannick a stack of bills. Dad just stared straight ahead and spoke. "Go, both of you. Go to Ace's. Drink, but not too fucking much, okay? No fucking talking. Just find peace with this however you fucking need to. But know that from tomorrow...from tomorrow, you step up. You want to be part of this family? This is how it happens. We make sacrifices...we do the fucking shit jobs. So tonight, you drink, find those fucking demons and make a pact, 'cause tomorrow we get down to business...and Jannick..." My cousin flinched as my father found his gaze in the rear-view mirror. "There will be no answering back on this, you understand me?"

Jannick just gave a nod, his eyes wide, his lips parted.

"Now go." Dad jerked his head toward the Chrysler as Cillian tossed Jannick the keys and growled, "Welcome to the fucking family."

I yanked open the door and climbed out. Jannick did the same, flinching at the headlights as Dad backed away, driving to where I didn't know. But he left us standing next to Cillian's Chrysler, my cousin clutching the money in one hand and the keys in the other.

"Let's go," he muttered finally. "I need a damn drink."

We drove to Ace's, one of the strip clubs our family owned. I'd been here plenty of times before, mostly tagging along behind Dad as he dealt with business. But this time, as Jannick pulled up and parked, it felt different.

The entire night felt different now.

Colder.

Older.

The howl of a siren nearby made me jump as we climbed out of my uncle's car and strode toward the back door of the club. Jannick cut me a sneer, then strode along the alley and lashed out, smashing his fist against the door. It opened in an instant. The bouncer peered at Jannick, then glanced my way before opening the door wide, allowing us entry. "Boys, been expecting you."

"Have you?" Jannick snapped. "Then Bethany better be fucking ready."

Jannick turned into a different beast when he stepped through the door. He became someone cruel, someone who got off on control.

"She is," the bouncer murmured, and motioned us forward.

Movement came from the corner of my eye. A shy little thing came forward, one I hadn't seen here before. She was young, younger than most of the strippers here, dressed in a pale pink nightie with fluff at the edges. The damn thing was see-through... and I could see *everything*.

Her tight little tits bounced as she walked, nipples darker, brushing the fabric as she took a step toward us. Heat rushed to my cheeks as my cock grew hard.

"Fuck, yes." Jannick muttered, watching her. "Take a good look, Bruno, take a good fucking look. I bet you never seen a woman like this."

I had. I'd snuck peeks at the strippers here and in Spade's and King's while they danced and spun, grinding on the pole in the middle of the platform. But this one...this one with her curly blonde hair and her innocent smile...she was different.

My cock twitched as she came closer. I caught the scent of some kind of perfume, cheap, sweet, and overpowering. She smelled like candy, the kind you had as kids.

"Jan," she murmured, and cut me a sweet smile. "Who's your friend?"

"Friend?" Jannick repeated, taking a step forward to grasp the back of her neck. "This is no *friend*. This right here is Bruno Bernardi, my cousin."

Her eyes widened. "Oh."

"Yeah, oh. This motherfucker's gonna be a goddamn badass, you just watch him." He turned and gave me a wink. "But right now, sweetheart," he muttered, that hold around her neck tightening until she winced. "*All* your attention should be on me."

"Yes, Jan." She broke our gaze.

She said it like it was scripted, as though somewhere in the dark past she'd learned the lesson of obedience. Jannick leaned close. "I'm about to fuck you like you've never been fucked before, sweet thing. I'm gonna shove my cock so deep inside you, you'll never want it to leave."

"Yes, Jan," she said, but she paled slightly, turning from flushed pink to a sickly shade of gray.

"Now, get in the fucking back, Bethany."

Her gaze lowered to the floor as she turned and left.

"You want to fuck?" Jannick asked like it was nothing.

"No," I answered. "I don't."

"Then have a drink, and when I'm done, we'll have a few more and get our asses home," he muttered, then cut me a look before reaching out and punching my shoulder before leaving.

I watched him for a second. But the others watched Jannick, too, the bouncers and the girls with their tits hanging out dressed, in G-strings and layers of makeup. They watched him with careful gazes filled with fear, then shifted that focus to me and smiled.

I went through the connecting door to the main club. The deep, throbbing music that reached me sounded more goth than sexy. White flashing lights against a pitch-black room, dancers spun around the pole, twisting around and around, tight tits on display. Images of tonight found me in the brilliance. The alley rose in my mind's eye, the splayed legs. The shine of his shoes gripped me.

"Mr. Bernardi."

I jerked at the name and almost looked for Dad. But the pretty waitress just stood there, a single drink in the middle of the tray, and I realized she meant me.

"You ready?" She motioned toward the hallway to the private room meant for family.

A room where we could fuck and drink. I licked my dry lips and grabbed the drink from the tray as the memory of that alley returned. "You might need to bring a few more."

"Right away," she smiled and gave a nod.

I drained the glass, handed it back to her, and tried not to cough from the burn before heading to the lounge. My steps were muffled by the heavy beat of the music. I strode along the hallway, swept the heavy black curtain aside, and stared at the dancer behind the glass. She was pretty, wearing a detached look on her face. I knew now how that felt.

I sat, drank when the waitress brought four more drinks, and waited until Jannick returned. When he did, he was beaming as he punched me in the shoulder. I knew he'd hurt her, I could see it in his high. His eyes sparkled with cruelty and he smelled like her, like Bethany.

"What did you do to her?"

He drained his glass, then lifted it to the waitress. "Another...on second thought, bring the bottle."

"Yes, sir." The waitress nodded and hurried to leave.

He drank and watched the dancer.

"What did you do, Jannick?"

I didn't know why I cared, why tonight of all nights I decided to understand the full extent of his sickness. And it *was* a sickness, one that was handed down from father to son, like a fucking legacy along with the name Bernardi.

Because I'd just seen my family murder someone tonight.

"Nothing she didn't ask for..." he answered finally, his voice growing deeper, darker as the waitress hurried back, this time carrying two fresh drinks...and the bottle. "Now drink your fucking drink, Bruno."

We drank in silence. I watched the stranger opposite me, then finally realized he wasn't a stranger after all.

I'd been the distant one.

The one who hadn't really seen my family for who they were. I'd thought I did, thought they were businessmen, making deals, shaking hands. But this...this savagery, this I didn't understand.

I drank until my thoughts blurred.

Drank until the horror of tonight faded into the background.

Then I rose and looked down at Jannick, who scowled and continued to watch the dancer, snatched a few of the bills my uncle gave him from the table ...and went home.

The taxi pulled up in the street outside my darkened home. The house was quiet when I shoved my key into the lock and stepped inside, just the low, throbbing hum from the club in my ears. I exhaled with relief, stepped inside, and closed and locked the door. I didn't want to see him, didn't want to see the killer in my father's eyes.

I didn't want to see that darkness staring back at me.

I dropped my head and turned for the stairs. But the moment I stepped onto the first stair, a deep rumble came from the corner of the room. "You think I'm a bad man?"

I flinched, my heart hammering. I hadn't seen him standing there...hadn't heard a damn thing.

This man wasn't my dad...not the one I knew. This man was lethal and unmerciful. He was dangerous...*really fucking dangerous,* and I didn't know how to handle it. "Yes," I answered, the truth burning inside me.

"I'm not a bad man, Bruno." He pushed off the wall and strode toward me in the dark. "Just a man. The sooner you figure that out about yourself, the better you'll sleep at night."

I knew what it meant to be on the bad side of him now.

What it meant to wrong a Bernardi.

My breath caught as Dad stepped closer. I couldn't stop the flinch as he lifted his hand, landing it on my shoulder. "Bad men in a badder world. But only bad men survive in the end. Get some sleep, son. Tomorrow, we make plans for an alliance."

An alliance?

"An alliance with *them?*" I couldn't stop the terror from spilling through.

That monster in the dark waited inside my head. Long black trench coat, soundless steps...menacing black limousine. My dad wanted us to be aligned with someone like him...*Valachi?*

"Sleep, Bruno," Dad murmured. "I'm fucking wiped, son."

My hand trembled as I gripped the banister. Everything crashed down inside my head, the killing, Jannick and that sweet young thing in the strip club, and it all swirled around in my mind with the alcohol.

This family...

This family were murderers.

This family was made of bad...bad men.

And I was one of them.

SUNLIGHT BLINDED me as the blinds were jerked open.

"Rise and shine, princess," Dad growled. I lifted my head and scowled at him as he cast clothes across the room to smack me in the face. "Have a shower and get dressed, we leave in two hours."

"Leave where?"

But he didn't answer, just strode from the room. I blinked, yawned, then winced as a throb grew fangs at the back of my head. A moan tore free as I crashed back to the pillow. *Leave... where the fuck were we going?*

Fragments pierced the haze.

A man striding across an alley.

Black boots shimmering under the moonlight.

Blood...the smell of blood so thick it made me flinch.

It had happened. *All of it.* Not just a bad dream.

It was real.

I shoved upwards on my elbow and listened to the sounds of pots and pans clattering from the kitchen. The smell of coffee wafted into my room. He was down there, making breakfast, acting like everything was normal. But it wasn't normal...not anymore.

I pushed upwards, fear bleeding into my world with the sounds from our kitchen. The sun didn't feel as warm now, the glare not as bright. I cast the covers aside, crossed the room, and closed my bedroom door. A tremor cut through me as I hurried for the TV remote, switched it on, and flicked through the channels...*until I saw him.*

The man from the alley.

"Senator Richard Harrison was killed last night in an upper-class area of Ikon. Reports are still coming in at this point, but seems to be a random attack, one his constituents are having a hard time coming to terms with. For now, it's back to you..."

I zoned out, staring at the face of the man I'd seen last night.

Senator Richard Harrison...

You should've kept your damn mouth shut, Harrison. You go to the fucking DEA about us? Dad's words resounded in my head.

You will die in this filthy fucking alley. Michele Valachi's words followed. *Like the dog you are. And your family will know all your dirty secrets. I'll ruin you...and I'll enjoy it.*

I stared at the image of Senator Richard Harrison and knew in my gut this moment would change the rest of my life. We were bad men...bad men in a badder world.

A world we were creating one body at a time.

I left the news report running and strode into the bathroom, cast the clothes Dad had thrown my way onto the vanity, and shoved down my boxers before stepping into the shower.

When I came out, a different news report was running, using the same smiling image of the senator, only this time they cut to an image of his family. His wife stood there shocked, tears streaming down her face as she clutched her daughter against her.

One look at the kid and I froze. There were no tears on her face. Just a stony, cold look of shock. She must be almost my age... almost my age and had just lost her father. I swallowed hard and glanced toward the closed door. *Because mine decided he had to die...*

I dressed, yanking on a white collared shirt and black ripped jeans, before tugging on my black boots and striding from my room. The smell of bacon and coffee hit me as I strode downstairs. It was late...later than I'd expected. A glance at the clock and I winced. "It's two in the afternoon?"

Dad just nodded and served me up a helping of eggs with a side of bacon and a couple of pieces of hot buttered toast. "You looked like you needed sleep. I didn't want to wake you."

Was that the only reason? He didn't meet my gaze as he slid the plate toward me. Instead, he kept busy, wiping those big hands on the towel, then stacked plates into the dishwasher. "I need to go to the warehouse for a while before our meeting. I was hoping you might come with me, I could use a second in charge of the shipments."

A second? So, not only did he not trust me on my own...he wanted to see if I could stand to be around him. "Sure." I stabbed the eggs, chewed, and swallowed, hating the fact that my belly still howled for food, when the idea of being around my family should sicken me.

But it didn't.

I ate my food and put the plate into the dishwasher while Dad got ready.

There was an awkwardness around us, a lull in conversation where there hadn't been before. Dad strode out of the house, and I grabbed my leather jacket and followed, climbing into the Audi. I understood what it meant to have cars like this now, what it meant to have the house and the clubs...and the connections.

"Michele Valachi," I murmured as Dad backed out of the driveway and turned the wheel, pointing us toward the warehouse. "He's dangerous, right?"

Dad cut me a glance, then focused on the road ahead. "Not as dangerous as the alternative."

The alternative. He meant the men the senator was talking to, right?

He meant the DEA.

"This alliance..."

"Don't worry, it's not you," he murmured, pulling out into the steady flow of traffic.

"It's not me what?"

He didn't answer, not right away, and when he did, he strangled the steering wheel. "It's not like you were asking to become the first son."

The words were a punch to my gut. I should've felt relief, should've felt anything other than menacing hunger inside me. *Not the first son*...not the one to take the lead with the Bernardi name. If not me, then it was Jannick. Jannick, with his cruel hands and sickening hunger, Jannick with the mouth that ran about how important he was.

"Tell me what you want him to do," I spoke as that formidable hunger rose inside me. "I want to know everything."

THREE

Evan

"You will not speak."

I swallowed hard as the laces were yanked at my back, tightening the bodice of my dress. I jerked forward, teeth gnashing with the impact, and tried to listen to that desperate growl.

"You will not fidget. You will not meet his gaze unless he asks you to. Do you understand me?"

A flare of defiance burned inside me. *Not meet his fucking gaze?* Still, I lifted my gaze to my father as he stood and those blue eyes met mine. "Yes," I answered. "I understand."

"This is important, Evan," he warned, his tone softening with love. "More important than anything you've ever done."

I glanced at my trophies for archery and dressage that filled the shelf of my room. Trophies I'd earned after years of training, and yet in this moment, none of that mattered. Because now I was reduced to this...to being a woman.

A woman who was to meet the man I was to marry. "Will you at least tell me his name?"

"Bernardi. That's his name."

I swallowed hard and tried to breathe. "Bernardi." The name resounded inside me, echoing like I was nothing more than an empty chamber waiting to be filled.

The lacing was yanked one last time and tied. "There," Jesse muttered before stepping back to admire her handiwork. I tried to smile, looking at her in the mirror, and winced instead. "It's tight."

"It's perfect," she announced.

The dress was a careful choice. The top flowed in long white sleeves edged with lace. The skirt was layered in soft waves that cinched in at my waist. I met my own gaze, my hard brown eyes looking out of place in something so feminine.

But I needed to be feminine.

For *Bernardi*.

"You look perfect," my father agreed and came close, reaching down to plant a kiss on my forehead.

My mom watched from the doorway, tears shining in her eyes. But she didn't step into the room, just forced a smile and turned away. I'd thought she'd stay, thought this would make her happy. That tremble of fear grew bolder inside me, overpowering any excitement.

"He needs to see your potential," Dad whispered, stepping closer. "Do you understand?"

Do I understand?

That's practically all he'd said since we started getting ready. My potential…I looked at the person in the mirror. Not a girl and not quite yet a women. "My potential?"

"Yes, as a wife…and a partner."

But not an heir?

That's what this was really about, wasn't it? I was a woman…a woman, and my father was a very powerful man. I wasn't stupid. Even if he kept me out of all the meetings and the private conversations, I knew more than he thought I did. I often snuck into his office, scanning the pages before he burned them, making a nuisance of myself when those deals went down, and hovering outside the study, or conveniently perching myself on the arm of his chair as he took those calls.

And lately the calls had been about the *Irish*.

Bernardi…Bernardi sounded Irish…

I turned to him, meeting those clear blue eyes, the ones that always reminded me of cornflower blue dresses and clear spring skies. "I wish *you* saw my potential."

He stilled, those eyes darkening for a second before he sighed. "Not this again, E."

"If you just…confided in me, trusted me. I wouldn't let you down and you wouldn't wish for a son instead."

He closed the distance between us and lifted his hand to caress my cheek. "I'm immensely proud of you, never forget that. But we need a line for this family, a male line. If I can't have someone to carry my name, then an alliance is the next best thing. *This* alliance, this is the next best thing. This is what *I* can do for you. This is how I'll make sure you'll always be safe. So I need you to be my girl now, can you do that? Can you be my girl and make this Irish bastard love you?"

I cringed with the words. Make him love me?

Make him love me.

This was his last desperate attempt to fix what was broken...and I was the one thing that was broken. A mold deformed in this violent world we lived in. *In the Mafia world,* a world ruled by men...and not women.

"Please, princess," Dad murmured.

His thumb brushed my cheek, drawing my gaze to his. I knew in that moment he'd never see me, not the real me. Not the woman I *could* be. If I didn't fix this...then Dad's last hope would be lost. "I'll try," I whispered.

He smiled, those darkened blue eyes turned to spring skies once more. "I know you will." He pulled me close. "Because you're a Valachi."

I'm a Valachi...

Those words boomed inside me. *I'm a Valachi...*

If only Dad could hear the sound. If only he'd could know how I trembled inside with excitement. If only he knew my pride. I glanced at the shelf once more, the one filled with trophies and medallions, all engraved with my name. *E. Valachi.*

Dad pulled away, adjusted his shirt, and collected himself. "They'll be here within the hour. I have some light refreshments planned and I thought a stroll through the front gardens for the two of you might be in order...to get acquainted, of course."

I glanced at the window, to the already darkening sky. I'd known something had been up all day. Dad had been locked in the study until a few hours ago, when he called Mom in by herself. He never *called* us in. We were always just *there*. But this afternoon, we'd been summoned, first Mom, then me, and Dad broke the news.

I was to meet the man I was to marry.

There were no questions, none he'd listen to, anyway.

It was done. A family of worth, one who occupied a seat on the Commission.

One who had only sons.

"Sure, Dad," I answered. "Sounds nice."

He smiled...*no, he beamed.* I understood now with cold, cutting clarity how he saw me. I wasn't a daughter, not one he saw as a legacy. No, to him I was a liability, a problem he needed to rectify as soon as possible, and it looked like his opportunity to do that was now.

Did my heart matter to him?

My will...

My desire?

"He's going to be the luckiest man on the face of this goddamn planet," Dad muttered, and took a step away. "He'll know that as soon as he sees you."

In an instant, he transformed. Gone was the doting father, and the proud parent. Those sky-blue eyes turned icy, hard and chilling. Maybe they always had been...maybe this was the real face of my father, the one lurking underneath the pretense of fatherhood. Maybe now I was only recognizing him for the first time.

I swallowed hard, forcing a smile as that chill inside me grew deeper.

"Jesse, you'll come and fetch Evan when it's time. But I want her to walk out on her own. I want the Bernardis to see what a prize they have at their reach. Maybe then they'll realize an alliance can be made by marriage as well as blood."

"Yes, sir." Jesse gave a slow nod of her head.

She was a few years older than me, more than a maid...a paid friend...as long as it suited my father. She was always dressed the same, a white collared shirt and a black pencil skirt that reached below her knees.

If you didn't know any better, you could almost forget she was there. It was like that with all the help. They were there, but never truly seen...*just like me.*

"Good...*good*..." he repeated as he glanced at me one last time and left the room.

The door closed behind him with a soft thud, then I was alone. Even if Jesse was there, I was alone, more alone than I'd ever felt before.

"Evan," Jesse murmured, and took a step toward me.

I swallowed the ache in the back of my throat. "That obvious, is it?"

"He's a powerful man," she started.

I just nodded and turned away, finding those hard eyes in my reflection once more.

"He's just doing what he thinks is right."

He'd never see me, not how I wanted him to. I smoothed my white dress down. Pure, that's how I looked. Pure and virginal. But that wasn't who I was. That wasn't the *real me*.

Make him love you...

My father's words resounded in my head as I turned away from the woman in the mirror and tried to forget who I truly was.

I paced the room, stopping when the glare of headlights cut through the dark and the sound of tires on the pebbled drive slipped through the open window. My knuckles ached as I twisted and squeezed my fingers.

"Relax," Jesse urged as she strode toward the door. "He's going to love you."

She was gone in an instant, leaving me all alone as I answered, "But will *I* love *him*?"

I stared at the door, aware of every flap of the blinds and every degree the night air plummeted, until finally a shadow cut across the bottom of the door. A soft knock and it opened. "It's time," Jesse said carefully.

My pulse spiked, and panicked breaths followed.

I stared at her with wide eyes as she swallowed and motioned me forward. "He's..."

"What?" I hissed desperately. "He's what?"

"Gorgeous," she answered, and exhaled hard. "He's gorgeous, E."

All the tension rushed out of me in an instant, leaving me lightheaded. The edges of my vision darkened, and my hands shook. "Thank. Fucking. God," I muttered, then winced.

My father hated it when I swore, hated it when I didn't act how I looked...*perfect*.

"Come on." Jesse grabbed my hand and tugged me forward.

She was rushing, her steps getting faster and faster as we raced toward the living room off the entrance. The faster we ran, the more I was swept up in her excitement. Fear bled to elation, then I found myself smiling, even laughing as she turned to me, her eyes wide. She was...*elated*.

"Blonde hair, deep brown eyes. An accent. *Holy shit, E. The accent,*" Jesse squealed.

I laughed and raced with her, my flat black shoes slapping hard on the tiled floor. Until we tore from the east wing of our home and headed for the front of the house. Then Jesse slowed and adjusted her shirt, composing herself. I smiled as she cut me a grin, her hand firmly clasping mine.

Then she let me go as we neared the entrance to the house. My hand cooled without her touch. I swiped my damp palm against my dress. I didn't know if it was me who was clammy...or her. But when I lifted my gaze to the towering entrance to the living room, a fresh wave of panic washed over me.

Low voices spilled from the room.

The deep, growling, thick Irish accent made me catch my breath.

My knees shook the closer I got.

I licked my lips and cast a panicked glanced at Jesse, who stopped, falling behind me. She gave a nod and a smile, urging me forward with a wave of her hand.

Make him love you...

I stepped into the room, barely noticing the three other males. My focus went to him...*to Bernardi.*

My father turned as I entered the room, those blue eyes glinting as he smiled. "There you are. Evan...this is Jannick. Jannick Bernardi."

Jannick took a step forward, scowled for a second, then swept his gaze up and down. "Fuck me..." he muttered, his accent thick and strong. "You're goddamn stunning."

FOUR

Bruno

My breath caught the moment she stepped into the room. A careful smile curled the corners of her mouth and I was captured by the movement, transfixed by those rose-red lips as they trembled. I wanted to touch them, wanted to slide my thumb across the surface. I wanted to feel her, to hold her...I wanted to fuck her, and it wasn't in the way Jannick fucked. I wanted to be part of her world, to be consumed by the scent of her sweat on my skin. I wanted to share her oxygen, to be touched by the same spill of moonlight that touched her.

I wanted to know how a woman like her felt underneath me as I thrust into her hard and slow.

Hunger gripped me, a kind I'd never felt before.

Until Michele Valachi stepped closer, gently cleared his throat, and called my cousin's name. Jannick looked her up and down and muttered. "Fuck me, you're goddamn stunning."

But she wasn't just stunning.

She was perfect. Shy, and careful, her cheeks reddening as she looked to the floor.

But for me...the world seemed to come to a screeching fucking halt.

She was too good for him.

The words were a roar in my head.

Too good for his filthy fucking hands. Far too good for what he was. My stomach tightened and my fists clenched. I'd never been jealous before, not of Jannick. I never cared about his whores and his stories...until now. Now I fucking cared...*a lot.*

Mine...a voice inside me growled, low and urgent. *I want her...I fucking want her.*

I needed to stop this, needed to find a different way for this alliance. I jerked my focus to Dad, but he just stared at Valachi, that deadly gaze picking apart every tone and every damn move. But it was Cillian who caught the movement, and his dark eyes met mine. There was a flare of confusion as he glanced at my fists then shifted that focus back to Evan.

"Jannick, it's nice to meet you." She stepped forward and lifted her hand.

No...don't fucking greet him, don't fucking *touch* him.

She tried to act confident, but I could see under the lie. Her cheeks burned a little hotter as my cocky cousin grabbed her hand, never once taking his predatory eyes off her.

He made her uncomfortable. Panic flared as she jerked her hand from his. But her father never intervened, just chuckled as Jannick stared at her like she was some fucking conquest.

"Evan," Michele Valachi motioned toward the open French doors and flowing white sheer curtains. "Why don't you show Jannick the gardens?"

She just smiled and nodded. But Jannick didn't take his eyes off her as she stepped away and headed for the doors. I took a step, unable to stop myself, as they slipped through the curtains and were gone.

"Adrian," my uncle called. "Why don't we talk in private?"

I caught movement from the corner of my eye as Dad nodded.

"I'm sure you can manage to occupy yourself, Bruno," Cillian murmured, drawing my gaze as he stepped close.

He reached out and grasped my shoulder, meeting my gaze. There was a knowing in his eyes, an urgency he was trying to unveil. He knew...he knew how she affected me, and was getting my father out of the way. Energy hummed through me as he dropped his hand and strode toward the others as they turned and left.

Leaving me standing there in the middle of the room...with no one but a female servant who took a step forward. "May I offer you some refreshments while you wait?"

I looked at her, scowled, and shook my head. "No," I answered, then headed for the damn door.

Their voices reached me as I shoved the curtains aside and stepped out onto the white stone terrace.

The place was massive. White and grandiose ,with potted white roses like a hedge along the terrace and the stairs as they led to expansive grounds. Moss stuck out from between slate gray stones as I stepped along the path, following her. But I didn't care about the damn opulence...I cared about her.

I kept my distance, scanning the darkened gardens that seemed to stretch out as far as I could see. Towering willows shielded the view of the city. Leaves drooped low, brushing the air with the breeze.

I caught the sound of her voice, careful and painfully nervous as she stuttered and kept moving. The faint scent of something sweet caught the wind, drifting to me. My mind turned to Bethany, the girl from Ace's. The one who looked at him like she was terrified.

Soon Evan would look at him the same way.

I couldn't let that happen. A glance over my shoulder at the house and I hurried, diverting around the thick row of roses. They were up ahead, and somewhere to the right. *Fuck.* I licked my lips, scanning the gardens. I didn't want them to see me. *So then why are you doing this?* That small voice questioned.

Because...

Because it mattered.

Because last night changed everything and now...

Now I knew who we really were.

"They told you, right?" Jannick's voice slammed into me. "Told you we're to be married?"

Her white dress floated on the breeze, making her look spectral in the dark. "Yes," she answered. "I was told."

He stepped forward, driving her backwards, and lifted his hand. "Then I want to know what I'm getting here, if this is going to be worthwhile."

I scanned for cover, then backtracked, heading for the floating curtain of a willow tree.

"What do you mean *worth—*"

Her words were cut short with a muffle...*a fucking muffle.* I knew what he was doing, knew before I stepped out and saw him kissing her. He had her pushed against the tree. One hand was above her head, boxing her in with his body.

Goosebumps raced across my skin as I watched them.

That icy burn of rage moved deeper as Jannick slid his hand to her throat. I stiffened with the contact, hating how his touch looked against her skin. He pulled his mouth from hers. "Have you kissed a guy before, Evan?"

She slowly shook her head.

"So, I'm your first?"

A nod, small, careful.

"A first kiss, nice. Have you been fucked?"

She flinched at the question, even from here I could see the curl of her shoulders before she tried to slide away. But he didn't let her, shifting with the movement to stop her.

There was a chuckle from my cousin, low and threatening, before he jerked her dress higher and slipped his hand underneath. "You don't mind if I check, do you?"

"*Stop!*" she cried out, and shoved against his shoulders. "*Stop that!*"

But he just leaned harder, crushing her under his weight, his growl turning lower, reminding me how he spoke to his whores. "You belong to me, right? That means I can do anything I want... *you hear me? Anything...I...fucking...want....*" His hand moved under her dress, reaching higher.

I clenched my fists and tore my gaze away. *You can't...they're to be married.*

"I want to fucking see your pretty little cunt.," Jannick growled, and yanked her dress higher.

A sob tore from her, drawing my gaze once more as he dropped to his knees. She shoved her hand onto her mouth, stifling her whimper as he lifted her dress, his focus between her legs as he jerked her panties aside. "'Cause it better be worth it."

"Please stop," she whimpered. "Don't do this."

"You're mine, right?" He yanked the fabric. "Spread your legs. I don't have time for a frigid bitch."

That's fucking it...

I strode forward, stepping out of the cover of the willow as she lashed out. The *crack* of her hand across his cheek sounded like a whip.

Jannick fell sideways, sprawling to the ground as she stumbled backwards, clutching her dress. "You...you *dare* touch me like that again and I'll make you sorry. I'll make you sorry, you hear me?"

Terror made her words tremble, until she stiffened and lifted her gaze.

She saw me as I strode toward them, my gaze not on the sprawling piece of shit I shared my name with, but on her. "Are you..."

She was gone before I could finish, tearing past me in a half walking-half running awkward gait.

I heard the sob tear from her as she left us behind.

And that sound punched a hole in my fucking chest.

"Little fucking *cu*—"

I lunged forward, yanked my fist backwards, and lashed out.

Fucking pussy.

Crack.

Bruno sucks cock.

Crack.

I punched him, driving my fists into his jaw until, with a roar, he shoved to stand, bearhugged me, and drove me backwards. His eyes were wild and wide. *"What the fuck was that for?"*

"For *you!*" I snarled, sucked in a breath, then lunged again, swinging my fist.

He reared backwards, my blow barely missing him. *"What the fuck, Bruno! Over her?"* he barked, stabbing his finger toward the house. "Over that frigid fucking—"

I let out a roar, but instead of swinging, I dropped my shoulder and charged.

We hit with a jolting *thud,* then hit the ground. I drove my fist upwards, the knuckles finding soft flesh. Something came over me, a kind of savage hunger tore free.

"Hey!"

I was wrenched backwards by my shirt, and lifted my gaze to stare into the dark, unmerciful eyes of my uncle.

"*What the fuck is going on here?*" Cillian roared.

Rage filled me.

Unstable.

Consuming.

My breaths were all that held me there. Hard. Sawing. Tearing in and out as Jannick moaned and rolled over on the ground, staring up at me, his mouth bloody. "You're fucking crazy," he moaned, and swiped his hand across his throat.

I wrenched away from my uncle's hold and met his gaze. Not once had I lashed out, not once had I felt the kind of anger that burned in me now. "He..." I gasped, my words punctuated by breaths. "Is *not* marrying her...not now...not *fucking* ever."

"Bruno," Cillian shook his head.

But I didn't want to hear it.

I didn't want to hear another fucking thing.

Instead, I turned, yanked my shirt back down, and headed for the car.

I was done. Done playing nice. Done putting up with Jannick's shit.

Done watching him touch what belonged to me.

FIVE

Evan

I ran across the gardens, tearing through the curtains in the living room in a panicked blur and ran smack into a wall.

A wall that barked, *"Fuck!"* with a heavy Irish accent.

Hands grabbed me...*just like he grabbed me.*

"No more...*no more,*" I cried out, and slapped. *"Get off me! I said, get off!"*

But it wasn't Jannick who held me. It was one of the others staring down at me with those hungry, bestial eyes.

They'd watched. *They'd watched while he did that to me...*

"Easy, now," mhe male urged, lifting his hands in surrender. "What the hell happened out there?" That gaze grew harder and more savage as he scanned me from head to toe.

But I didn't answer, just stepped around him, then lunged. My flat shoes slapped the tiled floor until the hallways were a blur. A sharp bark of laughter tore from my father's study further along the hall.

Tears blurred my way as I turned right, heading for my bedroom. *He did that...pushed his fingers.* My body clenched, aching from the intrusion. *He did that to me.*

I shoved the handle of my bedroom door and stumbled inside as a tear spilled free. Footsteps sounded in the hallway outside.

"Evan?" Jesse called. "Are you back already?"

I turned, leaning against the door, unable to answer. My throat was thick and throbbing, strangling my words.

"E?"

I closed my eyes and leaned my head backwards.

"Is everything alright?"

"Yes," I forced the word around the knot and tried to swallow. "I'm fine. I'm fine, Jesse."

"Will you let me in?"

I slowly turned and reached for the handle, but instead of opening the door, I flicked the lock. "I'm getting changed now. I'll see you in the morning."

"But E..." she chuckled. "You didn't tell me how dreamy your future husband is."

The tears trickled as I pushed away from the door, unable to lie. My thighs clenched as I walked, pulsing and clenching, like his fingers were still thrusting inside me. I wanted to take a shower, try to rid myself of the feel of his touch. But there wasn't enough heat to burn away the memory. And not enough promises to make it all go away. Instead, I crossed my bedroom, leaving the sofa and the expansive desk behind, and climbed into bed. I kicked my shoes free and pulled my knees closer to my chest.

I want to fucking see your pretty little cunt...

I'd never been so humiliated, so...*violated.*

I waited for the tears to flow, to stream down my cheeks and slide down my neck. But instead of a torrent...they stopped.

Spread your legs. I don't have time for a frigid bitch.

Those words returned to me as I stared at the window of my bedroom.

Make him love you.

Not this again E...

Need a line to carry our name.

Need an heir.

An heir.

I shoved upwards on trembling arms as the muffled *thud* of a car door sounded. I wasn't enough. I'd *never* be enough. I was fifteen, fifteen and my life was over. I'd never be anything more than a failure to him, never be worthy unless I was a man.

I crossed my room and stepped into my closet, grabbed my suitcase, and laid it flat on the bed. There were no more tears now, no more avoiding the truth. I grabbed some clothes, packing my jeans, tops, and shoes neatly into the bottom before I crossed to the set of drawers for my underwear.

"Evan."

I stilled at the sound of my father's voice as he spoke from the doorway.

"Honey, I heard there was an altercation."

An altercation? I swallowed the bark of laughter. There were no tears, no breaking down, no falling apart. There was just...*nothing*. But if I thought what burned inside me was emptiness, then I was lying. It wasn't *nothing* that churned in me. It wasn't shock, or anger...

It was...deep-seated rage.

My hands shook as I shoved down on the suitcase and pushed the clasps shut. My body trembled as I grabbed my bag and checked to be sure my wallet and keys were inside. I was barely legal to drive, my license brand new, my sky-blue beetle practically brand new. But all I knew was that I needed out of here.

I needed to be safe...and I wasn't safe here.

Not anymore.

I crossed the room, slid my shoes back on, and strode back, grabbing my bag as I went to the door. One click, and I yanked the door open, finding my father scowling from the other side.

He took one look at the suitcase in my hand, then the bag on my shoulder. "Are you going somewhere, Evan?"

"I'm leaving."

"*Leaving?*" He lifted those blue eyes to mine. "Leaving to where?"

"Anywhere, as long as it isn't here." I pushed past him.

There was a second where I thought I was free, where that shoved-down seething pain and fury simmered...until he lunged, grabbing my arm.

His blue eyes blazed with cruelty. I knew the man my father was…knew that vicious part of his nature lay buried deep. It came out on occasion with chilling clarity. It was that clarity I saw now as his lips curled in and he snapped, "What the fuck happened?"

"What do you care?" I screamed, wrenching my arm from his hold. "I'm *nothing* to you."

He flinched as though I'd slapped him. His brows furrowed as he met my gaze. "Is that what you think?"

"Yes," I whimpered, practically choking on the word.

A tear ran, tracing the worn line down my cheek. "I'm not good enough." I hated the sob that tore free, thickening my voice. "I'll *never* be good enough, because I'm not a man. But I'm no one's *whore*, Daddy. Not yours…*not anyone's*. I'd rather be dead."

I backed away, watching anger spark and clash in his eyes before I reached for the handle of the suitcase and left…

"Evan," my father called.

I quickened my steps, the sound of my suitcase wheels grinding on the tiles, and ran.

SIX

Bruno

19 YEARS OLD...

I STEPPED through the open garage door and into the stench of oil and grease mingled with blood and sweat, and maybe underneath it, tears. Loud grunts and the heavy *smack* of fists rang out as I tugged my sunglasses down and glanced around the old place.

It'd been a garage for what seemed like forever, stains from oil spills still marked the concrete floor, but the time for rebuilding cars had long gone. Now this place was in the market to rebuild people.

But if you came here to get in touch with your emotional side and unburden your fears...then you were very much mistaken. No, this place took all those fears, and all that hate and rage, and turned men into beasts. I scanned the four training rings which were filled by men sparring. Correct that, men and *one woman* sparring under a sheen of sweat, punctured with sharp commands of *"keep your damn hands up! Move...move, that's the way."* and caught the hard *smack...smack...smack...*of a bag being punished further in the back.

Heads turned toward me as I moved deeper. Careful eyes watched, but they said nothing. They wouldn't...because they knew who I was. My gaze found him further in the back, sunk deep in the shadows, which was where he lived now. Shadows and hate. A perfect fucking combination.

"Bruno." The mumble came from my right as Darragh heaved his old bones through the ropes and climbed down from the ring.

"Old man," I muttered, and jerked my gaze far back into the garage. "How concerned should I be?"

The deep, throaty chuckle came with a shake of his head as he neared and threw an old arm around my shoulders. "Kid...with that one, you should *always* be concerned."

He smiled, but it didn't last long. Under the pretense of shrugging off the worry lingered the fear. The fear that'd been growing in the old Irishman's eyes since Jannick had started coming here...right after that night.

The night our family plunged into crisis, the night I'd put hands on my kin and swore I'd kill him. Those words still lingered between us, roaring to the surface every time we looked at each other.

Which was the sole fucking reason I was here.

Smack.

Smack...

SMACK!

The sound pulled my focus as we made our way past the massive men, honed with aggression, as they pounded training mitts into each other. But none of them concerned me, not even the biggest made me turn my head and take a second glance.

No, my focus was for the most brutal of them. The kid that was always prone to cruelty and savagery was now the most dangerous man I knew...*and I knew a lot of dangerous men.*

The old man slid his arm from around my shoulders and hung back, leaving me to make my way to where my cousin worked the back. He was barechested, black gym shorts and bare feet showed a body made for violence. Hard muscles shone under sweat. The word *Bernardi* tattooed large in an arch across his back.

His fists drove into the bag a little harder, making the heavy thing jump. I imagined the thing as a body, imagined it was me. I was sure right about now he was doing the same.

"You didn't come to the family meeting last night," I declared, knowing full well he knew I was there. The punches were harder, faster...*more fucking precise.*

Smack!

"Or the one last week," I continued. "Or the one last month."

A hard bark of laughter came with that one. But the towering beast of a man never stopped. Hands up, shoulders hunched, he moved in for the kill, unleashing a combination that left the sound of pummeling to consume the room.

Only then did I realize they'd all stopped. The sparring and the training. Every single one in the garage watched him, but it wasn't with admiration. No, they knew a monster when they saw one...

The monster sucked in hard, consuming breaths and lowered his hands.

Before he turned.

I tried to hide the flinch as those dark, soulless eyes found mine. "You came here to remind me of that?" He took a step toward me. "Came to tell me how much of a failure I am as a son?"

"No, a damn heir."

He stilled then, those eyes twinkling before he dropped his head back and roared with laughter. "An heir? *A fucking heir?*" The laughter died, leaving him to shake his head as he turned and walked away.

But it wasn't fucking funny...

Anger burned inside me as I went after him. "You think this is funny?"

He didn't answer.

"Hey! I'm talking to you!" I roared.

He stopped then, grabbed a folded towel from a stack on the shelf, and faced me once more. Still he said nothing, just fixed me with a killer's stare. "What the fuck do you want from me, Bruno?"

I stepped closer, ignoring the panicked gasps behind me. Jannick wouldn't hurt me...*no matter how much he wanted to.* "I want you back," I growled. "I want you pissing off my damn father, and yours. I want you snarling and moody. I want you to fulfill your fucking role. Every fucking meeting you miss, you're just pissing them off a little more. They want the damn heir at the family fucking meetings, you know...*like fucking family should.*"

"You want me there?" he asked.

"Yes, I fucking want you there," I barked. "Why the hell do you think I dragged my ass all the way here? I don't get off on watching other men sweat."

"No...you don't." Jannick took a step closer, moving until he loomed over me.

Fuck, he was big...and getting bigger all the damn time.

Menacing.

Cold.

The eyes of someone who liked inflicting pain. *Have you been fucked?* Those words pushed to the surface. *I want to fucking see your pretty little cunt. 'Cause it better be worth it.*

I fought the flinch, but he saw it. He saw the past rise between us, saw that hate buried deep down. His lips curled into a sneer as a tiny bark of savagery tore free. "See...*that's* exactly why I don't come. I'm not the fucking heir, Bruno. I never was. Tell that to your father and maybe when you've taken the seat, you might stop seeing me as the cold, savage bastard from that night."

I swallowed hard.

I wanted to...

I really did.

But I didn't think that was ever going to happen. Because the woman I wanted refused to have anything to do with the Bernardis, even though the pact of marriage to my cousin still stood. *And I hated him for that.*

SEVEN

Evan

I stared at the map until my vision blurred, marking the boundaries, the players, and the fucking fools before I leaned back in my chair. There was room there, room to push into the market. Room to grow.

The door opened, drawing my gaze. Christi Marino scowled when he walked in, glanced at the mess on my desk, then dropped his shit on the desk and turned. "I see you've been here all night...*again*."

"I think I found a way we can take the east side of Hungerford."

"You do, huh?" he muttered, then gave a sigh.

I forced a laugh, fighting the flare of disappointment. "What, you don't believe me?"

"Oh, I believe you, Evan." He took a step, his hard brown eyes fixed on mine. "I can almost guarantee you've worked through every play a hundred times, the players, the field. I know we'll take that information and push harder, take a bigger piece of your father's pie, and as much as that used to fucking thrill me, now it just worries me."

"Worries you?" My voice grew deeper, darker...it always did when *he* was mentioned. "If earning more money worries you..."

"You *know* that's not what I mean, Evan. When you called me five years ago, I was excited to take you under my wing. I wanted nothing more than to take the only Valachi heir into my home and teach her everything I damn well knew. But you've outgrown us. You're too smart, too hungry." He waved his hand at the map. "You're too..."

"*Too...?*" I forced through clenched teeth.

"Important," he finished with a sigh. "You're too important, E. Not just for me, for yourself. You deserve better than the small pickings we get here."

"You took in over one-point five million last year."

"We did, and we've already surpassed that this year, because of you. You've made us more, cut our losses harder. You've made the Salvatores see me, and that's *never* happened before, not since I started working for Dominic."

My phone buzzed. I didn't have to look at the number to work out who it was. It was an *unknown,* always an *unknown.* I grabbed it, pressed the buttons, and blocked yet another fucking number. My father was relentless.

He didn't like it that I was in essence working for the competition, another family who occupied a seat on the Commission. It was always about business, about overcoming the problems such as having a daughter.

Christi just glanced at the phone as I pressed *block number,* and put it back down. "Sorry," I muttered.

But he didn't meet my gaze. This man...this man had been more of a father in the last five years than my own had been in my entire life. "You should take his calls, E."

My stomach clenched, the sting fucking brutal. "Are you kicking me out, Christi?"

He winced, then jerked his gaze to me. "If I did that, Luciana would have my goddamn balls. You're the daughter she never had. She fucking adores you. Hell, *I* adore you. Which is why this is so fucking hard. Don't you think you should be there instead of here?"

"I do." I lowered my gaze, hating how it still fucking stung after all these years. But here, here I knew I wasn't in line for the damn seat. My future wasn't a dangling carrot that I'd *never* be able to bite. Here, I had a purpose, even if it wasn't the kind of purpose I wanted.

Here, I learned.

Here, I became more than what lay between my legs.

Here, I learned how to be powerful.

Ding. The message came. *Missed call, view message.*

"Five years is a long time, E," Christi murmured, glancing at the phone. "Maybe he's changed?"

And maybe he hadn't...maybe my father would always be the controlling bastard he'd always been? The kind of man who was so fucking eager to marry me off to the best adversary, no matter how fucking cruel they might be.

Have you kissed a guy before, Evan? Those words came back to me from that night. *Have you ever been fucked?*

My pulse stuttered with the memory, my thighs clenched together as though somehow I was reliving that night. I could still feel his fingers inside me, hard, brutal, *stabbing*.

I shoved the phone away. *Fuck him.*

Christi's phone rang at that instant. He glanced at the screen, scowled, and pressed the button. "Mr. Salvatore...yes. Yes, sir. Yes, she's still in my employ. Sir, with all due respect, Evan makes her own...*oh, oh okay...*"

I jerked my gaze to his. There was a widening of his eyes, a look of concern.

"Yes, sir. I'll let her know right away. Okay...okay, thank you for ca—"

Christi lowered the phone threw one glance at me, and murmured, "E, you need to call your dad right away. It's your mom..."

"Mom?" I whispered as that anger inside me turned to fear.

I snatched my phone from the desk and with trembling fingers pressed my dad's number.

"Evan," he answered in an instant and sighed with relief. "Thank God."

"Dad, is mom..."

"She's sick, E," he croaked, his voice low, husky and raw. "I need you to get to Ikon Memorial right away."

I was already rising as the prickling brush of fear raced down my spine. "I'm on my way..."

"And E?" Dad murmured. "I love you."

My throat thickened in an instant. I wanted to say the words back to him. I wanted to forget the last five years of hurt. But I couldn't. "Hold tight, Daddy...hold tight."

I pressed the button and grabbed my bag, but Christi was already holding his keys and striding toward the doorway. "Ikon Memorial? Get in the car, kid. I'm driving."

WE MADE it there in a blinding blur. Still, it felt like it took forever as the early morning traffic closed in, strangling us as Christi laid on the horn and pushed the GTO harder than ever before. I hung on to the armrest, feeling trapped, adrift. My mind returning to Mom...*and all those calls.*

Calls I never took.

Calls where Dad had tried to reach out to me.

Or Mom. What if they'd been from Mom? A low tortured moan tore free with the thought. I wrapped my arms around my middle and rocked forward.

"What is it?" Christi snapped, handling the muscle car around a sharp corner then punching the accelerator, driving me backwards against the seat.

"What if they were my mom, Christi?" I met his gaze. "What if all those calls I ignored were Mom trying to tell me she was sick?"

"You don't know that," he said firmly, the fear in his eyes turning them stony and cold. "And you can't think like that, not now. Right now, they need you. They need you to be strong. Be fucking strong, E."

Be fucking strong...

I clenched my fists and tried to pull myself together, and in the distance the glint of Ikon Memorial Private Hospital rose. It was towering and gleaming, a hive for the best of the best. Christi hit the turning signal and pulled in, gliding the muscle car right up to the double doors, and braked hard.

"Christi..."

"I don't want to hear it, kid. Everything's going to be fine. I'm gonna be right here, waiting. So, you just call me, okay? You just call..."

I nodded, grabbed my phone and my bag, and yanked the handle. Valet parkers outside the hospital watched me with raised brows as I headed toward the double doors. But they said nothing as I strode through and headed for the reception desk.

The place was filled with the kind of panicked bustle you see at the Four Seasons. Elegant and opulent, just like my father expected. I stopped at the counter. "Erena Valachi." I murmured to the receptionist.

She scowled, punched in the name, then jerked her gaze to me. "Are you a relative?"

"I'm her daughter."

"Oh, of course. I'll need to see some identification please."

I handed over my license, waiting as she checked the details in her system.

"Floor fourteen, room twenty-six."

A nod and I was hurrying to the bank of elevators, stepping in as a door opened. It was only a minute or so until the elevator stopped, but it felt like forever. I raced along the hallway, searching frantically for room twenty-six until I saw him...*my father*.

He was outside a room leaning against the wall, staring at the floor. The door was closed, the blinds open. Inside was a woman...a woman huddled under white blankets and hooked up to machines. A woman who looked faintly familiar...

"Dad."

Instantly, he lifted his gaze, those blue eyes almost steel gray. He looked older than the last time I'd seen him, older and thinner, drawn. That's what he looked, drawn, as though the last five years had sucked the life from him.

"Evan." He shoved away from the wall, took a step, and froze. "I wasn't sure you were going to come."

The words were a punch to my chest. "Of course I came." I licked my lips and glanced into the room, at the tiny woman huddled under the covers. "You want to tell me what's going on?"

"She was fine, totally fine, then a month ago she started to get run down. I just assumed it was the stress. But last night she collapsed and we rushed her here."

Stress...oh, that's right, because of me.

I'd done this. I closed my eyes, rocked by my own fucking failure. *I fucking did this...*

"Here's the doctor now."

I opened my eyes to see a guy headed toward us wearing black pants and a brown knitted sweater. He didn't look like a doctor. Kind eyes met mine before he glanced at my father and forced a smile. "Mr. Valachi." Then he turned to me once more. "I assume this is Evan. I'm Gabriel Montgomery and I'll be looking after your mom. I'm sure both of you have a lot of questions, so why don't we go inside?"

He motioned to the room and for a second, I couldn't move. Go inside. The idea of seeing her like that terrified me. But Dad followed the doctor into the room and stopped inside, before glancing over his shoulder. "E?"

I swallowed hard and followed, closing the door behind me.

"We have the test results and I'm sorry, it's not good news. As you know, Erena's cancer is very aggressive. If she'd come to see me a year ago, or even six months ago, we might've stood a chance. But her body is very depleted, even more so than after all the pregnancies."

"Pregnancies?" I jerked my gaze to the doctor. *"What pregnancies?"*

He glanced at my father, who turned a shade of gray. "Evan..." he tried to console me.

"No, I want to know." Anger burned inside me. *"What pregnancies?"*

"I'm sorry." The doctor glanced at Dad. "I just assumed she knew."

"Dad?" I growled my mind racing, going back over all the times Mom was laid up in bed ill. She'd always been sickly, for as long as I could remember, usually sitting outside on the terrace while I ran and played. Always too sick to come to any of my dressage events, or watch me compete in archery.

"Your mother couldn't cope with all the miscarriages and the IVF. Years of treatments wore her body down."

The pain was crushing, cracking my ribs, pushing air from my lungs. IVF. *Because they were desperate for a boy.* I wrenched my gaze to my father. Agony filled his gaze. He was consumed by torture, riddled with regret. I could see it now. "And to think, out there I was blaming myself."

"Evan," Dad cried.

"And it was all you. You did this to her. You pushed her, drove her fucking mad, and all because I wasn't good enough."

"She wanted it too!"

"Oh, you're going to put this on her now? You're really going to put this on my mom who's in that bed because of you?"

"I don't think—" the doctor started.

I turned on him, hating how grief had turned me into an animal. "No, you don't think. You fix her. *Fucking fix her!*"

The doctor just shook his head, his voice soft. "I can't. I'm sorry, but I can't."

"I fucking *hate you!*" I screamed at my father. "I fucking HATE YOU!"

"No."

The word was a whisper. A hand rose from the bed, the thin fingers trembling. "Evan."

I pushed past the doctor and moved to her side. She'd always been so frail in my world, barely even there. But I loved her. I loved her and I missed her.

"It was me who wanted another child, not just a son. I wanted more, more for you. I wanted to give you brothers and sisters. I wanted all this...I wanted all this to not weigh on you."

Her big brown eyes filled with tears.

Mine flowed, spilling over as I lowered my head, resting my forehead against her. She brushed my hair, sliding those thin fingers through the strands. "Our life is a burden I'd never wish on anyone. So I hoped that if there were more of us...if you had someone to..."

She wheezed and coughed, forcing me to jerk my head upwards. The machine beside her beeped like crazy.

"I think that's enough for now," the doctor urged carefully.

I met my father's gaze and saw now why the guilt. He loved her. He truly loved her and he would've given her anything...*even if it killed her.*

I straightened, brushed the tears sliding down my cheeks, and stepped around the bed.

"Evan," Dad croaked as I reached the door. "Please."

"You won't accept me as I am and I'm done with being not enough for you," I answered, then glanced at my mother in the bed. "You might not have done this alone, but you failed as a husband and as a father. I want more, more than what you can offer..."

I twisted the handle and opened the door, but had only taken one step before he spoke.

"Okay, Evan. I'll give you what you want."

Frozen, my heart hammered. At first, I thought I was hallucinating.

"I'll give you everything, my legacy, the business. I'll teach you all you want to know. Just don't...don't leave. Don't leave us and work for the fucking Salvatores."

I turned slowly, meeting those blue eyes.

They thought Michele Valachi was a monster.

Maybe he was.

But I was his daughter.

No...I was his heir.

I closed the door and turned to him. "I want everything."

He gave a tortured smile and swallowed. "I know."

EIGHT

Bruno

Two weeks before...

THE PHONE RANG, loud and obnoxious, tearing me from an exhausted slumber. I cracked open my eyes and drew my hand from the edge of the bed as a low moan came from beside me.

"Fuck." I blinked and reached, snatching the damn thing from the bedside stand and answered. "Yeah?"

"We have a problem," Dad growled. "Get dressed and get to the Delegate *now*."

I shoved upwards, sleep falling away in an instant. "The Delegate?"

"Yeah, and Bruno? Hurry the fuck up."

I dropped the phone and turned to the woman in my bed. "Get dressed, I'll drop you home."

"Now?" she grumbled, sounding pissed.

"Yeah, Bethany, *now*."

I shoved from the bed, grabbed my clothes from the floor, and strode to the bathroom, switching on the light as I went. The Delegate was our whole damn operation. A set of warehouses crammed together almost as big as a damn city block. It had everything we carried legally, as well as a few things hidden in the back that weren't totally above board.

Tension rolled through me as I yanked on my clothes and ran my fingers through my hair before taking a piss and striding out. "Let's go."

She was already tugging down her dress, her heels in her hand. She smiled slyly and glanced at the rumpled sheets on the bed. "Bruno…"

"Later, okay?" I glanced away from the hope in her eyes. "We'll discuss it later."

I strode out of the bedroom and through my loft, snatched my keys from the counter, and headed for the door. Bethany followed, barely making a sound, and under the glaring lights of the hallway, I saw this for what it was…*a pity fuck*.

The only problem was, I didn't know who needed the pity more, me or her.

We took the elevator down to the underground parking garage. The sleek black Audi waited, lights flashing as I hit the button, unlocking the doors. I opened the door and waited as she slid inside, her black dress riding high, showing me the long line of a perfect thigh.

We had history between us.

A sad history, a comforting history. The kind I wanted to break away from, but I just couldn't, not yet. I closed the door and cut around the front, climbing into the driver's seat. Barely a minute later and I was punching the accelerator, tearing us through the garage and out onto the nighttime streets.

A brush on my thigh made me flinch. "Everything okay?" Bethany asked carefully. "With the call, I mean?"

"Yeah," I nodded, focusing on the traffic as I made my way toward the built-up yuppie neighborhood where she lived. "Fine."

I didn't talk business, not to the women I fucked, or to friends I hung around, not that I had many.

Life as a Bernardi was simple. *Work...then work harder,* and on those nights when the dark seemed too fucking lonely, I reached out to one of the women. Bethany had always been there, hovering in the background. I saw the way she looked at me, as though she was waiting for me to come to my senses and marry her.

I winced at the thought, my mind going straight to *her*.

Evan fucking Valachi.

The ghost of my past.

She still haunted me, even after all these years. I was still trapped there, in that night...in that hunger. I glanced at Bethany and pushed the car harder. It was always like this. My mind slipping back to that look of savage desperation in Evan's eyes as she tore past me that night.

I strangled the wheel, *haunted.* That's how I damn well felt. *Fucking tormented, more like.* I worked my way through the quiet streets, pulling up outside the apartment building where she lived, only this time, I didn't switch off the car.

"I'll wait until you're inside." I swallowed hard. A dismissal at best, an ending at worst. If only I had the balls to make it stick this time.

"Sure, and Bruno?" Bethany turned, leaning across the space between us to kiss me before pulling away. "I had a nice time."

I gave a smile, one that curled the corner of my mouth, and that's where it stayed. The sickly sweetness of her perfume hit me as she opened the door, clutching her bag and heels, then closed it behind her and hurried for her front door.

Like a gentleman, I waited until she was inside and the door was closed before I shoved the Audi into gear and pulled away. *Like* a gentleman. But there was nothing gentle about me.

It was the fucking reason I kept coming back to her.

That animal intensity inside me hungered to play.

And I knew Bethany sated that hunger. I knew as I gripped her throat and fucked her standing, she wouldn't turn me away. *Bernardis are all the same,* she'd said to me once, and fuck me, if that didn't burn. I wasn't a savage like Jannick, wasn't in the game to rape and ruin. But the bruises I still left behind didn't lie.

I was sick.

Sick, as my mind returned to that night with Jannick kneeling between Evan's legs. Her panties shoved crudely to the side as he drove his fingers into her pussy. My cock twitched, hardening once more. That's why I was fucking haunted. Because I wanted *that.*

No, I *craved* that. I fucking craved *her.*

That brutality. That invasion. That degrading fucking hunger.

And I couldn't fill it any other way.

I pushed the Audi faster, catching sight of a faint orange glow bleeding into the night sky. "Jesus fucking *Christ!*"

The glow grew larger and brighter the closer I got, and that ache inside me turned to anger. *Motherfuckers.* Who was it this time? The Salvatores? The fucking *Davieses?* I wouldn't put it past *any* of them...*maybe it was the Valachis?* The thought grew claws. The pact of marriage was still outstanding. Jannick refused to speak about it, instead he cut me a savage glare and stormed off every time my father spoke about it. So maybe the Valachis were done waiting? *Maybe this was revenge?*

Flashing lights blocked off the entrance to the street. I slowed the car and punched the button for the window, lifting my gaze to the young officer as he neared.

"Sorry, sir, you can't go through, there's a fire."

"I know," I answered coldly. "That's my warehouse."

"Mr. Bernardi?"

A nod, and the officer stepped away, grabbing his two-way hooked to his shoulder and called up his commander. A second later, he stepped close and motioned to the fire trucks parked in front of the loading dock. "You're cleared to go through, sir."

I eased off the brake, pulled the Audi in behind Dad's Ranger, and parked. I picked him out of the group of firefighters and police watching the warehouse burn as I strode closer, glancing at them before stopping at his side. "How bad?"

He met my gaze, that hard glint of rage reflecting the inferno. "Bad enough."

"Shit."

He jerked his head to where we could talk and I followed, watching the back of the building burn. "It's all gone. The money, the fucking coke. Everything."

Three million dollars.

Gone, just like that.

"Jesus." I felt the ground rock beneath me.

"Someone knew, someone fucking talked. Someone planned this to the nth degree," he snarled, watching our money burn. "I want to know who…and I want them to fucking pay." He turned toward me. "You hear me? I want them to pay."

I swallowed hard. "I hear you, loud and fucking clear."

The only problem was…*who the fuck was it?*

We stayed until the fire was out and until the last fire truck had left and when it was just the two of us standing outside the police caution tape, stepping through the remnants of what had been the biggest haul of our career, reality hit me.

"What the fuck," I muttered, staring at the burned-out area where the office had been.

"What the fuck, indeed. Come on, you come back to the house, we need to work this out."

"And Cillian?"

"Driving back from Darkfall now."

He'd be savage once he saw this. It had been years in the making, our whole operation to push out of Ikon and head south. Blood would be spilled…a lot of it.

My thoughts were consumed by the *who* and the *why*. By the time I pulled into the driveway behind Dad, I was convinced it was one of the other families.

It had to be.

One of the smaller factions, one looking to make a name for themselves. *Maybe it was Evan?* I'd heard she was working for the Salvatores, no, not heard...more like *I fucking knew it.* After she left her family, I'd had her followed to the other side of the city, where a small group of men loyal to Dominic Salvatore lived and worked.

There I found her.

I followed her for a while, sitting outside the rundown laundromats the family owned. Laundromats that regularly ran trucks north to where the Salvatores consumed a nice bite of the US pie. They were quiet about it, never once causing a fuss for the rest of us...but that didn't mean they weren't over there hatching some kind of retribution.

But if they thought the Bernardis were to be messed with, they were wrong.

I climbed out of the car, pressed the lock, and made my way into the family home. I'd moved to the loft over a year ago, needing my own space. It wasn't like Dad noticed much, anyway. I strode through the door, locking it behind me, then went to the kitchen, grabbed an energy drink and a leg from the roast chicken in the fridge, and headed for the office.

He wasn't there...then the shower turned on upstairs, so I hit the remote and waited.

The seven-year anniversary of that fateful night was next week...

I stiffened at the thought, chewed the bite of chicken, and swallowed. Goosebumps raced across my skin at the image, the same fucking image as they'd had that night. The woman clutching her kid against her as she wept for a husband that'd never come home.

A husband we'd put in the fucking ground.

NINE

Evan

"Ms. Valachi! Look at you with your power suit and your fine-ass self, come on over here."

I smiled at Bernie and walked over, giving the older woman a hug. "You like it, huh?"

She pulled backwards, scanned the brand new navy Chanel suit, and raised one brow. "Girl, you look like a runway model, where are we heading off to this time?" I strode toward her chair and flopped down. "Mauritius." Even saying the name sent a buzz of excitement through me. "I'm going to Mauritius."

"Oh, all that sun and sand. You're going to look gorgeous. Now tell me, what are we doing with your hair?"

I lifted my gaze, meeting hers in the mirror. I'd been coming to Bernie's for the last four years, and even after returning home, I still made the forty-minute trip to see her. "Something that makes me look powerful...and sexy."

"Oh, sexy, huh? Now that's a first." She grinned and gave me a wink in the mirror. "Are we impressing anyone in particular?"

"Everyone, Bernie...every damn one of them," I answered.

"Now *that's* what I'm talking about," she beamed as she grabbed the cape and secured it around my neck before she stopped. "You know, I was just thinking about you the other day. I was almost about to call you."

"Oh yeah?" I murmured, tearing my thoughts away from island breezes and the powerful Mafia families I was about to meet. Families who didn't even know about me...*except for the Salvatores*.

"Yeah, I was taking out the trash and I swore I saw you parked in a dark gray sedan across the street."

I gave a laugh. "A gray sedan, huh?"

"It was the spitting image of you, right down to your hair. Freaked me out for a second, but then she just drove off. So, you're telling me that wasn't you?"

"Wasn't me, Bernie. With these split ends, you can bet I'd be banging down your door."

"Strange," she said as she brushed my hair down and grabbed the scissors. "You have damn a doppelgänger then. Talk about freaky."

I tried to smile. "Sure is, the world can barely handle one of me."

But a tremor of unease tore through me...one I couldn't ignore.

"Okay, powerful and sexy." Bernie gave me a wink, and set to work.

An espresso and an hour of gossip later, I stepped out of the small beauty salon in the middle of Southside Ikon. My hair felt short... shorter than I'd ever worn it before, but I felt *powerful* striding through the parking lot as I headed for my black Mercedes. The sunlight glinted on the rows of cars, blinding me as I hit the button and climbed in.

My thoughts were on the Commission and the Valachi seat that was finally mine. A seat that needed no man, not when they had me. My father finally understood that. It'd only taken him my entire damn life. I glanced into the rear-view mirror and slid on my sunglasses before pressing the button and starting the car.

A seat on the Commission didn't need a cock to rule it...and neither did I.

Power was my aphrodisiac. Control was my desire.

An ache tore through me, leaving a tremble of soreness behind, one that lingered between my thighs. No man had touched me since that night. I'd made sure of it, driving the Valachi name harder, claiming my own power. I didn't need sex, didn't have time for it. The memory rose from the darkness like it always did, though.

Fingers.

Pain.

I want to fucking see your pretty little cunt...

Heat moved through me with the words. My nipples tightened, my fingers clenched around the wheel. *No,* I tried to push the past away. No, I wouldn't let those thoughts rule me, wouldn't allow then to make me wet and needy. I wouldn't allow myself to be reduced to *that*. To a cunt...a pussy, one any many could shove himself into anytime he wanted.

I closed my eyes as the memory of *him* returned. But it wasn't the dark eyes of the vile piece of shit who'd hurt me that lingered. The truth was, I barely remembered him at all. But the other one...*the one who watched in the shadows*. The one with blond hair and intense eyes. The one who'd looked at me with more than control and violence...*him, I remembered*.

The blare of a horn ripped me from the memory. I flinched, heart hammering, and glanced at the commotion as a dark gray sedan accelerated, the deep growl of the engine loud and savage, and as the car tore away and disappeared around the corner, I remembered Bernie's words. *You have a damn doppelgänger then. Talk about freaky...*

TEN

Bruno

Five days before...

"ANY NEWS?"

I ended the call and threw my cellphone onto the desk before meeting Dad's gaze as he strode into the room. He took one look at the phone, then met my gaze. "That good, huh?"

"Yeah, that good," I muttered, and let out a snarl, dragging my fingers through my hair. "I was sure it was them, could've almost bet my fucking ass on it."

"The Salvatores are clean, I told you that." He took a seat on the other side, lifting his legs to plonk his boots on the corner of the desk. "They've got their own problems to deal with and unless they think we're responsible for the hit on the wife, then it's not them."

I curled my lips into a snarl and shoved upwards.

"Jannick call in?"

"No," I grabbed the TV remote and switched it on. "He hasn't."

"He will...he's too much like his father."

And I was too much like mine. But Jannick had been with the hunting party since the fire and so far, he hadn't made a single damn attempt at relaying any important fucking information. Instead, I was left to speak to Ormond. Any other time, talking to the hitman wouldn't worry me, but who the fuck knew what shit Jannick was spouting behind our backs.

I didn't know for sure where his alliance lay...and that pissed me the fuck off.

"I have some news of my own," Dad muttered, drawing me from the TV as the same fucking news report came on. The woman held her girl huddled to her side as the scrolling text called for anyone who had information on the slaying of their father.

"Bruno..." Dad growled. *"Turn that fucking thing off."*

I hit the button, erasing the image, and jerked my gaze to him. I couldn't shake it...couldn't shake the fucking feeling inside me. The one that whispered it wasn't a coincidence that this shit was happening practically on the anniversary of that motherfucker's death, and Jannick refusing my goddamn calls didn't help.

"Evan Valachi is going to Cosa Nostra."

I froze with the remote in my hand and felt my pulse stutter. Evan Valachi...*fuck me.* The one fucking woman I couldn't banish from my goddamn life, no matter how hard I tried. "And?"

"And the arrangement still stands. Michele Valachi won't back out...*he can't back out.*"

Because if he did, then the deeds of that night could come to life. He was vulnerable, just as *we* were vulnerable. I dropped the remote to the desk and met my father's gaze. "She's to marry Jannick."

"She's to marry the heir," Dad said carefully.

Those dark eyes sparkled with excitement. He knew what that night had cost me, knew my blows against Jannick's face were just the start of the division. My fists clenched as I was sucked back there to the sight of his fingers deep inside her. "Then I'm going...I'm going to the fucking island."

"Is this what it's going to take, Bruno?" Dad slipped his boots from the corner of the desk. The same desk he'd sat behind my entire life. But he wasn't sitting behind it anymore...*no, that was me.* "Are you finally taking over?"

"I guess I am." I lifted my gaze to my father's. "And I'll make fucking sure the Valachis give me what I'm owed."

ELEVEN

Evan

One day before...

"ARE you still having the dreams, Evan?"

I lifted my gaze from the sofa. "Sorry?"

Doctor Jude Bailer leaned forward, his elbows on his knees drawing my focus to the rolled-up sleeves of his shirt. The taut muscles of his forearms flexed. Under the shirt, he was toned and fit, a hard stomach and thick thighs from all that working out. He was a difficult man to schedule, pro athlete, golf trainer. It'd be easier to find him in the gym, or the golf course than his office. He was rarely here...unless it was for me.

"Are you still having the dreams where you're sexually intimate with the faceless man?"

His eyes sparkled when he asked that. Maybe he was the one who needed therapy? It looked like he had a hunger buried deep down, a hunger it seemed like he wanted to explore.

"Yes," I answered. "Almost every night."

"And do you reach a climax?" he asked carefully.

My throat clenched, dry and thick, choking off the word. All I could do was nod as the memory reared, my own cry ringing loud in my darkened bedroom, the sheets fisted between my fingers, my panties soaked at my core as I tore from the dream.

Jude cleared his throat, his voice a little huskier as he asked, "And have the dreams changed? Last time you told me you were bound around your ankles and wrists while the faceless man attacked you."

"Yes." The answer was a whisper as the memory of the dreams returned. "They've changed."

"Oh?" One brow rose. "How so?"

Heat flared through me as I shifted on my seat.

Tight straps around my wrists. Gloved hands forcing my thighs apart. *Show me that pretty little pussy...*Fear pushed into my mind as my skin prickled. "He tears my dress, turns me over..."

"Yes?"

I closed my eyes, the words wedged in the back of my throat. There was no way I could say it...no way I would tell him what the faceless man did to me. "He consumes me," I whispered. "Mind, body and soul. He..."

Leather, stone, heat licking between my thighs...and...and...

"And you told me you were leaving on this business trip. Do you think this is connected at all? Stepping out of your comfort zone, being powerless in a way amongst men you don't know? Faceless men, when all the time you're still a..."

A virgin...

I opened my eyes as reality hit home. My lips were dry, my throat working, trying to wet the back of my throat. But there wasn't enough water in the world that could ease me. I dreamed about faceless men fucking me because, in reality, I couldn't bring myself to think about sex. Every time I did, memories of that night came rushing back, forcing me into the bathroom as the world spun and I forgot how to breathe. I leaned forward, took a sip of water from the glass and straightened, still clutching the glass. "Yes."

"And these dreams could be associated with what happened this morning?"

Water sloshed against the sides of the glass as my hand shook. *Flutter...flutter...flutter.* A pang tore across my chest. Panic pressed against the edges of my mind. It was the whole reason we were here. The whole reason I'd collapsed at the office this morning and locked myself in the bathroom. One urgent phone call, and Jude dropped everything to see me. I lifted my gaze, meeting his. "How can I fix this?"

"The same way we've fixed everything over the last year, we talk it out, explore it in a safe setting." He focused on my lips, then the open neckline of my shirt. "Exploration can be beneficial in these circumstances, even physically, bindings, playacting in a controlled setting. It might help you regain your power."

Was he talking about...*BDSM? Jesus.* "What about drugs?"

He gave a chuckle, lifting his gaze to mine. "I don't think—"

But the laughter in his eyes died as he realized I was serious. "No," I answered. "I want the drugs, Jude."

He sighed and stood, turning quickly so I didn't see the bulge in his pants. But I saw. He was turned on by the idea of binding me, of helping me *explore* the nightmares that'd plagued me ever since that night my life changed. I think he was more turned on by the fact I was still a virgin...still *unused* that way.

"The drugs will dull the effect, yes. They might even change the nature of the dreams, Evan. But they won't help your problem. You need to explore the underlying cause here and we both know what that is."

"My virginity..."

"Your lack of sexual exploration to start with. You still see the trauma, and sex can be so much more than that, if you let it be."

My thighs clenched, tightening. "Just write me the damn script, Jude."

"Evan..."

"Do I need to ask someone else?" I lifted my gaze to him.

He sighed, strode around the desk, and yanked his prescription pad toward himself. A few scribbles and a stab of the pen, and it was done. That was what I needed. A tiny little white pill. That would solve it all. The dreams, the institute...the damn panic attack. I leaned forward, slid the glass onto the magazine table, and rose.

My heels sank into the carpet as I crossed the room and took the script as he lifted it toward me. But he didn't let go...not yet.

"Think about my offer," he murmured, searching my eyes. "I can help you find the kind of therapy you need."

"I doubt it," I disagreed, and took the script from his hand. "But thanks for the offer. I'll call you if I need you."

"Enjoy your island, Evan. I'll be here when you need me."

I strode toward the door, yanked it open, and walked out of the office. Sunlight hit me the moment I stepped out of the building. I closed my eyes to the warmth, and tilted my face upwards before opening my eyes and striding down the stairs.

Deep down, I knew the reason for the panic attack. There was too much of a coincidence as I'd stared at the other names of attendees on the island...and stopped at one. *Bruno Bernardi.*

The blue-eyed faceless man from my nightmares.

The one who'd watched me.

The one whose face was branded into my memories.

Memories I wanted banished, and the little white pills Jude prescribed for me would to exactly that. I made my way toward my car parked further down the street and stepped down to cross the lane.

"Sonofa—" a woman snarled, trying her best to heave a rolled rug into the back of her parked Toyota.

She stopped and bent over, sucking in deep breaths. Blonde hair covered her face like a curtain.

I glanced at my car and took a step as a sob tore free from her.

She was crying...

"Please just go in. He's going to kill me if I can't—" she started to mumble at the carpet, then stopped.

Kill her if she can't? Can't get a damn rug into the car?

I licked my lips, glanced at my car once more, and sighed. "That looks heavy, do you need a hand?"

Massive dark sunglasses hid her eyes as she lifted her head. They looked so out of place in the shadows of the adjacent buildings. Most people would take them off...*unless she couldn't.*

She gave me a look up and down, taking in the perfectly pressed designer suit and heels. "I can't possibly ask, you'll get messy."

Purpose burned inside me, the kind I was made for. "You said he'd kill you," I murmured. "I'm hoping that wasn't the truth, but if you need help, I can help you."

She stiffened, then swallowed hard. One hand held the rolled rug against her body while the other went to those ridiculously huge sunglasses that covered half her face.

"So let me." I folded the script, placed it in my pocket, and stepped closer, moving away from the view of the street and stared into the open trunk. The car was an old, faded yellow. Rust spots marred the paintwork. "It'll only take a second."

"Well...if you don't mind," she assented as I stepped close and bent, grabbing the other end. "Hey, do I know you from somewhere?"

I forced a smile. "I don't think so."

But she stilled, straightening, leaving the bulk of the weigh to fall to me. I grunted with the effort, anger flaring inside me as I wrestled the damn thing to stop It from buckling.

"No, I'm pretty sure I know you." She stumbled toward me, but I couldn't look, barely catching her hand rise from her side. "You're Evan Valachi."

Something covered my mouth. I winced at the bitter tang as it flooded my nose and plunged down my throat. I jerked aside, dragging in a breath, and tried to push her away. But the world blurred around me, darkening at the edges.

My knees buckled and my grip slipped. I felt myself falling, until strong hands grabbed me and pulled me closer.

"Nice to meet you, Evan...we're about to become *very* good friends."

TWELVE

Her

"No!" She bucked and fought. Terror detonated in her eyes as she slapped feebly.

But the harder she fought, the faster the drug filled her lungs. Until her knees gave way and she collapsed against the car. I gripped her under the arms. One glance over my shoulder and I lifted her into the open trunk of the car. She was heavier than she looked, but then again, I'd never carried a body before.

Her head hit the bottom of the trunk with a hard *thud* before it came to rest. That was going to hurt when she awoke. *Good.*

The carpet was next. I lifted one end, then the other, unrolling it just a little so that it covered face, then closed the boot. Sunglasses down, I rounded the other side of the car and climbed inside. The Toyota was stolen, the plates swapped. As long as I didn't get pulled over before I got to my destination, I was home free.

Free...

The idea excited me.

"Soon, Daddy," I murmured, glanced into the rear-view mirror, and started the car. "Soon…"

The gears clunked before the old thing lurched forward. I tossed the sunglasses into the passenger's seat and pulled the Toyota out into the street.

What if she wakes up? Daddy murmured.

"That's not going to happen," I answered him. "I made sure it was strong."

Not too strong, though, right, princess?

"No, Daddy, not too strong. It won't kill her."

I focused on the road, glancing into the rear-view mirror as I made my way out of the yuppie part of Ikon to the industrial area, where stark gray landscape reigned supreme. Gone were the pretty parks and clean streets. This was the Valley, with ten-foot-tall barbed wire fences and muscled, black guard dogs. I kept on driving into the infested part of the neighborhood, where drug deals went down on the corner and if you didn't belong to a gang, you were an outsider.

But I was okay with that.

I'd been an outsider my entire life.

A low moan came from the trunk. I tapped on the brakes, slowing the car, and listened. But there were no more sounds, no crying, no screaming. Not that I expected any from her…no, that wasn't how Evan Valachi went down.

She went down fighting, throwing fists and threats like you'd expect someone like her to do…unless you had a rag dosed with chloroform. I turned the wheel, pointing the nose of the yellow Toyota toward the abandoned, half-built complex.

It was just a shell. Cracked concrete pillars and ruined walls lay discarded outside in the weather. It was supposed to be an apartment building. But not anymore. Now it was just a reminder of a life I might've had, if my father had been alive. I parked, climbed out, and walked to the towering gate, which was secured by a large chain. I shoved the key into the lock and unlocked the chain before swinging the gate wide.

I pulled the old sedan inside and parked around the back where no one would see. I climbed out, glancing at the gleaming dark gray Audi, as I hurried back to the gate. The street was quiet and empty, no sirens, no tail. My pulse quickened as I locked the chain and returned.

I opened the trunk and stared at the rolled-up carpet. One corner rose and fell with steady breaths. I pulled the corner out of the way, grabbed Evan Valachi, and lifted her from the trunk, settling her over my shoulders.

She gave a tiny whimper as I slammed the trunk closed and turned. But she didn't stir when I carried her through the remnants of the complex and headed for the darkened stairwell. One that would carry us to the basement below. I flicked a switch and the stairs were illuminated from the bulbs overhead.

The stench of damp concrete was almost suffocating, stealing my breath. Fire burned in my lungs as my knees shook. But I'd been training for this moment, building my core, focusing my intent... and it'd all been about her.

My phone gave a *beep,* drawing my focus as I found one stair, then the next. But I didn't reach for it, only sank lower and lower and lower, until I stopped at the closed basement door underneath.

Light spilled out from under the door as I leaned her weight against the wall and slipped the key into the lock. The door swung open and hit against the wall with a *bang* before starting to close. I heaved her up higher, hard breaths claiming me as I stumbled into the underground bunker and headed for the cot against the wall.

My knees locked, and unlocked, buckling me as she slid from my shoulder and hit the bed. My phone gave a *beep* once more. Insistent. But I needed the security more than I needed it. I crossed the space, closing the door once more and sliding the locks closed. *I did it...I really did it.* The room swayed before I threw out a hand and braced against the wall. *I. Did. It.*

I reached around and snatched my phone free, watched the steady rise and fall of Evan Valachi's chest, and hit the button.

"What took you so long?"

I closed my eyes at the sound of his voice. "Took a little longer than I expected."

"We went over this."

"I know," I answered, and licked arid lips. "I know."

"Send me a photo."

Panic flared. "What? Don't you believe me?"

His voice went low. "You know I do, I just want...Fuck, I just want to see it. To know it's real."

Hunger burned inside me. The need to please him scratched at the deepest parts of me. I closed my eyes, my thoughts jumbled and confusing, just as they always were around him. "You love me, right?" I whispered.

Fear moved slowly through me, twisting and winding like a gnarled root of a tree, strangling the very essence of who I was.

"You know I do." His voice was hard and cold, deepening as he murmured. "Put your hand down your panties."

Energy seared through me, quickening my breath. I knew better than to disobey. With one hand clutching the phone, I yanked up my shirt with the other.

"Open the button of your jeans," he instructed.

I did, my fingers fumbling.

"Your zipper."

"Pushed low," I hissed, shoving my fingers under the hemlines of my panties.

"Hurry" he growled.

The sound reverberated in my ear. I lifted my gaze to the woman on the bed. The woman I'd hunted for so very long. But I wouldn't have found her if it wasn't for *him*.

"Slide down your slit. I bet you're warm. Are you warm?"

I closed my eyes. "Yes," I whimpered.

"Are you warm for me?" he breathed in my ear. "Is it my fingers you're feeling? My touch, *my desire?*"

"Yes."

I heard him shift in the background, cloth on leather, and I ached for him, needing him here with me. "Lower, circle your clit for me," he instructed.

I did as he asked, circling the tiny nub over and over as I stared at the woman I'd just kidnapped off the street. *Not just any woman. The daughter of the man who'd ruined my family...*

"Inside," his voice commanded. "Now."

Her chest rose with hard breaths as I parted my thighs, driving a finger inside myself.

"Do you see her?"

"Yes."

"And you feel me?"

"Yes," I groaned.

"That's me fucking you while we watch her. Me sliding my fingers into that aching pussy."

I pushed deeper, slid out to circle my clit, and dove back in. Heat was building inside me, pooling low down in my belly.

"Enough," he snapped. "You're not to come, not unless I'm the one making you. Do you understand?"

A shiver of regret tore through me as my hand stilled. "Yes."

"Soon we'll be together," he urged. "I can't wait for you to get here."

My pulse sped with the words.

"Good. Now send me the goddamn picture," he snapped. "And be a good girl...for me."

The thunder in my chest pushed the ache away as I slid my hand from my panties as the line went dead against my ear. I held my phone between my chin and my chest, zipping my jeans closed and buttoning them once more. I took a snapshot of her lying there and I sent it to him, trusting him once more, then turned to the home *we* shared.

The stark concrete wall was filled with images of the Valachis and the Bernardis, and off to the side, the rest of the secret Commission. I had names and dates, and locations of buildings. Building's we'd firebombed in the middle of the night, racing through the cover of darkness to watch the place ignite.

He knew more than I did, finding all the information we needed, how they walked, how they sounded, their bank accounts and the money they had. Everything that could bring them down...one by one.

My gaze went to the Valachi whore. But he'd left *them* for me.

The ones I wanted...the ones who *had* to pay.

They will pay. My father's voice smiled through my mind as I rounded the concrete half-wall and stepped inside. A mattress lay on the floor. A punching bag hung deflated in the corner, the knife still embedded to the hilt. The sand that once filled it now lay in a pile underneath.

I dropped my phone onto the table and opened a can of peaches, grabbing the serrated butterfly knife and stabbing a piece before lifting it free and eating. Juice dripped down my lips to my chin. I ate and watched her, knowing it was finally time. Time for me to take my place.

I glanced at the other photos. The ones of Evan...every outfit she wore, every place she visited, from her hair salon to her damn shrink. I knew every color and brand she wore, even knew the size of her bra. I placed the can down and turned, dragging my old white tee-shirt over my head, then my old bra, jeans, and panties, before walking naked to where the clothes were laid out on the bed, next to the suitcases.

I took my time, sliding on black lace panties and the matching bra. Transforming myself. Just as I had done for the last five years. The nose I wore wasn't mine, neither were the high cheekbones. I glanced at the images and got to work, turning to the array of makeup and illuminated mirror, smearing and blending before setting the foundation. Contacts were last, turning my hazel eyes brown. By the time I was done, I looked like perfection. *Mafia perfection.* My blonde hair was smooth and shiny, cut to my shoulders. I rose from the seat, pulled and on the black Chanel pants and black sheer lace top, and smoothed it down over my stomach.

Like this building, I was just a shell when he'd found me. But he built me from the ground up, remaking me into his angel...an angel of vengeance. My Louboutins were next, black and high. A moan came from inside the bunker, low, painful.

I smiled, pulling on my jacket and fastening the button as the moans grew louder.

"What the fuck?" The slurred words reached me.

I grabbed the handle of my suitcase and strode out. As I walked past the doorway, I pulled my knife and the last piece of peach from the can.

"There she is," I murmured, watching her slowly turn her head and wince. "Sorry about that, you're a bit heavier than you look."

A flare of confusion crossed her face as she splayed her hand beside her and pushed.

Her gaze swept the room and stilled on me as she drove herself to her feet, wobbling. The fact she was standing was damn well impressive. I'd seen grown-ass men flat on their back for hours after a dose like that.

"What the fuck?" she hissed.

Now she saw me.

Now she understood.

I let the handle of my suitcase go and closed the distance. "Thanks for making it so goddamn easy.," I sneered, and went closer.

"What...what's easy?"

"Your death," I answered, and jerked my hand forward, driving the knife in my hand into her stomach all the way to the hilt. "One down...*one to go*," I exulted.

She just froze for a second, then looked down.

Her shrill scream was piercing in the underground bunker as I grabbed the suitcase once more...and walked out. After all...*I had a plane to catch.*

THIRTEEN

Bruno

The wheels touched down on the Mauritius airstrip. I leaned forward and reached for the clasp on the seatbelt as the warning lights blinked overhead. The ride had been smooth…and long. But I wanted out of this goddamn tinned can with its walnut paneling and plush leather seats. I wanted out and I wanted…

What did I want?

Her. I wanted her.

Tension rolled through me like a storm, tensing the muscles of my shoulders.

"Mr. Bernardi." The stewardess made her way toward me as the jet slowed. "We've arrived, sir. Is there anything else I can do for you?"

Her voice was low and husky, her smile sly and seductive. I just gave a shake of my head. "No, thank you."

There was a flicker of disappointment. One that played out on her face before she gave a nod. "Enjoy the sunshine."

I stabbed the clasp and pushed out of the seat. Clear skies called my name as the jet's doors opened. I strode forward, turning to slide my body along hers. She held my gaze as I went, her tight breasts brushing against my chest. My cock twitched and my balls let out an ache.

"We'll be waiting for you, Mr. Bernardi," she said with breathless intent.

Fuck me if I wasn't tempted. I still had warm blood in my veins and time to kill. But I wasn't here just for pussy. I was here to claim a woman. A woman who wasn't like a random piece of ass. I wanted it unmistakably clear what I intended, so my mind had better be sharp.

Still, the stewardess licked her lips and curled a strand of hair around her ear as she lifted her gaze to mine. "Right here, I'll be waiting," she whispered. "All alone."

I dropped my gaze to her mouth, imaging those perfect lips wrapped around my cock. I grew harder at the thought, but swallowed hard and turned away. "Good, 'cause I want out of here as soon as possible."

I forced myself out of the fucking jet and into the warm Mauritius sunshine. Stepping down the stairs, I glanced at the Ford Explorer waiting for me. The door opened and Deviouz stepped out. I winced at the sight as my boots hit the asphalt. He glanced at the porter carrying my bags from the jet and jerked his head toward the back of the four-wheel drive.

"Why are you here?" I growled.

"Didn't think we'd let you come alone, did you?" he muttered.

We...the word wasn't lost on me. Still, my gaze moved to the passenger side. "Are you alone?" I asked as I met the enforcer's gaze.

He just gave a shrug. "For now."

For now...

The words didn't sit well. I was the fucking heir here. Didn't they answer to me? I clenched my jaw and strode toward the passenger's side.

I yanked the door open and climbed in, scanning the two bags on the backseat as the back door opened and my bags were loaded in.

First the warehouse on fire.

Then this fucking island.

I felt torn...between the world and *her*.

The driver's door opened and Deviouz climbed in and started the car. "We headed to the marina?"

One nod and he shoved the four-wheel drive into gear. "I have a man waiting to take us across."

He pulled away, leaving the jet behind, and nosed us toward the water. Blue sparkled in the distance, tightening my stomach. I didn't like the idea of Deviouz being here, especially with the reason why I'd come here in the first place.

Evan Valachi filled my thoughts as we skirted the glitz and glamor of Mauritius and headed straight for the boat. I wanted to be on the island as soon as possible. I wanted to be waiting...*for her.*

We pulled in hard to the marina and parked. I shoved the door open, climbed out in silence, and moved around to the back. Movement came from behind the gates as a young guy headed my way.

"Mr. Bernardi."

I glanced toward the steward and heaved one of my suitcases from the back of the four-wheel drive.

"I'm Caleb, I'll be the steward on your trip to the island."

I glanced past him to the cruiser waiting for us. "Get it started," I ordered, and turned away. "I want to be gone."

"Yes, sir." He gave a nod, stepped forward, and grabbed one of my bags before reaching to take Deviouz's duffel bag in his hand.

"Not these," the enforcer growled with a shake of his head, making the steward pull away in an instant.

The enforcer just stared and the young guy scurried away before the snarling bastard just glanced my way. "You sure you want to do this?"

"You mean claim what's owed to me?"

"To the Bernardis," he corrected.

I didn't like him correcting me…didn't like it one fucking bit. I took a step closer to the hitman, meeting those unflinching eyes. "Do you know something I don't?"

He was testing me, pushing against my control, forcing this fucking divide. I stepped closer, until we were barely a breath apart. "While you're here, Deviouz, you answer to me, do you understand me? Not the other way around. If you don't like it… I'm quite happy to have you replaced…*permanently*."

There was a twitch at the corner of his mouth.

One that told me all I needed to know.

He didn't like me, that was plain to see, and he was hiding something. I saw it dancing behind the savage glint in his eyes. I was betting my father didn't know about this 'additional protection', and I sure as hell knew if he didn't…then there was only one man who did.

Jannick.

Hate moved through me as I stared into his eyes. Jannick had sent him, still playing heir even from the fucking sidelines. Well, he'd given up that seat when he decided to go full fucking mercenary. "Are you and I going to have a problem, Deviouz?"

"No, *sir*," he snarled.

"Good. 'Cause I have no fucking tolerance for you *or* my cousin's bullshit right now."

I grabbed my bags and turned. "Check in with the harbormaster before we leave. I don't want any surprises."

I left him behind, striding toward the boat as he swore under his breath. But the moment I strode through the gates and headed to where the steward waited on the jetty, I gave the command. "Throw the ropes…we're leaving."

"Now?" he glanced behind me.

"You have a problem with that?"

"No, sir," he met my gaze and gave a careful nod.

I headed for the boat, stepping over the divide and onto the boat as it rose with the swell. Barely a second later, the ropes were tossed into the back of the boat and the engine throttled.

"*Hey!*" Deviouz barked, striding through the gates and along the jetty.

Hate twisted his mouth into a snarl. But we were already pulling away.

"I'll take your bags, sir," the steward said, taking them from my grasp.

I stood in the middle of the deck, watching my cousin's enforcer curse and snarl, then finally drop his bags at his feet. If Jannick thought he was going to send some fucking asshole to spy on my every goddamn move, then he was very much mistaken. I turned around as the engine throttled harder and we pointed into the endless blue.

I made my way into the cabin, pulled out my phone, and searched for a signal, punching out a text to my father. *On the boat. Will be there in the next few hours. Any word on the search?*

I waited for an answer, checked the information coming in from the island with a simple text to Mateo Ristani, the island's Commander. *On the boat.*

Mateo: I know. See you soon, Bruno.

I smothered a smirk. I'd met Mateo twice before when I attended the Institute and every time, he'd been a cold, cutting sonofabitch. He reminded me a lot of my dad.

Dad: No word. Focus on the island and leave this to us.

In other words, don't come home until I made good on this deal with the Valachis.

I shifted on the seat, remembering her that night. The night I'd stood in her family's home as a damn kid, watching as she stepped through the doorway and smiled at Jannick. I hadn't felt it then, hadn't felt how much she'd fucking consume me. But the woman was a damn earthquake, one that started slow, making me feel unsteady as the faint tremble shook my world.

The moment I saw him kneeling at her feet, her dress yanked up and her panties shoved aside, the tremors grew stronger. It was those tremors I felt even now...those tremors that I knew were more than a shift inside me...they were a gaping fucking hole.

She'd come to us hopeful that night. But the hope had long ago died in her eyes. I knew that for a fact. I pressed my phone, but instead of messaging my damn family for no fucking information, I opened my gallery, finding the latest picture of her, one taken as she stepped outside of Harlequin's Restaurant. She looked stunning, tall, powerful, dressed for success in a royal blue suit. She wanted to pretend she was a man, wanted to believe she now held all the power.

I swallowed hard looking at the image of her and felt my cock come alive. But this desire wasn't like the one I'd felt for the stewardess. It wasn't just physical or fleeting. It was consuming, so consuming that I couldn't think about anyone else, only Evan Valachi.

I rose from my seat, scanned the cabin, and spied the door that would take me below deck. This is how much the woman had me worked up. This was how much I fucking wanted her. I stepped down the stairs, and made my way along the hall, opened the closed door to the stateroom, and stepped inside.

Hunger rolled through me and my cock hardened even more. I flicked the lock and jerked my zipper down. I could barely wait, pulling my cock free and opening up her photo on my phone. Her with her business fucking suits. Her with that hard gleam in her eyes. I closed mine, letting myself drift back to that night, her spine pressed against the fucking tree and my cousin's fingers deep inside her.

Should've been my fingers.

I wouldn't have hurt her. I would've made her feel good, would've had her panting and moaning. My own moan tore free as I worked my length, gripping tight and sliding all the way to the tip. I would've made her look down at me bathed in the moonlight, and see everything we could have together. I would've showed her what real power was.

Power over me...

I felt dangerous about that.

Power over my body, my heart, and my soul. Power over my mind. I didn't have to give her that...she took it. I stared at her picture, then looked down, watching my cock twitch in my hand. A drop slipped from the tip, one lone fucking tear as I pumped my hand harder. Evan...*Evan was...mine...*

I came hard, cum shooting as my balls grew tight and emptied. I wanted it inside her. Wanted it coating those creamy thighs. Wanted it buried deep, filling her, so that all she felt was me...*forever.*

I closed my eyes and swayed as the boat rocked.

An earthquake.

That's what she was. I opened my eyes and stared at her photo. I'd forever feel the shocks she left behind. Forever realize how ruined I was by her.

"Mr. Bernadi," came the steward's voice from the other side of the cabin door. "We're about to dock, sir."

"Thank you," I answered, yanking my zipper up. "I'll be right there."

I stepped into the bathroom, washed my hands, and stared at myself in the mirror. It was time to find her, time to make her remember what her family owed...

FOURTEEN

Evan

Agony roared. I tried to open my eyes. The pain radiated, pulsing and throbbing as it reached through my body, darkening my world at the edges. But the pain...the pain was terrifying.

I fought the darkness and forced myself to surface.

Bright lights buzzed and hummed above me...blurring and blinding. I tried to remember where I was...but there was *nothing*. I pushed against my memories, remembering Jude...*yeah, Jude*. I went to see him, went to talk about...*the island*. I licked my lips and tilted my head, looking down, my gaze stopping on the knife sticking out of my side.

A knife...

In me.

Pull it out! The need roared to the surface. *Pull it out...NOW!* I lifted my hand, fingers trembling as I grasped the hilt. But the moment I touched the weapon, a fresh wave of agony ripped through me, tearing a low, wounded moan free.

No…no, I can't do it. My hand hit the floor with a *thud*. I…can't…do…it. What the hell happened to me? Tears welled, blurring my vision. I swallowed, trying to focus on the fact I was still alive, and glanced at the knife once more. My shirt was bloody, cold, and stuck against my skin. But the blood…there wasn't a lot, less than what I'd expect. *It missed an artery, for now.*

For now…

I closed my eyes as relief swept through me, as fleeting as it was. I sucked in a deeper breath, then froze, aware of the movement now that I had a sharpened hunk of steel in my middle. I needed to get out of here, needed to find someone to help me.

That looks heavy, do you need a hand?

The words rose from out of nowhere…and with them came the panicked racing of my pulse. There was something about those words. Something that triggered me. I took a hard breath and lifted my head, dragged my arm under me, and pushed…

Pain screamed, howling and shrieking, tearing through my mouth as I pushed and pushed, driving upwards. Darkness pushed in, blurring my vision as the room around me bled to gray.

"Hold on…*hold on…*" My words were nothing more than a mumble.

Still, I gripped hold of the burn in the back of my throat and pushed.

That looks heavy, do you need a hand?

An alley forced its way into my head as I pushed to a sit. The agony stabbing...*stabbing*. I looked down, *I'm pretty sure I know you*. The words came with the rage of pain. *You're Evan Valachi.*

Out of nowhere, she came.

Blonde hair in my exact shade.

A face that could pass as mine.

A face that could pass as mine...

I looked down at the knife in my stomach, then at the room. It wasn't a room...it was a bunker. There were no windows, just one door. I swallowed hard and focused on that door, driving the heel of my palm against the floor. My arms trembled and desperation howled as I focused on that door and slowly pushed to stand up.

White...

White-washed...

That darkened to gray.

"No." I pressed against the wall, steadying myself, and tried to breathe. The room dulled, then slowly brightened, sharpening in the middle. All I had was that tunnel...and as I focused on what I could see, a doorway came into view. The room where *she'd* come from.

The walls were painted white. Pictures were stuck on the wall. It was those photos I focused on as I took a step, wobbling as my knees trembled. But they held, locking in place to keep me from falling. I took another step and reached for the doorway.

My hand smacked concrete. I held on and stepped into the room, staring at photos of me.

Photos taken outside Jude's office.

Photos of me stepping inside my salon. Bernie's warning rose like a wave inside my head. The car she saw parked across the street... a dark gray Audi. The memory of that alley pressed in. The grimy old yellow Toyota. I bet it was stolen. A prop she'd used to lure me...*but who the fuck was she?*

I moved closer, drawn by the photos and the information scrawled underneath, stopping at one photo in particular. One that felt like this fucking knife had plunged into my heart.

It was me...standing over the grave of my mother on the day of her funeral.

My father stood at my side, frozen and stoic, while I wept. I was dressed in a black dress, big black sunglasses hid my eyes, but they did nothing to hide the shine of tears on my cheeks, nor the image of my fists clenched tight at my sides.

This...*bitch* had invaded me.

In my most personal fucking moment.

Rage rolled through me like I'd never felt before. Ignited by agony, this hunger plunged deep. I wanted to *fucking kill her*. I took a step...I wanted her *dead*. I shifted my gaze to the next photo and froze. It was *him*. Bruno Bernardi.

Older than I remembered him, with long, dirty-blonde hair. A hard body was hidden underneath his shirt. My gaze dragged down him and my heart thundered a little harder, driving the ache in my side a little deeper. I winced, pressed my hand to my side, and took a step closer.

One swipe of my hand, and I ripped it from the wall, taking the clear packing tape with it. I looked down at it, desperate to wad it into a ball in my fist.

But I didn't.

I gripped the corner and shoved it against my side, folding it roughly, then stuffed it into my pocket as the room swayed.

"Easy," I whispered, waiting for the room to brighten once more.

I needed to get out of here. Needed to find somewhere...

A hospital. You need a damn hospital. That voice inside me urged.

But thought of a hospital wasn't what fueled me as I stumbled along the wall. No, urgent care wasn't what drove me toward that door and lifted my gaze to the locks. I ground my teeth and slapped at the lock, feeling it wedge tight as her face burned in my mind. Her *fucking* face that looked like mine. *"Fucking bitch! Take what's mine...and try to kill me?"*

No...

I would not let that happen.

I closed my eyes and slowly made my way back inside the room, finding nothing but a bed, more images taped to the wall, and an empty can of peaches. Nothing I could use to pry the door open. I'd be stuck down here forever. *My phone...*

I glanced to where I'd awakened and found nothing. But I needed something to pry the door open, something strong and sharp. I looked down at the steel stuck in my side. Fear made me shiver, crawling like insects across my skin, driving me back to that door. There was no way out of it, no other way to *survive*.

"Fucking *bitch!*" I barked, and grasped the hilt of the knife.

The wave of agony was unbearable, making me scream. The knife trembled with the shudder. I couldn't do it. Couldn't tear it free...

"NO!" I grasped my wrist with my other hand and leaned against the door, and with one savage yank, I pulled the knife free.

My knees buckled and my head smashed against the door. I stayed like that, leaning into the door as the pain rose and rose...*and rose*. I focused on my breaths and the rise and fall of my chest, the only thing that told me I was still alive. I don't know how long I stood there, how long it took for the pain and the rage to dull.

It burned like a furnace inside me.

Until I lifted my hand and slowly pushed myself upright. The knife was bloody and slick in my hand. Warmth trickled from my side. I didn't dare look down. Instead, I lifted the point of the blade to the crack of the door where the lock was wedged tight and, using all my strength, I forced it through the gap.

The gap widened, wedged aside by the blade. I kept pushing, holding my breath as that warmth slipped further down my side. "Come on..." I begged, forcing the hilt of the knife over until the gap widened...

And I slipped, falling hard against the door.

It popped open, smashing against the wall with a resounding *bang!*

I flew forward, stumbled and tripped. A blast of pain tore through my shins as I hit the jagged edges of the concrete stairs. I barely had time to protect my face...but my side hit hard.

I retched with the pain. My stomach clenched as the wave of darkness slammed into me and this time I couldn't hold on...

FIFTEEN

Bruno

Others disembarked from luxury cruisers onto two other docks further along the island. More flew in their helicopters overhead, invading the island like ants all around me. I stepped to the side of the boat as we slowed and stopped, workers securing us with thick ropes to the smaller dock designed for smaller boats like this one. The ramp was dragged into place before the steward scurried to carry my bags across.

"Thanks," I murmured and stepped over, my boots touching down on the island...*finally*.

I scanned the buildings in the distance. Which one was hers? I looked down at my phone and fought the need to check with Mateo to see if she'd arrived. I didn't want to go running to the Commander every damn time I wanted information about her. I needed a better way to hunt my prey.

And Evan Valachi was my prey...make no mistake about that.

I grabbed my bags and headed up the rise of the Institute's grounds. I'd been here before and roughly knew the layout. My phone gave a *beep*, forcing me to juggle my bags and reach for it.

Deviouz: You must've missed me at the dock. So I grabbed a charter. I'm right behind you.

I winced at the text and went to tuck my phone back as it gave another *beep*.

Institute Security: Your floor is available, Mr. Bernardi. Building 6: Floor 4, Penthouse Suite.

Building six. I lifted my gaze to the towering rows, five accommodation buildings sat amongst the learning blocks right in front, six more would be to the east and I was betting building six was at the far back corner. Giving me the longest walk.

Beep.

A map followed the text. Yep, the far corner of the damn island. I glanced behind me to the steward as he heaved my other bags from the boat.

"Mr. Bernardi, sir."

I turned at the sound of my name to find one of the island's security staff striding toward me. "Yes?"

"I'm here to assist you to your building. Seems there was a mix-up with your guard's arrival and he's sent a request to escort you."

I smiled. "Sure, whatever."

"Your keycard, sir." He handed me a white plastic card and grabbed a bag from my hand, taking the larger suitcase. "If you'll follow me."

I waited for him to walk ahead, following along the path that carried us over the rise and toward the towering buildings in the distance. Laughter cracked out to my left. A woman's laughter and that hunger inside me drove me forward, matching the bodyguard's steps. "How do I find out information about an arrival?"

He glanced my way. "As in, one of the *others*, or a Commission member?"

I licked my lips. "A Commission member."

"Then that will have to go through the proper channels, sir."

Proper channels. So I'd need to go through Mateo anyway. I grabbed my phone, punched in my code, and opened my texts. *I want access to CCTV and arrival information for Evan Valachi. Make it happen.*

Barely a second later, my phone rang. "You realize the situation you're putting me in here, right?" the Commander growled. "*You know I can't give out access to other Commission members.*"

"*I'm* a Commission member...*and* an heir."

"So is *she*, Bruno," Mateo snarled. "If she wanted to spy on you, would you allow it?"

Heat tore through me with the thought. Her watching my every move, watching me hunt her. "Yeah," I murmured. "I would."

"*I* specifically can't allow the request. But the control room is open to *all* serving Commission members," he said carefully. "And as an heir, you have full access to gather the information for yourself."

I smiled, understanding what he was telling me. "Then I guess I'll be visiting the control room."

"Enjoy your stay, Mr. Bernardi," Mateo said curtly, and ended the call.

My smile stayed as I followed the guard past the first towering apartment building and headed across the open grounds in the middle. The place was manicured and opulent. Glass sparkled with the sunshine. Lush gardens surrounded the entrances to the state-of-the-art buildings. The island's guards were everywhere, dressed in dark suits marked with the island's emblem of a shield topped with a skull and a crown. It was a Cosa Nostra emblem, one worn by the founding members.

Like my family...

The Bernardis had a tumultuous past as part of the Commission. We'd been members forever, but something happened years before, something that drove my family back to Ireland. That's where the Bernardis stayed, until my father and uncle decided to split their future between the homeland, and the US.

"Bernardi!"

I jerked my gaze to where Finley Salvatore strode toward me. I glanced at the guard. My gut clenched as I faced the son of Dominic Salvatore. "Finley," I answered.

Had he known his father was hiding Evan Valachi all these years? Did he know the bastard took great pride in tucking her away with one of the gun-running families working for his father?

"Good to see you," he muttered, reaching out to grasp my hand.

"When did you get in?" I asked.

"Few hours ago. I flew in while the others came by boat."

He glanced toward the dock, watching the others disembark.

"Looking for someone?" I followed his gaze.

He flinched and jerked his gaze toward mine. "No one you need to worry about. Catch you around?"

"Sure."

He strode away, trailed by his guards. One was built like a goddamn tank and rumor said he'd been a SEAL. The other was older, met my gaze, and gave a nod. I nodded back, then headed after my luggage. By the time I found building six, my thighs were starting to burn. I swiped the card against the reader tucked on the wall behind the mammoth green palm.

The doors opened, leaving me to stride in and ride the elevator to the penthouse suite. The grind of a zipper came from the bedroom as I made my way inside the opulent suite that faced the back of the island. Through the window-walls, I saw the island stretched out in the distance.

There were no views of other buildings here, just grass, sand... and the sparkling blue water.

"Someone will be arriving soon to unpack your bags, Mr. Bernardi." The guard met my gaze as he stepped from the bedroom.

I just gave a nod as he went toward the door. "Wait, the Control Room."

"Building one, s, between the Commander's offices and the infirmary."

A nod, and he left, leaving me alone.

Beep.

I reached for my phone and dragged it free. *"Class schedule?"* I winced, remembering where the hell I was.

I'd come to meet with Evan, to make her see sense and *give in*. She was promised to the Bernardis. I was here to make sure she made good on that promise. But class schedules? That wasn't on my list of things to do. I tucked my phone away. My to-do list had one name...and I wanted to spend my entire time here doing her very...*very well*.

I took the elevator down to the lobby and stepped out, crossing the grounds as I headed for building one. Halfway across, I caught the commanding stride of someone pissed off and glanced back toward the bodyguard as Deviouz headed to our building. Pity he'd find it empty.

I strode along the path, glancing to where the Salvatore building sat back from the rest of the compound. I wondered who Finley was so interested in finding? Better not be Evan...I glanced over my shoulder, finding the cruisers heading back out to sea. The sky was starting to darken. No doubt they'd be back soon enough with a new group of passengers.

I stepped up to the door of building one as it opened. I wanted to be in first, get the information I wanted, and be out of there, away from the rest of the horde. The rich had invaded our institute, led mostly by a VanHalen. I neither knew her, nor cared.

"Mr. Bernardi." A guard nodded as he strode past.

I have a nod and moved deeper into the building, heading for the Commander's offices and past the conference room where I'd seen my father attend once before. *Where I'll attend in the future.* The Heir, the title rolled through me as I lengthened my stride.

I'd never wanted this title.

Not after *that* night.

The night that had changed everything for me.

I still saw those fucking shoes in my nightmares, still saw the dark pool of blood spilling under his body, and Michele Valachi's face as he strode past me and climbed into that black beast of a car. The night was black and white to me. And *we* were the blackest of them all.

I stood by and watched my family kill a man, and I've stood by many times since then. Drug deals. Guns. Beatings, you name it, and I've watched it happen. I winced. I even contributed...for the sake of the family. My pulse sped with the words. *For the sake of the family...*

Like we lived in the homeland once again.

Where violence was served with your morning breakfast and you had to fight every fucking day to survive.

Only here, we survived by reputation—and this...*the Commission.* No one dared come after you when you were part of the five families. *No one dared.*

I lifted my gaze to the doors marked Infirmary and glanced along the corridor that led to Mateo's offices. The Control Room had to be around here somewhere. A door sat to my left, sunken back from the hallway, like it didn't want to be disturbed.

I took a step, rapped my knuckles against the door, and waited. Nothing, until the camera over my head moved. The heirs were granted more power here than the others, we could go where they couldn't, access the kind of information they wanted. I'd never needed this kind of invasion, never hungered enough to know.

But that all changed the moment Evan Valachi's name was on the attendance list. Now I'd use my position and my power to take all I could where she was concerned. I grabbed my keycard and swiped it over the sensor on the door, hearing a *click*. Then I yanked it open and strode inside, melting into the shadows.

SIXTEEN

Her

I clenched my grip on the table's edge, forcing a smile as one of the other women chattered and laughed. *Pretend. That's all you have to do. Pretend to be like them and get to the island.* I lifted my gaze to the darkness all around me. *Won't be long now.*

Won't be long and I'll be exactly where I'm supposed to be.

Until then...

I had to wear a mask, had to become someone I wasn't, had to forget the voices in my head for just a moment...

Except for me, right, princess?

"Yes, Daddy," I answered, earning a sideways glance from the others around the table. "Except for you."

My throat was dry, my hands shook. The lights in the cabin of the cruiser were unnaturally bright, glaring in my eyes.

"Don't you think that's *too* funny?"

I glanced at the brunette at my side and just stared at her for a second. The laughter died in her eyes and her smile fell, crashing as she stared at me. *Snap out of it,* that voice pushed at me. I curled my lips, trying to understand what she'd just said. But in my head...all I thought of was *him*.

He told me I could do this.

He had never let me down.

He and I were *in love*.

In love...

My smile grew wider, leaving the brunette beside me to frown, slide off her stool, and back away...*slowly. Maybe too wide.* Don't ruin this. Don't ruin all we've done together. I let my mouth go slack, smothering the pretend happiness in an instant.

The boat rocked, rising with the crest of a wave as the faint sparkle of lights shone in the distance. That slow, aching *thud* in my chest hit harder, driving me from my own seat on the outside of the party. And as I watched the bright lights grow a little brighter, I thought of the woman I'd left behind. The *real* Evan Valachi.

I'd wanted to do more than stab her. So much more. I had plans. Dreams filled with sharpened hooks and a honed blade. I had a life of rage and betrayal screaming at me to make good on my promise. *But he didn't want me to.* He wanted me to leave her to die in that basement. He wanted me to leave her where no one would find her...and take her fucking face.

I glanced to my left, to the gleam on the widows of the boat and caught my own reflection. I did take her face. I took her name, and her clothes, as well. I took her *everything*.

He liked it when I did. Liked me looking like her.

He liked fucking me like this.

I liked it, too.

Movement came all around me. The armed guards moved in an instant, striding toward the deck of the boat. My heart hammered as I scanned the others. *They found her...they found her...and now they've found me.*

"Ladies and gentlemen." One of the guards stepped forward, calling everyone's attention.

But they ignored him, drinking their champagne, laughing at their shallow jokes. Even the brunette turned away, reaching for the bottle of Dom.

"There's been a shooting," the guard continued.

All heads turned then, hard gazes snapped his way. Laughter died and conversation ended mid-sentence.

"But I want to assure you we're doing everything in our power to ensure your safe arrival," the guard attempted to reassure us.

"What the fuck does that mean?" one of the guys barked, rising from his seat as he scanned the darkness. "What kind of shooting?"

"I can assure you—" the guard tried his best to placate the murmurs and panicked glances that filled the boat. "We are taking all precautions."

"I was assured the island was safe?" the brunette murmured. "Are you saying it's not?"

The asshole that had spoken up just glared at the guard.

But all I felt was relief. I closed my eyes and felt the boat rock. Crashing, consuming relief. The kind that made me unsteady. I reached out, grasping the edge of the table a little harder. My breaths were suddenly light...*too light*. Like the weight of this started to lift...*like I was almost free.*

"It's okay," the brunette murmured beside me. Someone to my left rested their hand on my arm.

I opened my eyes to find their wide shocked gazes and it took all I had not to smile at their fear. Couldn't they see? *Didn't they understand?*

This was all for me...

For me.

"We'll be okay," the brunette whimpered, her eyes shining and filling with tears as the boat rocked and those sparkling lights in the distance grew clearer.

Yes, I will...

I'd thought for a moment I was done, thought everything I'd worked for was over before it had barely begun. My heart beat harder, I could almost feel the slap of the handcuffs as the lights of the Institute hovered just out of reach.

The one place *we'd* been fighting to get to all these years.

I took a step forward as the guard tried his best to give what little information he could.

But I left them all behind, moving out of the glaring lights of the cruiser's cabin and toward the darkness, catching the glint of the boat's lights shining against the murky waters. But it wasn't over.

Not by a long shot.

The engine of the cruiser throttled louder, driving us toward the illuminated docks. Buildings rose out of the darkness. I watched, mesmerized as the Island grew bigger and bolder. Glass glinted like stars. It was everything I'd dreamed of. Everything I'd hoped. A place where justice would finally be served...and it'd been a long time coming.

It's finally here, the whisper rose in my head.

"Yes, Daddy," I answered, watching the buildings grow in the distance. "It's finally here."

SEVENTEEN

Bruno
———

"Sir?" The guard behind the desk rose as I entered.

I glanced around the rows of monitors against the wall, finding images from the docks and across the grounds. Images flicked from each angle, moving through building after building.

"Mr. Bernardi?"

I met his gaze, trying to find the right words to make this seem... not so invasive. But there were no words, none that could paint this as anything else other than what it was. "I want access to someone...is there a way you can do that?"

"Access?"

I flinched, my jaw clenching tight. He was going to make me say the words, wasn't he? I met his gaze. "I want access to Evan Valachi's apartment, her fucking bedroom. I *want*...access to her."

He swallowed hard, searching my gaze, making sure he'd heard correctly. "You want to spy on an heir of the Commission?"

"Yes. Do you have a problem with that?"

My pulse was roaring in my ears, the sound deafening. I waited for him to tell me to fuck off. For him to be disgusted and outraged. For him to look at me like the piece of filth I was. To spy on another guy was one thing…but to spy on a woman. To *invade* her like that. A bead of sweat gathered at the nape of my neck and slowly trickled along my spine. I reached up, massaging the back of my neck as he searched my gaze.

"No, sir." He sat back down. "Evan Valachi, you said?"

"Yeah," I answered, my voice husky and raw.

I glanced back to the monitors as he brought up a screen of information. A few keystrokes later and an empty apartment filled the monitor.

"Seems she hasn't arrived yet, sir."

I was mesmerized by the layout, even without her being there. "That's fine. Is there a way you can send this live to my phone?"

"You want me to set up a separate connection through our servers?" One brow rose.

I heard the disdain, and chose to ignore it. I licked my lips, unable to tear my gaze from the cameras as it scrolled from the living room to one of the bedrooms…*her bedroom.* "Yeah, I do." I swiped my thumb across the screen, unlocking my phone, and handed it over.

"I've never…I've never had to do anything like this before."

"Yeah, well…there's a first time for everything," I muttered, falling to a new fucking low.

He worked on my phone, loading an app to connect to the cameras of her apartment and bedroom, and handed it over.

"Her bathroom—" I started.

One brow rose. His gaze glinted with a hard glare, killing the rest of my words.

"Yeah. Maybe a bit much."

"You think?" he snarled.

"This stays between us," I snarled back.

He just shook his head and the tight curl of his lips said it all. "No can do, Mr. Bernardi. After this, they'll all know. This information goes out across the private Commission network. So what we do for one heir, we can do for all. I wonder if you'll be as forgiving if Ms. Valachi requests access to your private quarters?"

The thought of that slammed into me.

Evan…watching me. While I slept, while I…fisted myself.

That bead of sweat gathered at the small of my back as excitement raced along my skin. "Yeah, I would," I answered, turning away from him.

I made my way back along the darkened hall to the door. I liked the idea of that a lot. The only thing I'd like better was if she heard me growl her name as I came all over the sheets. *Now that'd make me happy.*

Beep.

I looked down at my cell, reading the text. The guard was right, here it was, in black and white. My dark, dirty needs sent across the private network for all the heirs to read. *Now they'd all know.* I couldn't fight the smile as I strode along the hallway, heading back to the front doors. By the time I stepped out, it was full dark. Voices drifted toward me on the wind. I lowered my head, shoved my phone into my pocket, and made for my building.

"Bernardi." A growl came as I crossed behind one of the buildings.

I stiffened and whipped my gaze toward movement as Cole Hunter stepped out of the shadows. He glanced around, searching for *something*, then settled his gaze on me. "Thought I'd seen you skulking around."

"I don't *skulk*, Hunter," I snapped, my focus shifting over him. The rich asshole was dressed to blend in with the night. Dark blue blazer, black pants, and polished shoes that glinted as he stepped forward. Memories of shoes shining in the night threatened to surface. I swallowed hard, pushing the memory away. "This right here." I waved my hand his way. "Looks a lot like skulking to me."

He gave me a grin and cocked his head to the side. "Care for a game of blackjack?"

"Not a fucking chance." I walked beside him. "Last time you cleaned me out fifty K."

He grinned my way. "Last time you were a chump."

"Fuck you."

Hunter might not be Mafia, but we had a kind of alliance. One born from both of us having to share a suite here at the Institute once. Before I became heir, that was. Now we wouldn't take a chance of someone like Hunter learning the kind of information that could be used against us...or get him killed. But it didn't stop the asshole from turning my place into the seedy strip club he liked.

"I heard Salvatore's making an appearance."

"I heard the same," I answered.

"Fucking sucks about his mom," he muttered.

I winced. Cian Salvatore was from the homeland, a cousin to the Kilpatricks, and my kin's sworn enemy. But no matter what bad blood lay between the Bernardis and the Kilpatricks, there was no denying Cian Byrnes came from good stock.

Her father was quiet, hardworking, even honest, if there was such a thing amongst our kind. A world away from the cold, ruthless Salvatores. But one look at her dark red hair and the fire smoldering in her green eyes, and Dominic Salvatore had been smitten. He wanted her…and look where that got her.

Six feet fucking under.

"Come on." Hunter strode forward. "Blackjack?"

I smothered a laugh. It was always my fucking building that sank to all-time lows here on the damn island. My suite where the cards were played. My fucking bedrooms that were invaded by orgies and drugs. Of all the fucking times…

"We keep it quiet, right?"

"Right," Hunter lied. "Anyway, I heard we're about to be invaded. You might snag an heiress and can ask her for a fucking loan…" He gave me a playful punch to the shoulder.

"For what?" I chided. "By the end of the night, you'll owe me."

"Doubt it, schmuck," he muttered, and glanced over his shoulder. "What were you up to back there, sneaking out of the Commander's building?"

I flinched, answering slowly. "That's none of your fucking business."

His grin just grew wider.

I followed him past the other buildings, heading to mine. I would shut him down in an instant, but the image of Deviouz striding across the Institute's grounds with steam coming out of his ears made me give in. If anything, the loud music and strippers might piss him off enough to go running back to my cousins with his tail between his legs.

Now *that* made me smile.

"Heard you stepped up," Hunter murmured as we cut across the grounds and headed for building six. "Congratulations."

"Yeah, well..." I started, my mind returning to the real reason I was here. I fought the need to open the damn app on my phone and check her suite. "It was either me or Jannick, and he seems busy of late."

"That's one scary fucking dude." Hunter shook his head, casting me a careful look. "No disrespect."

I gave a nod. No disrespect taken. He *was* scary...no, Jannick was downright terrifying.

And gaining momentum every second of the fucking day.

I pressed my card against the reader outside my building and strode toward the elevator with Hunter at my side. *Bang!* A fist smacked the glass wall of the foyer. I jerked my gaze toward the sound, finding Hudson Pierce pressing his face against the glass.

One glance toward Hunter said it all.

The asshole just grinned and hurried forward, punching the button to open the door from the inside.

"What's up, fuckers?" Hudson strode inside with two of the newest recruits of the island on his arms. "This is Stacey Jade and Ebony Smith." He nodded toward Hunter, but those careful eyes moved to me.

"Hi," the brunette smiled. "Stacey."

I just nodded, focusing on Hudson.

"Hunter." The idiot who couldn't keep his word stepped forward and reached out, taking each girl's hand.

"Ebony," the stunning blonde answered, her gaze fixed on me. "And you?"

"Not impressed," I muttered, casting Hudson a glare. "We keep this quiet, okay? I don't want it to turn into the island's own fucking strip club."

He lifted his hands in mock surrender. "Anything you want, Bernardi."

"Bernardi?" The blonde took a step closer, leaving Hudson's side. "With an accent like that you have to be Bruno."

As if she *didn't* know who I was. But I never flinched, just held her stare as she reached up and brushed the lock of my blonde hair from my face. "Fuck me, you're gorgeous," she whispered.

Blonde. A banging body. I could almost pretend she was someone else. Someone who cursed me a long time ago. Maybe she wouldn't care she was being used? Maybe she was just like Bethany? I smiled as my phone gave a *beep*.

I looked down, finding a text from Jannick.

Don't be a fucking asshole. He's there to protect your pathetic fucking ass...now that you're the heir.

My lips curled in a snarl, a flare of hate mingled with self-righteousness. "Fuck you."

"Excuse me?" the blonde questioned.

But I ignored her as I closed out the text and found the brand new app on my phone, the one that connected to the cameras in *her* room. And all of a sudden, I didn't give a shit about playing cards, or sleeping with lookalikes. I wanted the real thing...even if it was through a goddamn camera.

"Just one game, okay?" Hunter urged.

I looked up, meeting his gaze. Hope danced in his eyes...and there was always Deviouz.

"One, I promise." He just smiled as chatter started and the brunette shivered, wrapping her arms around her body.

The movement couldn't be more obvious. So I turned and headed back toward the elevator, watching as Hunter sent a text to someone. "Just organizing some refreshments," he muttered.

An hour later, and those *'refreshments'* were starting to make my head spin.

"Have another," Hunter urged, sliding a tiny pink pill toward me from the other side of the card table. Music pounded and the lights were dimmed low. My apartment was suddenly filled with familiar and unfamiliar faces. I shook my head to the pill and downed my Scotch as the beat of the music thrummed, crawling under my skin.

The brunette was suddenly naked, striding through the apartment with her bare pussy showing and all. Still Hunter grinned like an asshole.

"I told you to keep it quiet," I growled, a moment of sobriety hitting me like a freight train.

"This is quiet," he grinned. "Now, fucking deal. I'm not leaving this table until you owe me at least ten K."

I just stared at him. "I...I need a fucking drink."

I didn't remember how it had happened. But then again, with Hunter, I never really did. I rose from my seat, swallowed, and waited for the room to stop spinning before taking a step. Movement came out of nowhere, slamming into me. I growled as the redhead stumbled backwards, her eyes widening with fear.

"What the fuck—" I barked.

"S-sorry," she stammered, took a step backwards, and smoothed down her dress.

"Hey," I scowled. "Don't I..."

"I don't think so." She spun and scurried away from me.

But I was sure I knew her...I was sure...a name hovered at the edge of my mind. *Kat...Kat VanHalen*, the billionaire heiress. "Well, fuck me."

I stared after the redhead, then turned, running smack into a fucking wall striding after her.

"What the fuck—" I lashed out, grasping the guy by the shirt. *"Watch where you're fucking walking!"*

He tore his gaze from the redhead scurrying away and glared down at me. Hate moved behind those cruel eyes. I knew the gaze of one who liked to deal out pain. One I saw every time I saw Jannick.

"Fucking asshole," I shoved him, watching him stumble backwards, then straighten, backing away carefully, shifting his focus to the redhead striding away.

"You okay?" Hunter was beside me before I knew it.

"Who the fuck was that guy?" I stared after him.

"Damon Zakharov," he answered as the asshole left.

But there was something about the asshole who hunted the redhead. Something that set my teeth on edge and made the darkness in me rise to the surface. "I don't like him."

"Not many do," Hunter added, staring after the fucker.

"There you are."

I caught the flinch from Hunter before he swallowed hard and slowly turned. "Vad.," He muttered, and licked his lips. "I was just coming to find you."

"Of course you were."

I turned, catching the glint in the asshole's gaze. "Vad," I acknowledged.

He just met my gaze before turning back to his prey. I fought the urge to flinch, knowing the vindictive asshole would take pleasure in the reaction. Calling Vad Kardinov a shark was offensive to sharks. But there was no other word for him. Cold blooded. A fucking savage and not one I wanted striding through my place. "Why are you here, Kardinov…I'm sure the hole you crawled out of is lonely."

He just cut me a stare. "It's collecting day, and Hunter here owes me two."

"Two thousand?" I took a step closer. "Piss off..."

"Two *hundred* thousand...*with interest.*" He cut that glinting stare back to Hunter. "Or would you like me to explain how we acquired the little habit you seem to have trouble kicking?" He swiped his nose with his thumb.

"No," Hunter answered, paling under the dimmed lights. "I wouldn't."

"Hunter," I said, not taking my gaze from the Kardinov. "You okay here?"

He licked his lips, then forced a smile for me. "Yeah, grab your drink, B. I'll be there in a minute."

I didn't want to leave him, not knowing how Kardinov and his band of nasty brethren worked. Whispers of a *skin trade* for the island surrounded him. Wouldn't surprise me with someone like him. I knew he trafficked drugs and guns for the Commission. They fucking owned him somehow, although I could never figure out why.

That shit was never spoken about.

Skin trade or not...I didn't like him coming around, which was just another reason to shut this party down. I strode toward the counter and refilled my glass, making my way back to the table. Out of the corner of my eye, I watched them. Kardinov's lips curled in the corner as Hunter shook his head and massaged his temple. He was nervous about something. Something he didn't want me to know about.

You name it and I'd seen it. Hell, I'd probably had a hand in it.

But this...this had put Hunter on edge.

He turned away from Kardinov, pacing the floor before stopping in front of the asshole once more. His shoulders sagged, a resigned nod of his head. I tried to focus on the cards in front of me, playing with my stack of chips as Hunter finally returned and slowly slid into his chair on the other side.

"Bernardi," Kardinov muttered.

I didn't answer, just lifted my gaze to Hunter as he sat there, sweating like a bastard, until the shark finally swam away, seeking more blood in the water. The way Hunter sat there and stared at the middle of the table, unable to meet my gaze, told me this game was over.

I waited until the asshole was gone before speaking. "You in trouble?"

Hunter flinched. "Don't...okay? Just don't."

"If it's money you need..."

Hunter just gave a hard bark, something unhinged echoing in the sound. "No, it's not about just about money." He licked his lips and exhaled hard, finally meeting my gaze. "I'm okay, B. Thanks for the offer, but I'm okay."

I wanted to believe him...I really did.

But I knew when the asshole was lying.

And right now...he was hiding something.

Something big...

EIGHTEEN

Her

"The *infamous* Evan Valachi."

I stepped into the apartment, lifted my gaze to the voice in the dark, and stilled. My heart hammered as the porter carried my bags to my bedroom, leaving me behind. I'd known this moment was coming, had gone over it in my head. But planning was one thing...being here was something else altogether.

Warm amber lights illuminated the living room floor, but the rest of the place was plunged into darkness. Darkness was what she liked. Sex, seduction, and dark deeds in darker corners. That was Xael Davies's world. Movement came from the sofa as she slid her feet from under her and rose.

Wild ebony hair framed the kind of face men got hard for, with pouty, perfect lips and kohl-lined, glittering eyes. My pulse sped as she took a slow, seductive step toward me and, even though I'd only ever known *him,* heat raced through my body.

"Here I was thinking they made you up," she murmured. "The precious Mafia Princess tucked away in her ivory castle, never to see anyone for as long as she was pure."

I licked my lips, my mouth suddenly dry. I was prepared for this...I was prepared for *her*.

He'd prepared me, unearthing all her secrets from the years of research. From the number plate on her cherry red Lexus, to the reason she was expelled from the prissy all-girls Ivy League college she'd attended months before.

Seducing her English Lit Professor was one thing, but posting pictures of Rosalie Hartford's perky breasts and the creamy inner thighs on the internet for her husband to find was another.

Her family tried their best to shut the story down. But there was one thing about Xael Davies no one was able to manage...

She didn't give a fuck.

Not about everyone knowing she liked men *and* women, or who her daddy was. In fact, I think she liked it.

Careful, princess, Daddy whispered in my head.

Only this time, I couldn't answer. I had to be careful...had to be *very* careful where Xael was concerned. I swallowed hard. "It's me..."

"In the flesh," she murmured, stepping close...a little too close.

I took a step backwards as she advanced, until I hit the end of the kitchen counter with my hip. Pain smarted for a second, but then she reached around, placed her hands on either side of me, and stared into my eyes.

All I could see was her lips, and smell the dark, erotic scent of something that reminded me of midnight blooming flowers and raw, rich earth.

"Umm..." I whispered as she leaned in, her breasts barely an inch from mine. "I don't...I don't l-like women..."

Her lips curled into a smile before she dropped her head backwards and chuckled, pushing away. "I'm just messing with you. Fuck, I know that." She turned her back to me, then froze, glancing at me over her shoulder. "But then again, I don't really know anything about you, do I?"

Panic reared. My voice was husky, my throat dry as I answered. "I guess you will now...seeing as how we're sharing an apartment."

"True," she agreed. "How nice the girls have to share, but the dudes get a suite all to themselves."

My nerves were starting to hum and fray. "I saw others in the elevator. Looks like the ones below ours are taken, as well."

"As long as they don't wake me in the mornings, I don't give a fuck." She spun toward me, piercing me with a deadly stare. "You're not an early riser, are you?"

"God, no," I muttered, knowing full well a party girl like her slept until well past noon.

"Thank fuck," she sighed as she turned away. "Or I'd have to knife you in your sleep."

My darkness escaped, a little at least. "You can try."

Her smile grew wider and her lips parted, showing perfect white teeth. "I like you already, Valachi. You and I are gonna get along just fine." She strode toward the elevator and stopped as the porter headed back toward us. "Oh, and make room for me in your busy schedule. I have a friend I want to introduce you to. Don't worry, you'll like her. She's filthy fucking rich and not pretentious."

"Oh?" My heart thrummed. Meeting others was a hazard. "Who?"

"Kat VanHalen," she called out as she followed the porter into the elevator.

A VanHalen? My pulse stuttered and raced. I heard the elevator *ding,* leaving me alone...on my first night on the island. Panic and elation swept through me. I did it...*I did it.* My lips curled and in that moment, I didn't give a fuck if my grin was too wide, or if I made others uncomfortable.

I didn't give a fuck...

"I did it, Daddy." I stepped away from the edge of the counter and spun, taking in the sparse, elegant surroundings in the penthouse suite. "I made her believe."

Of course you did, princess. There's nothing you can't do...

Laughter spilled out of me, sounding too high-pitched and strange. But I didn't care. I made my way through the apartment and opened the refrigerator door, seeing food other than canned peaches filling the shelves, and opened the cupboard. There was food there, too. A chef would bring us the kind of foods I liked. A cleaner would wash and dry our clothes. Someone else would take care of our bathrooms and make our beds...*they'd make our beds...*

I jerked my gaze toward the bedroom, hurrying as I stepped through the door and hit the light. My suitcase had been opened and my clothes were hanging in the walk-in closet. "No," I whispered, opening the closed, stowed away suitcase, and felt the weight. It was heavy...too heavy for it to be fully unpacked.

The apartment was silent behind me. I stilled for a second before lifting my suitcase onto the bed. My phone gave a *beep*. I pulled it free and looked down, reading the text before freezing.

I read it again, just to be sure.

Then I straightened, aware of everything around the room. Every movement, every hum...and slowly lifted my head to the smoke alarm on the ceiling in the center of the bedroom.

Careful.

I unzipped my suitcase and reached inside, feeling for the false floor. A jerk of the velcro corner of the lining, and I angled the suitcase to the side. With my heart hammering, I pulled out my weapons and slowly knelt, covering my movements with the lid. I'd need a better place to hide them, especially now.

Heat raced across my skin and burned in my cheeks as I slipped them under the mattress and rose. I could feel him...feel him *watching*.

"I don't want to do this," I mouthed the words.

I didn't. I didn't want to do what *he* wanted.

Revulsion rolled through me as I closed my eyes. My hands shook as I grabbed my purse and opened it, taking out the bottle of small white pills. I twisted the cap, shook out two tablets, and popped them into my mouth.

The thought of Bruno watching me...of him, *wanting me,* made the darkness rise. Even if it wasn't really me he wanted. I ignored the tang of acid in the back of my throat, fighting the urge to gag, and swallowed, forcing the tablets down.

The thought of pretending was almost too much to bear. Panic pounded in my ears as I looked down, rereading the message.

*You will do this...*he wrote. *For me.*

I'd come all this way, done all those *things*. The dark, dank basement rose in my mind. The place he'd hidden me after the hospital, with all its rules and pills. Pills that made my head fuzzy and my dry throat ache. Pills I still needed, even if it was just to force the darkness away. In that basement, I'd found clarity. In that basement, I'd found *him*.

And we made the plan...

The plan that was almost over...almost *real*. Then we'd be together *forever*.

Then we'd be free...

I smiled, knowing that was where I'd left her, the real *Evan*.

And now I had one more person to put in the ground. One more *heir* to tear apart...like *they*'d torn me apart.

I would do this...for *him*.

Because that's what love was...

My knees trembled as I rose and stowed my suitcase back in the closet. Heels sank into the carpet, then clacked against the tiles as I made my way into the bathroom, not switching on the lights. Illuminated by the bedroom lights, I gripped the basin and stared into the mirror. Was he watching me in here? I had to expect that now...I had to expect everything.

A shiver coursed along my spine.

I'd only every known *him*. His body. His hunger. His *lust*. Desire pulsed through me. He'd been my first, and I only ever wanted *him*. But could I do this? Could I do more than look like her... could I entrance like her, as well?

Could I seduce...*Bruno Bernardi?*

I thought of the knives under my mattress, and the way *she* looked when I'd plunged the steel in deep. I thought of how it would feel when it was Bruno. I could almost hear his screams. He'd bleed like *she* had. He'd panic like *she'd* panicked. His eyes would widen and he'd look at me so confused. He would know... that this was all a lie. Desire coursed through me, shoving revulsion aside. This I could hold onto. *This I wanted.* My mother's haunting gaze filled my mind. She was broken after my dad died, crumbling into nothing when they came and took everything.

Our house.

Our car.

Our *future*.

Seduce Bruno Bernardi?

I had a better idea.

Not seduce...*entice*.

How a rattlesnake makes a sound, drawing out its prey...right before it struck.

I smiled, staring into the mirror for a second, then turned for the bedroom.

NINETEEN

Bruno

"Thanks for this, man..." Hunter slurred, one arm draped around my shoulders, his blazer discarded somewhere, his shirt unbuttoned. "I owe you."

"Sure." I just walked him to the elevator, and removed his arm from around me. "No problem at all."

But it was a problem. A *very big* problem. I wanted this goddamn party over and to be alone...*with the fucking app on my phone open.*

She had to be in her room by now. Holed up safe and sound... within reach.

Christ, I was aching to watch her, to see her...to *fucking touch her.*

"You seem to owe a few people, Hunter," I growled, meeting his gaze. "Kardinov isn't the kind of man you'd want to owe *anything* to, if you get what I mean."

He just licked his lips and swayed. Desperation echoed in his eyes as he gave a nod. "I know...I know. It's just..." he started before his frown deepened and his gaze shifted. "Never mind. You don't need to worry about me, Bernardi."

For a second, I thought he was going to tell me just how deep he was really in, until he swallowed hard, and straightened his spine. "Thanks, man. I appreciate it. You're a true friend, B...a true fucking friend," he muttered, turning away and stepping onto the elevator.

The others followed, filling the car.

The lights were dimmed, but the music still played, filling the apartment with the slow, steady pulse of an erotic track. It was the kind of music you fucked to. Grinding, riling...hot and heavy, making my cock hard with the thought of it.

I crossed the space and hit the button, ending the sound, leaving my ears to hum in the wake. Glasses littered the counters and a small baggie lay discarded on the arm of the sofa. I picked it up, glanced at the contents, and fought the urge to take a taste. But I didn't want to be dulled while I watched her. I wanted to be sharp, to etch into my mind every fucking minute of her.

I tossed the baggie into the garbage, shutting off the lights to the apartment as I went. Grabbing the keys from my pocket, I unlocked my bedroom door. No fucking way was I allowing others to fuck in my bed. It was bad enough I'd let them invade my space. I massaged the back of my neck as I stepped inside and closed the door.

Beep.

I glanced at my phone.

Deviouz: Any more coming up tonight?

I winced, having almost forgotten he was up, and punched out a text. *No, no one comes up tonight...*

Unless it was Evan. My pulse raced at the thought. I should be so fucking lucky. But I had a feeling it wasn't going to be so fucking smooth between us. After all...we had history.

A Bernardi. My wince was almost a smile.

It didn't matter who it was. Jannick...me.

She hated us all.

My heart pounded as I stepped into the bathroom and undressed, aching to open the app and watch her on the cameras. *Not yet...*I stepped out of my shoes and draped my pants on the vanity. I stepped into the shower, adjusted the water, and dropped my head. Heat washed down my spine. I grabbed the washcloth, running it over my body, and cupped my balls. My cock twitched in my hand, my nerves were on fire, my balls tight and aching. I leaned my head backwards and let the water run down my chest until I couldn't wait a second longer.

I turned off the water and stepped out, grabbed a towel from the rack, and dragged it across my skin. My phone waited. I grabbed it, sliding my thumb across the screen and opening the app. My gaze was riveted to the screen as I dropped the towel to the floor and strode naked into the bedroom.

I scrolled through her apartment, taking in the layout, and flicked to the camera in her bedroom. Energy coursed through me as I found the outline of her body in the dark, black on creamy skin. I stopped at the edge of the bed, taking in the tiny black negligee she wore.

Fuck me...

Her long legs scissored against the sheets as she shifted on the bed. Was she awake? More importantly, did she know I was watching? She had to, right? Had to have read the text sent from the Institute. Had to know it was me…

But it hadn't specifically said who'd requested access to the internal monitoring equipment…or who they were watching. Excitement flooded my body, hitting me harder than any drug, as her nightie rode high, showing the sweet curve of her ass.

I sank to the mattress and slid under the sheets. Fuck, I wanted that ass, wanted my fingers sinking into her flesh. I wanted to expose her, wanted to touch her, finding the parts of her aching with heat. I swallowed hard and reached under the sheets.

But nothing compared to the image in my mind. The one that never failed to get me off. Her standing with her back against the tree. Her perfect white dress billowing behind her as Jannick knelt between her legs, shoving her panties aside, exposing her pussy.

But it was my fingers that sank into her…warmth up to my first knuckle, sliding into the tightness.

And in my vision, she didn't look at me in horror. She looked at me with *need*. Biting her lip as she dropped her head backwards, opening her legs a little wider as heat rolled through her body.

"Fuck," I growled as the vein running the length of my shaft pulsed and blood rushed, sending a bead into the tip. I opened my eyes and looked at the screen as she shifted again, tossing and turning, unable to sleep.

I bet that virginity is weighing heavy right about now…

I knew she was…pure. Knew how she'd vowed to never let another man have her. I knew she both clung to and hated her virginity. She used it and honed it, working harder, becoming colder. She didn't need sex. Didn't need a man...sure as hell, didn't want a husband.

There was only one problem...*the deal was already done.*

"I fucking own you," I whispered, drawing my clenched fist all the way to the tip and sliding back down. *"You hear me, Evan Valachi? I fucking...own...you..."*

The fantasy morphed from the garden of her home and moved into her bedroom on the island. I stood at the doorway of her room, watching as she tossed and turned in the dark, her nightie riding high, just as it did right now. Through the cameras, I watched as she parted her legs, her hand moving to the juncture between her thighs.

My breaths came hard and heavy. "Fuck yeah," I moaned.

Black lace against her creamy thigh, she rubbed along the crease, clamping her legs tight against the sensation as though she didn't want to feel what her body craved. But it did. It *ached* for fingers running against her pussy, *burned* for a cock buried deep. She *hungered* for the release. It was a release I wanted to give her.

I *wanted*...

"Fuck," I barked as my cock twitched, spilling against my fucking hand.

Hard breaths consumed me as I came down from the high. Still she rubbed, holding her hand still and rocked her hips forward, her thighs closed around her fingers.

She was dangerous, this one...

More than I'd fucking realized.

And I wasn't talking about business.

She was dangerous to me.

I laid my phone down, leaving the app open. In the dark, I watched her lips part and face contort. She was heated and raw, chasing a high her body craved, but as her hips jutted forward and a frown drew between her brows, she stopped.

Exhausted. Frustrated. She drew her hand from between her thighs and lay there staring up at the ceiling. Then slowly, her gaze moved as she looked directly into the camera. Light glinted in her eyes. The reflection of the camera at night like a hunter's scope.

My pulse raced at the sight.

I watched her even after the glint died away and she closed her eyes. Watched her as my own breaths slowed and sleep finally came. Even in the darkness, I watched her...over and over again.

VOICES SPILLED along the hallway of building two. I glanced at my phone for the sixth time in as many seconds, and glanced toward the entrance. She should be here by now...*so why the fuck wasn't she?*

I'd awakened with her on my mind, reaching for my goddamn phone as my eyes watered and stung. But she wasn't in her room. Her bed was neatly made and the apartment was quiet. From the camera in the kitchen, I could see Xael Davies still in bed with the blinds drawn. But there was no Evan...

She was on the class schedule. One I'd checked a hundred fucking times now. Supposed to be here for some bullshit class on psychology. But she hadn't shown.

"Waiting for someone?"

I glanced toward the growl as Finley Salvatore strode toward me, looking just as pissed off as I felt. His jaw flexed as some woman called out his name. But he didn't glance toward her, just shoved his hands into his pockets and stopped at my side.

"Yeah," I answered. "I am. You?"

He didn't answer, just glared as a group of rich assholes headed toward us. So that was a big fat yes.

"Didn't think you were coming," I muttered, watching the same group as they stepped through the doorway, casting us nervous glances as they went.

"Yeah, well." He turned and met my gaze. "Plans fucking change, Bernardi."

"That they do, brother." He lifted his gaze to a brunette as she scurried toward us, clutching an iPad to her chest.

She froze when she saw him and her eyes widened. One panicked gaze to the open doorway, and she slipped inside the classroom...and Finley Salvatore followed. I waited for a second, until the lecturer closed the door.

His voice spilled through the cracks in the doorframe. Still, I didn't hear a word. Instead, I pushed off the wall and opened the app on my phone, finding her apartment still fucking quiet. "Where the hell are you, Evan?"

I spent all day searching for her, going to all of her classes, but she never showed. And when Xael finally dragged her ass out of bed at two in the afternoon, she was still nowhere to be seen.

Where the fuck was she?

I massaged the back of my neck as I strode toward my building. Movement came from the corner of my eye. I glanced up, finding Deviouz watching me from the other side of the grounds. My lips curled at the sight. Hate rolled through me. He hadn't come near me after I left the fucker behind. The text from Jannick had gone unanswered.

I didn't trust him...*or* the fucking bodyguard.

My sour mood just grew as the day wore on...and when night came, I sat on the sofa in my apartment in the fucking dark and stared at my phone...

I couldn't eat. Scotch was the only thing that helped stave off my hunger for her. I blinked and zoned out. Rage was like ice in my veins. When the elevator door in her apartment opened and she strode in, I leaned forward, my grip clenching around the phone as I growled, "Where the fuck have you been?"

TWENTY

Evan

The faceless man took a step forward. *"Take off your clothes, Evan,"* he growled. *"You know you want me...why are you fighting so hard?"*

He grabbed my arms and yanked me against his chest. Still his face was murky, blurring as I turned my gaze away.

"Get the fuck off me!" I fought, shoving away from him.

"I'm not here to hurt you. I don't want to hurt you, Evan."

His grip slipped as I tore from his hold. Desperation roared as I jerked my gaze to look behind me. Emptiness waited for me back there...I focused harder, squinting.

Something shifted in the dark. Black on black moved, spiking my pulse.

Something waited, something *watched me.*

"That looks heavy." A woman's voice spilled out of the *nothingness*. The tone deepened before morphing into a low, sickening chuckle.

The sounds spilled through the emptiness, standing the hairs on my arms. She was mocking...*me*. I tried to remember saying the words, deep down knowing they were the reason why I was here, in the dark. *"THAT LOOKS HEAVY!"* she roared.

I flinched, my heart smashing against my ribs as I stumbled backwards.

Movement came again, only this time it came toward me.

A whimper wrenched free as I stumbled backwards and turned my head, desperate for help from the faceless man. But he wasn't there...it was just me...and...*her*.

Her...

"Evan!" A deep growl wrenched me awake.

I opened my eyes, my pulse thundering. A scream trapped in my throat as the bright lights overhead speared my vision.

"Evan. *Thank God.*"

I jerked my gaze toward the familiar voice, and as my eyes adjusted, a familiar face came into view. "Dad?"

Concern etched his face, adding to the wrinkles at the corners of his eyes. "It's me." He leaned closer, grasping my hand. "It's me, honey."

Behind him, someone stepped into the room. Her face crumpled as she neared the bed.

"Jessie," I whispered.

She gave a little wave as tears ran down her cheeks. Her lips parted, but there were no words, just torment as she stared at me and wrung her hands. I glanced at Dad, searching his gaze for answers.

"What happened?" I whispered.

A machine beeped beside me. An IV drip was attached to the back of my hand.

"That's what we'd like to know," he answered.

Danger etched his words, and slowly the fear in his eyes was pushed aside. He gripped the railing on the hospital bed and searched my eyes. "What do you remember?"

Remember?

I shifted my gaze to the foot of my bed, my mind a blur. "Nothing."

"You were stabbed, Evan," he growled. "Bleeding out when they brought you to the hospital. You're lucky to be alive, you understand that, right? You're lucky *to be alive.*"

"Stabbed?" I repeated, and shifted my gaze to his. "How?"

There was a twitch at the corner of his eye. "That's what I'd like to know."

"Here she is." A guy strode into the room, iPad in hand, a stethoscope draped around his neck. Tall and gorgeous, his brown eyes sparkled as he smiled. "Evan, I'm Doctor Terrance Brillene. I was the attending when you were brought in from Ikon General." His voice deepened as he set a warm gaze on me. "You gave us all a bit of a scare for a while, so it's good to see you awake and talking."

Ikon General...

What the hell was I doing there?

I licked my dry lips and tried to swallow as the doctor glanced at my father, then Jessie. "Mr. Valachi," he said carefully. "How about I check Evan and see you outside for an update?"

It was the politest way of saying 'please leave' that I'd ever heard. Dad held my gaze, then gave my hand a squeeze before rising from the chair, glaring at the doctor as he motioned for Jessie to leave. "Make sure she receives the best care."

"Of course, sir," He bowed his head slightly as they left the room, until the door closed.

Then he turned toward me, not moving for a moment, and smiled. "Your dad's one scary guy."

My lips twitched at the corners. If he only knew.

"Now, questions." He unwound the stethoscope, placing the ends into his ears and came closer. "Hit me."

"Dad said I was brought in with a stab wound.," I responded, lifting my gaze to his as he pressed the cold metal over my gown.

"Quite a substantial one," he commented, bending over, his gaze unfocused. "Half an inch to the right and I'd be having a very different conversion with your father. One I never get used to. But we were lucky, they were able to stabilize you at Ikon General and brought you here."

My pulse raced, sweat beaded at the nape of my neck. *There's something else wrong with me...something...*

But he leaned back and removed the stethoscope from his ears. "Want to tell me what happened?"

Confusion flared. My pulse pounded with the question as I searched my mind. Only darkness waited...*darkness*...a cold shiver raced through me as the memory of that emptiness returned. Something moved in the shadows. Something that was waiting for me.

That looks heavy...

The words slammed into me as he leaned closer and patted my arm. "It's okay...if you can't tell me. I'm here to make sure you're okay, physically at least. The mind is a beast of its own..."

But his words drifted away.

I was frozen with fear as inside my mind an alley rose from the murky depths, dragging with it a woman standing at the open trunk of a car.

A cold sweat raced down my spine.

"But you might want to talk to the police," the doctor continued, oblivious to the fact I wasn't there anymore.

I'd been dragged back to the moment I'd stepped down from the curb and the resounding words found me. *"That looks heavy."*

"What?"

I jerked my gaze to the doctor as I was thrust into a room, a room that smelled like cold and wet...and *concrete*. My heart pounded, the sound filling my ears as I fisted the sheets.

Concern flared on the doctor's face in front of me as the machines at my side started to beep and howl.

"Evan?" The doctor leaned closer, grasping my arm. *"What's wrong?"*

I shook my head as my memory sharpened. Footsteps followed from that room, thundering in time with my racing pulse as the glint of a knife shone.

A knife...

A cry ripped from me. My hands flew up in a defensive pose as my body shook and shuddered. The machine was howling beside me, and the room started to blur.

"*Evan!*" the doctor barked beside me.

I could feel his hands, and hear his voice. But the image of that knife...*had me by the throat.*

Pain carved through my middle as the hospital room started to darken at the edges. From the corner of my eye, the door to my room flew open and the wrath of Michele Valachi stormed inside.

"*What the fuck is going on here?*" Dad roared.

I lifted my gaze to the panic in his eyes as the machines howled and squealed beside me. *Daddy*...the word hovered on my lips as the doctor grabbed me by the shoulders and pressed me back against the mattress.

"Breathe, Evan," the doctor ordered. "*Breathe!*"

Air rushed in, cold and chilling. I closed my eyes and tried to push the image of that knife away.

But instead of driving it back into the darkness and staving off the crumbling of my world, the rest of the memory slammed into me...*all of my memories.*

Her face.

Her *hate*.

Her moaning and whispering into the phone as I surfaced from the darkness.

And finally...the photos in that room.

One photo stuck inside my head.

Of Bruno Bernardi...

"No!" I growled, and shoved against the doctor's hold. "NO!"

The room brightened as hate forced the darkness aside. Hate for *him...and her.*

Bruno's face burned in my memory. His long blonde hair. The quirky smile on his face. Eyes that held nothing more than hunger and greed. Deep down, I knew who he was...and it wasn't just a monster. He was the reason why I needed therapy, the face of the man who haunted my dreams.

I closed my eyes as the squealing of the machine suddenly ended.

But it wasn't his face, was it? He *was* the *faceless* man.

He was the one who made me feel sick and dirty.

The man who made both my pulse race and my body hum. My fists gripped the sheets tighter.

"Evan..." the doctor started, staring into my eyes.

"I'm okay," I gasped, and opened my eyes. "I'm okay."

"What the fuck was that?" Dad barked.

His hate and power filled the room. *Suffocating me.* What was it? The memory of what happened to me. I remembered it all. Every terrifying moment...the only thing I didn't know was...*why?*

Why me?

Who the hell *was* she?

The photos inside that room filled me once more. Photos of me, my hair salon, my therapist. My mother's funeral. *Who the fuck was she?* I found my father standing beside me. Rage sparkled in his eyes. One word and I'd unleash him. One word, and he'd become the man most people in our world feared. The man who did terrible things in the pursuit of power.

For a second, I imagined how it would feel to watch him destroy the world in my name...and I didn't like it. The power would be his. The wrath...*his*. And I'd be nothing more than a ghost occupying the seat of my father. I'd *never* become an heir. Never be what I wanted to be.

Purpose burned inside me, stealing the panicked thrum of my pulse and slowing it down.

Thud.

Thud.

Thud...

"Evan?" The doctor pressed his penlight and shone the glare into my eyes. "Want to tell me what that was?"

"Determination," I growled, and unfolded my fingers from the sheets and pushed them aside. "I want out of here. *Now.*"

The doctor's eyes widened as he stumbled backwards. I didn't bother to watch my father as the doctor shook his head. "That's not happening. Back to bed, Ms. Valachi."

I stiffened at the sound of my name and glanced at my father. But it wasn't fear I saw when I looked at him. I winced, grabbed the bedrail, and pulled my feet toward the edge. "Are you going to lower this thing?" I met my father's gaze.

There was a twitch at the corner of his lips as the doctor spluttered, "Evan, this isn't a joke. You were stabbed."

But Dad just stepped forward, stabbed the button, and lowered the railing.

"No. You're not leaving," the doctor insisted as I clenched my fist on the side of the mattress and slid my feet inch by agonizing inch toward the side.

Dad never helped me, but never made a move to stop me, either. He just took a step backwards as I pressed my hand against my side, clenched my teeth, and shoved forward.

"I'm telling you, you'll cause yourself some serious damage by doing this," the doctor warned curtly.

"I know," I forced the words through clenched teeth. "Whatever I need to sign, doc, I'll sign. I just can't... stay here."

"*Talk* to her." The doctor jerked his gaze to my father.

One brow rose on the old man. The doctor had no idea *who* he was talking to...or *who* he was talking about.

"My daughter is old enough to understand the consequences of her actions. Aren't you, Evan?"

I just gave him a look and gripped the bed as I scanned. "I need someone to take this damn thing out of my hand." Then my gaze stilled on the doctor.

His gaze sharpened and his lips narrowed into a thin line. "If you insist. I'll need you to sign a waiver."

"If *you* insist," I replied, reaching over my shoulder to yank the ties on my gown.

The IV line pulled tight as I leaned forward, until the doctor gave a sigh and pulled the metal stand around. That room waited inside my head. Bright lights. The cold, heady scent was cloying. "My phone," I muttered, and glanced around the room.

"You didn't have anything with you when you were brought in." The doctor strode toward the door, then stilled, glancing over his shoulder at me. "Are you sure about this?"

"Sure as I'll ever be," I answered.

I wasn't just sure.

I was *determined*.

That...*bitch had* left me for fucking dead.

She hadn't counted on me surviving.

I guess her investigation hadn't told her I wasn't so fucking easy to kill.

The doctor yanked open the door and disappeared, leaving us alone. I jerked my gaze to my father. "Dad, I need your phone."

He frowned.

"Don't look at me like that," I grumbled, wincing as pain throbbed in my side. "I *know* you track my phone. So hand it over."

He took a step, reaching inside his pocket. "Let me do this."

"Not this time."

"E," he said, calling me by the name he'd used when I was a kid, when he wanted me to do what he said.

But I wasn't a kid anymore, and doing things to please him wasn't high on my agenda anymore. But doing them out of spite...and fury...*now that was right up there*. My hand shook, but still I held it out. "Don't push me, Daddy."

There was a second when I thought he'd fight me, when he'd push me to the point where I left him *again*. But he didn't.

Instead, he stepped forward and placed his phone in my hand. "The code is the most important date in my life. Just promise me you'll be careful."

"I'll promise you I'll make you proud, how's that?" I slowly met his gaze.

"If you only knew how much that terrifies me."

Oh, I had a fair idea.

I was guessing it was the reason I was here, with a damn knife wound in my stomach. A badge of honor from having the Valachi name. I grabbed the phone in one hand, the metal IV stand in the other, and shuffled toward the door as Jessie pushed in.

She clutched an overnight bag as she strode into the room. "Evan...Evan, they told me you..."

"I need clothes, Jessie."

Confusion narrowed her gaze as she looked at me, then to my father. She didn't realize I knew she'd been keeping his bed warm since my mother, didn't know I knew all about their dark and filthy little secrets. The games they played...*and the clubs they attended.*

My father might be older...but he wasn't dead.

She'd tried her best to hide it from me, tried to not *'taint'* the memory of her before my mother died. But I didn't care. In fact, I was glad. "I'm not asking, Jessie," I urged. "I need to do this."

"E." She shook her head, trying the same tactic my father had as she met his gaze and stilled. Her eyes widened and her lips parted.

Yeah, they were definitely fucking.

"Just give it to her," Dad said behind me.

I took the bag as she lifted it. "Thanks." And I made my way slowly past before stopping. "And I'm really glad you two have each other."

I left them behind, bracing my hand against the wall as I made my way out to the nurse's station. One of them headed my way, a scowl on her face.

"Save it," I told her. "I'm not changing my mind."

I was prepared for an argument, but the middle-aged woman just gave a nod and handed me a sheet of paper. "If you'll just sign this, Ms. Valachi, and I'll take that cannula out of your hand and get you underway."

Just like that?

I signed my name before she led me to a treatment room. Barely fifteen minutes later, I was pressing my hand against my side and shuffling down the corridor.

"Wait," the doctor barked behind me. I glanced over my shoulder, to find him striding toward me. I readied myself for another argument, searching my hazy mind for something other than *'because I have to'*. But instead of trying to get me to stay, he just handed me a pill bottle. "Take those if the pain gets too bad...and believe me, it will get bad."

I grabbed the bottle of pills in his hand and glanced at the label.

"Just try not to tear your stitches, okay?" he muttered.

In another life, he might've been dating material. God knows, with all the guns and the knives and the backstabbing that happened in our lifestyle, having a doctor around was probably a good thing.

But when I looked at him, I saw everything I didn't want. Instead, I gripped the pills and smiled. "Thanks, and I'll try."

His gaze was heavy as I turned and painfully made my way along the corridor to the elevators. There was no way I could stay there a second longer, not when she was out there...

My mind returned to that underground bunker, and the picture of Bruno Bernardi.

I knew in my heart who was next to feel the point of her knife.

As much as I hated him...I hated her more. I pressed the button for the elevator and waited it to open. My own haunted reflection glared back at me in the shine of the doors. "I'm coming for you..." I whispered. "As soon as I find out who the fuck you are."

TWENTY-ONE

Bruno

Evan was avoiding me, and not just to speak to, to even look at.

I waited for her outside her building the next day, and stalked her fucking classes. Hell, I even hosted a fucking party tonight just to get her to come. Xael attended, like the tornado she was, cleaning me out of eight grand in blackjack while downing tequila shots and eye-fucking the guy at the table next to ours. *But there was no fucking Evan.*

Even when I pushed Xael, urging her to send her roommate a text, she just gave a shrug and muttered something about *'not being her fucking keeper'*.

I winced and yanked the neckline of my shirt, feeling the sweat beading and running down my damn spine, and pushed back from the table. Bare skin drew my gaze as Xael reached across the table for the nice stack of hundreds I'd just thrown away. I stared at the swell of her breast barely contained within the leather halter top she wore.

"Again?" she asked, smiling with a glint in her eye.

"Fuck, no. You're a goddamn shark," I snapped, and grabbed my phone.

She just clutched the bills with one hand and sucked on her middle finger with the other.

"Fuck, too, Davies," I muttered, and rose from my seat as I opened the app on my phone.

"What do you have there?"

She was beside me in an instant. The woman was a goddamn shadow, spilling over my shoulder as she glanced at the screen.

"Nothing." I yanked my phone away from her sight.

"You're spying on someone." Her lips curled onto a slow, sly smirk. "Got our apartment wired, huh? Better not be watching me fuck, Bernardi. Not unless that gets you off?"

"Watching *you?*" I growled, jerking my gaze to hers. "Not even remotely, Davies."

She just laughed, shook her head, and turned, shoving her ass against my thigh before walking away. I wanted to laugh at her, wanted to be playful and take her up on another round of cards. But my nerves were frayed, twisted and wrapped around the fucking fist inside my stomach.

Beep.

My phone vibrated in my hand. I looked down at the text.

Finley: Baldeon's getting out of the infirmary. Party's at Zakharov's.

So Baldeon was getting out...poor bastard had been shot in the shoulder after one of the boats was attacked getting to the island. I glanced around the apartment as everyone else's phones lit up. Xael grabbed her phone, stared at the screen ,and smiled, then met my gaze. "You coming?"

Would Evan be there?

I didn't think so.

I looked around the emptying apartment. She wasn't anywhere I said I'd be.

Exactly....

I jerked my gaze up. "Xael...wait."

She stopped halfway across the living room and, glanced over her shoulder.

"Send Evan a text that I'm going to be there."

Her brow rose and her red lips pursed. "What are you playing at, Bernardi?"

I drew in a deep breath, my mind racing. "Your favorite past time...*hunting.*"

She just chuckled and gave a nod. "Okay, this *one damn time*. I'm not in the habit of setting up my goddamn friends."

"I'm your fucking friend," I growled, fighting the urge to add. *I was here first.*

I'd never tapped Davies. None of us had, I didn't think. We didn't hunt in our own pool, not where Davies was concerned. She was one of the guys, like my own sister. I watched as she punched out a text and turned away, striding for the elevator. "Have a good night, Bernardi."

I dragged my teeth across my lip, waiting as the last of the others left, strippers from the mainland and all. Half-filled glasses and empty bottles were left behind. I grabbed my glass from the table and drained the contents.

"Seems like it's just you and me."

I jerked at the deep growl and turned, to find Deviouz leaning against the wall. I hadn't seen the asshole come in, hadn't seen him at all, really. I glanced his way. "Sure, maybe you can text my cousin that?"

He just pushed his massive frame off the wall and strode my way. "I'm not here to spy for him, Bruno."

"Of course you're not." I fought the twitch as he reached past me, grabbed the empty bottle from the card table, and walked around the end of the counter into the kitchen.

He dropped the bottle into the recycling bin and came back, moving through the apartment, cleaning up as he went.

Beep...

Davies: Trap has sprung. She's not coming.

The corner of my lip curled as my pulse sped. She wasn't coming, so that meant she'd be staying at her place or going somewhere else. Now I just had to narrow that down. I slid my phone into my pocket, reached over, and grabbed my leather jacket.

"Going somewhere?" Deviouz glanced my way as I made for the elevators.

"We have an island full of security," I growled. "You're not needed."

His glare burned into the back of my neck as I strode to the elevator and punched the button, waiting for the doors to open. But there hadn't been a problem since the attack on the boat. Baldeon had been released tonight, by now the party for him was in full swing. A party I was supposed to be at.

The elevator doors opened and I stepped inside. But I had no plan on where I was going. No, I was done with this evasive fucking bullshit Evan was handing out. I wanted to see her face to face...to finally, after all these years, *torment myself a little more.*

My breaths came harder as the elevator descended. I went through the meeting in my head, knowing she was going to fucking *hate* what I was about to say. But I'd come here for a reason. She'd been supposed to marry my cousin, but I was having her instead.

I lifted my head as the elevator doors opened, and I strode out, carving through the foyer, and stepped out into the night. I lowered my head, slid my hands into the pockets of my jacket, and cut across the Institute's grounds, keeping to the shadows.

First, I'd make sure she knew there's no sense in hiding from me, that one way or the other, she was leaving this island at my goddamn side. I had the jeweler at Cartier on standby, all I needed was her to pick out the fucking ring and it was a done deal.

Christ, the thought of that made my blood hum. Bethany and all the other women faded away. For me, there'd only ever been one. Evan Valachi. I lifted my gaze to her building in the distance. The penthouse was alight with dull amber lights that melted into the shadows. I searched for movement, desperate to see a glimmer of hope.

A flicker of fear tore through me. The hairs on my arms stood on end as my gaze was drawn to the building in the distance. Shadows caught my gaze before movement came closer. I jerked my focus to the right, finding a lone figure striding forward.

Lazarus...Lazarus Rossi.

My gut clenched at the sight. "Sonofa—" Hate rolled through me, shoving the fear aside.

That bastard wasn't supposed to be here. If he was, that meant Finley needed to know. I gripped my phone and pulled it free, punching out a text.

Rossi is here.

I waited for a response, getting one a second later.

Finley: Yeah, I know.

"Fuck." I dragged my fingers through my hair, that's all we needed.

The Salvatores and the Rossis had bad blood between them, especially since Lazarus put one of Fin's crew in the fucking hospital after beating him at Fin's mom's funeral. The last thing we needed here was a goddamn war. With Lazarus being here, that's what was coming.

I ground my teeth and glanced once more at the Stidda asshole as he froze, his gaze fixed on the building in the distance...*Baldeon's building*. I was sure of it. Something was happening out there...I clenched my jaw and jerked my gaze toward Evan's apartment.

That hunger burned inside me, pulling me forward. Whatever bad blood lingered between Lazarus and Finley, I wanted no part of it. Besides...there was the fucking code.

A code we all lived by.

A code they wouldn't break...not unless they wanted to piss the Commander off.

And none of us wanted to deal with that wrath.

Fuck 'em...let them deal with their own bullshit.

I forced myself to turn and head toward the front door of Evan's building, catching a shadow shift against the window of her bedroom. I swallowed hard as my pulse raced.

She's there...

Suddenly feeling awkward standing outside her apartment building, I yanked my keycard from my pocket and slammed it against the reader on the wall, waiting as the doors opened to her foyer. I strode inside, and hit the button for the elevator.

Tension coiled inside me as I stepped into the elevator. Goosebumps raced along my skin, making me shudder as the doors closed behind me and the elevator rose.

Panic set in as I tried to think of what I'd say.

Give me your fucking hand, seemed a little too forward. How about, *Evan...Evan Bernardi, that's who you are now.* The Irish in me was desperate to take her to fucking bed. I closed my eyes and took a deep breath. That woman was going to break me.

I jerked open my eyes as the elevator came to a stop and listened...

My heart thundered as I took a step inside her apartment. Suddenly this felt...*wrong.*

Invasive. A...*betrayal.*

As though the Bernardis hadn't betrayed her enough already. I licked my lips and stopped at the entrance to her apartment. "Evan."

Fuck, I hated how my voice reverberated in my chest, sounding ruined and raw. But that's how she made me feel... *ruined...and raw.*

The silence was deafening, and I felt like ants were crawling along my skin.

"Evan...I know you're in here." I started forward, hating how that tug-of-war inside me shredded my resolve. I didn't want to wait any longer, I *needed her.*

Boom!

The sound of a slamming door hit me. The fucking stairwell. *"Fuck!"* I roared, swiveled on my heel, and charged back toward the elevator once more. But I kept going, lunging for the stairwell door. She must've already been running as the elevator rose.

Running from me.

"You can't get away from me." I yanked the door open and strode into the murky light, letting the door slam behind me with a deafening *thud.* "Not for fucking long."

I was the hunter in that moment, tearing down the stairs. The faster I went, the more I wanted her. By the time I shoved through the last door and charged across the foyer to the exterior doors, I was savage.

Cold night air hit me as I stepped out.

Movement came from my left as I headed for the other buildings.

"Bernardi!"

I jerked my gaze toward the roar, finding the Commander sprinting across the grounds. "There's been an attack. Get the fuck back to safety *now!*"

I froze with the words. "What?!"

But he was gone, his boots pounded into the ground, driving him forward, and his men followed not more than two steps behind. I stared as they left, then slowly lifted my gaze to the building they'd entered. *Baldeon's building.*

There'd been an attack?

"No…" I whispered, and started forward, my heart hammering.

"Bruno!"

Deviouz was hauling ass across the grounds, his massive thighs straining, his arms punching through the air as he scanned the grounds for movement.

"What the fuck is going on?" I growled.

But he grabbed my arm and yanked me forward, dragging me toward our building. "We're locking this shit down *now!*"

"Wait!" I yanked my arm from his hold. "What the fuck is happening?"

The bodyguard stopped, jerked his gaze toward Baldeon's , and met my gaze. "Marcus Baldeon is dead."

"No." I rocked backwards with the words and shook my head. "You're fucking lying."

Movement spilled out of the buildings in the distance. Deviouz jerked his gaze toward the movement and took a massive stride forward, closing the distance between us. "Would I fucking be here if it wasn't the truth?"

A scream rocked the night, low and guttural. A male in agony. Coming from Baldeon's building.

"This place is going to be locked down tight. They could still be on the island, Bruno...*now are you going to listen?*"

I wanted to follow him, wanted to think about saving my own ass.

But as more screams rose and cries of *"No!"* rang out, all I thought of was Evan.

"I have to find her." I started back across the grounds. "I have to make sure she's safe."

"Fuck!" Deviouz barked as I scanned for movement, spotting Xael racing across the grounds, headed toward Baldeon's building...and raced after her.

TWENTY-TWO

Evan

Find the building.

Find the room.

I pressed my hand against my side and took a shallow breath. The low throb in my side turned savage, tearing across my middle. The world around me flared bright as I caught my breath. A low groan rumbled in the back of my throat. But it didn't escape. Instead, I swallowed it down. All the way down, into the back hole of retribution inside me.

The pain made me regret leaving the hospital...*almost*.

But drugs and comfort meant nothing against a crazy bitch who wanted to end me. And it was only a matter of time before she realized I wasn't in the hole in the ground where she'd left me. *Then she'd be back.*

Someone like her didn't stop...not until it was over. Not until it was over and everyone on her goddamn wall was dead. I had one chance at this...one chance to find *her* before she came back for me.

I intended to make every second count.

Cars were parked outside the hospital. Sunlight glinted against their windshields, blinding me for a second, until someone stepped into the glare. My pulse sped at the sight of Kyle as he strode across the parking lot. The towering former linebacker was now my father's private security detail. He was all danger, pure intimidation.

Powerful thighs strained the stretch of his pants as he consumed the distance between us, carving through the low hedge and stepping across the driveway of the hospital as he headed my way.

"Ms. Valachi." He scanned me up and down, his gaze lingering on my hand clasped to my side.

There was a flicker of annoyance. His lips pursed, fighting the urge to curl against his teeth.

I just swallowed, watching the sun suddenly eclipse behind him. "Kyle."

He bent and wrapped me in a strong, but very careful hug. "Asshole." The deep, reverberating sound rumbled like thunder in my ear.

I just smiled and hugged him with one arm.

"You scared the shit out of me." He pulled back and glanced at my hand pressed to my side. "*And* you shouldn't be out here."

I shook my head. "Don't you start on me, too. I can't stay in there, not after what happened—"

"I know," he murmured, bending down to grab my bag. "Come on. Tell me what you need."

"But Dad..."

He stilled and met my gaze, one brow rising. "Who do you think sent me?"

A tremor of gratitude coursed through me. Of course he did. He'd barely made a fight when I told them I was leaving. This was why. He knew I'd be protected no matter what and for the first time, all I felt was relief about his careful control.

I let Kyle carry my bag as he turned and headed across the driveway to my father's dark blue Range Rover. I tried to keep up, but my steps were slower., the pain grabbing and twisting with every step now. Kyle slowed, moving to my side as a car drove toward us, slowing until we made it beyond the crosswalk before passing.

He dropped my bag on the backseat and opened the back door, reaching out to grasp my hand as I carefully slid inside.

"You're in pain," he growled. "I don't like it."

"It's keeping me sharp," I groaned, dragging my feet inside before he shut the door.

He climbed into the car and started the engine, meeting my gaze in the rear-view mirror. "Your father said something about tracking your phone?"

I swallowed the agony, leaned to the side, and pulled Dad's cell from my pocket. My fingers slid along the screen, punching in the numbers of my birthday, and unlocked his phone. I'd known he watched me, known it was more for my protection than anything else. And any other time, I might've been pissed. But now...I was relieved.

I opened the tracking app, finding not one but two numbers being pinged. One was mine and the other...was Jessie's. A surge of betrayal coursed through me. It was going to take a little time to get used to how much they cared about each other. He cared, in his own controlling and possessive way. I shifted my gaze from her number and opened the details on mine, scanning the cell towers my phone had connected to in the last forty-eight hours, and stopped at one tower that was south of us.

I pressed on the map, opening the coordinates. "Hargraves and South."

"The industrial estate?"

I lifted my gaze. "That's what it says."

A nod and he backed out of the parking space and headed for the outskirts of the city. I tried to remember where I'd been, but everything after stepping into that alley was a blur of nothing. Memories of the dream rose in my head, that beast in the darkness tore a shiver along my spine. *I almost died...*

I swallowed hard as panic rose. Kyle turned the wheel and braked, slowing as we merged with the traffic accelerating onto the on-ramp. The snarl of the four-wheel drive's engine filled my ears. It'd be so easy to give into the fear, so easy to tell Kyle everything, to curl up in a ball and let the men in my life protect me.

But that wasn't the life I wanted.

That wasn't the path I'd chosen.

So I closed my eyes and turned inward to face the darkness. "I'm coming for you.," I whispered. "I'm coming."

I released my hand from my side and opened my eyes as we exited the freeway and headed south. Fear waited for me in the murkiness of my mind. But I pushed through it, grasping hold of the flickers of sunlight that blinded me as I forced my mind out of that hole in the ground.

The choking scent of concrete swept through me. I stiffened and jerked from the memory as it flooded my mind. "It's a building… apartments or something, but it's not finished. Just a shell…a steel fence blocks it off from the street."

"Could be anywhere," Kyle grumbled, then glanced into the mirror. "I have an idea."

He grabbed his phone, divided his attention between the road and the cell, and gave a command. "Call Rusty."

"Calling Rusty," the automated voice answered as a phone started to ring.

Kyle slowed the car, pulled off the on-ramp, and pointed us toward the industrial part of Ikon as the call was answered with a bark. "Kyle, you big bastard. How the hell are you?"

In the mirror, I caught the smile on my bodyguard's lips. "Good, buddy. Listen, I need a favor."

"Hit me."

I looked out the window as he talked, trying my best not to listen too hard as Kyle asked about the forgotten building. I gathered Rusty had some kind of mechanic shop on the Southside and knew men who might know about the building. He hung up after saying he'd ask around and get back to Kyle.

So we headed for the graffitied chop shops and the storage units surrounded by ten-foot fences topped with razor wire. Drug deals went down on the corners there, and gangs ran the streets. It was a dangerous neighborhood, but still, I knew the life. It was the same as mine.

Dangerous.

Desperate.

The only difference was the money...and the pretense that came with it.

We drove for an hour, taking street after street while I searched for anything remotely familiar. But there wasn't anything, not the guarded glares from the people as we drove past, not any half-demolished building that doubled as a crack house. The longer we drove, the more desperate I felt.

I checked Dad's phone, finding us pinging from that same cell tower, and stared harder through the windows. I even called Ikon General Hospital and asked for information on the man who'd brought me in. But there was nothing. No name given, no cell number I could call. Just street after street.

Until Kyle's phone gave a *beep*. He pulled the four-wheel drive over to the side of the road and glanced at the text. "Might have a possible location." He dropped the cell and swung the wheel, but instead of sticking to the south side of the cell tower, we headed north.

It had to be in the same radius, but it could be anywhere. But the moment we turned into the newer and quieter neighborhood, I felt a charge of excitement course through me. We passed streets filled with neat but generic houses, low-cost, affordable housing designed to lift the Southside out of the bad reputation it had.

And as we turned onto one of the streets, panic raced through me. "This is it..."

I leaned forward, staring at the end of the street, to where the sun glinted on the towering fence blocking the construction site from the rest of the street. "That's it! Right there...*that's the place.*"

Kyle pulled the Range Rover over and killed the engine. "I want you to stay right here," he commanded, reaching inside his jacket and pulling his gun free.

"No." I shook my head as terror tore through me with an icy touch, chilling me to the bone. "Don't make me stay here on my own."

"Evan..." he started.

"I know what's down there." I met his gaze in the rear-view mirror. "I need to do this."

Muscles clenched in his jaw before he gave a nod. "Stay close."

"Don't worry, I plan on it," I assured, and grabbed the doorhandle.

I forced myself to hold my side and push the door open. Taking it slowly, I eased myself out of the car, catching my breath when my feet dropped to the ground with a jolt. But Kyle was waiting, standing in front of me as I eased the door closed and lifted my gaze to the gap in the fence, remembering the terror as I'd pushed my way through. A bright smear of blood was on the fence. Kyle glanced at it and lifted his gun.

I followed him slowly inside, fighting off the panic as it rose, and pointed to the rear of the empty concrete carcass. "Over there."

Kyle strode forward and I'd never felt so comforted by his massive presence as I did in that moment. His big hand gripped the door and yanked, pointing the gun into the darkness. I hung back, watching over my shoulder for movement as he descended the concrete stairs, then disappeared.

My pulse sped, booming in my ears as I waited.

"Evan, you can come down," he called finally.

I stepped down, fighting the terror as that cloying scent of concrete filled my nose once more, and made my way back into that room. It was different this time. Kyle made it different, driving back the terror with his presence alone. I kicked something and looked down, catching it skid across the floor and hit the wall.

I froze. It was a knife...*the knife.*

Blood still coated the steel, darkening around the edges. Kyle stepped toward me and knelt, grasping it from the edges, then looked up at me, his gaze moving over my hand pressed against my side. "You're fucking lucky to be alive," he growled, taking in the knife with its serated edge once more.

She'd eaten peaches from that knife minutes before plunging it into my side.

I never wanted to see peaches again.

I left the knife behind and made my way into that other room, where the pictures of me still plastered the walls.

"Jesus," Kyle almost groaned.

My gaze moved from the photo of me standing beside my mom's casket to the one of Dad and Jessie taken not long ago. They were sitting in a restaurant, holding hands. My Dad was looking at her with love and kindness, a different look than he'd given my mom.

But I knew in that moment that they were a target. They both were.

Other photos were taped beside them. My gaze met the cold, calculating eyes of Adrian Bernardi and his brother Cillian. Underneath him was the savage stare of a killer...a cruel, savage, vicious man I hated. I clenched my fists, strode toward the wall, and ripped the picture of Jannick Bernardi down.

But Bruno was there.

Bruno, with the same cold, brutal gaze.

Only he wasn't the same. I hated him, *loathed him*. He was the man in my dreams, the one who'd hurried toward me as I ran that night. I could still remember the sting of my hand, and the haunting *slap* I'd hit on Jannick's cheek.

But it was Bruno whose memory haunted me, Bruno whose yells had burned into my memory as I'd scurried inside, Bruno who I'd heard beating his cousin bloody that night...because of what he'd done to me.

I stepped toward Bruno's photo and peeled it from the wall. Written on the back of the photo was times and dates and the name...*Cosa Nostra Institute*. "I'm going to the island."

"What?" Kyle barked. "No way..."

I turned toward him and met his gaze. "That wasn't a request," I started, my mind racing. "And I'm going alone."

"No," he growled, striding forward and grabbing my shoulders.

One glance at the wall of information and he shifted his gaze back to mine. "Let me come."

I shook my head. "No, Kyle."

"I'll take leave. I'll go without your father's permission if I have to. But I won't let you go alone."

"And having you at my side would draw too much attention."

"Then I'll stay hidden. You won't even see me once we hit Mauritius."

"Kyle..."

"With or without your permission," he insisted.

I stared into his hard gaze and finally nodded. "Okay. I'll leave tomorrow. Go home, make what plans you need to, and I'll call you when I have the flight plans.

"Promise?" he murmured.

It wasn't the first time I'd lied, but God, it felt like a betrayal staring into his eyes. "I promise."

An hour later we were driving home after stopping off to grab me a replacement phone swapped with my spare SIM card.

"I'll call you as soon as I can," I murmured as we pulled into the driveway and stopped at the front door.

Kyle was out of the car first, opening my door and reaching for my hand. Agony roared through my side, making me freeze halfway. I swallowed and clenched my jaw, waiting for the wave to pass.

"E..."

"I'm fine," I whispered, and met his gaze, forcing a smile. "Just tired."

He walked me to the door without saying a word. I knew he was going to call my father the moment I stepped inside.

Dad was a patient man, especially when it came to me. He'd let me push this, but for how long? How long until he took the decisions from me, forcing me to step back. After all, I wasn't an heir...*not yet.*

I pushed off from the door, grabbed my phone, and made a call. "Jared, how fast can you get me to Mauritius?"

"I thought the trip was cancelled." The low murmur came on other end of the line.

"No, not cancelled, momentarily suspended. So, how long?"

"Give me an hour to log the flight details and have the jet ready. We can be in the air in ninety minutes, how's that?"

Relief swept through me. "That sounds perfect, Jared. I'll meet you there in an hour."

"Sure," he answered. "See you then."

Ninety minutes...and I'd be on my way. I reached into my pocket and pulled out the folded picture of Bruno Bernardi, the faceless man in my dreams. It'd take me twelve hours to reach Mauritius, twelve hours just to get to the mainland.

A flare of pain ripped through my middle, drawing my focus to the wound in my side. She'd go after him...there was no doubt about that. I had a feeling what she had in store for him was something far more terrifying.

My pulse sped at the thought. I turned and headed for my bedroom at the far wing of the house, forcing myself to push through the pain. I had to get there...had to get to the island, and hope to God I wasn't too late.

TWENTY-THREE

Bruno

CHAOS DESCENDED THE DAY AFTER BALDEON'S MURDER. We walked around stunned, moving with a savage sense of helplessness. Fights broke out amongst us, but mostly our anger was directed at the Commander.

We were supposed to be safe here, supposed to be *protected*.

But we weren't...not here on the island with its useless fucking security, or at home. It was a hard damn lesson to swallow. But we did...swallow it. Looking at each other with the same stunned expression that said *'which one of us is next?'*

Deviouz was more persistent than ever, shadowing me when I finally attended the goddamn classes. I couldn't move without the brute being behind me, armed to the goddamn teeth with guns and knives.

Everywhere I turned, there were armed guards invading the foyers of every building as they waited for another attack. I'd tried to find Evan last night, even sending her a goddamn text to make sure she was okay. But there was no reply, and as the day wore on, my doubt and anger grew.

"Where the fuck is she, Davies?" I strode along the hallway, hunting.

Xael gave a shrug as she stepped out of the classroom, slipping her arms into her leather jacket. "I'm not her keeper, Bernardi. So stop fucking asking...you're sounding pathetic."

"*Pathetic?*" I snarled, hating how the anger drove me. I grabbed Xael's arm, pulling her toward me. "She fucking ran from me last night like a terrified kid, and today...today she's nowhere to be found *again*. What the hell is up with that?"

Davies lowered her gaze to my grip around her arm, then met my gaze. The corner of her lip curled into a sneer as she turned on me, stabbing my chest with her short, blood red nail. "You need to stop dragging me into your fucking mess, Bernardi. Fuck her, don't fuck her, I don't give a goddamn shit. I'm not your relationship counselor, *or her* goddamn warden. She comes, she goes. Where? *I. Don't. Care.*"

My face burned as she barked at me. Others glanced our way as they crowded out of the classroom behind her. Even Salvatore saw the way I had Davies in my grip and scowled at me.

I released my hold. "Fuck, Davies. I didn't mean..."

"Yeah, you did," she snapped, straightening her jacket. "She haunts you, doesn't she?"

I raked my fingers through my hair, trying to fight the truth from showing all over my damn face.

Xael stepped closer and lowered her voice. "This has to stop, Bruno. You can't keep chasing what's not going to be yours. So make it happen, or let her go. But do it fast, okay? Do it and be done, and get some fucking sleep, okay? You look like shit."

She jerked her gaze to one of the guys who'd lingered in the hallway, listening.

"What the fuck are you listening to?" She strode toward the asshole, who hurried away. "You know who I am? The fuck you listening to my conversations for?"

She left me with her words. As brutal as they were, they were the truth.

I had to make it happen...or let Evan go. I couldn't keep living like this, half alive...half fucking tortured. I raked my hair back once more and glanced toward Deviouz. *"What?"* I barked, striding toward him. "You think this is entertaining?"

"Not at all," he answered, his amber eyes glinting as he looked down at me.

I clenched my fists, anger seething inside me. "I wouldn't be in this fucking position if it wasn't for..." I froze, the words burning in my chest. But the last thing I wanted to do was hurt Evan even more by airing our dirty laundry. "You know what?" I snarled. "Never fucking mind."

I just strode away, charging along the hallway and into the foyer of the lecture building, then headed out into the afternoon. *Fuck her...don't fuck her.*

The words resounded inside me. I clenched my jaw and dragged my phone from my pocket, opening the damn app. I hated the sight of her empty fucking room. But I hated this compulsion even more. This...*drive*. It wasn't normal. It wasn't something I wanted...but it wasn't something I could shake.

I needed to break the spell she had over me, needed to figure out a way to get her out from under my skin. I strode across the grounds, heading for my own building as the sight of my hands around Davies's arm rose inside me.

Fingers clenched, driving against the flesh, I'd probably bruised her. But I had a feeling Xael didn't bruise that easily. She sure delivered a savage blow. If I was any less of a man, I might even be tempted to go there, to find out just how fucking wild Xael Davies really was.

Welsh and Irish. What the fuck could go wrong?

It'd be explosive, that was for sure.

But as soon as the thought rose inside me, it turned cold and empty. Not even a flicker of excitement, not even a twitch of my cock. I pressed my keycard against the reader outside my building, listening to heavy steps behind me as the doors opened. I needed to get my mind off her, needed to drown my fucking ache. I punched a text into my phone and sent it to the group of contacts.

Party my place, bring your own fucking alcohol. I need to get drunk.

The replies were instant. Excitement, desperation, anything to get our minds off what was happening around us. I made my way into the elevator, moving to the back as Deviouz stepped in. "There's a party tonight."

"Figured," he replied, staring straight ahead as we rose and came to a stop.

"You might want to bring earplugs," I muttered, stepping around him. "Seeing as how you're coming. It'll most likely get loud."

He said nothing as the doors closed. But it felt like an uneasy truce between us. The truth was, after last night I was almost glad he was here, even if he reported back to my cousin.

My phone vibrated in my hand as I walked in. I glanced down, then answered. "Dad?"

"I'm flying in," he announced, the sound of the jet's engines in the background. "They've called a meeting of the Commission. We left early this morning to get there on time. I should be touching down in a couple of hours. We need this shit locked down tight. First our fucking warehouse is set on fire, then Jannick...now this..."

"Jannick?" I stopped walking. "What the hell happened?"

He seemed to forget himself for a second. Silence filled the airspace, then he mumbled a curse. "It's nothing. He's fine, just banged up a little, nothing he can't take. But it seems like someone out there has a goddamn hard-on for our fucking name right now. Which is why I need you to be fucking smart about this. Keep your head down, and that goddamn bodyguard close. You hear me?"

"I hear you," I muttered.

"I'll be there soon, and Bruno...this is one of those times where you trust no one, you hear me?"

I licked my lips and nodded. "Yeah."

"See you soon, son." He ended the call, leaving me to exhale hard.

He was on his way and I didn't have a fucking thing to tell him. I hadn't even seen Evan, let alone carried through with the plan to align our families. If I didn't do this soon, then others would scent blood in the water. A Commission family with no male to lead? They'd come for her soon enough. Then it wouldn't matter a fuck what I wanted.

She wouldn't be mine, not then…*not ever.*

My heart tightened at the thought as the elevator door opened. Deviouz strode out, followed by Hunter. A very pale looking Hunter. He forced a smile for me, and the show started.

"Buddy." He lifted his hands, clutching two bottles of Scotch. "Let's get this fucking party started early, okay?"

"Beats drinking alone," I answered, and strode for the kitchen, grabbed two glasses, and waited as Hunter poured.

Trust no one, that's what Dad had told me. And as I drank and felt the burn slide all the way to my belly, that thought fucking hurt. I watched Hunter as he drank and smiled, then started spouting some bullshit about a woman he had back home. I listened, because the silence was just too fucking raw.

The party started slowly, as a waitress came carrying trays of food. Others spilled from the elevator with their own drinks. Music started as the sun went down.

We drank and talked, and tried to forget there'd been one of us murdered mere fucking yards from where we stood. I sat back on the sofa, watching them all come and go. Zakharov prowled through the fucking party. I caught a glimpse as he moved behind a group of others, then he was gone.

The ache in my chest started to ease the more I drank. I rose from the sofa, heading for my bedroom, and caught sight of Kat VanHalen pressed against the wall. That sonofabitch Zakharov had his hands around her throat.

The room swayed and the shadows blurred. But the sight of that pissed me off. I licked my lips as Zakharov jerked his gaze over his shoulder, saw me coming toward them, and released his hold on her throat. It was all she needed to run, scurrying away from us.

"I don't like you." My words slurred as I stepped into his path, blocking him as he tried to head after her.

Rage sparked in his eyes as he lowered his gaze to mine. "Yeah?"

"Yeah," I answered, and stepped closer, making a move on the fucker. "I don't like you at all. I don't want to see you, not here, not fucking anywhere."

He just barked a laugh. "We're on a fucking island."

My lip curled as that savage side of me rose to the surface.

"Or what, Bernardi?" he pushed.

I licked my lips and moved again, pressing my chest against his. "Or you might just find yourself on the wrong side of me...and that's a *very bad* place to be."

His eyes widened for a second, before his lips curled into a sneer. But it was all for show as he lifted his gaze to the others and muttered "This party blows anyway." Then he stepped around me, slamming into my shoulder as he passed.

I watched the fucker leave before I made for my room, unlocked the door, and slipped inside. The party was slowing anyway, pretty soon it'd be over and I'd be alone...*again*. I made for the bathroom, then took a piss and flushed before reaching for my phone.

Movement filled her apartment. Xael was drinking with others. But as I watched, two of them rose, bent to give her a kiss on the lips, then made for the door, leaving Xael and one other woman behind. I glanced at the time, almost three in the morning. Exhaustion weighed me down, and loneliness lingered behind it. The party outside turned quiet, until silence was all that was left.

But Evan wasn't drinking with Xael. *Where the hell was she?* I flicked my camera to her bedroom, finding her curled up in bed. Fists clenched, as rage burned inside me.

She lay there, safe and warm. I didn't know what hurt more, her fucking avoiding me, or *being right in front of me and not giving a fucking shit*. She didn't want to see me, she fucking snubbed me, like I wasn't good enough for her.

She fucking owed me...

I strode out of the bedroom and grabbed a bottle of Scotch as I passed the kitchen.

"Hey, B," Hunter called from the sofa, underneath a blonde with her legs wrapped around him. *"Bernardi, where the fuck you going, man?"*

I didn't answer, just kept striding for the elevator.

Fuck her. Don't fuck her. Make it happen or let her go. Xael's words resounded in my head. I couldn't escape them, couldn't escape *her*. I lifted the bottle, took a swallow, and waited as the doors opened.

A guard stood in the foyer, his arms crossed on his chest, watching the night outside. He turned as I strode toward him.

"Mr. Bernardi..." he started forward.

Until I stopped him with the wave of a hand. "You're not needed."

"Sir." He strode after me, until I stopped, swiveled, and met his steely gaze. "You don't want to be around me right now."

He just shook his head. "No one's allowed to be on their own."

"I got this," came a growl from behind me.

Deviouz strode toward us, shrugging into his jacket. "He's safe with me."

I met my bodyguard's gaze. "What the fuck are you playing at?"

He just gave a shrug. "My job, I thought...*if you'll fucking let me.*"

"So you can report back to Jannick? No fucking thank you, I'll go on my own."

"You really are a spoiled little brat, aren't you?"

I froze, hate mingling with the burning in the pit of my gut as I slowly faced him. "What the fuck did you say?"

He took a step closer and reached into his pocket to pull his phone free. One swipe of his thumb and he handed it over, unlocked. "Check the texts."

I looked at the cell. "No."

"Check the fucking texts, Bruno."

I hated it, but I took the phone and opened his texts before stilling. It wasn't Jannick whose texts were at the top...it was my father. I jerked my gaze to his. "Dad?"

He just gave a chuff and nodded. "Who else would want his son protected by the fucking best?"

Dad had sent him? *Why the hell hadn't he told me?* I lifted my gaze as everything I *didn't* want to see hit me. Of course he knew my every fucking move. He was the one getting Deviouz's texts. I handed my bodyguard's phone back to him.

"Now are you going to trust me?" he growled as he took the damn thing.

The burn of the alcohol had eased. One swallow from the bottle, and I grabbed my own phone. "One motherfucking word," I muttered. "And we're done here."

What the hell was I even doing? I strode through the door as the image of her in bed rose. *Her...that's what was I was doing...her.* Thunder boomed in the sky overhead as I headed across the grounds toward her building.

Fuck her. Don't fuck her. Then let her go. "Fuck you, Davies," I slurred as my vision blurred.

I needed to put an end to this, needed to make a move...needed to do something *bold and forceful.* Lightning flickered in the distance as the wind picked up, slamming into me as I ducked my head and made for her building.

I was just going to see Davies and apologize for the way I'd reacted earlier today. I licked my lips as the wind died away once I was sheltered by her building. I pressed my keycard to the lock of her door and stepped inside, lifting my gaze to the bodyguard standing in the foyer.

He took one look at me, then shifted his gaze to Deviouz. "Mr. Bernardi. Would you like me to announce you to Ms. Davies?"

"No," I answered, heading for the elevator. "I wouldn't." But I couldn't go up, not unless he swiped his keycard against the reader of the elevator. "You gonna do this, or am I going to have to take the fucking stairs?"

Deviouz just stared at the guy, waiting. "Maybe this isn't the best way to go about this?" My bodyguard glanced my way. "Tomorrow is better, then you're sober and this doesn't look like what it looks like?"

Hate rolled through me as I took a step toward him, my fist clenched around the neck of the bottle. "And what does it look like?"

"Like you're about to make a big fucking mistake," he answered. "And reinforce the impression that the Bernardis really are fucking monsters."

I flinched at the words, swallowed hard, and looked down at my phone. I didn't need to open the app, didn't need to see her lying in bed three fucking floors above me right now. Laughter spilled through the air a second before the elevator doors opened.

Xael stumbled out, laughing with several others, and shifted her gaze from the bodyguard protecting her foyer to me. And all of a sudden, the spark in her eyes died away. "Bernardi," she said carefully. "What are you doing here?"

I strode toward the elevator. "She's up there, right?"

Xael moved fast, stepping in my way and placing her hand on my chest. "Not going to happen, Bruno."

I clenched my grip around the bottle. "The fuck it isn't. You said it yourself, fuck her or forget her. So get out of the goddamn way, Davies."

Her companions watched us, their gazes burning on the back of my neck.

Xael moved close, all laughter dying in her eyes as she lowered her voice. "You really want to do this? You really want to be *that* guy?"

"Why the fuck not?" I barked, moving so close I pressed my chest to hers. "I'm done waiting. Done being *owed*. I fucking want it...*I fucking want her.*"

A cold blast cut through the foyer as Xael's friends scurried like mice, leaving before it all went to hell.

"I don't believe you," Xael murmured, searching my eyes. "I don't think you've got the stones, Bernardi."

I clenched my jaw, leaning close. "Step out of the fucking way and find out."

So she did...

Adrenaline tore through me at her movement. I held her gaze as she stepped aside and motioned to the empty elevator. "Go on... become the fucking monster she always thought you were."

I shoved the half empty bottle of Scotch into her chest and strode forward. Desperation and hunger were in the driver's seat now, forcing me into that elevator. My fucking fingers trembled as I punched the button and turned, finding their gazes as the doors closed.

What the fuck was I doing?

I didn't have time to find the answer...*because there wasn't one.* None that would paint me in any other kind of light than the fucking bastard I was. I invaded her. I watched her...*spied on her.* I was a fucking bastard. A *cold,* fucking bastard.

The doors opened as silence waited inside. My boots were so fucking heavy, weighed down like blocks of cement. I forced myself to move, and with every step I took toward her bedroom, that seething desperation inside me grew colder.

I'm the fucking monster she thought I was...

No better than Jannick.

I stopped in the middle of her hallway. *I. Was. No. Better. Than. Jannick.*

My pulse leaped at the words. I lifted my hand and my fingers dragged through my hair. My gaze found the open door to her bedroom. She was in there...curled under the sheets. Her body warm and soft, *pliable*. But it was her will that was a razor's edge. Her will honed to sharpened steel. Her will that was all Valachi...

Fuck!

Xael was right. Three more steps and I'd change this forever. Did I want to take her like that? I closed my eyes, remembering the fear in her eyes as she'd looked at Jannick that night he attacked her. I could still hear the slap as her hand connected with his cheek, still hear her threatening words ringing in my ears.

If I did this...*we were over.*

TWENTY-FOUR

Her

A FLASH OF BRILLIANCE MADE ME OPEN MY EYES. BUT IT wasn't a slash of lightning in the midnight sky that drew my gaze. It was my phone...illuminating with a text. I slowly reached up and turned the cell toward me.

Him: Bernardi is inside your apartment.

My heart lunged, slamming against my ribs as the screen went dark.

Bernardi...*is here?*

I jerked my gaze to the doorway of my bedroom. Shadows fell where they hadn't been before, spilling across the hall. How the hell did he find out? Panic rose as I searched for a moment where I'd slipped the disguise and pushed my fingers under the mattress.

Cold steel kissed the tips of my fingers as I grasped the hilt of the knife and pulled it free. *Now*...my pulse boomed. *It's happening now.* My phone illuminated with another text. I glanced carefully at the camera in the smoke alarm. *Was he watching me?* My breaths deepened with the thought.

I could end it here and now, plunge the knife deep into Bernardi's chest and watch as his life slipped away. All I had to say was I'd defended myself when he attacked...*who would know?* Excitement coursed through me.

My phone illuminated again. The sound was on silent. I ached to read his text, hungered for any part of *him*.

He'd been avoiding me since I arrived. I understood the need for secrecy, but still it stung. My texts went unanswered, calls went to voicemail. I'd tried to find him on the grounds, waiting for hours in the dark, until I came home *alone*.

I swallowed hard and inhaled. But he was reaching out now.

I risked a glance over my shoulder and dragged the knife close as I rose. My feet hit the cold tiled floor and my lace negligee spilled to mid-thigh. But the sound of footsteps in the hallway made me stop. Bruno Bernardi wasn't heading this way...*he was leaving?*

Panic filled me. Did he know it was me? Or did he think I was her...*Evan Valachi?* I stepped around the end of the bed, gripping the knife, and stopped in the doorway. I licked my lips, my mind racing with thoughts on how to take advantage of this. I could end this now. Kill him and walk away. We both could. We'd leave this island, and this whole fucking vendetta behind.

And be together. That's what I really wanted...*just the two of us*. Evan and Bruno would be dead, their families's legacies in tatters. A life for a life...from each family.

My grip clenched around the hilt of the knife as I stepped out of the doorway. The slow *clunk* of the elevator doors sounded as I moved faster, striding through the kitchen and headed to the entrance.

But he was gone.

I clenched my jaw until my teeth cracked. *Gutless bastard...*

What do I do? How can I finish this? I jerked my gaze back to my bedroom and moved. I hurried, slipped back inside, and moved to my closet. In the dark, I yanked on black pants and a dark hoodie before sliding my feet into dark sneakers.

End this.

The urgency hummed in my veins. I rounded the bed and grabbed my cell phone, pressing the button to read the texts.

Him: Are you there?

Him: Do not do anything stupid. Let me deal with this.

Him: You know I love you.

My pulse thrummed with the last text. His love hit me like a tsunami, consuming me as I slipped the knife inside my hoodie's pouch, then headed for the hall. A quick scan of the darkness and I stepped out, heading for the stairwell door. Every creak of the door made me wince as I opened it carefully and slipped out. My fingers fumbled on my cell, pressing the button before the bright light lit up the space. I moved quietly, hurrying down flight after flight, my sneakers silent on the concrete stairs.

My thighs were burning by the time I made it to the bottom, my breaths deep and heavy. The rush filling my ears. I pressed the button on my phone, turning off the light, and yanked the hood low over my forehead, covering as much of my face as possible before turning the handle and opening the door.

The foyer was empty except for the island's bodyguard. A knee jerk reaction to the chaos unfolding...chaos I was part of...*chaos I'd caused.*

And it was all for *him.*

I slipped out of the stairwell, ducked my head low, and gently cleared my throat. From the corner of my eye the guard swung his gaze toward me. "Ms. Valachi?"

"I'm...going out for a run."

"Ma'am, *you need an escort,*" he barked.

But I was already hurrying for the door and slipped out into the night, away from their prying eyes and their panicked stench. My pulse was thundering, the sound spilling out of my body and across the sky. *He was out here...somewhere.*

I moved fast, dragging my cell free and hurried around the corner of the building, hiding amongst the giant leaves of a tropical plant. My fingers moved across the screen as I typed...*where are you?*

The low, throaty groan of a woman's desire made me pull my finger away from hitting send. The sound came from around the back of the building mere feet from where I stood.

"Christ, that feels good," Xael groaned.

I knew her voice now. Hungry, velvety, and rich, deeper than a woman's normal tone.

"Why the fuck can't you come upstairs again?" she moaned.

I stepped closer as the sound of a zipper came through the air. Heat moved through me. I wasn't immune to desire, aching for the one I craved.

"You know I can't," the male growled.

I froze at the sound. Cold plunged deep, impaling me to the spot. I couldn't move, couldn't think...*no, it's not him.*

"Fuck, you feel good," he murmured.

Xael caught her breath, then commanded. "I want you inside me."

The words drove me forward and my sneakers skimmed the ground as he commanded, "Turn around, hands against the wall."

Agony plunged deep as I peered around the corner of the building...and watched my lover fucking another woman.

TWENTY-FIVE

Evan

He waited for me in the darkness with his sandy blonde hair and intense dark eyes. Eyes that nailed me to the ground as he stepped out from under the weeping willow tree and strode toward me.

You're mine, a snarl came from behind me. I didn't need to turn my head to know who it was, the piece of shit who wanted to hurt me.

Don't look at him, Bruno commanded with a shake of his head, his gaze slipping behind me. Fear widened his eyes before he focused on me once more. *Don't turn your head, Evan. Just keep coming...keep coming to me. You don't belong to him anymore. You're mine now...*

"No," I whimpered. "I don't want to...I don't want..."

His arm was around me, drawing me close against his body. *You don't want me?* He stroked my hair and wrapped his other arm around my waist, pressing against the small of my back.

My pulse was racing as I came alive. In the blink of an eye, he became the faceless man of my nightmares, turning me in his hold...his hand sliding up to cup my breast. *You don't want me?* He murmured in my ear as my hunger came alive. My nipples tightened under his hands as he reached under my shirt, his fingers delving under my bra to graze the tight peaks. *I think you do...I think you want me as much as I want you.*

I closed my eyes to his touch, knowing this was all just a fantasy, all just a dream.

A dream I'd had over and over, and it always ended the same.

Me giving in to him.

"No," I whispered, playing my part of the illusion. "I don't want you."

I think you do...let me show you how much. His hand dipped lower, sliding out from under my shirt to dive inside the waistband of my pants. Calloused fingers grazed tender skin as he found the elastic of my panties and plunged inside.

It was just a dream.

Just a savage, unmerciful dream. I trembled as that heat grew between my thighs, imagining the touch of his fingers and the warmth of his tongue. My body quaked with the fantasy. My breaths grew heavy as that hunger took hold.

I wanted him...*I wanted him.*

I. Wanted. Him.

"Ms. Valachi?" I rose from the darkness. *"Evan?"*

I shivered, cold to my core, and opened my eyes. "Yes?"

Jared just smiled a slow, sad smile. "There you are. You okay?"

"Yes...*why?*" I blinked, sleep slipping away.

"We arrived almost an hour ago," he said carefully. "We haven't been able to rouse you."

"Rouse me?" I tried to understand what he was saying and remember where the hell I was.

I pushed up from the leather seat of the jet and stiffened, catching my breath as a slash of agony roared through my side. Memories came with the pain. Flashes of panic and fear. I pressed my hand against my side, probing the thick bandages underneath. *I was stabbed...and left for dead. Now I'm...I'm here.*

"We've reached Mauritius." Jared's brows narrowed. "You sure you're okay?"

"Yes." I forced a smile, clenched my jaw, and forced myself to move my feet. "Just tired."

"You've been cleared through customs and I have a man waiting to take you wherever you need."

Wherever I need...

I tried to wrack my memory. I had no car, no hotel...no bodyguard. Guilt flooded through me as I thought of Kyle. I swallowed, nodded, and forced myself to move. Cold swept through me as a bead of sweat trickled from the nape of my neck to slip down my spine.

"Thank you," I whispered ad I passed Jared.

The inside of the cabin seemed to blur as I walked, forcing myself to head toward the open door of the plane. Dark, broody skies waited, shielding me from the glare of the sun.

"Evan, you sure you're okay?" Jared asked behind me.

"Sure I'm sure," I muttered as the world outside seemed to tilt and sway.

I reached out, grabbed the railing, and held on for dear life. Voices dulled and sharpened, one tight breath, and I forced myself to move again, stepping down until my flats hit the asphalt.

"Ma'am." A man stepped closer and motioned for me to follow. "My name is Igor and I'll be your driver, anything you need, I'm your man. Please, right this way."

I followed him, forcing myself to keep it together. I wanted to be out of here, find a hotel, have a shower, and some sleep... God, I needed sleep. Then when I woke up, *when I woke up what?* I tried to think as my hand moved to my pocket. The hard edge of something tucked away drew my attention. I pulled out a folded six-by-four photo and stared into the eyes of Bruno Bernardi.

Bruno...

He was out there...on the island with the bitch who'd tried to kill me. Was he dead already? Was she hunting him like she'd hunted me? The image of that alleyway filled my mind. The way she'd struggled with that rolled-up rug at the trunk of her car. She'd been playing me, watching me, waiting for the perfect moment to strike.

A slick bead of sweat stuck my shirt against my back as I followed the man into the airport and through security.

"Ms. Evan Valachi," he told the official at the door.

I reached into my bag and handed over my passport. All of a sudden, it hit me. There was someone else out there pretending to be me...someone with the same face and the same hair.

Someone who'd shoved a knife into my belly and left me for dead. *Someone who* thought *I was dead...*

I swallowed as the guard scanned my documents, then met my gaze. Did he see my terror? Was my fear written all over my face? I'd never been afraid like this, never been so...*alone.*

"Have a nice time in Mauritius," the guard said, handing back my papers.

I left him behind, striding for the double doors of the airport and outside. A black Chrysler waited, the trunk open, my bags stowed inside.

"Ma'am." My escort motioned me forward. "Our driver will take you anywhere you need to go."

A nod and I stepped closer, slipping inside as the driver opened the back door. The driver's door opened and closed. "Where can I take you, Ms. Valachi?"

I almost said the harbor, ready to climb onto the boat and...*do what?* No one knew me, not really. First my father had kept me away from everyone remotely attached to the criminal enterprise that was his life, then, after that night when I was promised to the Bernardis, I'd just disappeared.

I'd spent the next few years hiding, learning, and rebuilding myself into the kind of woman who belonged to no man. But now I was stranded, helpless at the hands of a woman who'd stolen my identity. Without my family by my side, how could I prove otherwise?

"I need a hotel. Somewhere quiet, comfortable, and near the marina."

He gave a nod. "I know just the place."

Rain splattered the windshield as we pulled out and into the airport turning circle. Horns blared behind us, but the driver paid them no mind, pulling into the flow of traffic as we headed toward the city. I'd been to Mauritius once before when I was a kid. All I remembered was the ocean, the salty scent heavy in the air and the people, smiling…happy. Like there wasn't a care in the world.

But now I knew different.

I pressed my hand against my side. "Do you think we can stop at a drugstore on the way?"

"Of course," he answered instantly.

I sat back in my seat, watching out the window as the gray skies grew darker and the rain turned persistent. We drove into the city, pulling up outside a small white building. I glanced at the ramshackle place, then the driver as he reached across the seat, grabbed an umbrella, and got out, rounding the rear of the car.

The umbrella shielded me from the rain as I stepped out. Pain carved deep, plunging like the knife was still in my side. I licked my lips, pressed my hand against my side, and walked to the closed door. The lights were garish, buzzing overhead, as I stepped inside and approached the counter.

"May I help you?" the man behind the counter asked, his white lab coat blindingly white.

"I need some painkillers and dressings for a wound."

"Of course." He pushed his glasses back, turned, and made his way along the aisles of drugs.

I waited while he pulled bottles down from the shelves and loaded up the counter with gauze dressings, sterile packs, and bottled solution. "And antibiotics, will you be in need of those, too?"

"Yes, please," I answered.

I cursed myself for not filling the prescriptions the doctor had given me when I left the hospital. Cursed myself more for leaving Kyle behind. A little bell chimed as the door opened behind me.

"Get this and get back to the island," a man growled behind me.

I glanced over my shoulder, suddenly aware of how vulnerable I was here. But the man's accent at my back wasn't Creole, it was Bronx. He just lifted his gaze to mine. I turned away, grabbed the items on the counter, and moved to the checkout counter.

"Can't risk another attack," the guy muttered. "One more, and we're getting the hell out of there, Institute or no damn Institute. One death is enough."

My pulse leaped at the words. They had to be speaking about Cosa Nostra. *One death?* Don't tell me I was too late? I opened my wallet, slid a fifty dollar note along the counter and grabbed the bag with my supplies. "Keep the change."

I was out of there, walking as fast as I could. My driver opened the door as I neared. I slid inside, my mind racing as I glanced at the door of the drugstore as it opened. The two guys strode out, one lit up a cigarette as the one who'd been talking looked at the car as we pulled away.

He saw me...

He saw me and he knew me.

I shook my head. There was no way. But one death...who were they talking about? I grabbed my phone, pressed the screen, and listened to the phone ring back home.

"Evan," Dad answered with a mumble.

It must be night there. I woke him. "Dad, I'm sorry."

"Don't be," he replied, sleep slipping from his tone. Behind him, Jessie's muffled voice came. "Yes, it's her," he answered, his voice clearer as he spoke to me. "Are you okay?"

"Yes. I'm fine, we landed about an hour ago. But Dad, I overheard someone in the drug-store. There's been an attack?"

He didn't answer right away, and when he did, his voice was deeper. "Just a minute." Sheets rustled in the background before the heavy thud of his steps as he stepped out of the bedroom.

I could almost see him moving, tracking every step until the thud of his study door sounded. "Evan, Marcus Baldeon is dead."

"Marcus Baldeon?" I knew the name but not the person.

"He was shot when they were on the boat heading to the island and survived, but they must've been waiting, biding their time until he recovered and was discharged from the damn infirmary."

I pressed my spine against the seat as the car turned, my mind shifting to the bitch who'd stabbed me. "Do they know who attacked him?"

"CCTV footage shows three men. It was organized, whoever it was."

It couldn't be a coincidence. "And now?"

"Now there's security everywhere. I've been waiting to hear from you, ready to call the Commander and have that fucking bitch arrested."

"No," I answered instantly, my mind racing.

There were too many things that didn't make sense, too many threads untethered. My mind returned to the moment I'd woken up in that bunker, the sound of her voice, deep and husky as she spoke into the phone. Three men had attacked and killed someone on the island. And she was there now, pretending to be me. "It can't be a coincidence."

"I agree," Dad answered carefully. "Which is why I haven't said anything and waited for you to call. Tell me what you want to do, Evan, and I'll do it."

"I want you to wait," I declared. "Wait until I get there, until I say."

"You're the heir," he responded, his tone etched with pride.

The car pulled into the driveway of a sleek and stylish motel. One glance out the window and I found the deep, broody blue of the ocean. "I've got to go, Dad. But I'll call as soon as I can."

"Okay, and Evan? Be careful."

"I will," I answered. "Goodnight, Dad."

"Night, honey." He ended the call as the driver climbed out.

Porters hauled my luggage from the car as I grabbed my drugstore bag and carefully climbed out.

Barely twenty minutes later, I was standing in the living room of a suite facing the ocean. I emptied the bag from the drugstore and grabbed what was labelled as painkillers, then antibiotics, downing them with a gulp of cold water from a bottle, and turned to the bedroom.

I felt like sleeping for a week. My body shivered with a low-grade fever and my limbs grew aching and heavy. I stumbled to the bed, my eyes already closing. I just needed sleep, a little sleep and I'd feel better. I pressed the button for the curtains.

Black-out blinds shielded what little sunlight there was. I stepped out of my shoes, tugged down my pants, and climbed under the covers, As I closed my eyes, the last image that stuck in my head was of Bruno Bernardi.

TWENTY-SIX

Her

He betrayed me....

Warm tears slipped down my cold cheeks as I watched the shadows melt into one another outside my building. I was unable to turn away, frozen in agony as I stared at hands splayed against the wall as pants were pushed low.

My stomach clenched at the sight. Even though I couldn't see his face, I didn't need to.

I knew it was *him*.

Knew it by the way *he* moved. By the way he kissed and growled. By the way he fucked and as I stood there watching him fucking Xael Davies, I knew everything had changed.

My chest was empty as I quietly made my way back to the front of the building. The space where my heart had once been was now ice cold, hollow from the inside out. I shivered as I used the keycard and stepped through the doors into the foyer.

"Ms. Valachi, everything okay?

I crossed the space on autopilot, pressed my card to the elevator and waited as the doors opened before I stepped inside.

"Ms. Valachi?" The guard stepped closer.

I lifted my gaze as the doors closed and the elevator took me higher. But I didn't see the guard any more than I saw Xael. All I saw was *him*. The reason I was here, the *one fucking good thing in my life*. I closed my eyes, squeezing the tears free and let them run, before opening them once more.

I lashed out and my palm met my cheek as the brutal *slap* filled the space.

Fire found me. The burn was good...*too good*. I yanked my hand back and unleashed again, this time hitting harder, until my teeth gnashed together.

Slap...

SLAP.

I wasn't thinking, or feeling. Only action mattered in that moment, *only revenge*. Hard breaths consumed me as fire gave birth to pain. I *wanted* him to know I'd seen them, wanted him to feel that weight of panic that swelled inside me now. I wanted him to fall and fumble, to realize what he'd been doing with Xael was *wrong*.

Because there was only one right for him.

And that was me.

My fingers shook as I punched out a text.

I saw you tonight. You betrayed me.

My hand hovered over the send button and, as the doors opened, I pushed it. Guilt wrapped around me as that crushing feeling clenched tight. I couldn't breathe, couldn't think. All I could do in that moment was *feel*.

Feel shattered.

Feel heartbroken.

Feel like I was spiraling, because that's exactly how I felt. Everything was twirling around me, slipping from my fingers. The plan we'd had was now nothing more than a blur. *Everything was a blur.*

My hands trembled as I stepped out and made my way through the apartment. One I shared with the woman who was sleeping with the man I loved, and stumbled for the bedroom. This out-of-control sensation wasn't new. I'd felt it many times before. Before when I was *sick*. When I'd had no purpose. But I had a purpose now, one *he'd* given me.

I glanced at the empty screen on my phone and stepped into the closet, yanked open the suitcase, and buried my hand inside. I searched for the false floor release, and the small bottle of pills taped underneath.

Drugs that had helped me before.

Drugs I needed right now.

I shook two tablets out and tossed them into my mouth, swallowing them dry. In the darkness of the closet, I fell backwards, my ass hitting the tiled floor, and that's where I stayed. My feet curled under me, I leaned backwards against the soft chiffon fabric and designer gowns.

Clothes that belonged to another woman.

And not me.

Because *nothing* belonged to me. Nothing but anger and rage and heartache...I pressed the button on my cell phone. My eyes skimmed the messages as I swiped, finding the camera app before pressing the button. Tiny cameras were wired into the entrance of the bunker. And right now, I wanted to see the bitch whose clothes I wore lying cold on the concrete floor.

I wanted death.

Wanted pain.

I wanted to relive that moment when the knife plunged into her belly and watch surprise fill her eyes. Anything was better than this *nothingness* I felt now. Anything was better than the images of Xael's hands against the wall and him driving between her thighs that were inside my head. *Anything was better than that.*

But the moment I loaded the camera app, I found the bunker empty.

She was gone.

I pressed the button, shifting the angles, finding the door cracked open. *They'd found her already...*

Adrenaline coursed through me as I punched her name into the search engine and waited for the results to load. If they'd found her, there'd be a statement.

But there wasn't.

No reports of Evan Valachi dead.

No mournful pictures of her father as he wept over his fucking heir.

Panicked thoughts collided with a barrier as a wave of calmness washed over me. Of course they wouldn't tell the media, not yet anyway. They'd want to keep the death of a monster's daughter quiet…for the moment, at least.

I closed my eyes as my phone vibrated with a text.

But right now, in this moment as the drugs flooded my system, taking that crushing emptiness inside me and making it fade, I just wanted to sleep and remember the moment Evan Valachi died. The happiness I'd felt. The *calmness*. I wanted that calmness back, wanted to right this tilting mess I found myself in. It'd only ever been about killing them…the Valachis and the Bernardis. Only ever about repaying the debt owed to me and my mom.

That's my good girl, my dad whispered in my head. *We're back on track now. Find the Bernardi bastard and make him pay.*

"I will, Daddy," I whispered. "I will."

TWENTY-SEVEN

Evan

Darkness consumed me. I tossed and turned, flitting in and out of consciousness, waking in a cold sweat to faded light spilling in from the doorway before crashing back under the wave of exhaustion once more. By the time I surfaced long enough to remember where I was, it was full dark. The kind of dark that made you question if you were still asleep. It took me longer than normal to realize I wasn't.

I blinked as my phone illuminated beside the bed and then darkened. My hands felt like blocks of lead as I reached, smacking the corner of the table and hissed in pain. But I captured the corner of my cell and dragged it back to the bed, where I blinked and tried to focus my eyes.

Fifteen missed calls...and they were all from Dad.

Panic carved through me. I pushed myself up from the pillows and stabbed the button, listening to the phone ring before it was answered.

"*Thank fuck, Evan,*" Dad barked. "Where the hell have you been?"

"What do you mean? I've been asleep," I answered, stifling a yawn.

"All this time?" he asked, exhaling into the speaker.

"Yeah, all this time, Dad. What's going on?" I slid my feet from under the covers as a gnawing cramp consumed my abdomen. How long had it been? A few hours, if that...

"The last time we spoke on the phone, Evan, was almost twenty-four hours ago."

Twenty-four hours? "What?" I muttered, and shoved my panties down as I sat on the cold toilet seat. "That can't be right."

"It is, and while you've been asleep, there's been another goddamn attack on the island, which is why when I couldn't reach you..."

"You freaked out," I finished for him. "What happened?"

Warmth spilled from my body. The pang of agony eased as Dad started talking.

"Katerina VanHalen's been kidnapped."

I stiffened, searching my mind for an image of her. Redhead, quiet, controlled, and filthy fucking rich. "Holy shit."

"Yeah, holy shit," he breathed, the sting in his words easing.

A male's bark drifted in through the closed glass doors, reaching me in the bathroom. I wiped, rose, and flushed the toilet, wincing, knowing my father was hearing *everything*. Pain moved through my side, the ache deeper, *hotter* than it was before. "Tell me everything."

"I just finished a conference call with the other members of the Commission. It seems as though the real target was the Stidda asshole."

"Lazarus Rossi," I growled, hating how rivalry burned in my father at a time like this.

I swapped my phone to my other hand and pressed against the knife wound in my side as I headed out of the bedroom and across the suite to the glass doors facing the ocean. "So they came for him and took the redhead. Do we know why?"

"Convenience, I think. Apparently, the St—Rossi boy has a thing for Ms. VanHalen. They were seen together, and that apparently was enough for the intruders to take her instead of the heir."

"Looks like it's hunting season," I muttered, channeling Elmer Fudd as I pulled aside the curtains and opened the sliding glass door.

"What?"

"Nothing, Dad." Warm ocean air hit me in an instant.

The male roar came from somewhere. Angry. Desperate. *Where is she?* I faintly caught the words before they were gone again. "So they came for the Rossi heir and took Kat. Have they demanded a ransom?"

"Not yet."

"Okay, good. I need to get onto the island, and soon. They'll be distracted. The *bitch* who stabbed me will be distracted."

"Evan...look," he started. "I think you should just—"

"You tell me to come home now, and the Valachis are over. You get that, right? Even if the Commission survives this...whatever the hell *this* is, we'll be seen as the ones who fucking hid when war was declared. We'll be a damn laughing stock. Our legacy will be over, and I *refuse* to have that happen."

"Evan, you've been stabbed."

"And I'm still fucking standing," I forced the words through my teeth as I stared out into the night. Moonlight glinted off the water in the distance. "I'm right here. If you think I'm going to pack up my bags before I find out who did this and why, then you don't know me well enough to decide for me, do you?"

"There are things about me...*about us*...the Commission, you don't want to be part of. Things that were done well before you or I sat in the seat. Things done in the Valachi name."

"And I'm only hearing about this *now?*" I snarled.

"I thought I could save you."

"You mean, you thought I'd never find out. It's not the same thing and never has been. By saving me, you put me at risk."

"It wasn't just us," he muttered. "Everyone on that Commission had a part to play here."

"Then you're no better than the rest of them. Or wait...I bet the other heirs know, don't they? I bet they all know and I'm the last one to find out."

My father was silent...and he was rarely silent, except when it came to the truth. I sighed, swallowing the burn of anger I felt toward him and shoved it aside...*for now*. "And you think that is what's happening here? The attacks?"

"It could be," he sighed, sounding beaten. "I don't know. Until we find the bastards who did this, we won't know."

But *she* would, wouldn't she? If she was part of this attack on the Commission, then there was only one way to find out. "I'm getting on that island, Dad, and I'm going tonight. But I'm going to need you to do something for me. So I'm going to call you when I'm almost there, and I need you to call the Commander and have him…and *only* him, meet me on the beach."

"Okay, Evan. Okay, we'll do it your way. But if you're doing this, I want you goddamn armed, you hear me? The *first* sign of trouble, I want you to shoot first and worry about the cover-up later."

"Oh, believe me," I growled as the man's roar from outside grew fainter. "I won't be taking *anymore* chances where my safety is concerned."

But it wasn't the bitch who'd stabbed me I thought of. It was Bruno…and Jannick and all the other assholes who thought I was helpless and weak. Who thought their hands around my throat would make me whimper in fear. Who thought a woman had no place occupying a seat on their precious fucking Commission.

And those assholes…I'd prove wrong.

I hung up the call, closed the door, and made my way back into the bedroom. I might be hurt, but I wasn't over. I lifted my phone and hit the number for the driver, listening as he answered on the second ring.

"Ms. Valachi, can I drive you somewhere?"

"No, thank you," I answered. "But I do need your assistance. How soon can you get here?"

"Give me twenty minutes?"

"Good, see you then."

I hung up the call, grabbed clean clothes, and head for the bathroom. Twenty minutes later and I was showered and dressed in black jeans and a black bomber jacket. My hair was still a little damp and piled into a loose bun on the top of my head as I waited inside the door to my suite, my bags packed and ready at my side.

A knock, and I waited as he spoke his name. I opened the door and quickly told him what I wanted. I had to hand it to him, he barely flinched. Instead, he gave a nod, pulled his phone out, and stepped away.

Barely five minutes later, he returned. "It's done. We're meeting at the marina." He picked up my bags and strode toward the front of the hotel. "But I need to warn you...the weather, it's turning bad."

I glanced up at the swirling night sky. The clouds were darker, thicker, building up to something more savage. It *was* turning bad...and everything else along with it. But I had no choice now, I was deep in the trenches...buried up to my neck in blood. My side pinched, agony waiting for me to acknowledge it. But I didn't. Instead, I just put my shoulder to the task.

I made my way to the reception desk, finalized my room, and smiled, nodding to the receptionist. "Yes, everything was perfect, thank you."

Heat moved through my side as I forced my stride to lengthen and headed for the car. But I refused to wince. Instead, I popped two more painkillers and slid into the backseat as Igor opened the door. I screwed the top of the bottle closed and glanced out the window as he pulled out, drove down the road, and slowed at the marina.

We met a guy, who knew a guy. I gave a nod, watching as he handed over the money in exchange for a gun. Not just any gun.

The serial number removed, no trace of it in any register. I grabbed the weapon, checked the magazine, and tucked it into the rear of my waistband. I shoved the spare clip and a box of bullets into the pockets of my jeans. It was enough to do some damage, enough to cover my own ass.

"You sure you don't want someone watching your back on the island?" Igor asked, his dark eyes glinting with anticipation.

"I'm sure, Igor.," I answered with a smile. "Besides, I'm going to need you here for me. When I call…I might be in some trouble."

"Trouble is my middle name, Ms. Valachi," he said with a chilling smile. "I live for it."

"Unfortunately, so do I," I answered, and looked out over the sparkling dark waters.

The throaty sound of a motor cut through the darkness.

"That sounds like your ride," Igor murmured, rounding me to haul my bags from the trunk of the Chrysler, and headed for the docks.

I followed him, the gun rubbing against the small of my back, drawing my focus. Fear mingled with adrenaline, creating a dangerous cocktail. Igor helped me onto the boat and spoke in Creole to the captain, who just nodded.

"He said he knows the island." Igor turned to me. "And the smaller dock where you won't be seen."

"Thank you," I murmured. "I appreciate everything you've done. I'll call you soon," I added as the boat's engine grew louder and we slowly pulled away.

Igor just nodded, standing on the dock, watching me as we pulled away and sped through the dark waters.

I tried not to think about what waited in the murky depths underneath and instead turned my mind to how this would play out once I arrived on the island, a little late and in a very different circumstance than what I'd originally planned. It was supposed to be my fucking moment. My power play to Bruno Bernardi and the rest of the damn Commission. It was supposed to be the opportunity I'd been longing for all these years, the one where I became not just a daughter, *but an heir.*

I wanted to make Bruno Bernardi crawl on his hands and knees toward me, then I was going to make him pay. *Make him beg first, then bleed.*

Marriage or not, if he thought I was going to succumb to his goddamn demands, he'd find out soon enough, this was one of those times where the sins of the father didn't fall to me. If they wanted to marry a Valachi so fucking bad, then they could marry my dad.

Hours of therapy were wasted on me. The faceless man in my dreams wasn't some repressed hunger, no matter how much Jude wanted to psychoanalyze every moment into some kind of sick and twisted desire.

I dropped my hand, feeling the hard edge of the photo inside my pocket. It wasn't desire that drove me to Bruno Bernardi, it was rage, cold, savage rage. One that had started that night I'd slapped his damn cousin in the face, and had haunted me ever since.

I don't know why I didn't think of Jannick, especially after what he'd done. It wasn't his face that was etched into my memory, it was the man who'd stood in the shadows, watching as my clothes were ripped and my body exposed.

He'd watched it happen...and that was worse.

I bet he'd enjoyed it, too.

Heat moved through me as seaspray slapped against my face and we throttled harder, jumping the waves. I turned my head and held on. Time seemed to slip away, timed by the rise and the slam as we crested wave after wave, until finally, after what felt like hours, I caught the glint of lights in the distance.

I grabbed my phone, punched out a text to my father, and waited.

The closer we came to the island, the more I saw. Someone waited for us…a lone figure dressed in black stood on the smaller dock. I sucked in a breath, glanced at my phone, and pressed the button, calling my father as we slowed…and headed for the shore.

TWENTY-EIGHT

Evan

THE COMMANDER WASN'T QUITE WHAT I'D EXPECTED. HE was younger than I'd imagined for one, *fucking gorgeous,* for another. Dark, sultry. Brooding. One scowling look at me, and his brows furrowed. I held out my phone and disembarked from the boat, wincing as I strode onto the dock.

The boat's captain hefted my suitcases onto the dock before the boat slowly backed away. The wind was howling, slamming waves against the island's shore with a deafening roar. I felt the building storm, even if the clouds were thick, heavy and unmoving. It was in the wind where the panic was, the brutal, thrashing gusts wound the tension tight inside me until I thought I'd snap.

The gun cut into the small of my back as I moved, drawing my focus to the weapon as the Commander took my phone and lifted it to his face. Dad's video cut in and out as he brought him up to speed. But given that he and the Commander had spoken only hours before, it was only to reassure him that I was the real Evan

Valachi...and the woman on the island who'd stolen my name was an impostor.

"I understand., Mateo muttered, and stared into my cell. "Discretion is needed at this time. But as you're well aware, Michele, I cannot put one family's safety above everyone else's."

"We have no idea who that crazy bitch is," my father snapped. "We don't know if she's acting alone. We don't know anything other than the fact she tried to kill my daughter and is out for blood. I want your full assistance with this. It's a fucking priority."

"I understand, but, as you know, we have another crisis on our hands, as well."

"The VanHalen girl, any word?"

One shake of his head was all that was needed. "I'll do my best to assist any way I can," the Commander assured, then lifted his gaze to mine and handed back the phone.

"E," Dad started as a violent wind gust drove me sideways. "Be careful out there."

"I will!" I shouted.

He said something else, something I thought was *I love you*. But then he was gone in a pixelated blur and the connection ended.

"It's the storm!" The Commander moved close to roar in my ear. *"A damn typhoon is headed toward us."*

A typhoon? I stared at him, dumbfounded. "Of course, what fucking more could go wrong?"

"What?" he roared, shaking his head.

I leaned close. Closer than I was comfortable with, but desperation was the only thing driving me now. *"Bernardi, is he still..."* Alive...safe...what did I want?

"He's safe. We're all on lockdown and escorted by island personnel!" he yelled. "This card will get you into all buildings. It's registered to the Commission, so it won't show up with your name. Your father said no security, but Ms. Valachi, I don't think you understand how dangerous this place is at this moment."

I straightened. Didn't understand? I reached the zipper of my jacket, yanked it low, and lifted my shirt, revealing the taped dressing on my wound with one hand while I grabbed my gun and drew it free with the other.

His gaze dropped to the movement, his eyes fixed on the dressing that was sticking to my skin with dried blood. I didn't need to look down to know even more blood had seeped through the barrier as I roared, *"I understand better than you might think!"*

TWENTY-NINE

Her

Him: *It's not what you think.*

I stared at the text as tears slipped down my cheeks.

Him: *Talk to me.*

My fingers trembled across the screen, then stopped. Agony roared through my chest, carving all the way to the very center of us.

You don't need him, pumpkin, Daddy whispered in my head. *You never did. It was better when it was just the two of us, wasn't it?*

I tried to remember, tried to find the answer through the pain. I closed my eyes, but I couldn't get through the barrier. I couldn't feel anything other than this betrayal. All I saw was her hands on the wall...all I heard was his growl in her ear. The creak of her bed sounded in the room next to mine and I swore I heard her sigh with contentment. The sound was faint as I sat curled against the wall of my closet. I knew what I wanted to say now.

Knew what I wanted him to see.

Did you enjoy fucking her?

I hit send as the words blurred under a sheen of tears.

Was she nice and tight? Did she moan just the way he liked it? Did she make him feel how *I* made him feel? Was she loyal...loyal enough to kill for him? Loyal like me?

Him: No.

My heart thumped as I read his message.

He was lying. *LYING!* I shoved the phone away and wrapped my arms around my knees, tears burned against my cheeks. He was trying to break me, trying to hurt me somehow. Was it something I'd done? Something I'd said?

My phone vibrated, the ringer on silent, and the caller ID was *Unknown.* But I knew who it was...the only one who'd call me.

Don't answer it, my father urged.

But that aching void inside me screamed for him. For this to all go away, for everything to go back to the way it was before, when we were in love.

Still, I stared at the phone as it hummed, bouncing against the tiled floor. I moved before I knew it, grabbing it and pressing the button. My heavy breaths blew against the handset, but silence filled the space. My senses were on fire, fear pounding inside my head.

"I want you to go to him."

The words resounded in my head, low, controlled...*demanding*.

"You'll send him a text and tell him you want to come to him. I want you to seduce him."

"No." The answer was instant. "Please don't make me do that."

"You will. And you'll do it for me."

I closed my eyes at the words, and my throat thickened. "No." Silence. Cold. Cruel. Heavy. It weighed me down, pushing me under the weight of it all. "You fucked her." The spell was broken as a sob tore free. Tears fell thick and slow. "You betrayed me."

"I betrayed *nothing*," he barked in my ear. "You think me sticking it to some fucking bitch changes anything?"

His words were cruel and haunting, etching into my mind. "Y-you...y-you *b-betrayed m-me*."

A heavy sigh came through the phone, then slowly, "Stop acting like a child, Sophie."

I stiffened, the sob trapped in my throat. He called me *Sophie?*

He said my name...

"Think of the bigger picture," he urged. "The *real* picture, the one where you and I are together for good."

I swallowed the lump in my throat, hanging on to every word he said.

"She means nothing to me. She's a fucking pawn...nothing more. But you...you, my love, are my future. When we're done with this, it'll all be over for *them,* but it'll be just the beginning for us. It'll be the start of our lives together. You want that, right? You want us to be together when this is all through?"

"Yes." The answer was quiet and careful. "Yes, I want that."

"I do, too, which is why we need to play the game now. That's what this is, my love, it's just a game. A game where there are—"

"Winners and losers," I answered for him.

"Yes. Winners…and losers."

How many times had I heard him say those exact words to me? Whispered, grunted, driven deep inside me as he thrust between my thighs.

"So you understand now. You see the bigger picture?"

The tears on my cheeks grew cold. "Yes, I see."

"Good, and you'll do exactly what I said, won't you?"

"Yes," I answered, hope warming me from the inside. He really did love me…he was doing all this *for me*.

"Now, you'll text Bernardi and this is exactly what you'll say…"

THIRTY

Bruno

My phone gave a *ding*, waking me from the washed-out gray haze inside my head. I groaned and opened my eyes as the faint illumination on the screen died. Didn't matter. I wasn't asleep anyway, not really. I rarely slept anymore. Instead, I lay in bed, tossing and turning, listening to the howling wind outside and felt that savagery deep inside before I finally gave up.

I rolled, reached, and grabbed my phone, pressing the button to read the text.

Evan: I want to see you.

"What the fuck?" I muttered, re-reading the text again. "You want to meet...*now?*"

My mind raced as I tried to make sense of the complete fucking turnaround. "You fucking avoid me, you run from me, you make no attempt to acknowledge I exist, and now you want to *meet?*"

Anger burned through me. I'd found myself re-evaluating my future the last few hours, trying to come up with some kind of outcome where I could walk away from this unscathed. Evan Valachi might be promised to marry a Bernardi heir, a promise that was to be enforced by my father, as well as Evan's. But Evan had made it *very* fucking clear she wanted none of it.

And the last time I looked, a wedding...needed a goddamn bride.

So I sighed, licked my lips, and punched out a reply. *Then by all means come and see me.*

Barely a second later, there was a response.

Evan: I'm on my way.

"What? *Now?*" I shot upwards, sliding my feet from the bed, waiting for her text once more. *She couldn't be coming now...it was...*I glanced at the time—it was almost midnight.

But there was no follow-up text. No scheduling of a time, just *I'm on my way.* I slid out of bed and pulled on silk pajama pants, at least. I didn't think she wanted to see me buck fucking naked. I ran my hand through my hair. Was this an ultimatum? A truce, maybe? Fucked if I knew. Maybe she was leaving. Maybe this was her way of saying this was never going to happen between us and this was goodbye and good riddance?

I shot Deviouz a text: *Evan Valachi is on her way up, show her in.*

D: Will do.

That was fast. I hadn't expected him to respond so fast. Was he even asleep? Panic pushed the grainy sting from my eyes. I rounded the bed and made my way into the kitchen, flicking on the lights as I went. There was no party last night, had been none since the report that Katerina VanHalen had been kidnapped.

Fuck, this trip had gone all to hell. First Baldeon, and now Kat. Both attacks left nothing but destruction behind. Lazarus Rossi was savage, a fucking beast tearing into everything in his way. The last I'd heard, there was a meeting with Kat's father, and some kind of asshole who was engaged to marry her.

It all sounded goddamn messy.

But wasn't everything lately?

Just look at my own fucking life...

I grabbed a glass, poured a splash of Scotch into the bottom and tossed it down. The heat burned along my throat and filled my stomach as a faint rumble came from the elevator.

My pulse sped as the elevator doors opened. Shadows moved, spilling along the floor before the doors closed and ended the glare. She came around the corner, her head lowered, her face shadowed by the hoodie she wore. I stiffened, my hand clasped around the empty glass as I watched her. It wasn't what I'd expected at all.

"You wanted to see me," I urged, trying like hell to stop from staring as she came closer.

The faint light from the living room spilled across her face, but I couldn't quite see her, couldn't look into her eyes. "Well, here I am."

Look at me.

Her gaze followed my hand as I reached for the bottle, and for a second, it wasn't pissed-off frustration I felt. A cold sliver of fear cut through me as though I was looking at a stranger. This wasn't the Evan I remembered, not the one from my dreams, not the one filled with fire and power. This one was cold...*and a little fucking scary*. I tilted the bottle and poured before setting it back down and grabbing the glass. "So, what did you want to talk about?"

I barely had time to lift the glass to my lips before she moved, striding toward me fast. Scotch burned my lips before she pushed my hand away, grabbed the nape of my neck, and pulled me down to her. She kissed me, hard, her teeth grazing my bottom lip before she let me go.

Fuck me. I lifted my fingers to my lip and licked, tasting blood. *"What the fuck was that?"*

She didn't answer, just attacked, driving her body against mine and grabbing my neck, pulling my mouth to hers once more.

"Whoa, there," I muttered against her mouth, and pushed her away. "What the hell is this?"

"What the fuck does it look like?" she growled, lowering her gaze to the floor.

I wanted to look into her eyes, to figure out what the fuck was happening here. But I couldn't get a read on her.

"You don't want me?" she asked.

And the panic inside me grew. This was what I wanted, wasn't it? What I'd been desperate for all these years, and now…right when I had her in my fucking apartment asking me to fuck her, I was going to, what? Choke?

She turned, moving away.

"Wait," I growled, stopping her. "Just…I didn't say that. Give me a minute to think here."

"There's no thinking," she said, and turned toward me. "There's only action. That's why I came, Bruno. I thought that's what you wanted, too."

Her hands worked the zipper on her hoodie, but she didn't push the hood aside, just left the hoodie open as she worked on the buttons of her blouse underneath. I wanted to tell her to stop, that I needed to think this through. That there was more than just sex hanging in the balance between us. But that wasn't it, not really.

Something wasn't right here...

Like something I'd forgotten, something important.

No.

Something pivotal.

Her black blouse parted, revealing the creamy skin of her belly and small, hidden breasts covered by the lace cups of her bra.

"You want this, right?" she whispered, and slid her hands over her bra.

My body responded, my cock grew thick and heavy. But there wasn't the rush I expected, wasn't the craving I'd hoped for. It was like Bethany all over again. Maybe it was me...maybe I was the broken one? Maybe I was chasing a ghost that'd never been there, a hunger that was in my imagination. Maybe that was all there was. A physical sensation. A triggered response to a woman offering herself to me.

Not just any woman...Evan Valachi.

She moved closer, grabbed my hand, and placed it over her breast. I didn't look up, didn't meet her eyes. Fuck her, give her what she came for, fulfill my part of the bargain. She pressed my hand harder against her and curled her fingers over mine, forcing me to paw her...as I met her gaze.

But something inside me balked.

A hunger that wasn't ready to wither away.

"Fuck me and make me yours," she whispered. "I'm right here... ready for you."

My body took over, hunger was pushed aside for victory. She wanted this...and I wanted to claim a goddamn wife.

I grabbed her, slid my hand around the back of her neck, and pulled her into me. Kissing her for all the times I'd fucking dreamed of her and all the times she'd made me fuck another woman when all I wanted was her...

It was always her...

Always her.

Now, I'd have what was mine.

THIRTY-ONE

Evan

"This keycard gets you into every building," the Commander said as he handed me a white keycard in one hand and my cell phone with the other. "And your phone now has an app for the cameras. I've set you up with my security clearance, as you requested. You now have access not even the heirs do. So don't make me regret this."

I gave a nod and grabbed my phone, checking the time. It wasn't far off midnight. I was desperate to find her, desperate to see her once more. I wanted to look into the face of the monster, more than that...I wanted her to see mine.

"Will you have your man take my bags to the apartment?" I asked.

A nod and a wave of his, and a man dressed in black strode forward. "Take Ms. Valachi's things to the spare wing in building one."

"Yes, sir," he grabbed my suitcases before turning to leave.

"I want regular updates." The Commander held my gaze, letting me feel the force of his urgency. "I want to know where she is and what she's doing. I have a tracker assigned to your cell and I'll have access to a regular log of everything you access. Believe me when I say this, Ms. Valachi, your security is paramount. I'll have no hesitation in taking out this…imposter and anyone else she comes into contact without a second's hesitation."

I believed him. Anyone who looked into those bottomless eyes would. He was the man I knew him to be. A cold, merciless killer. An Albanian, I was told, and a ruthless one, at that. "Understood," I answered.

"Good. Happy hunting, Ms. Valachi. I'll be waiting for your updates," he repeated, then turned and strode away, leaving me standing there on the small dock in the howling wind.

A storm was coming. A typhoon, it seemed.

What a damn night to hunt a killer.

I shoved my hands into my pockets, along with the keycard and phone. I'd have a room to sleep in and wash and plan. But sleep and rest were the last things on my mind. I pulled out my phone and opened up a map of the island. The fake Evan Valachi was sharing a penthouse suite with Xael Davies.

I knew of her, the wild daughter of Taran Davies, Welsh-born and impossible to tame. The idea of anyone from the Commission being tainted by the traitorous bitch who'd left me for dead filled me with rage. I wanted to scream and howl into wind. I wanted to slam it home with every fucking bullet in the loaded magazine at my back and let the fucking carnage speak for itself.

How dare she…

How fucking dare she!

How dare she...touch what was mine.

The words resounded as agony ripped through my side. I pressed my palm against the wound, trying to find relief with the pressure, and kept on moving. It was time to see where the fuck she was. I glanced ahead and pulled my hood down low, covering my face.

With the access the Commander had given me, I pulled up the cameras for my building, the one where she was currently a squatter. Night-vision cameras made the screen light up like day, just in green. Seemed when it came to security, no expense was spared. I flicked through the rooms, finding a naked brunette lying sideways across her bed, asleep.

That wasn't her.

I moved the camera to the next room...with a bed that was currently empty. Silence lingered behind the static. I stared into the murky gray of the room, then closed out. *Where the hell are you?*

I walked toward the lights sparkling in the distance, the same buildings I'd watched now almost within reach. Fear gripped me. She was out there somewhere...somewhere I couldn't see her. *But could she see me?*

My breath caught as I jerked my gaze to the glinting buildings and listened to the crash of the waves. I couldn't hear anything else but the ocean and the wind, Mother Nature at her ferocious best. But it made me nervous. I glanced over my shoulder, fought the panic back down, and hurried forward.

She had to be somewhere.

But where?

My mind shifted to another person here on the island I wanted to see. *Bruno Bernardi.* Guilt rose inside me as I pulled up the camera details on my phone once more. But instead of my building...I brought up his. Two floors showed as being occupied, the lower floor...and the penthouse.

I clicked on the penthouse and caught movement. Bruno Bernardi rose from the bed naked, the tight contours of his ass casting shadows until he slid a pair of satin pajama pants over his body. My heart thundered, and my throat went dry. I forced myself to watch where I was going before glancing back.

I clenched my jaw as he rounded the bed and made for the kitchen, flicking on the lights in his path as he went. My steps grew slower and my breaths became deeper, until I just stopped walking. *Hate him...fucking hate him.* I shut off everything else. But there wasn't the burn inside me I wanted. There wasn't that inferno of rage. Instead, I couldn't look away.

His sleek, muscled frame flexed as he moved, lifting his hand to comb his hair back, and stopped at his kitchen counter. The long blonde hair fell back across his face as he poured himself a drink and lifted the glass to his lips. I was drawn to his body, remembering the kid he'd once been. But he wasn't a kid anymore. He was a man, with the body of a man.

My eyes drifted down every inch of him until he lifted his head, his focus fixed on the entrance to his apartment as the elevator doors opened...then closed. Shadows spilled across the floor as a woman stepped in, dressed in a hoodie that hid her. But there was no mistaking the curve of her body underneath, and the seductive way she walked toward him.

Was she his lover?

Jealously ripped through me, making me clench my fists. If she wasn't already, then she wanted to be. His lips moved as he poured a drink. I wanted to hear his voice, wanted to remember just what the demon in my dreams sounded like. But as much as I wanted to watch him, she was the one who drew my gaze as she crossed the space between them and kissed him.

The movement was savage and fast. My pulse spiked, and panic pushed in.

It's her...

I don't know how I knew. Maybe it was the way she moved, the way she attacked as she kissed him. But I knew, I knew without a doubt...*this was the woman who'd stabbed me.*

Sweat broke out across the back of my neck, and my stomach clenched tight. I jerked my gaze to him, to the way his hands went to her arms before he pushed her backwards, breaking the kiss. Did he know...*was he in on this?*

I moved before I knew it, lunging in a half-walk half-run, gripping my phone with one hand while I reached around with the other, my thoughts frantic, and headed for his building. I didn't know what to think, all I knew was this wasn't happening...*no fucking way.* I brought up the map of the buildings and scanned the towering apartment blocks in front of me, settling on the one at my far right. That had to be it...that had to be building six.

I stepped off the pavement and onto the soft grass, feeling it sink under my boots as I raced toward the bright lights of the building's foyer. *What if they wouldn't let me in?*

A surge of panic pushed high as I skirted the thick tropical gardens and headed for the doors, catching sight of the guard dressed in a suit standing sentry in the foyer. *Please work...*

please...I yanked the card the Commander had given me and slammed it against the reader outside.

The doors to the foyer opened instantly and the guard stepped forward.

"*Stop,*" I commanded, drawing every forceful part of my nature into my tone. "You *will* not speak, not even acknowledge I'm here. I'm acting under the orders of the Commander."

His brows rose, surprise filling him as he started forward. But I gave him no chance to argue. Instead, I brought up the cameras of Bruno's apartment upstairs on my phone, watching as she shed her clothes in front of him and pulled him across the space toward the bedroom.

But I wasn't heading to the elevator, nor was I lunging for the stairs. I headed for the little red box against the wall, twisted, and slammed it with my elbow before pulling the handle for the fire alarm, and prayed I wasn't too late.

"*You say nothing, do you hear me?*" I roared over the blare of the alarm "*Our lives are at stake!*"

The guard just gave a nod as I turned and lunged for the doors.

THIRTY-TWO

Bruno

"Take me," Evan urged, pulling me toward the bedroom. "It's what you want, isn't it?"

Is it? The thought rose as I followed her around the end of the counter and headed to the bedroom, feeling the weight of my responsibilities. I *wanted* to want her...I really fucking did. But as I lifted my gaze to hers, her lips curled in a sad smile, her face still hidden by that fucking hood, she felt like everyone else I'd fucked.

There was *nothing*. Not even the heat of desire. *Just...nothing*. My cock was soft, slapping against my thigh under the silk pajamas as I moved. The small flare of lust I'd felt seconds ago was now cold and stale.

She was just a woman...

Just another *responsibility*.

Not even one I wanted. How the fuck was I going to marry her now?

"Take off the jacket," I demanded as she stepped into the darkness of my bedroom.

She didn't obey my command, just pulled me toward the bed, her pale breasts exposed through the opening of her blouse. I fixed my gaze on the shadows of her face. And a cold, careful feeling washed through me.

Something was wrong here. Something I couldn't push away. I lifted my hand to her hood.

She moved fast, slapping my hand away with enough force to fling my hand through the air, leaving a sting behind. *"Don't fucking touch me,"* she barked.

I took a couple of steps backwards. My gut clenched in warning as the piercing blare of an alarm cut through the air. She jerked her gaze upwards to the tiny red lights blinking on the fire alarm, her lips curling in savage rage.

I saw her now, saw her as the faint light fell across her cheeks and the tiny upturned point of her nose. I saw those empty eyes that looked faintly familiar, and that warning in my gut screamed something I couldn't quite understand.

That isn't Evan...

"Bruno!" a roar boomed from the entrance of the apartment.

I wrenched my gaze from her and stumbled backwards. Still, she never moved. She was frozen with rage as she stared at the blinking red light.

"We have to evacuate," Deviouz shouted over the alarm as he ran toward me. *"NOW!"*

The wind battered the windows outside, drawing my gaze. This wasn't right, *none of it*. I jerked my gaze to my leather jacket slung over the back of the stool and lunged, yanking it free as I turned to the stranger in my bedroom. "Evan...*Evan, we have to go now!*"

Deviouz dragged me toward the stairs. But she still stood there, transfixed by the fucking alarm as she screamed, *"I DID WHAT YOU WANTED, DIDN'T I?"*

"What the fuck?" The words barely left my lips before I was hauled through the stairwell doorway and into the murky gloom.

"I can't leave her!" I roared, yanking from my bodyguard's hold, and lunged for the bedroom.

My bare feet stung as they slapped the tiles before I skidded to a stop in the doorway of the bedroom. But the room was empty. *She wasn't there...*

I scanned the space, lunging for the closet. *Where the fuck* was *she?* But there was no one in the closet and no one in the bathroom, either. My heart thundered, the sound mingling with the piecing squeal of the alarm.

"BRUNO!" Deviouz roared.

I gripped my jacket, lunged for my boots, and hurried for the stairs once more. *"I can't find her!"* Panic mingled with the kind of eerie fear I had when I watched psycho thrillers in the movies. Evan wasn't there...*she wasn't anywhere.*

I barrelled after him, grabbing the railing as I hauled my ass down four flights of stairs, barefoot and barely clothed. My calves were screaming, my feet burning with the friction. But I didn't have time to yank on my boots, only to lunge down two and three stairs at a time as I hurried after Deviouz.

He jerked his gaze back at me. His dark eyes shone in the dimness then, as we neared the bottom, he reached around his waistband and drew his Sig free. My heart lunged, fear punching through, as he charged forward, using all his six-foot-four raw power as he yanked the foyer door open and charged through.

He was gone in an instant. My pulse was deafening as I waited for the crack of gunshots. But there was nothing…just the piercing squeal of the alarm and the blinding light as I raced after him into the foyer, my boots in one hand and my jacket in the other.

"Bernardi!" the Commander's guard called, motioning me forward.

There were more of them in dark suits charging through the open doors of the foyer, their eyes wide, guns drawn, ready for an attack. I scanned the darkness as Deviouz grabbed my arm, dragging me closer.

"Don't just fucking stand there!" he roared at the guards. "Search the goddamn building!"

They scattered…*all but one of them.*

The one assigned to protect me by the Commander himself. He just watched me and the commotion around us with utter shock. I sucked in harsh breaths and braced my hands on my knees as the other bodyguards scurried like we were under an outright attack. For all I knew, we could be.

Evan filled my mind. She was in my fucking bedroom one minute and the next, she was gone. "She's up there!" I roared at the other men as they ran for the stairwell door. "Evan Valachi is still up there!"

"You just left her?" one of them asked.

Christ, if those words didn't stab deep, carving through every thought of who I was as a man. *You just left her?*

Deviouz gripped my arm, dragging me backwards toward the exterior doors. *"Move!"*

It was us against everyone else. My protection was all he cared about, and I knew I'd made a mistake about him all along…

It wasn't Jannick he answered to, it was my father.

Because my safety was the only thing he cared about, hiring a man to protect me at all costs. I met Deviouz's gaze, finding nothing but cold, unflinching determination as he pulled me out of the foyer and into the night.

"We need to find somewhere secure," his voice a roar in my head now we were out of the piecing blast of the alarm.

I scanned the night, finding movement in the distance. A woman stood at the corner of my building, cloaked by shadows. A surge of adrenaline ripped through me as she moved, stepping out into the foyer lights.

It was her…HER!

But it wasn't…

She reached up and pushed the hood back from her face.

A face that was so damn familiar.

One I saw in my dreams.

My feet moved on their own. My bodyguard's grip fell away.

Desire, rage, and *hunger* found me.

"Wait," I yelled, tearing from my bodyguard's hold as I stepped forward. But she took a step backwards, pressing a hand against her side.

I was transfixed by the sight. It was her...the *real* Evan Valachi. Her gaze pinned me where I stood as she lifted her hand and pressed a finger to her lips.

Shhh...

I could almost hear the whisper, almost feel her urgency. She glanced through the glass wall of the foyer as it filled with more of the Commander's guards, then stepped backwards, sinking into the shadows once more.

"Bruno," Deviouz growled, drawing my gaze, but he was staring at the same spot where she'd disappeared.

But the moment I turned back she was gone.

What the fuck was going on here? I tried to understand what was happening as a couple of the Commander's men strode toward me. If that was Evan Valachi...*then who the fuck was in my bedroom?*

"The building's clear," the Commander called, charging toward us. "There's no sign of a fire."

"Then what the fuck happened?" Deviouz barked as he scanned the night.

"I don't know.," the Commander answered as the shrill sound of the alarm ended. But he fixed those dark, glinting eyes on me. "You said Evan Valachi was in your bedroom?"

I scowled, my mind a fucking mess. *I thought it was.* "Yeah, I mean, I don't know."

"You don't know?" the Commander questioned.

I found the darkness where she'd disappeared once more. I needed to find her, needed to try to understand what was happening here. "Have the other floors been searched?"

"They're finishing up as we speak."

I nodded, my mind whirling. I dragged my fingers through my hair as Deviouz looked at me with a confused and pissed-off glare. But he knew not to speak out of line. He knew no matter what he saw, he stayed quiet, until *I* told him not to. "Then we're all good?" I asked.

A crackle came from the two-way in the Commander's grip. He lifted the handset and spoke, relayed the information as the guards spilled out of the stairwell door and back into the foyer once more.

"Looks like we're all clear." He met my gaze. "There's no sign of a fire, *or Ms. Valachi.*"

The way he said her name pissed me off. Did he think I made up the fact she was in my damn apartment just to panic his guys a little more? He shifted those beady fucking eyes over mine, picking me apart in his head.

"Okay, then," I muttered. "That's that."

"That's that," Mateo repeated carefully.

I felt his damn gaze as I strode back into the building. The guards filed out, nodding at me as I stepped around them. My mind raced as I pressed the button for the elevator, the heavy ringing in my ears making me swallow. But I was desperate to be alone, desperate to think and figure this shit out. The wind outside howled, slapping the palms against the glass as the elevator doors opened and I stepped inside.

I hadn't imagined the blonde outside, hadn't fucking imagined the fire in my chest when my gaze found hers. I closed my eyes as exhaustion hit me like a freight train. I hadn't slept properly for fucking days, and there'd been too much partying, too many drugs. I needed to get my head clear, needed to figure this all out.

Something was happening here...something I wasn't part of.

Until now.

THIRTY-THREE

Evan

I PRESSED MY HAND AGAINST MY SIDE AND RAN. IT WAS him...Bruno Bernardi, standing outside his building. *And he'd seen me.* My pulse roared in my ears.

But did he finally understand?

I fucking hoped so...for his sake, at least.

The howl of the wind still sounded as I moved around the edge of the building and slowed. Hard, heavy breaths lit a fire in my chest. The gun was cutting into the small of my back. I stopped, pressed my spine against the wall, and closed my eyes for a second.

She was in his apartment, that vindictive bitch who'd used my name *and my damn face*. I opened my eyes and lifted the cell, opening the app to the cameras in his apartment, and stared at the grainy image once more.

I hadn't seen her come out, not with the security, or following Bruno and his bodyguard as they'd burst from the stairwell.

Fear unleashed a tendril inside me. One that snaked around my stomach and gripped tight. If she hadn't come out, then she still had to be in there. *With him.* I stared at the screen, flicking through camera after camera, and searched his building. Desperation mingled with frustration as I flicked through apartment after apartment and room after room. "*Where the fuck are you?*"

I needed to know where she was, needed a way to flush the bitch out. I lifted my gaze to the bright foyer lights of the buildings in the distance. I needed to get out of the open, needed a place where I could get out of the wind and think.

The keycard the Commander had given me was in my hand, and a room waited, a room where no one went. One which only one guard knew was being used and a place no one monitored. Right now, that sounded perfect. I peeked around the corner of the building, made sure my hood was pulled low, and hurried across the grounds.

I slapped the card against the reader outside the doors and slipped through, stepping into darkened hallways and sucking in hard breaths. I glanced at the image of the rough, hand-drawn map the Commander had sent me and moved, heading for the rear of the building.

A CCTV camera moved against the wall, scanning the interior of the building. I stilled, bent my head down even further, and hurried underneath it, moving through the hallway and past the conference rooms up ahead. The screen on my cell illuminated with a text. I glanced down.

Mateo: Bruno is secure. No sign of imposter.

No sign of imposter? Just like I'd thought when I scanned the entire building. She'd just disappeared. I hurried along the hallway, heading to the door marked *Private* just like the Commander had said, and pressed the keycard to the scanner, waiting for the *clunk* of the lock before I slipped inside into total darkness.

I fumbled for a light switch as panic rose. But the second I felt the connection and hit the lights, it all eased. The place was perfect, with a small living room that led into a small kitchen. I made my way through the space, stepping into the bedroom, and found my suitcases beside the bed. There was a connecting bathroom . I stepped into the doorway and hit the switch, flooding the room with light.

I'd spent too much time in the dark lately, too much time in fear and agony. I winced and looked down, lifting the corner of my shirt to find the bloody gauze. I needed a shower, and a fresh dressing. As my belly let out a growl, I added food to my to-do list. Yeah, food would be good.

I carefully lifted my bag, set it on the bed, and unpacked the essentials before kicking off my boots and heading into the bathroom. I placed the gun next to the sink. One sound and I'd be within reach. So, this is what it felt like being the heir of a Mafia family. This is what it felt like to be a Valachi.

I pulled my shirt over my head and carefully peeled the dressing from my side, looking into the mirror at the ugly, oozing mess. That bitch had stabbed me. She'd stabbed me and now she was after Bruno. I couldn't let that happen, couldn't let her get away with hurting...

A sickening feeling washed over me. Hate mingled with desperation to form some kind of noxious hunger, one I didn't like at all. I shoved my jeans and panties down, then unhooked my bra and stepped into the shower. The sting was instant when

I turned on the water, making me hiss. But the longer I stood under the spray, the more the warmth eased my muscles.

After I washed and dried, I gently applied antiseptic cream to the wound and a fresh dressing before taping it up. I pulled on clean jeans, a t-shirt, and a hoodie. I needed to be as far from my real self as possible, and I needed to be ready for an outright attack. I glanced toward the door of the apartment...I guessed it was only a matter of time before either I found her, or she found me.

I paced the floor and kept myself busy flicking through the cameras on my phone until the battery blinked and I put it on charge. Then I ate and lay on the bed, staring at the ceiling, and thought of *him*. Bruno. Right now, he was probably confused as hell. Had he recognized me? Did he even have a clue what was going on? I turned over, curled my arm under the pillow, and closed my eyes.

Bang!

I woke with a jolt. Panic made me shove upwards, and agony followed, tearing through my side.

"Shit!" I looked down, feeling the throb, and shivered.

An icy blast tore through me. I dragged the covers higher, huddling, and listened for the world outside. It couldn't have been more than an hour since I'd gone to sleep. I tried to settle, but the gnawing pain in my side grew worse, forcing me from the bed. I stumbled into the bathroom and dug through the painkillers from the drugstore, swallowing two before I found the antibiotics.

I downed a couple of those, too, and went back to bed, yanking the covers high, and fell back to sleep with a shiver. When I woke again, I felt worse. The sheets around me were damp with sweat. I dragged myself out of bed and peeled the clothes from my body.

I didn't need a doctor to tell me I was in trouble. In a haze of fever, I stumbled for the kitchen in my underwear and grabbed my phone. I punched out a text, hoping to God he understood as my stomach cramped. I let out a moan and doubled over, cast my phone aside, and staggered for the bathroom, sinking to the cold tiled floor.

I must've passed out, because when I woke, two men stood in the bathroom with me. One was dressed in black, leveling a glare at me. He strode forward and knelt. "Evan? Can you hear me?"

I blinked and stared into the Commander's eyes. He looked worried, *really worried*. With a glance over his shoulder, he muttered, "Can you help her here?"

"I can try," the other guy replied, and stepped closer, taking the Commander's place in front of me.

", I'm Neale Grey, the island's doctor. I'm going to take a look at your wound, okay?"

I could only nod as the Commander rose to his feet, watching as the doctor peeled the dressing back and probed my side. "It's infected, as you'd expect. You really should be in a hospital, you know that, right."

"Not going to happen," I muttered, holding the Commander's gaze.

"Can you give her a shot of antibiotics?"

"I can." The doc pressed the tape back again. "It'll help for the time being, but she really needs to rest, and any movement..."

"Just give me the shot." I forced the words through clenched teeth.

The doc just rose and headed for the bedroom, but the Commander stopped him with a hand on his arm. "She was never here, you understand me?"

There was a second of silence before the warning hit home and the doctor slowly nodded. "Of course."

The sound of the door opening and closing filled the space. But the Commander didn't move, just stared at me as I huddled on the bathroom floor. "You're tough," he said. "Tougher than you look. You remind me of my brother, Edon."

"Oh, y-yeah?" my teeth chattered with the words as I wrapped my arms around my middle. "Don't feel so tough right now."

"You never do," he responded as the door opened behind him once more. "Not until it comes down to the wire. I hope you make it, Valachi. You'll be interesting to watch."

"Great, thanks," I growled, a fat lot of good that'd help me.

The doc stepped in and knelt down, unsheathing a big goddamn needle. I turned my head with the sting, biting down, then he straightened once more. "You'll need a follow-up injection in twenty-four hours, but if the fever gets worse and you slip into a coma, I'm flying you out of here, code or no fucking code. It's not worth dying over."

I let out a bark of laughter. One that earned me a glare from the doc.

"Glad you think this is funny," he practically snarled, then turned on his heel and strode out.

Funny...

Hell, this whole thing was fucking hilarious. I'd been stabbed and left for dead in a goddamn underground bunker that was the thing of nightmares, and I'd survived. I was already a walking fucking ghost here, already living on borrowed time. How much longer that time was? I looked down at the redness peeking out from under the dressing, who the hell knew.

"The woman who was kidnapped..." I muttered, and lifted my head. "Have they found her?"

"Not yet," the Commander answered as he turned to follow the doctor. "But they're closing in."

Relief flooded me with the words. *"Wait."*

The Commander stopped halfway across the bedroom and turned.

"There's something not right. Something that's bugging me. She wasn't there in the apartment when it was searched. She wasn't anywhere, which means she has a way of getting in and out of places no one knows about."

His gaze darkened, but there wasn't a flicker of surprise. He'd been thinking the exact same thing, I was willing to bet on it.

"There's only one way that can happen..." I urged, pushing myself upwards until I stood on shaky legs. "They have access to the cameras."

A hard sigh, and his jaw muscles clenched. "I thought the same thing."

"So it has to be one of us, someone with access. An heir."

"Maybe..."

"I need to see him...Bruno. I need a way to talk to him without anyone knowing and I need it to happen without the damn cameras."

A nod was all he gave. "Sounds like a perfect opportunity to do a camera check after the false fire alarm."

"I was thinking the same thing."

"I'll set it up tonight and text you the time," he answered, striding out. "Get some rest, Evan. You're going to need it."

With that he left, closing the door behind him. His footsteps echoed, then faded away. I looked over my shoulder, staring at my own reflection in the mirror. I'd wanted a meeting with the monster in my dreams...and it looked like I was about to get it.

THIRTY-FOUR

Her

My phone let out a *beep*, but I was too afraid to look. I knew who it was, knew without glancing at the text. So I stayed where I was, curled up in the far corner of the closet, out of sight, and stared at the phone on the floor.

Feet hit the tiles in the room next to mine, and a groan of exhaustion followed. Hate burned inside me, making me curl my lips as the sound of her steps grew louder.

"Hey, E?" Xael called from the doorway of her room. "You in?"

But I didn't move from where I was, just clenched my fists and burned with rage, imagining how it would feel to stick *her* with a knife. For a second, the fantasy unfolded. In my head, it wasn't the blonde bitch I smothered with a cloth soaked in chloroform and stuffed into the back of the stolen Toyota—it was *her*, the woman fucking the man I loved.

I closed my eyes as his words resounded. *Think of the bigger picture.*

I tried to do what he wanted, tried to take my emotions out of this, tto *be* the cold, ruthless killer he wanted me to be. But every time I thought of *them,* the ones who'd taken from me, all I felt was uncontrollable, burning rage. And now the fire had spread to *her,* the fucking bitch standing outside my bedroom, the one who thought I was just like her. But I wasn't...I wasn't anything like her at all.

Kill them...kill them all and be done with it, Daddy murmured.

I lowered my gaze to my hand. Steel glinted on the sharpened edge.

Kill them and be done. *He'd* be angry. But in the end, he'd see I'd done this for *him.* I licked my lips and quietly pushed to stand up.

"You still asleep?" Xael called, the sound of her voice coming from the kitchen.

I stepped into the doorway of the closet as my cell illuminated on the floor. "Yeah, must've slept in," I answered, and shifted my gaze to the smoke alarm over my bed. "What time is it, anyway?" as I adjusted my grip on the knife.

Stab the bitch...stab her...

I could be out of the building and in Bruno's bedroom before they even knew...

My phone vibrated again, on silent. The only sound was it bouncing against the tiles. He'd moved from texts to calling now. I stared at the blinking red light, hidden away in the smoke alarm. So that's what it took for him to see me? For me to want to murder his little Mafia *slut.*

I smiled and bent down to grab my cell, and answered.

"Don't you fucking dare," he growled in my ear.

I just smiled at the camera and lifted my knife. I *would* dare, that was the problem. I *would* dare very...fucking...much. "She means that much to you?"

Silence.

That fire burned inside, scorching my lungs and blistering my need.

"You do," he answered finally. "You mean that much to me, Sophie."

"You lie," I snarled. "You've lied this entire time."

"Then let's do it" he said carefully. "Let's kill them all...every single one of them, *together.*"

My pulse sped as footsteps sounded in the kitchen, heading this way.

"An espresso will help get the old brain working," the dead bitch called out.

"But we do it together," he urged in my ear. "That's if you *want* to be together, Sophie."

The thought of him by my side as I stuck the bitch was too much to resist. But being without him? A pang tore through my chest at the thought. "You know I do."

"Then put down the knife."

My pulse thrummed as I lifted my gaze to the alarm once more.

"Put it down, Sophie. Put it down and we can do it together. We'll bathe in their blood..." he whispered in my ear as a form filled the doorway. I stepped forward and just opened my hand, letting the knife fall. It hit the soft fabric of my suitcase.

"There you are. Figuring out what to wear to a fucking typhoon?" Xael smiled as she stepped closer and held out a tiny cup of espresso.

"I wasn't sure if D&G was going to cut it," I answered, taking the cup from her hand.

She just stared out the window of my bedroom as the palms across the institute's grounds flailed in the air, oblivious to how close she had come to having a knife in her neck.

"Anyway, I'm going to drown myself in a long hot shower," she declared, and strode out of my bedroom.

"Sounds perfect," I murmured, and sipped my coffee.

My cell lit up with a text. This time I didn't hesitate to read it.

Him: Security will be down in Bld 6 after the fire. Fuck!

I stared at the text and tried to think what that meant for us. They were shutting off the cameras, so that meant no more spying...for a while, at least. I glanced at the time. It was late, almost twelve. There were no classes after the kidnapping and security was on high alert. Made it hard to move...and harder to kill.

THIRTY-FIVE

Evan

When I woke, it wasn't to cold shivers and fever. I felt better, cool even. I raised my hand to my forehead. There wasn't the sickly damp like there was before. The fever, it seemed, had broken. I rolled over, groaned at the deep, flare of agony through my side, and checked the time. Pity the fever didn't take the goddamn pain with it.

It was nine PM. Two texts waited from the Commander.

Mateo: Cameras will be down from nine PM until midnight.

Another sent five minutes ago.

Mateo: Cameras are off...make your move, Valachi.

Make your move...

I dragged myself out of bed and made for the bathroom. A different fever burned inside me now, one that had sandy blonde hair and a wicked smirk, who'd haunted me all these years. I stripped off my clothes and climbed into the shower, taking my time to wash my hair.

Shit, whatever the doc had given me was fucking amazing. I felt better than I had since I'd walked out of the damn hospital, and even that felt like a lifetime ago. I rinsed and stepped out, then dried my body and my hair, taking the time to comb it through. I strode from the bathroom, pulling out dark jeans and a black top. Nerves hummed through me as I stared at the clothes.

I was taking far too long with this, caring too much what I wore to face the demon. And he *was* a demon. The only difference was…I was supposed to marry him. "Just get it done," I mumbled to myself. "Tell him about the bitch out to kill him and let him freak out. I know what I want…" I pressed my hand against my side, then tucked my blouse and the gun into the waistband of my slacks.

I wanted the bitch in handcuffs and I wanted to know *why*.

Why us.

Why me…

That deep, seething rage splashed through my mind, bubbling and spewing like a volcano inside me. I was about to face the faceless man in my dreams. About to exorcise the demon who'd haunted me all these years…and I was ready.

I yanked on my boots, lacing them tight, and slipped into my jacket, taking one glance at myself in the mirror as I strode from the bedroom. I looked like myself, Evan Valachi, dressed in nightmares and stab wounds.

I slid the keycard into my pocket and grabbed my cell, scanning the cameras in this building before I cracked open the door. I stepped out, kept the collar high on my jacket and my eyes low, then, moving against the wall where the cameras were, passed underneath.

I was gone before the cameras barely moved, slipping out the entrance of the building and back out into the night. I checked the time, it was after nine-thirty, and time was running out. I couldn't take a chance the cameras would stay off. I couldn't take the chance of anything, not now.

The wind was brutal, slamming into me as I stepped from the protection of the building and headed across the grounds. The same guard was on duty in the foyer of Bruno's building. But there were others, the Commander's men, by the look of their black shirts. I pressed my card against the reader outside the door and stepped through as they opened.

The guard from last night glanced toward me and stilled. His eyes widened as the other men moved around him, checking cameras and viewing the angles on their laptops. None of them looked my way as I neared. If anything, one spoke to the guard, drawing his attention, and gave him a command.

They knew who I was...and knew not to pay me any mind.

My heart thundered as I stepped up to the elevator and pressed my card against the scanner, slipping inside as the doors opened. In a second, I was fifteen again, standing in my bedroom while Jessie fussed over my hair, prettying me up like a lamb to the fucking slaughter. The Bernardis were monsters, *all of them.*

You wono't speak, my father's command rose inside my head. *You won't fidget. This is a big deal, Evan, you understand that, right?* "Sure, Daddy," I murmured as the elevator came to a stop. "A big fucking deal."

I stepped out of the entrance to his penthouse suite and into a brick wall of pure muscle. The bodyguard scowled as he faced me and lifted the gun in his hand.

"Don't bother," I said, barely registering the flare of determined anger in his glare. "If I wanted him dead, he'd be dead already."

"The fuck..." the snarl came from behind the bodyguard.

I'd dealt with security all my life. This guy was no different. "Bernardi," I growled, and stepped around the bodyguard. "We need to talk."

Bruno strode out of the bedroom, barefoot, dressed in tight black jeans and an open collared white shirt. He carried a half-full glass in his hand, that I could see had been put to good use, as was the scowl on his face.

But the moment he saw me he froze, his brows furrowing. *"You?"*

"Me," I confirmed, my hate howling like the destructive winds outside.

I *wanted* to kill him, wanted to hurt him, wanted to gouge his memory from my mind. But as he strode toward me, his bare feet padding on the cold tiled floor, I wanted to do something else. Something that was born from that darkness inside my mind. Something that made my pulse race and my breaths quicken.

Those lips...*don't look...don't see him.*

But my mind and body were at war and I lowered my gaze to his mouth.

I wanted to kiss him...

The thought burned in my mind as he crossed the living room. "Want to tell me what the fuck is going on? And *who the fuck was in my bedroom last night?*"

His words riled that rage inside me, forcing me to step closer. "Maybe you need to be a little more *selective* who you take to bed."

He shot his bodyguard a look. "I'm fine, D."

"Maybe I'll stick around," the bodyguard resisted, completely invested in what was playing out in front of him. Until Bruno shot him a look that said *like hell you will.*

I didn't shift my gaze, just nailed the sullen, broody fucking brat with as much hate as I could. "Stay, go. I don't give a fuck. But you want to know one thing before he leaves." I slid my hand under my jacket and reached around, dragged the filed Glock free, and laid it on the counter. "We're at war, whether you like it or not."

Bruno didn't flinch. Hell, he never even missed a beat. "Leave... now" he commanded. "But don't go too far."

The bodyguard gave me another glare before he left. Bruno waited for the elevator doors to open and close before lifting the glass to his lips. I couldn't look away as he pressed his lips to the rim and swallowed.

"I take it the fire alarm was you?"

"You're welcome, by the way," I sneered, saved his ass and he couldn't manage a damn *thank you.*

"And *this,*" he pointed to the cameras tucked away in the fire alarm that were no longer blinking red, "is you, too?"

I just glared at him as he came closer. He'd changed, *a lot.* Gone was the pimply-faced kid that had stumbled out of the darkness, scared shitless, after I'd just slapped his cousin...no, *this* Bruno was fucking *beautiful* and stubborn as hell. My mind raced as he raked his stare over me, moving down my body.

"I want to know *everything*," he murmured, his voice thick and husky.

He wanted, did he? I clung to that burn inside me, glanced at the gun on the counter, and tried to imagine how I could end two problems I had this very night. Murder Bernardi, set it up as the psycho bitch, then kill her, too.

Then I'd be free...*to marry whoever I wanted.*

My body responded as he came closer, my nipples tightened, hardening against my bra as he met my gaze. "So, I think it's best you start at the beginning."

"The beginning when?" I snarled, hating that the heat between my legs grew bolder. "When your cousin tried to rape me, or do you want further back than that?"

"*My cousin*," he snapped. "*Not* me. I'd never—"

"Force me into anything, right?" I stepped closer, stopping right in front of him. I clenched my fists. "Like marriage, for example?"

His breaths deepened and his dark eyes glinted with something dangerous. He moved fast, grabbing my shoulders and driving me backwards. I stepped, until I hit the wall.

"You want to talk about *forcing* anyone?" he barked. "I was a goddamn kid, just like you. If you have a problem being promised to *anyone*, Evan, then maybe you need to take it up with *good ol' daddy*?"

"*Fuck you...*" The words tore from my lips.

He stilled, and his gaze moved to my mouth. "Fuck me?" He moved closer, pressing his body against mine. "You finally ready to lose that V card, are you, Evan?"

My pulse spiked, thundering in my ears, making my t race. He knew...*he knew I was a virgin?*

"You fucking haunt me," he growled, brushing some hair from my cheek. "You know that, right?

I jerked from his touch, hating how my body was a battleground for his desire. "Don't you...don't you fucking touch me."

"Fuck, I want to kiss you," he almost groaned. God, if I didn't want the same thing. "You want me, too, don't you?"

"No," I lied.

"You remember that night?" He lowered his head so that his voice was a growl against my ear. "You against the tree with Jannick between your legs."

Hate and fear ripped through me, thundering in my head.

"I wished it was me." He pressed against me, his hand moving between us. "My fingers sliding into that pretty little pussy. I'd touch you so good, Evan. *So fucking good.*"

I couldn't stop the moan from tearing from my chest. Heat flooded my cheeks. God, I burned.

"My fingers coming away slick and warm." He continued, then let out a ragged moan.

My clit throbbed.

He spread my jacket away from between us, exposing my shirt. "It's *all* I can think about. *All* that gets me hard anymore." His breath was heavy and hot against my ear.

It hadn't stopped him last night. He *had* to have known it wasn't me. The words were a bucket of icy water, dousing the flames between my legs. "Fuck you," I snarled, and shoved him backwards, punching him hard in the chest.

He stumbled backwards toward the living room, a cruel smile instantly making him even more brutally fucking gorgeous. "Just like that, huh?"

"It didn't stop you from fucking *that bitch* last night."

Hate burned inside me, the image of him kissing her etched into my mind. But it was the pang in my chest that hurt. That ache that pissed me off, that howled with desire and all the sick, twisted things Jude had warned me about. But with the hunger came the rage.

He stilled, the smile slipping from his lips. "I thought...I thought she was you."

"Did you?" I growled, and strode toward him. "Did you really?" The truth shone in his eyes. *He knew it wasn't me...*

"Who the fuck *was* she?"

My fingers trembled as I yanked my shirt free, revealing the ugly taped dressing. "The fucking bitch who tried to kill me...and who came here to kill you."

He just stared at my middle, then lifted his gaze. "Jesus fucking Christ."

"I saw her...with you. You're fucking lucky I did, you know. Or you might not've survived like I did."

"When?" He jerked his gaze to mine. "When did that happen?"

"The day before I was to come here."

"Jesus." He turned away, dragging his fingers through his hair.

He paced the floor, ignoring me...*what the fuck?* "It's her," he muttered. "It *has* to be."

My anger went cold. "Her *who?*"

He just cut me a glare, then stilled, frozen as he searched my gaze. "The senator's daughter."

What senator? My chest tightened.

"You don't know, do you?" He stepped toward me.

"*Know what?* What goddamn...senator?"

"The one your father helped murder."

All the air left my lungs and for a second, didn't return. My voice was raw and husky. "Murder?"

He strode toward me, and this time there was no stopping him. "Yes, *murder*. Why the fuck do you think your family and mine are to be joined? Just like this whole fucking Commission, no one trusts, no one fucking believes." He reached up, his hand sliding around the back of my neck. "They wanted to make sure we were protected *from each other.*"

I stared into his gaze. "But I don't know anything about a murder."

He just smiled a slow, sad smile. "If you think there's not an envelope somewhere with some cop's fucking name on it, then you've learned nothing working for the Salvatores all these years."

I flinched. *He knew about that?*

He moved closer, his hold around me softening. But his gaze was hungrier than before, sparking with intensity. "You need me. *I need you*. We were both dragged into this fucking mess, with no way to escape. You were *always* going to marry a Bernardi one way or another, Evan...better it was me."

I looked into his eyes, that hate still there, seething and savage. But there was hunger, too, the kind of aching lust that made me tremble. One that was born from the darkness of that night. One I couldn't escape, not even in my dreams.

"You hate me. You hate me so fucking much. You don't wear your virginity as a shield...you wield it as a weapon. You use it to drive you harder, to make you more savage." He lowered his gaze to the open collar of my shirt and lifted his other hand, his finger working the top button until it opened, displaying my breasts against the lacy black push-up bra. "You're not pure, Evan. No matter what that empty ache between your legs says. You're just as fucking sick and as twisted as the rest of us. You just haven't enjoyed the pleasure that comes with this fucking life." He lifted his gaze from my breasts to my eyes. "I'm going to enjoy teaching you that...*as your husband.*"

THIRTY-SIX

Bruno

As your husband.

The words echoed inside me, resounding deeper than anything I'd ever said before. *Her fucking husband,* that's what I was born to be. I wasn't letting her get away, not now I finally had her. But that hate...fuck me, the hate that burned in her eyes was chilling.

"My husband?" she snarled, then lunged, grabbing my shirt and fisting it in her grip. Her tone was venomous. "You think I'm here to marry you? I came to *hurt* you, did you know that?"

"Did you?" I licked my lips, my pulse thundering. A ring. A bullet. The choice was hers...

Fuck me, it was like playing with a lioness, a dangerous, uncontrollable beast that purred one moment and ripped your face off the next.

"I thought about it...thought about killing you, then her. I'd be free then, free from all of you." She straightened her spine, the movement jutting her breasts.

My cock hardened, imagining sliding between those beautiful fucking mounds. I wanted to fuck her more than I ever wanted anything in my life. I wanted to slide between her tits and into her sweet, virginal pussy. And fuck me...I lowered my gaze to the flare of her hips. Her ass...I wanted that fucking ass, too.

If I didn't have her...*I'd go insane.*

"Who are you punishing, Evan?" I whispered, and dragged my gaze upwards. "By holding onto all that rage?"

She just gave a wicked smile and dropped one hand to cup my cock. My body twitched at the contact, aching and throbbing. "Right now?" she whispered. "Feels like I'm hurting you."

I licked my lips and pressed against her, driving her hand against her thigh as I ground my length against her fingers. "Want to hurt me a little more?"

Her lips parted, breathless. But her grip around my erection curled.

"Where are you staying?" I slowly thrusted against her.

"What?" she was breathless.

"Where are you staying, Evan?" I closed my eyes and bit my lip, lifting my hands to brace against the wall, caging her in. "Where on the island?"

"Building one," she answered, her grip sliding along my fucking length as I grew harder. "There's a room in the back..."

I shook my head. "Too risky, someone will see you."

"There's nowhere else."

I opened my eyes and pulled away, meeting her gaze. "Stay here, with me." Panic flared in her eyes for a second. Fuck me, she was beautiful when she was afraid. "I'll have the cameras shut off. The fire alarm was tripped by burned wiring or something. I don't fucking know...*and I don't fucking care.* We can protect each other here...let me fucking protect you, Evan."

She swallowed hard and I was drawn to her throat. I couldn't stop myself, not even if I'd wanted to...*and I didn't want to.* I shifted my body until I kissed her ear, then moved lower, dragging my lips along the side of her neck. One nudge of my nose against her jaw and she tilted her head. Fuck, she smelled good.

Her hand went slack against my cock, but I didn't care. It was all about her anyway. "The cameras are off," I murmured against her next, and felt her pulse flutter. "One word and I can have your things here in ten minutes."

"And what...share your bed?" she growled, dropping her head to push me away. "I don't think so."

"You don't want to? Fine, there's a spare room." I nodded toward the hallway.

I hated the thought of that, having her a room away felt like torture.

"Okay," she answered. "I'll stay...*in the spare room.*"

There was the teeth. Evan Valachi wasn't just any woman...*she was a Mafia heir.* I pushed away and grabbed my cell, pressing the button before she had a chance to rethink what she'd agreed to.

"Yeah?" Deviouz answered.

"I need you to come and get Ms. Valachi's security card and do a job for me."

"I'm on my way."

I hung up the call and watched as her eyes widened. "What are you doing?"

"What does it look like? Playing the white fucking knight." I stepped closer and held out my hand. "Card, Evan."

I had her off balance here, fighting to stay in control. She could fight all she wanted to…I liked a challenge. The elevator doors sounded and a second later Deviouz's heavy boots thudded.

Evan reached into her pocket and withdrew the keycard. "It's not under my name," she explained. "So you need to be careful with the cameras. No one can trace it back to us."

I glanced over my shoulder as Deviouz just smiled. "Stealth, huh? I like it."

He strode forward and took the keycard from her hand.

"My suitcases, and the bathroom things."

"It'll be like you were never there," the bodyguard assured before turning and heading for the elevator. But he stopped to glance over his shoulder. "And Ms. Valachi, it's nice to finally meet you."

There was a hint of a smile on her lips before the big oaf was gone. When the *clunk* of the elevator doors sounded, I let my gaze roam down her body. "I knew it wasn't you." How the fuck could I have thought otherwise? "She avoided looking at me, kept her face shadowed with that hood. But deep down, I knew."

"Sure looked like that when I saw you with your tongue down her throat," she snarled.

Was she jealous? I fought the urge to smile. I wanted to, but I also liked my balls where they were.

"Anyway, I'm not here so you can fucking undress me with your eyes, Bernardi. I'm here because, like you said, we need each other. I'm going to make a call to the Commander to keep him updated, then I want to hear everything you know about that murder."

She wanted to know about the senator? The flicker of amusement died inside me. She didn't wait, yanking her phone from her pocket and stepping around me as she made her way into the living room. "Mateo," she murmured.

Anger ripped through me at the way she said his name. I turned, my gaze fixed on her. Her lips, her fucking breath. I watched it all. Did she have a thing for the Commander? The bastard was good-looking enough, if you liked them savage enough to bite your hand off. The thought of her wanting another made me feel fucking dangerous.

"I need the cameras left off in building six. Make up something, burned wiring, whatever you think…yeah, that sounds good. I'll be staying here with Bernardi." I clung to every word she said as she turned her back and murmured. "Yeah, I think it's a good idea. I get that. His bodyguard is collecting my things now. I'll keep you updated. Thank you, Mateo, for everything," she said carefully, and hung up the phone.

"So…" I tried to keep the sting from my tone. "What's *everything?*"

She looked up, glaring at me as I rounded the counter, grabbed a glass from the bar, and poured her a Scotch.

"You don't get to be jealous, Bernardi." She stalked closer.

"Don't I?" I murmured, sliding a glass with a splash of Scotch her way. "Pretty fucking sure you belong to me."

"I belong to you. Do I?" She neared, grabbed the glass, and raised it to her lips.

"Yeah." I rounded the counter. *"You do."*

She let out a bark of laughter. "Fuck you, Bernardi." But the moment she lifted the glass, she froze. Panic widened her eyes as she swayed on her feet.

I lunged, grabbing her arm as she reached for the counter. "What the fuck?" I growled.

She paled a little under the soft amber lights. "I'm okay," she insisted, breathless. "I'm fine."

"Like hell you are." I dropped my gaze to her side and the fresh wound she carried. "You need to sit down."

"What I *need* is to fucking survive," she snarled, hate burning through the flare of agony in her eyes. "That starts with you telling me the truth about that goddamn senator."

She was stubborn, I'd give her that. Still, I yanked out the stool next to her and waited until she gave in, sliding that perfect ass into the seat. I raked my hand through my hair, and dredged up the darkest moment of my past.

"I just can't believe this is happening…deep down I always thought it might. I wanted to forget that night. I *still* want to forget it." I jerked my gaze to hers. "It took a lot of fucking therapy to keep it all buried."

She said nothing, just sipped while I wrestled with the demons of the past, remembering clearly the night it all changed, for all of us. "Senator Richard Harrison." Saying his name put loud made me feel fucking sick. "He was a friend of your father's, a good friend it seemed. And through your dad, he became friends with my father and my uncle."

"You mean Cillian?"

I nodded, drained my glass, and rounded the counter. In an instant, I was fourteen years old all over again. Just a fucking punk sitting in the back of my father's car, still bruised and aching from Jannick's fists. "But he was feeding information to the FBI behind our backs."

Her breath caught as I grabbed the bottle and poured, reaching over to splash more into her glass. Christ knows we needed it.

"Jesus," she whispered, her skin paling for a different reason now. "What did he tell them?"

"Who knows." I drank, letting the burn slide down the back of my throat. "It can't have been much. Whatever secrets he had died the night my father kicked the living shit out of him and your father cut his goddamn throat."

"I can't believe it." Her hand trembled as she reached for her glass and drank. It took her a minute to find the words. "I knew he was fucking ruthless...*but a murderer?*"

"Believe me, it happened. I wished to fucking God it hadn't."

"And you were what, told about it?" She met my gaze.

"*Told?*" I shook my head, leaning closer. "I was right fucking there. I saw *everything*. Including your father wearing the senator's blood."

She flinched at the words, her gaze unfocused and strange. "He killed her father and now she kills us."

On the anniversary of her father's death, of all times.

My pulse sped with her words. "No, we're not dying because of what they did. That bitch is going down. It's either us or her."

She met my gaze and swallowed hard. "How...how do we do this?"

I understood what could drive a man to commit an act like that now...it was the need to protect. As I lowered my gaze to her side, I knew there was no limit to what I'd do if I ever saw that bitch again.

"We need a plan," she urged. "We need a way to trap her. Maybe Mateo--"

"No." I shook my head. "This is our mess, we can't involve anyone else. Besides, there's enough shit going down right now, if you haven't heard."

"Marcus Baldeon and Katerina VanHalen."

I nodded. "Yeah, who the fuck knows who else is out there ready to attack? So we deal with that bitch, nice and quiet, and forget this ever happened, okay?" The elevator rumbled, drawing my focus as I rounded the corner and gripped her chin, forcing her attention to me. "Okay, Evan?"

Fear glinted in her eyes, but she didn't fight me *this time*. "Okay," she agreed as the doors opened and Deviouz strode out wearing a black hoodie pulled low.

He pushed the cover back and met her gaze. "Your things."

"Thank you." She slid from her seat, pulling away from my touch, leaving her gun on the counter next to me, and grabbing her bag from my bodyguard.

"The Commander assigned another guard and issued a statement the cameras to this building are down because of the fire. So, you wanna fill me in here?" He glanced from me to Evan.

So I did, relaying what had happened and why the need for the Commander's response.

"Fuck me," Deviouz muttered, taking it better than I'd expected. He just glanced at Evan. "She left you for dead?"

She nodded, lifting her shirt to expose her middle. "In a bunker with a locked door."

I didn't like him looking at her like that, *or any way, for that matter*. "You're hard to kill, Valachi," he rumbled, respect glinting in his gaze.

"Thank God for that," she replied with a wink.

"I'll take double shifts," he volunteered. "No one's getting past me."

She just marched to the counter and grabbed her gun. "We take shifts *together*. While one sleeps, the other watches. God knows *he* needs someone to make sure he doesn't climb into bed with a damn killer and I feel like it's going to take the two of us."

"I like you," the bodyguard declared, and cut me a savage stare. "You'd better step the fuck up, Bruno. She's too fucking good to marry Jannick."

He headed to the elevator and was gone, with those words hanging in the air.

She *was* too good for Jannick.

THIRTY-SEVEN

Her

He's a liar, pumpkin, Daddy whispered in my head. *Once a liar, always a liar.* I closed my eyes and tried to push the voice away. The voice that'd been growing louder, swallowing my thoughts until it was all I could hear.

"No, he's not," I protested, and crossed my bedroom to the closet. "He's doing this for me."

Don't be stupid. He's doing this for himself. It's only ever been for himself. From the moment he found you, it's only ever been what he wants. You remember that, don't you? You remember where he found you?

My breath caught as I reached into the suitcase, feeling my way under the false bottom to the small bottle of pills. Yes, I remembered, sometimes a little too well. The bite of the antiseptic. The howls and screams that bounced along the hallways in the dead of the night. The locked doors and secured beds. The place where they gave you a plastic spoon to eat driedout mashed potatoes, for fear of you killing yourself with a fork.

I remembered alright.

I remembered it all.

Remembered his eyes through the plexiglass barrier as he watched me day after day. I remembered the first words he said to me. *"Take your pills, Sophie. They'll help, but they won't give you the freedom you crave. I can help with that."*

Won't give me freedom...

That's all I remembered from that moment. It's what resounded in my head over and over, even piercing through the tiny white pills. I dragged my hand out of the suitcase, gripping two of the pills in my palm.

He'd invaded the haze in my head that day, and every day thereafter. I started to look forward to medications, to the moment he was so close. One brush of my hand as he handed me the tiny white cup with my medication, and my heart was racing. He saw me. Saw the *real* me and not the broken little girl who clung to the casket of her father as they lowered it into the ground.

He didn't see me as the girl at all.

But the woman.

One who couldn't sleep at night on their thin mattresses. But I could think of *him*, remembering the brush of his hand and the way his gaze pierced me where I stood. I touched myself to the memory and found myself slipping from the hold of the drugs they gave me. Our visits grew more frequent, but we had to keep it from prying eyes. *They won't understand,* he told me. They wouldn't. They'd call it wrong, maybe send me away, or maybe they'd take *him* away.

So we had stolen moments in the murky gloom of the janitor's closet and, under the guise of environmental therapy, he took me outside the walls to the park across the road. There he told me about the future he saw for me, one that included him.

We could be unstoppable together, he told me.

I was so in love.

I still was, desperate to feel that brush on the back of my hand once more. I downed the pills in my hand and tried to slow the panicked beat of my heart. Through the windows, the world was chaos. I moved closer, drawn by the terrified tremors inside me as another memory came roaring back to me.

One that wasn't filled with the heady rush of love.

But with nightmares.

It wasn't always hazy thoughts and stolen kisses in that place they called a *therapy center*. It was endless nights...nights where the nurses would be away from their desks...and the guards would roam the halls looking for their next victim.

They locked me in the storage room and turned out the lights, then in the darkness they did things to me, things with their hands across my mouth so no one would hear me scream, and when they were done...I knew I had to get out of there, *or die trying*.

But *he* was there for me, enraged when I told him what the guards had done, and what they said they'd do to me when they came back. Instead of revenge, he helped me hatch a plan, one that'd see me outside those walls...never to return.

Still, I was shattered by those dark moments, unable to get out from under the smothering holds over my mouth and the pain. It still terrified me, the emptiness...the fear. As I stood at the window and looked outside, that's all I saw coming for me, darkness and death. My pulse raced, punching through the void in my mind.

He won't help you this time, pumpkin.

"Yes, he will, Daddy," I answered that voice in my head. "Yes, he will."

I clutched the pill bottle still in my hand. He would come for me...I knew he would. *He had to.* The apartment lights hummed and buzzed, growing brighter.

My cell vibrated in my hand.

Him: Take a breath, Sophie. It's all okay. It's just the storm.

See...I wanted to tell my father's voice in my head.

Palm trees slammed against the ground, uprooted by the howling wind as it tore the island apart. The sound inside the apartment was terrifying, screaming as it slammed against the walls. I stepped closer and pressed my hand to the double-glazed glass. The building was strong, but was it strong enough?

Not even he can help you now.

"Shut up," I whimpered as the voice battled the roar of the gusts. "Just please, Daddy, shut up."

He's going to leave you.

Leave you...

Leave...you.

I closed my eyes and slammed my fists against the side of my head. "No! *No...no...NO!*"

"Hey!"

I spun, terror slamming into me as a woman stood in the door of my room. *No, not just a woman...it was her...the bitch who'd fucked the man I loved.* She came closer, confusion making her gaze narrow as she glanced from the window to me. "You okay? I heard you screaming."

"Yes." The word was hoarse and husky. "I'm okay."

But the moment I lowered my fists from my head, the lights in the apartment flickered. I let out a shriek, yanking my hands back to my temples. But as the lights came back on, the bottle slipped from my hand and hit the floor, rolling toward the bed.

Xael came closer, bending to pick it up from the floor. "Sophie Harrison?" She glanced at the label, then at me. "Who the hell is that?"

"No one," I snapped, and lunged for her, snatching the bottle from her hand. *"Don't touch things that don't belong to you!"*

Her eyes widened at my outburst. But when the lights went out, and this time didn't come back on, I knew I had to fight...or die in the dark.

THIRTY-EIGHT

Evan

The lights flickered overhead, making my pulse stutter then race.

I jerked my gaze to Bruno, taking a step before the apartment was plunged into darkness. "Bruno?"

"I'm here. Walk straight ahead," he said, his voice a beacon.

I headed for the sound, reaching for him until I brushed his outstretched hand. His fingers curled around mine, before he drew me against his side. "It's just the storm," he murmured, sliding his hand along my back, pressing me against him. "It'll be back on in a second."

But the longer I stood there listening to the cyclonic gusts of wind against the windows, the more terrified I became. "It's her," I whispered, my panic getting away from me. "I know it is."

He tilted my chin, forcing my gaze to his. In the faint light, I saw him, the outline of his chiseled jaw, that intense look of hunger glittering like stars in his eyes as his phone illuminated with a text. "It's not her," he reassured. "Look." He turned us toward the window.

The entire island was dark. There were no lights from any of the other buildings, not even the security lights that surrounded the walkways shone in the night. We were nothing in that moment, insignificant and alone, far away from anyone.

"All we have to do is wait," he murmured as the screen on his cell went dark.

His voice sent shivers along my skin. His breath was warm against my neck. In an instant, the fantasy that had plagued me all these years came alive. The one where he became the faceless man in my dreams, the one who licked and touched...and took from me, making me hot and wet, slick between my thighs.

My body trembled, his gaze pinning me to the spot. I became aware of him, of the heat that radiated from his body and the predatory desire that seemed to consume the room. His phone lit up once more. In the glow, he saw me, saw the fear and the desire. Confusion narrowed his gaze. I hated him, hated the boy who'd stepped out of the shadows that night to come to my rescue. I hated him even more after I found out he'd beat his cousin bloody...and he'd done it for me.

"I'm not going to marry you." The words spilled free.

There was a twitch at the corner of his mouth as determination filled his gaze. "We'll just see about that," ge growled.

He dropped his hand from my chin and lifted his phone, scanning the text as my own cell buzzed in my pocket. I turned my back to Bruno, but didn't dare take a step.

Mateo: Power's out to the entire island, we're working on it. Best to hole up and wait it out. I'll come for you if you need.

I scanned the text twice, slowly becoming aware of silence behind me. The hairs on the nape of my neck rose as he murmured, "Do you want him to come for you?"

I spun, the heat of anger filling me. "You make it a habit of reading other people's text messages, do you?"

There was a cruelty in his eyes, a glint of savagery born out of jealousy. He loomed closer. "When the woman *I'm going to marry* texts another guy, yeah, I get fucking jealous."

Heat flooded my body with his words. He was a beast in that moment as he snatched the phone from my hand. "What else have you been discussing with the Commander?"

I jutted my chin in the air, defiant. "Wouldn't you like to know?"

"Yeah," he snapped. "I would."

I stumbled backwards, fear and anger colliding inside me. In an instant, we were back in that whirlwind of hate and hunger once more. He was the bastard I didn't want…and I was *all he* wanted. "You Bernardis are all the goddamn same, aren't you?"

He flinched as though I'd slapped him. But he didn't stop, reaching out to grab my throat as I stumbled and fell back against the wall.

"You think that, huh?" His grip on my throat was snug, pushing me backwards. "That I'm just like my cousin? Just a goddamn piece of shit that takes what he wants and doesn't give a fuck about anyone else? This is what you want, right?" His other hand cupped my breast, kneading me roughly.

Panic froze me until anger punched through. I clenched my fist, ready to lash out. But his hand around my throat didn't cut off my air. It was just there, forceful and demanding, drawing my focus to the stroke of his thumb over my racing pulse.

"Is that what you think of me?" His touch against my breast turned soft and desperate. His weight pressed my spine against the wall. "Taking what I want..."

His harsh breaths turned urgent. My fist dropped as he lowered his head, his hand stilling over my breast. Through the thin fabric, his thumb grazed my nipple and I hardened in response, a shiver carving through me, with a charge of excitement.

"Just a beast, right?" his tone deepened, his focus fixed on the slide of his thumb before he lifted his gaze to mine.

In the darkness, I saw him more clearly than I'd ever seen anyone else before. He wasn't a monster, not the one I wanted him to be. He was just a man, fighting his own goddamn demons.

His fingers worked the buttons of my blouse and slid in. "Is this what you want from me, Evan?"

I flinched, his caress electric as he delved under the edge of my bra. My nipples hardened at his touch, absorbed by the feel of him.

"Fuck me, I want you," he growled.

The tortured sound did things to me I'd never imaged. My hand lowered, fingers unfurling, until it hit the wall. Silence grew between us, and in the emptiness, came the truth. I wanted him to be the bastard, to trigger my hate until it ignited into something else...something carnal that had started between us all those years ago.

His fingers worked a few more of my buttons until, with one yank, he pushed the blouse aside, exposing my bra, the swell of my breast barely contained.

"Jesus," he growled, staring at the faint outline of my body.

I could barely see anything. But he saw it all, every tremor, as he dragged the strap of my bra lower until I spilled free. "You're so goddamn beautiful."

I shivered with the cool air, closing my eyes as he lowered his head. *You're not pure, Evan.* His words resounded with the lick of his tongue. *No matter what that empty ache between your legs says. You're just as fucking sick and as twisted as the rest of us. You just haven't enjoyed the pleasure that comes with this fucking life.*

I let out a moan, trembling through my core.

He lifted his gaze. Need sparked in his eyes. He was all beast in that moment, all consuming hunger, and God, I wanted him, more than I'd ever wanted anything before.

"You fucking hate me, right?" He arched his spine and slowly thrust between my thighs.

Cold licked where his mouth had been. Christ, he was hard and demanding, driving his cock against my core. I dropped my head backwards, my hate seething, turning into something else... something that made me drag him closer. "*Harder,*" I whimpered. "For God's sake, *harder.*"

He drove between my legs, hitting just the right place. Tremors tore through me as I imaged him thrusting inside me, savage and brutal and unforgiving. I clawed his shoulders, desperate for him to be closer. But then he pulled away, taking a step backwards.

No! I trembled with anger, but it was a new kind of hate that found him in the dark. The winds battered the windows, shrieking with rage, mirroring that bestial growl inside me.

"You fucking want me?" he murmured, reaching up to unbutton the rest of his shirt and peeled it from his body. "All you have to do is say the words...say you'll marry me."

I shook my head. *No...never.* The words were on the tip of my tongue. My pulse was hammering.

"Say the goddamn words, Evan." He dropped his shirt to the floor. "And I'll take care of that ache between your legs right now. We don't even have to fuck, if you don't want to. Let me make it all about you."

Heat found my cheeks, turning me icy in places and in others burning with need. "No," I whispered. "I won't..."

"You won't, huh?" He dropped his hands to the waistband of his pants, fingers working his belt. "Why, because you don't want me, is that it? Don't want me coming home to you every night... crawling between your legs as I fuck my way to heaven? You're all I think about." He drew his belt free and reached down to cup his cock through his pants. My core clenched at the sight. "You're all I want. Tell me you don't want me," he murmured as he dropped his hand. "Tell me you don't want me to protect you tonight and all the fucking nights to come."

Lightning tore through me at the words. "You don't want to do that." The ache in my side whispered...*no...not him, not for me.*

"Don't I?" he answered, leaning closer. "I have no relationships, no future, not one I want without you, at least. Tell me, Evan. Tell me you haven't dreamed of this, and I'll stop right now. I'll put that shirt back on and won't touch you ever again. Tell me you haven't thought of us together and it'll be done."

He touched me, his fingers finding the lower buttons of my blouse. I couldn't move, breathtakingly aware of how close he was, and how much I needed him to be closer. He dragged my blouse lower until it dropped to the floor. His hands went to my pants, working the button before I knew. "You can't, can you?"

I closed my eyes, hating the fact he was right. *Stop*...that panicked voice inside me cried. But the sound never reached my lips as he dropped to his knees. "No," I whispered. "I can't."

"Because you *crave this*." His hands slid down the backs of my thighs, pushing my slacks low until they dropped to my feet.

"You're mine, Evan." His fingers danced along to the backs of my knees, then my calves, before he gripped my boot and pulled it free before moving to the other. "Mine to fuck and to marry and to build a fucking legacy with. The Valachis and the Bernardis. Together we'll be unstoppable."

The Valachis and the Bernardis.

"You want me because of obligation." He peeled my socks free and my voice shook as I my lowered my barefoot to the floor.

My fear spilled free. If everything he'd said was true, the intention of marriage had been born from blood...and fear.

"Is that right?" He lifted his head, his gaze finding the black lace of my panties before meeting mine. "I think I'll enjoy reminding you of that after I put our third baby inside you."

I flinched at the words. *A baby?* Heat moved through me at the thought.

He surged upwards, grabbing me around the waist and lifting before I had a chance to cry out. But my body responded. My arms went around his neck and my legs wrapped around his waist as though it was the most natural thing in the world. "You think I want you because of our goddamn fathers? I wanted you the moment you slipped through that goddamn doorway the night you met my cousin. I wanted you before you even saw him, before you uttered a word from those pretty lips. You fucking hit me like lightning...you were just too busy with Jannick to notice."

His erection rubbed my core as he moved, striding around the living room wall and into the bedroom.

"All these years you hated us. I tried to see you, tried to speak to you. If you'd've given me the chance, I would've shown you I was nothing like him. I would've shown you love," he whispered, lowering me to the bed, his gaze moving to the dressing at my side. "I'd give anything to have been there."

My hands slipped, my fingers danced over his taut shoulders and along the muscles of his arms.

Warm lips kissed my belly beside my wound. "I'd kill her with my bare hands and leave the bitch in the bunker where she belongs. To think I almost fucking lost you..."

An ache tore along my side, constant and gnawing, as he went lower, and lower, kissing the top of my panties. "Wait," I whispered, grabbing his arms and stopping him. "I'm not ready."

"It's okay," he murmured, lifting his gaze. "We don't have to do anything you don't want to." One stroke of his fingers along my core made my pulse race. "Let me take care of you."

Take care of me?

He moved lower, gliding the tips of his fingers along my center. "Oh...Oh God." I bit my lips and my hands fisted the sheets as that heat came roaring back.

"That's it," he urged, his lips finding the top of my panties. "Close your eyes. Let yourself go."

THIRTY-NINE

Bruno

She gave a shudder, then did exactly as I'd said, letting out a moan as I grazed my fingers along the core of her. Christ, she was perfect. Even if I couldn't see her clearly in the dark, I could goddamn feel her. Firm, fragile, just as I'd always imagined. I wanted to give into myself, to slip under the edge of the elastic and dive in deep.

I wanted my fill of her. But I was afraid that might never come. There was no future where I wasn't kissing her, fucking her...*owning her*. Desperate for more, I'd waited long enough. "This was inevitable," I whispered as she arched her back and my fingers skirted the warmth of her. Fuck, she was warm, radiating heat through her panties.

The more I craved this, the hungrier I became. *Inevitable*. That's exactly what we were...

"More," she sighed. "Bruno, give me more."

"More?" I groaned, my voice low and husky as I moved up, dancing around the tiny nub at the top of her crease, but never over it, just around and around and around. Enough to make her whimper and lift her hips to meet my touch.

In my head, I was watching Jannick touch what was mine. I'd hated him that night and all the nights to come. I hated him for laying a single fucking finger on what belonged to me.

"This." I opened my hand and cupped her sex hard enough to make her shudder. "Is mine. You get that?"

She let out a gasp and gripped my arm, her nails biting into my skin. I dropped my head and licked, finding the peak of her breast in the dark. Her nails eased as her other fingers fluttered against my skin. I inhaled, the scent of her desire filling me, and took more of her.

"Jesus," she moaned. "Oh, Jesus."

"He's not going to help you," I growled softly against her warmth, sliding my touch over her core until she was writhing.

I traced the line of her panties' elastic, then pushed, sliding underneath to what I wanted. Warmth waited for me, slick and wet. I slipped along her core, finding her clit. She jerked with the caress, her body spasming, growing heated, knowing exactly what it wanted. My cock, sliding in deep.

My own body responded, punching against my zipper. I'd fuck her nice and slow, take my time breaking her in. Fuck me, the thought of that made me moan around her breast. I opened my mouth and drew her deeper, my teeth grazing the puckered flesh. I wanted that...wanted to wear her fucking virgin blood with honor.

Not yet...

I pulled away from her breast and slid my fingers from her pussy.

"No," she whimpered, lifting her head from the pillow. "Why are you stopping?"

"I'm not stopping, Evan." I gripped the edges of her panties and dragged them over her hips and down her thighs. "Only getting started, sweetheart."

I felt the heat of her gaze as the wind battered the windows. She was hungry...*fucking ravenous*. And I had what would sate that need. She drew her feet back. Her panties slid over her knees and down her legs. It was all her in that moment. All her need making her lift her feet to discard her panties.

All she had to do was say no...*and she wasn't*.

I smiled, lowering my head as I cast her panties to the floor, and kissed the inside of her thighs.

"Bruno." Her hand on my head stopped me.

"It's okay," I urged, moving closer and closer, nipping her flesh with my lips, the heat of my own breath radiating back at me.

My cock throbbed. Fuck, I was on fire, desperate to drive into her cunt. I wanted to fill her, fuck protection. I wanted to see my cum trickling from that pussy when I was done. The thought made me moan as I moved my mouth over her core.

"Oh...*my*...*God*," she hissed.

I opened my mouth, my tongue dancing along her slit before I moved upwards as I tasted her. Salty and warm, the scent of her not sweet, but fuck me, it was drugging. I never knew what I'd craved until now.

Now I knew.

I pushed my tongue in deeper, finding that swollen hood, and curled the tip of my tongue over it before I moved deeper, sucking her into my mouth.

"Oh, God. I'm going to come," she cried, her fingers gripping my hair.

"Not yet, princess," I disagreed, pulling away. "Not yet."

Her scent grew stronger. I closed my eyes, fighting the urge to cover her with my mouth and fuck her with my tongue. But she'd waited all this time, hating me...there was no fucking way I was letting her get off this easy...not yet. Instead, I trailed the tip of my tongue along her crease and sucked her lips, drawing them into my mouth, then I released her and rose.

I grabbed her hand and guided it to my cock. "Feel that?" Her breath caught. "That's for you."

"Christ, you're hard," she breathed. In the dark, I caught the lick of her lips. "I want to...I want to touch you."

I clenched my jaw, letting her hand slip from under mine. She worked the button of my pants, then slid the zipper low. I moved higher, bracing my fists on each side her head as she gripped my cock and moaned.

"Fuck, you feel good." She ran her grip along my length and widened her legs as though she knew exactly where I belonged.

Not yet...she's not ready.

Fuck this sense of decency. Fuck this need to make her want me as much as I wanted her. I could just take her right now, fuck her hard and give her body exactly what it craved. But would she want me tomorrow? Would she look at me with hate-filled eyes, or would she hunger for more?

Give her just enough to crave me.

She pushed my pants low, letting them slide down my thighs until they hit the floor. I lifted my foot and climbed onto the bed to straddle her. Her hand slid from my cock to slide down my thigh, then upwards. My stomach tensed with her touch, trembling. "You don't know what you do to me," I moaned.

I leaned over her, letting her touch where she wanted. She slid her hand higher, up my chest to grip the back of my neck and pull me down to her. "Then show me," she demanded. "Show me exactly what I do to you, Bernardi."

The way she said my name, hard and needy all at the same time. I knew in that moment that as much as she tormented me, I tormented her just as much. She both hated and wanted me. A dangerous kind of passion, like a double-edged sword.

I took her mouth, kissing her deep and hard, and lowered my body to hers. My cock pressed against her mound. She opened wider, leaving the shaft to find her warmth. I slowly thrust against her, stoking that fire between her legs, and slid my hand under her head, fisting her hair before I broke the kiss. "When I fuck you, Evan, you're going to feel it a week later. I just want to make sure you understand that."

She cried out with the shock as I pulled her head backwards, hard enough for her to know who was in control here. "I fuck you when I want it. I *fuck* you…when you need to be reminded who's in charge here."

I rose higher on the bed and grabbed her breast as I arched my spine, sliding my cock along the valley between her breasts. Warmth slid against the tip. Fuck me, I wanted to come, to spill all over her, to see her slick and shining with my seed.

She let out a whimper and panted. Her thighs widened as I fucked her tits. I let go of her breast and reached behind me, finding her hot and slick...*and ready*. "Open your mouth, Evan," I commanded, my grip tightening.

She did as she was told, like a good little princess.

My Mafia Princess.

I thrust my hips forward and sank two fingers into her pussy, guiding her head forward to meet the tip of my cock. She let out a moan, the sound deep and *primal* as I slid into her mouth.

"This." I sank my fingers deep inside her. "Is what should've happened that night."

I fucked her mouth and her pussy, the sensation overwhelming as I sank deep in both places. She gripped my thighs, sliding her hands around to grab my ass and pull me forward.

Her tongue worked my length as she sucked and licked, driving me wild inch by goddamn inch. She sucked, pulling away. "I need you to fuck me," she gasped, her hips rising from the bed to meet the slow thrust of my fingers. "Or I'm going to die."

I pulled away, sliding my slick fingers along her crease. "You're not going to die, princess," I assured her, pulling out of her reach. "We're just getting started."

I sank down the bed, over her splayed legs. "'Cause I've got choices here."

She jerked her head upwards, anger bleeding into her tone. "Oh yeah? What *fucking choices, Bernardi?*"

I sniggered, enjoying the heat of her anger. "Do I fuck you here." I lowered my head and licked her folds, driving my tongue deep.

She moaned and thrust against my mouth before I swallowed, groaning at the taste of her, and lifted my head. I pounced, gripped her hips and gently rolled her onto her belly. "Or here," I said as I plunged my fingers between the cheeks of her ass, sliding down until I reached her pussy, then back up, leaving a trail of her wetness in my wake.

She lifted her hips from the bed, unleashing a sound of torment. *Fuck, yeah.* "You wanna keep that V-card, princess?" I taunted, and eased back onto my thighs, lowering my lips to the sweet curve of her ass. "We can do that."

"I...don't...want...to," she moaned, and dropped her head as I slid my fingers back down, teasing at her entrance. But this was the game...make her take it for herself. I dragged some slickness to her ass. "Breathe, Evan," I whispered, and pressed against that muscle.

She quivered, pliable and heated, desperate for me to take and keep on taking. I sank my finger inside. Jesus, she was tight. *So fucking tight.* I pushed in harder, feeling her body fighting me. I slid back out, lowered my head, and worked the spit in my mouth, then let it trickle free, finding the crease of her ass.

"Oh God, what is that?" she whispered, lowering her forehead to the pillow.

"Perfection," I answered, sliding my finger out to my saliva and thrust back in.

I worked her body, driving deeper, until I slid two fingers in. "You ready, princess?"

"*Yesss...*"

I smiled, rising upwards, and guided my cock along her core, taking her slick around the tip. "Breathe for me, baby." The command was desperate as I lifted higher, pressing against her entrance.

I didn't give her mind time to register what was happening or her body to fight. Just pushed in, spreading her wide, listening to the sharp hiss before I eased back out.

In and out.

Nice and slow.

I invaded her body, claiming every part of her. She lowered her torso, driving her ass into the air. If only Jannick could see her now. Jealousy burned inside me, making me thrust deeper.

"Oh God." She clenched around me and whimpered. "I'm going to come."

"Then let go, princess," I urged. "Take what you need from me."

She drove her fists against my pillow, slamming her ass against my cock, driving me deeper and harder, before she stilled, shuddering and panting. I gripped her hip with one hand, holding her tight against me and thrust, taking what I needed.

Desperation roared inside me, turning me into an animal. "Mine," I growled against her ear as my cock jerked. "You hear me, Evan? *You...belong...to...me, and don't you forget it.*"

She cried out underneath me, bucking and moaning, her body tight as I spasmed, coming hard, then eased out of her. Harsh breaths filled the air, mingling with the roar outside and the panicked thrum of my pulse.

I slowly slid down beside her on the bed, leaving her facing away from me. The sound of our breaths was the only sound, until I licked my lips and tried to get my mind working. "You okay?"

She was slow to respond, making me panic a little, until she rose on her elbows and turned her head. "You fucked me in the ass."

A chuckle tore from me, rumbling in my chest. "Yeah, I did. Was that okay?"

"Yeah, more than okay. I kinda liked it."

The chuckle turned deeper, forcing that flicker of nervousness away. I reached for her, hoping to Christ she wanted to be held. She did, sliding her ass closer until she slid into the crook of my arm. "When can we do that again?"

"Fuck me, woman," I groaned.

"Hey, you were the one all *'when I fuck you, you're gonna know it, Evan.'*"

She mimicked me, chuckling.

The woman mimicked me...then laughed. With a growl, I shoved upwards, rolling on top of her and ending the laughter in an instant.

I slid my feet along the insides of her legs and shoved them wider, driving my cock that was already hardening, between her legs. "You want me to fuck you?" I stared down, meeting that terrified excitement in her eyes, and gave her the ultimatum one more goddamn time. "Then say you'll fucking marry me."

FORTY

Her

My knife...get my knife! I jerked my gaze toward the bed in the dark and lunged, desperate to stab and scream and get the hell out of there.

"Fucking lights," Xael snarled as a blinding glare shone from the back of her phone right into my eyes.

I jerked my hand upwards, blinded, and stumbled sideways. *"Get it out of my eyes!"* I roared, blinking.

Rage consumed me as white sparks danced in my eyes.

"Fuck, *sorry*," she barked. "Just trying to help."

But in the haze behind her, something moved. A shadow sharpened, growing bolder until *he was there.* The light shot upwards to the ceiling, then slammed down as her phone hit the floor with a *thud.*

"*What the fuck!*" Xael screamed as her steps scuffed against the floor as though she was staggering. "What the hell hit me?"

My heart was hammering, tracking the slow thud of his footsteps under the roar of the wind. A hand clamped across my mouth, a low growl in my ear. *"Don't scream."*

With his hand over my mouth, he yanked me forward. My shoulder hit the wall as Xael yelled from the floor. "Where the fuck is my phone?"

She scurried, searching, as I was dragged past her and out into the hall. I fought against his hold, flinging my head from side to side as I tried to suck in air around his fingers. But his grip was cruel, smashing my lips against my teeth, forcing me hard against his body. My heart hammered as desire battled the need for air. He was here…he was here for me.

He dragged me along the hall, letting go of my arm for only a second. I caught the faint scent of stairwell air around his hold before I was yanked inside. I waited for his lips, for his strong desperation. I waited for him to make sense of the betrayal with that bitch. The door closed with barely a sound before his hand slipped from my mouth to clamp around my throat.

"What the fuck were you doing, Sophie?" he growled against my ear.

The sound of my name in the open air panicked me. "What?"

"You heard me. I saw you go for your fucking knife. I know what you were about to do."

I couldn't see him…couldn't see his eyes. I swallowed hard, feeling his fist clamp tighter around my throat.

"You were going to kill her, weren't you?" he snarled.

I closed my eyes as he pressed his body against mine, so strong and warm. His words resounded inside me like a hollow drum.

Kill her? Yes...yes, I was going to kill her because she tried to take what was mine. Love bloomed deadly inside me, the scent suffocating and sweet, consuming.

"You were going to kill her, weren't you? You were going to kill her and ruin it all, all because of your goddamn jealousy."

"Ruin what?" My voice was a whisper as love turned desperate and I fisted his shirt. "Talk to me. Tell me what you're planning. You know I can help."

He stilled, his warm breath blowing against my neck. I waited for his lips to find my skin, for him to talk to me, to tell me the things I needed to hear. "Tell me you love me. Tell me...how important I am to you."

But he didn't say the words. He just pulled away and dropped his hand from around my throat. "You fuck this up for me, Sophie, and it won't matter what you *think* you are to me." I caught the shift of his head as he searched for my gaze in the gloom. "You fuck this up and you're dead."

The words were a dagger to my chest. My body jerked from the blow and my breaths seized in my chest. "No," I whispered, but it sounded like a whimper. "Don't say that...*don't you dare say that to me.*"

"I have men on the island," he said. "Men who don't even know you exist. You got that?" He took a step down, moving away from me. "They have their orders and they won't stop, not until this is done. So I'm warning you now. Stay out of my way." He glanced at the door to the apartment. "And stay the fuck away from Xael, you got it?"

His phone lit up with a text as the emergency lights flickered on. In the glow of envy, I saw him as he lifted his cell and read it, his lips curling...saw him for the monster he really was. He didn't care about me. He might've once, doing enough to get what he wanted. But not anymore. He hadn't come to save me...*he'd come to save her...that bitch, Xael.*

It wasn't the agony of betrayal that stung...it was fact he'd played me...I was just a trigger, right? All those words, all those promises, they meant nothing. I closed my eyes, remembering all the time he'd plotted with me, pushing me to go after Evan Valachi. He wanted me to kill her and leave her in that bunker, wanted me here on this island, too. He wanted me to *be* her. I lifted my hand and touched a face that was barely recognizable. *My face.* But it wasn't my face any longer. Now I looked like a dead woman. My cheeks burned as he raised his head, turned and took another step down. "Stay out of my way, Sophie. This is your last warning."

I watched him take a step backwards once more and turn his back on me. Cold moved in swiftly. Maybe it'd always been there all along and I was numb to it? Maybe the cold wasn't his absence. Maybe it was his touch. Icy right to my core. I slowly wrapped my arms around my body.

But the cold moved deeper, making my teeth gnash and chatter.

Until I clenched my jaw.

He'd used me...

He didn't want me.

He didn't care about me.

He only cared about himself.

"Stay away," I whispered as Xael called out a dead woman's name in the apartment, searching for me. "Stay away or I'm dead, right? Fuck that."

You know what you have to do, pumpkin, Daddy whispered, his voice resounding in my head. *You know what you came for. Focus on that now. Focus on killing the man who betrayed me. Fuck what he says.* "Fuck what he says," I repeated, and took a step, going after the bastard I'd come for, Bruno Bernardi.

FORTY-ONE

Evan

"Marry me..." Bruno lowered his head, his words hot and breathy against my ear. "You know it's going to happen one way or another. Why make it so goddamn hard on yourself?"

One thrust of his hips and that fire ignited inside me, making my pulse skip. My body hummed with promise, clenching and pulsing like an engine ticking as it cooled.

"Bruno, I..." I started until in the corner of my eye, my phone illuminated with a text.

His lifted his gaze to the glow and let out a snarl of annoyance. I let out a chuckle and reached for my phone. "Saved by the text."

"You think so, huh?" he , and slid his weight from mine.

The wind picked up, howling as something screeched from outside the building. *Boom!* Something slammed into the side of the building below us, making me flinch. The floor vibrated, racing through my toes as my feet touched down and I grabbed my phone. "It's Mateo." I moved to the window, still naked, and read the text. "He's got the power back on..."

Something ignited with a *pop!* Outside the building, sparks arced from a light pole uprooted from the ground. I flinched from the sight, jerking my gaze up as I stepped backwards. "What the fuck..."

The lights inside the apartment came back on. Bruno rose from the bed, moving closer to the bright glare outside. But in the glow, something moved. Something dark, scurrying from the water's edge and over the sand to cut across the pavement. No, not *something. A number of somethings...*but as they grew closer, heading this way, I froze with fear.

They were men...men dressed in black from head to toe, carrying machine guns. "Bruno," I hissed, riveted to what I was seeing.

But he was there in an instant, stepping closer to the window. "Get dressed, Evan..." he warned, turning to me. *"Move!"*

I clutched my cell and hurried, lunging around the bed, grabbing clothes as I went. My fingers trembled, panic made my mind race as I yanked on my panties and bra. There were men...not our men...not armed like that.

The first *crack* of gunfire outside was barely audible, unless you were listening. I jerked my gaze up, heart hammering.

"Fuck!" Bruno barked, punching out a text, and yanked on jeans and his boots. I did the same, my fingers barely working as I fumbled, before turning to my bags. I searched for anything warm and dark, sliding my arms into a black windbreaker I used for riding as Bruno slipped his phone into the back pocket of his jeans. "D's on his way." He yanked down his shirt. "I don't know what's going on out there, but Evan...get your gun."

I nodded, stepping around him as he reached for his own jacket. The *beep…beep…beep…* of his safe sounded as I hurried from the bedroom. Terror spiked, making me cry out as another *crack* of gunfire sounded, only this time it was closer. "Bruno…"

"It's okay….we're going to be okay," he declared.

But I could hear the doubt in his voice and saw the way he watched the elevator door. I slipped my gun into the back of my waistband, then raced for the small backpack which had a spare magazine.

"Grab everything you need, we're not staying here waiting for them to pick us off one by one."

I froze, his words hitting home. That's exactly what we were here…*dead*.

FORTY-TWO

Bruno

Protect her...the need surged through me, dark and savage. I jerked my gaze up as she neared. Her eyes were wide, her skin pale. *Crack!* The echo of a gunshot was faint through the windows, but still I heard it. So did she, flinching at the sound.

I gripped my gun in one hand and reached for her hand with the other. "Come on."

Movement came from my right. I dropped her hand and stepped in front of her, lifting my Sig.

"Easy," Deviouz growled, glancing at me, then scanned the rest of the apartment as he pushed open the stairwell door. "We move...*now.*"

My fucking heart was thundering as I gave a nod and followed. We made no sound, stepping into the gloom of the stairwell, and hurried down. I listened for her steps as my mind raced. First the attack on Baldeon, then Salvatore, and Katerina VanHalen. Now it was our turn.

Fucked if I was going down without a fight.

My phone vibrated with a text. But I didn't have time to look.

"The Commander," Evan whispered. "He's sent out a global warning. We're under attack." I came to a stop and glanced over my shoulder as she read his message. *She'll go to him...I know she will.* But she didn't reply, just slid her phone back into her pocket and met my gaze. "What?"

I stared at her for a second, my jealous fucking heart pulsing in the back of my throat. There was no hint of confusion in her gaze, no wavering of intent, as the heavy thud of boots came from somewhere above.

She'd made her decision...and that was to stay with me.

"They've breached," Deviouz murmured beside me. "We have to hurry."

I pushed forward, driving closer to D to give her enough room to hide, and motioned her against the wall. If anyone was coming through the door above, then they wouldn't see her, not at first. Maybe seconds...but seconds were all I needed to make a shot count as we hurried down flight after flight, slowing near the end.

"Ready?" D asked, and lifted his gun, reaching for the handle on the door of the ground floor.

Evan's breaths were like gunshots behind me. She was all I focused on, lifting my gun before I muttered. "Go."

Deviouz was through in an instant, spilling into the foyer as a team of men in black moved toward us.

Bang!

Bang!

Bang...

The deafening sounds filled my ears. I trained the muzzle toward movement on the other side of the glass and squeezed the trigger. *Bang!* Glass cracked with the shot. *Bang!*

The roar that followed was all the sound I needed. Wind howled through the hole the gunshot left behind, filling the foyer as we hurried, moving toward the doors. Deviouz was out first, scanning the entrance and turning.

One attacker was still alive, crawling along the ground. Flecks of blood shot in the air as he coughed and crawled until D neared, kicked the gun out of his hand, and pushed him over with the toe of his boot. "How many?" he growled.

I grabbed the guy's weapon and checked the clip before hitting the safety on mine, and slipped it into the waistband of my jeans.

"Bruno," Evan whispered.

I glanced over my shoulder, to see movement in the distance. Someone was running toward building one. "D, we have to go."

The second I turned back, I watched my bodyguard rise from the ground, the knife in his hand dripping with blood. But where the fuck did we go?

The glow of Evan's phone was like a neon fucking light in the dark. "I have it," she whispered, and stepped closer. "There's a bunch of abandoned cabins on the other side of the island."

She shoved her phone toward us, cupping her hand around the screen to shield the glow. Deviouz grabbed her phone, scanned the map detailed on the screen, and lifted his gaze. "Well, we can't stay here."

"Then we go," I decided. "Hide out, figure out what the fuck is going on."

"Seems pretty fucking obvious," Evan muttered, pocketing her phone, and pulled out her weapon. "They want us all dead."

She winced and pressed her hand against the wound on her side. It was easy to forget she'd already survived one attack, and here we were, under attack once again.

"This fucking trip," she muttered, settling the backpack snug against her back. "Can go to goddamn Hell."

Deviouz glanced at her hand against her side and met her gaze. "Can you run?"

"Yeah." She gripped her gun and gave a hard nod. "I can fight too, if I have to."

"Good," he growled, and scanned the night. "Stay close."

He moved quicker than his big frame should allow, sprinting around the rear of our apartment building. Movement came from inside the foyer as we took off from the corner. I didn't have to stick around to find out what their next move was. The sharp crack of gunfire came across the grounds. We ran with our heads down into the roaring wind and left the Institute behind, not stopping until we were running in the dark.

Deviouz slowed, sucking in hard breaths, and reached out to Evan. "The map."

She fumbled, punching in the code and bringing up the map of the island. But it was the faint roar far behind us that had me lifting the muzzle of my gun as I turned. Gunshots rang out, barely reaching me through the deafening roar of the wind.

My hair lashed my eyes, making them water. The brutal gusts weren't easing, if anything they were getting stronger. Evan fought to remain upright, stumbling sideways before she turned her face into the wind. My gaze went to her hand pressed against her side, then shifted to the buildings behind us once more.

"Over that way!" Deviouz roared.

I gave a nod and started walking, moving between her and whatever came for us. We hurried into the darkness, boots scuffing as the grass gave way to sandy loam. Thick brushes rose in front of us. We hurried for the cover, plunging between the overgrown palms and island shrubs.

"They'll realize we're not there," Evan gasped, ducking to scurry under a branch.

"By then we'll be long gone," I answered, close behind.

We ran, spearing out of the thick brush to a worn track. Deviouz slowed, then stopped, sucking in deep breaths as he scanned the area around us. We were moving deeper into the other side of the island now, far beyond the towering view from the Institute.

Part of me wanted to turn back, to hunt and kill.

"Bruno," Evan called my name.

I jerked my gaze toward her, finding her concern. I wanted to go back, but I wouldn't, not yet. Not until I knew she was safe. I moved closer, placing a hand against her back. "I'm right here."

She reached for my hand, grasping it as Deviouz took off, moving along the track in front of us. The thicker we were in the brush, the quieter the wind. I scanned for movement and followed D, until in an instant Evan stopped, jerking my hand from her grasp.

I followed her gaze, catching the faint moving blur, and froze. Something moved through the brush, something dark...moving fast toward Deviouz. I jerked my gaze toward the bodyguard, my heart hammering. They may not have seen us yet, but if I yelled a warning, they would for sure.

I jerked my gaze to Evan, motioning her with my hand. "Stay down."

There was nothing I could do but to leave her behind. I lowered my head, gripped my gun, and lunged, driving myself into the direct path of the attacker as he raised his gun and took aim.

Protect her...that's all that drove me in that moment.

All I thought about.

All I knew.

FORTY-THREE

Evan

No!

I lunged as Bruno lowered his head and slammed into the guy as he charged from the bushes. The *thud* reached my ears, sickening and chilling. Terror was all I knew as Bruno raised his gun, wrestling with the attacker. But the guy was bigger, throwing Bruno to the side, and instead pulled a knife from his belt.

"Bruno!" I screamed, and lunged forward.

The wind pushed me backwards. Still I drove my boots into the sand, using every ounce of strength I had to propel me forward. Agony ripped through my side, making me catch my breath. But I couldn't worry about that now. Not as the attacker slashed the air in front of him and fixed his gaze on Bruno.

"Evan, *run!*" Bruno screamed, jerking his wide, panic-filled eyes toward me.

Run...and what, leave him here to die? I didn't think so.

I reached around, drawing my gun from my back, and jerked my gaze behind me. Something drew my focus, something that plunged onto my senses. A flash of movement in the darkness... my heart slammed against my ribs. *Was that blonde hair?* I sucked in hard, panting breaths and forced myself forward, lifting my gun to take aim. Grunts tore through the air as Bruno swung his fist and charged, hitting the guy with his shoulder.

They moved too fast. I tried to take aim, but one wrong shot...*and I could kill him.*

I couldn't do it, couldn't take that chance. I shoved my gun back into my waistband and let out a howl of rage, lunging to slam against the fucking asshole with all I had.

Black eyes peered back at me from the eyeholes of his balaclava. Rage was all I felt, rage and desperation. *"Get the fuck off him!"* I clawed his face, tearing at his eyes. There was a grunt before we fell backwards. I wrapped my legs around him, clenching my thighs tight.

Ten years of riding unbroken geldings and pain-in-the-ass mares and I knew how to stay on. I squeezed my thighs with all I had, listening to the *crack* underneath me as we hit the ground.

Agony roared through my side. All I saw was stars.

"Fucking *bitch!*" he roared, and rolled, shoving to his feet.

Darkness rose in front of me as he straightened, the glint of a gun neon in the night.

"Evan!" Bruno screamed my name as I stared at the muzzle pointed right at me.

Until the assassin was hit from the side. *Boom!* I jerked as the gun went off. *No...no...no...no...*they hit the ground. But only one of them pushed from the ground and stood.

Pitch black was all I saw as the attacker spun and stumbled to the side. My mind wouldn't function, senses shut down. I was frozen as I lay there in the sand and the sticks and slowly turned my head to where Bruno lay motionless.

I'd just killed him...

It was all I could think of. *I just killed...him.*

"Fuck," the attacker gave a grunt and collapsed to the ground.

A low moan came from Bruno. I shoved forward at the sound and crawled toward him. "Bruno..." I whimpered. "Bruno."

"I'm here," he answered.

I glanced over my shoulder at the motionless asshole, finding the hilt of the knife sticking out from his chest. He was dead...*dead*. I jerked my gaze back to the man who'd just saved my life and reached for him.

"What the fuck happened?"

Deviouz barked in front of us. The thud of boots resounded in the night, but all I cared about was running my hands over his body until I felt the slick warmth. "You've been shot," I moaned.

"*Fuck!*" Deviouz snarled.

"Yeah, no thanks to you." Bruno shot him a glare as the bodyguard dropped to his knees and yanked Bruno's shirt up.

"You were supposed to be behind me."

"He was coming for you." Bruno winced and moaned as Deviouz pressed against the side of his chest. "What the fuck was I going to do?"

"You were *supposed* to stay the fuck alive, that's what you were supposed to do. You're damn lucky. It's just a graze."

"Just a graze," Bruno muttered. "Fuck you."

But I couldn't swallow, couldn't speak. If breathing was voluntary, I wouldn't be able to do that, either. He was shot because he'd lunged at the attacker as he took aim at me. He'd been shot because that bullet was meant for me.

The wind didn't roar inside my head anymore as Deviouz grabbed Bruno's shirt and dragged him to his feet. It was my world imploding, burning up at its core. I moved without thinking, watching as Bruno glanced toward me. "Evan?"

I grabbed him, pulled him hard against me, and kissed him.

Hard.

Deep.

And part of me gave a shudder. I wrapped my arms around him, feeling his hands around my waist, pulling me hard against him.

"Ahem." Deviouz cleared his throat, forcing me back into the moment.

I broke away, sucking in deep breaths, and stared at Bruno. He looked different somehow. Harder, older. Solid and safe. He drew me in, like gravity. I was helpless to fight.

"We need to find you somewhere safe," Deviouz muttered. "We're not far from the cabins. This time, stay close, okay?"

"Yeah," Bruno answered automatically, but his gaze didn't shift from mine.

Something had changed between us, a monumental shift we both felt. He winced with the movement as he grabbed my hand, pulling me with him. I glanced toward the trees as we hurried, this time staying closer to Deviouz.

"What is it?" Bruno followed my focus.

I shook my head, unsure of what I'd seen before in the moments before the attack. Maybe it was my own personal demons, or the movement of the trees. But for a second before, I thought I'd seen her, seen the shine of blonde hair. "Nothing." I shifted my gaze back to the trail.

We ran harder, Bruno wincing with every step, reminding me just how close to death he'd come. A fraction or two, maybe even less, and I'd be running on my own...desperate to survive once more. And Bruno...Bruno would be back there dead because of me.

I pressed my hand to my side and kept on moving as a new hunger burned inside me. I didn't just want revenge on the bitch who'd stabbed me now, nor did I only care about leaving Bruno behind...now I needed to keep him alive. Keep us *both* alive and him close to me.

The thought hit me hard as the track seemed to stop in the middle of nowhere. Deviouz kept moving, shoving his arm upwards as he cut through the brush. Bruno kept me against his side, gripping my hand and pulling me with him as we stumbled free of the trees and finally saw the ocean on the other side of the island.

The cabins weren't what I'd expected. Forgotten was one thing, but these were decrepit. Some of them were nothing more than wooden stumps set back from the ocean's reach. Others were still little more than wooden carcasses, The buildings themselves washed away by relentless, consuming waves.

"Over there." Deviouz pointed further along the tree line to where darkened blurs waited.

We kept moving, skirting around the trees as the sand gave way to stone. I ducked, and winced as the spindled branches scratched my back before we were through once more. The further we walked, the clearer they became. More sheltered than the others, most were standing, at least.

"Find one and hole up for the night." Deviouz glanced at Bruno as he slowed. "I need to go back."

"That's fucking crazy," Bruno exclaimed. "You go back there and you'll get yourself killed."

"I *don't* go back there and we'll *all* be killed. Who knows how many have invaded the island and what they're planning? I'll find the Commander and come back for you."

I didn't like it. But he had a point. A nod toward the cabins in the distance and Deviouz muttered. "I'll come for you as soon as I can. You have weapons. Stay alive, stay out of sight and try to stay dry, okay?"

"We will," I muttered.

Bruno tugged me toward the buildings as Deviouz headed back the way we'd come. If felt like hours we'd been walking. The trees had blocked out the grayish black, streaky sky, but out here the dangerous clouds looked lighter, like morning was fast approaching.

When that happened, we'd be visible, more than what we were now. I hurried forward, catching up to Bruno as he neared the first small cabin, then kept going, heading for the next and the next. I shifted my gaze to the spindly, wind-battered brush that grew on this side of the island and tried to navigate the boulders.

"The last ones look like they're set back from the water, and higher up." Bruno pointed toward a few darkened blurs growing clearer in the distance.

Waves crashed hard against the rocks, sending the seaspray in a foggy haze. He was right, the last two cabins were higher, but not quite out of reach. I glanced over my shoulder, seeing the headland jutting out behind us. But we'd be sheltered, for a little while at least.

I hurried forward as Bruno slowed, waiting for me to catch up. "Watch the rocks, they're slippery," he called over his shoulder, then stepped, navigating carefully.

He moved slowly enough for me to follow, placing my feet in the exact same spots. But there was no way he was holding out his hand for me, no way he was making me feel like I was the woman in need of saving, *even from my own damn feet*. A tremor in my chest grew stronger, warmer, making me stare at him a little longer.

Long enough to find more things I liked.

That was becoming a problem.

I focused on the climb, grabbing the slick surfaces and rounding the boulders, balancing on rickety stones and glancing down as the black stony surface dropped away to the ocean. Waves crashed, battering like fists against the island. I breathed in the salt, tasting it on my lips as Bruno made it to the top and stepped toward the cabin.

The last one was further back and higher, almost out of reach of the spray. I knew he was headed there before he even glanced toward it. I knew because that was the one I'd pick, too.

I sucked in a harsh breath as I reached the top and looked backwards. We'd see them coming, long enough to fight any way we could. The other side of the island seemed like a whole other reality. Towering, perfect buildings, the luxury of it all. Bruno tested the wooden stairs, gripped the railing, and climbed.

From here, it was almost like we were stranded, like we were the only ones alive on the island. For a second, I allowed that fantasy to take hold as Bruno put his shoulder to the door and pushed it open with a *thud*. He disappeared into the gloom.

*Bruno...*I waited with his name trapped in my throat, the sound too damn desperate. But he was back, stepping into the doorway and scanning the rocks and the trees. "It's safe."

I moved inside, brushing his chest as I passed. The place was dark and smelled of salt and rotting wood.

"Stay close to the edges." He closed the door behind us, dulling the roar of the waves down below. "Just in case the wood is rotting."

I pulled my pack from my shoulders and turned as he neared. "Your shirt...take it off."

He glanced out the window and turned with a surprised look on his face. But I just grabbed the first aid kit from inside the pack and motioned him closer with a jerk of my head. "Shirt, now."

He slid his jacket free, dropped it next to my pack, and yanked off his shirt in one fluid motion. His gun was next. He checked the safety and bent, placing it on top of his shirt. My gaze went to his chest, then to the bloody groove on his side. I forced my gaze down, finding an antiseptic wipe, and tore the packet open. "This might sting," I muttered, and moved closer.

So close I felt the warmth radiating from his body.

So close I was drawn into his stare.

And that tremor inside my chest grew bolder, thundering with a beat of its own. This man had protected me, fought for me...taken a bullet for me. I lifted my gaze, meeting his, and swallowed hard.

"Welcome to the club," he murmured as sparks danced in his eyes.

My pulse was booming, driving heat through my body as I lifted a shaking hand and cleaned the wound. But he didn't move, didn't shift his gaze. He never even flinched, and the longer the moment lasted, the more I felt myself slipping.

This was never meant to happen. I'd come here for revenge, on both him and the bitch who'd left me for dead. But this...this felt too much like...*lust*. Sure, lust. I stared into his eyes. The kind of lust that felt like falling. The kind that shook me to my core.

The kind that terrified me.

I was falling in love with Bruno.

The kind of love that'd take a lifetime to get over. He lifted his hand and brushed a strand of hair from my cheek. And I knew that somehow I'd never really left that night, that part of me had stayed there. But it wasn't with Jannick. It was with *him*.

With the kid who'd stepped out of the shadows.

The one who'd beaten his cousin twice his size bloody minutes after he hurt me.

He was stuck there, too, unable to move forward. I saw that now, saw how this wasn't a game to him, wasn't anything he'd planned. This was something neither of us had anticipated. Yet, here it was.

But I wasn't going back to being invisible. Not after everything I'd been through. "I came to the island for retribution, to kill *her* and to hurt you, but now...now I realize that's not what I want at all. I want you. I want to be with you. But I won't be a trophy wife, Bruno. If you want me, you take me as an heir and everything else that comes with the Valachi name. I won't stand in the shadows, not any longer. So think long and hard before you commit to me, because if you break your promise and my goddamn heart, I'll kill you myself."

"Don't you know by now that's all I've ever wanted?" He grasped my face, cupping it in his big hands, and drew me closer. "You won't stand behind me, Evan. And you won't be in my goddamn shadow. You'll be beside me...where you've belonged all this time. Together we can be unstoppable. Together we can be fucking fire. I want you and everything that comes with you. Your power. Your hunger...your fucking lust."

He kissed me hard and deep.

The first aid kit slipped from my fingers and fell against my pack on the floor. He moved against me, driving me backwards until I hit the wall. His mouth claimed me, his hard chest pressed against mine. "I want all of you, Evan. I always have. You haunt me, drive me. You *consume me*."

I closed my eyes and let out a tortured sound as his hand dropped to cup my ass and pull me against him. I broke the kiss and opened my eyes. "I want you, Bruno. I want you so fucking much I can't think about anything else."

And with a sly smirk, he whispered, "Thank fucking Christ."

FORTY-FOUR

Bruno

She stepped closer, her fingers skimming my stomach, then pressed against my chest. Need in her eyes. It wasn't timid or scared this time, wasn't hovering at the edges...*it was her.* Consuming, bleeding and raw from the inside. Just how it felt for me.

She was ready...

And I wasn't waiting anymore. Faint light fell from the window next to me, cascading down her body. I lowered my head and kissed her neck as the memory of that gun came roaring back to me. She almost died...she almost died.

She almost fucking died.

I kissed her neck and yanked at her zipper, sliding it down low. Her fingers speared through my hair, gripping the back of my neck, pulling me against her. Her jacket was gone and her shirt was yanked open, leaving me to drop my head into the warmth of her. A moan rumbled in the back of my throat as I reached down and worked the button of my jeans before pushing down the zipper to free my cock.

"Bruno..." she whispered, drawing my gaze.

I pulled back, my breaths hard. "Yeah?"

"You don't have any...you know, protection. Do you?"

"*Fuck!*" I pulled away as reality set in. "I don't...I..."

Something passed through her gaze, fear, determination. She exhaled hard and pulled me back. "Don't stop. Don't fucking stop."

I scowled and fixed my eyes on her. "It's okay, we can do—"

"No." She shoved her shirt free and unhooked her bra, her fingers working fast. "We're doing this."

We're doing this? I shoved my fingers through my hair as panic rose inside me. This wasn't just anyone, this was Evan. *My* Evan. The woman I wanted to goddamn marry. The woman I'd dreamed of all these years.

No one else compared. No one I'd hungered for...not like this.

But could I take her like this? Like a goddamn beast rutting against the wall in a goddamn decrepit cabin while men armed to the teeth hunted us? Could I be so fucking callous...for her first time?

The cyclonic wind howled through the gaps in the cabin walls as I turned her, forcing her to brace her hands against the wall. "Mine." I leaned against her back, kissing the long line of her shoulder and cupped her breasts from behind. "You get that now?"

She leaned backwards, reaching for the back of my neck. Her body trembled as I cupped her breasts and my fingers slid across tight nipples that hardened with my touch.

"Bruno," she moaned as I rolled them gently and kicked off one boot, then the other.

She was impatient, the desperate need to feel more than fucking terror driving both of us. I knelt, grabbed her pants, and yanked, sliding her jeans and her panties down on one savage move.

I couldn't be gentle in that moment, couldn't give her the perfect fuck she deserved. All she got was the fucking storm…a goddamn *cyclone*.

She moaned, grinding my hands against her breasts and pressed back against me. But I was done not seeing her and I'd waited long enough. I wanted to look onto her eyes when I fucked her for the first time. I spun her, driving her backwards, she tripped, one foot still trapped by the leg of her jeans.

It didn't matter.

None of it mattered.

Not if she stumbled.

Not even if she fell.

I grabbed her hips, catching her weight, and pulled her against me. "I got you."

The connection roared between us. I'd always be here. Right where she needed me to be. To protect her, to catch her. "I told you that you were mine." I lifted her, sliding my hand down the back of her thigh and forced her legs wider, staring into her wide, panicky eyes.

That's where it started and ended, right here. I leaned in and kissed her mouth, kissing her before whispering. "It's okay, we don't have to—"

"I want to," she urged, tears welling in her eyes. "Before..."

Before a gunman came out of those fucking trees and took aim.

Before we were both dead...

The image fought for purchase in my mind, but I shoved it away. I refused to let that happen...refused to even entertain the idea. *Protect her.* That hunger burned in me, beyond any limit I could control. A single tear slipped down her cheek. She stood there naked, with the howling wind cutting through the gaps in the walls, so desperate and powerful all at the same time.

"Don't cry," I murmured, and thrust against her, pressing my cock against the warmth of her crease. "How can I fuck you if you cry?"

She let out a bark of laughter, the sound at war with the sadness in her eyes. I'd just found her...there was no way I was losing her, not now, *not ever*. She stilled, her breaths becoming deeper as that connection roared between us, burning in my veins like fire. My pulse boomed louder as the salty air plunged deeper, moving through my chest.

I licked my lips and moved against her, sliding back to slowly thrust forward. She clung to me, her gaze fixed on mine as I rocked my hips. Warmth met the head of my cock. Slick and warm. I was desperate for her, hungry beyond anything I'd ever felt before, aching with the need to feel her, to taste her...to pleasure her. I pushed deeper as that surge of claiming swept through me...until I could go no further.

I was barely in, the warmth of her a kiss around the head of my cock. "Hold on to me," I murmured. "Hold on."

I slid out, leaving that warmth. *No!* My body roared as I angled my hips and drove in harder. Her eyes widened and her breath caught until a low moan tore free. The tortured sound was a knife plunged into my chest. "Evan?" I held her, pulling her against my chest.

She just closed her eyes. "Keep going, don't stop."

Hate and desire surged through me as I slid out. I looked down. In the gloom, I saw the darkened smear of blood, then pushed back inside. Rage turned into something else. Something harder, something bestial inside me. I moved slower, thrusting in and out, easing that icy sting of pain and turning it into something else.

Something that warmed between us. Each thrust stoked that fire, building and building, until she drove her nails into my shoulders and met my body with a thrust of her own. She moaned again, only this time it was harder, *more urgent.* "More, Bruno."

I gripped her hips and drove upwards, gaining inch by sweet goddamn inch, and closed my eyes. This was what heaven felt like. It felt like her. It smelled like her, *moved like her.*

That need built inside us, crashing and building like the surge and the crash of the waves outside. Each *boom* was like thunder inside my chest, driving harder, faster. She wound her arms around the back of my neck and held on while I took her over and over...*and over.*

She was mine now.

Mine.

Her body, her mind, *her soul.*

She had to be.

"Evan," I growled, unable to hold on a second longer.

"Do it," she moaned. "I want you…"

My body jerked with her words and heat rushed through me, pulsing and throbbing as I emptied inside her. A moan ripped from me, low and guttural, sounding like a beast. Hard breaths moved between us. I tried to gather my thoughts as something moved at the edges of my mind. A knowing…a *disappointment.*

She hadn't come.

I sucked in air and came back to reality. *She didn't climax.* I pulled back, even as she clung to me. "You didn't…"

But she didn't move, just held onto me, the rush of her breath loud against my ear.

"Shit, Evan, I'm so sorry."

She turned her head and darkness glinted in her eyes. I tried to map the stars, tried to understand what she was thinking. But I couldn't.

Thud.

A low sound dragged me back to reality. Evan turned her focus to the door as the low thud came once more. I lowered her to the floor and spun, grabbing my jeans and yanking them upwards. "What the fuck!"

Panic drove me. Evan hurried, yanking her pants back on as I bent, grabbed my gun off my shirt, and moved to the doorway.

Deviouz lay against the steps, still, his chest rising sharply before falling back down with a sickening wheeze. I moved down the stairs, scanning the trees as Evan called out behind me. "What is it?"

"D," I answered, stepping down as I kept scanning for movement. "He's bad. Grab the gun and shoot anything that damn well moves."

The thud of her steps echoed through the cabin before she was back, standing on the top step as I neared him. It could be a trap, could be anything. I leaned down. "D?"

The hot metallic scent of blood mingled with the choking scent of the ocean. I grabbed his shirt, finding the wetness against his side. He'd been shot. Bad, by the looks. "D?" I growled a little louder.

He opened his eyes and winced. "Didn't make it back. More coming. Need to run."

My pulse sped as I searched the sheer cliffs in front of us, then shifted my gaze to him once more. "Shit."

I grabbed him, lifting his head from the stairs.

"Don't." He barely shook his head. "Bother. Lung...gone."

The hard wheeze was brutal as he shoved me away. He jerked his gaze toward the trees. "Run...don't know if I lost them."

Evan was already hurrying down the stairs, yanking her pack onto her shoulders. She met my gaze, then looked at Deviouz.

"Go," he pushed upwards, and tried to suck in a deep breath. "I'll hold them off for as long as I can."

The wind picked up, slamming against my bodyguard as he fought to rise.

"Bruno," Evan called my name, drawing my gaze, and reached out her hand. "We have to go."

I met Deviouz's gaze. Desperation and respect raged in his eyes. "Thank you." I gripped his shoulder.

A nod, and the bodyguard turned, lifting his gun. "Stay the fuck alive, Bruno. Don't make this all for nothing."

FORTY-FIVE

Her

I PLUNGED THROUGH THE TREES AND STOPPED, SCANNING the darkness. Harsh breaths punctured my chest. They were here...*they were here.* Voices. I'd heard them. One that slipped through the trees, but now they were gone. I clenched my grip around the handle of the knife. *No.*

I'd find them...I'd find them. *I had to.*

"Daddy?" I whispered. "Daddy, are you there?"

But there was no answer, nothing but the stillness in my head, one that scratched and clawed. I lifted my arm and slammed my fist against my head. *Smack...smack.* The knife's handle slammed against my head. "Daddy, where are you?"

The wind howled, shrieking and whistling through the branches. *Snap!* I jerked my gaze upwards. My breath stilled in my chest. In the murky gloom I saw him. A man...running.

Crack! The echo of gunfire made me flinch.

Boom...boom...boom.

More shots followed and tiny sparks of orange drew me forward. The attack was fast and brutal as two guys opened fire in front of me. I lowered my hand and stepped closer, grasping a branch in front of my face. One guy hit the ground and didn't move. I looked toward the other as he neared, his weapon still raised. Through the gaps in the trees in front of me, he stumbled sideways, then looked down, pressed a hand against his chest, and let out a low moan.

I knew him...knew him well. My heart hammered with the realization. *He was the bodyguard. Bruno's bodyguard.*

Snap.

I jerked my gaze toward the sound in the distance then back to him. He'd heard the same thing too. There were more of them... and they were coming *fast*. I glanced the way the bodyguard had come. There was no way he'd run off on his own. No way he'd save himself, not even with the invasion.

I took a step forward as another *snap* pierced the gusts to find us. The bodyguard pressed his hand against his side and lifted his head, scanning the trees all around him, and met my gaze.

My heart leaped, slamming against my chest. *He saw me...he saw me.* My hand clenched around the knife, but then he shifted his gaze. One step and he seemed to stumble, then he fell.

He hit the ground hard on his knees, then fell forward onto his hands. *Kill him...kill him now.*

I took a step, the knife clutched tight in my grip. One blow was all I needed. The sharpened blade would slice deep, blood would flow like it always did, then it'd be over. For him, at least. I took a step, moving toward the edge of the tree line toward the worn track.

Snap.

The sound came from behind me. The bodyguard glanced over his shoulder. If he looked the other way, he'd see me...*he'd see me.* Bruno's face rose in my mind. The face of a monster. *Evan?* His voice echoed. "No, not Evan." I whispered as the bodyguard shoved against the ground and rose.

He took a step, stumbling sideways, then another.

I hunted him along the track until he stumbled off it. I moved faster through the trees, hugging the track until I couldn't anymore. I squinted into the gloomy darkness, searching for movement.

Crack!

A gunshot exploded. Something whipped past me, shattering the branch near my face.

Crack!

I lunged backwards, the knife slipping in my hand.

Crack.

Pain slammed into my hand. I lunged backwards, slamming against the trunk of a tree as I fell. My heart was thundering in my ears. *Or was it footsteps?*

My thoughts were slow, hovering at the edges until they rose up and slammed into me.

MOVE!

I rolled, then shoved upwards as movement came through the trees. But it wasn't from the bodyguard that had shot at me...*it was someone else.*

Boom!

The bullet whipped past, tearing the shoulder of my jacket, and the sharp stench of burning fabric filled my nose. The bodyguard...

I stumbled backwards, turning to lunge...and ran for my life.

FORTY-SIX

Evan

I swore there was movement through the trees. "Bruno," I whispered, tearing my gaze from the brush and descending the stairs. "We have to go."

I met the bodyguard's stare and found the savage determination to survive. One I knew only too well, as I'd seen it in myself every day since the attack. It was desperate and choking, fear sparkling in the depths. I swallowed hard, knowing full well the kind of uphill battle he was facing. To be stabbed in the side in the middle of a metropolitan city with a team of highly trained doctors and nurses mere minutes away was one thing. But to be shot in the chest all the way out here and on the distant side of the island, far away from any kind of medical help was another.

He wasn't going to make it.

He knew that.

"Go, Bruno," he wheezed, falling backwards against the stairs. "You were a pain in the ass to mind anyway."

Bruno flinched, swallowing hard as Deviouz grasped his gun. "Move it."

"Bruno." I gently grabbed his arm, pulling him away.

"Fine," he snarled, and leaned down, meeting his bodyguard's stare. "You better survive this."

"Yeah?" D murmured, his face growing pale in the brightening sun. "I better."

Bruno let me ease him away, lifting his gaze to the trees as we hit the last stair, and gripped his gun. "Come on." His left hand gripped my sleeve, fingers brushing my arm.

Anyone else and I'd pull away from them. I touched no one, needed *no one*. But with Bruno...*it felt like the most natural thing in the world*. I gripped the waistband of his trousers and scurried along the rocky surface, leaving the last cabin behind. The trail leading back to the Institute was behind us, back toward the way the bodyguard had come, and seeing as how we weren't half dolphin, that only left forward.

"Watch your step," he growled, his hold around my arm tighter as I hurried across the smooth rock.

I wanted to look over my shoulder, to find the murky outline of the cabin in the dark. I wanted to go back there and start all over again. *You didn't...*

Bruno's words rose in my head as he slowed, scanning the thick trees and thorny brush, trying to find a way forward for us. Panic grew inside me as he stopped and stepped closer.

"No," he growled, turning his gaze toward me.

Crack! The shot came behind us.

"No. We're not doing this, not fucking running, not anymore. Fuck this shit." Electricity surged inside me. "Bernardis don't fucking run." He pulled me closer, his eyes filled with brutal hunger. "And neither do the Valachis."

I licked my lips and gave a nod, the gun firm in my grip.

"Got your spare clip?" he asked quietly, searching my eyes.

I swallowed hard and nodded, letting his trousers go to find the magazine in my pack and slipped it into my pocket.

"Stay behind me," he warned.

I jerked my head up, the words *'like hell I am'* burning on the tip of my tongue before he lifted his hand. "If you think I'm allowing the mother of my fucking children to be shot in front of me, you've got another think coming. We survive this first, then worry about you kicking my ass later about it, okay?"

I couldn't fight the wave of relief that hit me. I could deny it all I wanted. But I was scared. Maybe I'd been scared all along, *terrified* more like it. But right now, in this minute, was the first time someone had seen past the mask.

"Okay." He reached and brushed a strand of hair from my face. "I'm not letting anything happen to you, not now...*not ever.*"

A pang tore through my chest. My heart thrummed, filling my head with the sound.

What the hell is happening to me, I stared into his eyes. *No, this can't happen. Not with him...*

But it didn't matter. I still felt myself slipping as he dropped his hand to mine and stepped even closer. "I promise you're making it out of this, you hear me? You're making it out."

He dropped his hand, then stepped away. But the way he was talking made it seem…

No, no that can't happen.

But he walked away, raising his gun, and headed back the way Deviouz had come. As we neared the cabin, my gaze went to Deviouz…but he was gone. My heart clenched as panic spiked. Bruno stared at the same spot, then scanned the rocks. But there was no sign of him. One glance my way, and Bruno moved forward, putting distance between us as he hurried ahead.

The realization hit home.

He didn't expect to make it.

Not this day, not this island.

Not me. He didn't expect to make it past me.

"Bruno." His name was snatched from my lips by a sudden gust of wind as he bent over, sliding down the rocks.

Until in an instant, it died away.

Everything died away.

The roar in my ears, the sting of my eyes. I lifted my gaze to the clouds as they slowly swept over us. The eye of the storm. That's what this was. The center of everything. I hurried after Bruno, lifting my gun as he moved down the rocks to the sandy terrain below.

It didn't take us long to be back at the entrance of the trail, but in the sudden stillness, it all felt wrong, like in that moment death had swept its uncaring gaze across the world and finally noticed us. *There you are,* it whispered…*there…you…are…*

I jerked my focus to Bruno, taking a step toward him. My hand trembled at my side, desperate to reach for him. To touch him one last time as he scanned the trees for movement, then met my gaze. A shuddered breath, and he reached toward me, seeing my fear.

Something shifted inside me, the slide monumental...*and lifechanging.*

Crack!

The sharp sound of a gunshot drew my gaze. I scanned the trees, trying to track the sound, until Bruno lunged, tearing off through the thick brush and leaving me behind. But it wasn't away from the sound...*it was toward it.*

FORTY-SEVEN

Her

"I'M NOT THEM!" I SCREAMED AND SPUN, STUMBLING backwards, only to find the dark blur lunging through the trees and slamming into me.

I was hit hard, the air knocked from my lungs as I was knocked to the ground. He was a dark silhouette, grasping my neck with big hands as he straddled me. Everything was a blur, the fight, the chase. I let out a gasp as his grip tightened.

I'm not them...

"I tried to warn you, Sophie," he growled as he squeezed. "But you didn't fucking listen."

No! I thrashed, beating my fists against *his* head. *No...no...NO!* "Stop." The word was a sudden gasp as fire lashed my face. "You're hurting me..."

My heart was thundering. The rush of blood in my ears...*deafening*.

Until everything died away.

Darkness blurred at the edges of my vision. My blows went wild then my nails raked down his arms. *Knife...get the knife.* Desperation and heartbreak forced me to drop my hand. It hit the ground before I twisted to my side, my fingers growing numb as I reached for the handle tucked into my waistband.

"You don't ever fucking listen," he snarled, his dark eyes all I could see now.

They were the night...the endless night.

"Tried to tell you to stay out of my way, but you didn't fucking listen," he repeated, rising above me to bear down. "You *never* fucking listen."

The darkness whirled, blurring the world around me. Fragments of seconds slipped before reality roared back with a vengeance. I couldn't feel my fingers. All I could do was grip *something* and shove upwards.

He bucked above me, roaring, and shoved to the side. As he jerked his gaze to my hand, air rushed into my lungs, sweet, salty air that pushed the darkness away. I sucked in hard breaths, still feeling his hands around my throat, even though I knew it was a lie.

"You fucking stabbed me?" he howled, looking down to his side, then lifted his gaze to me. "You *fucking bitch!*"

His black shirt was sliced, and pale flesh and blood peeked out. I shoved away from him, rolling slowly. My heartbeat boomed in my ears as I shoved upwards. "You...you just stay the fuck away from me." My hands slipped, my movements jerky as I rose, the knife trembling in my hand. "Don't make me hurt you."

Kill them, Daddy whispered in my head. *Kill them all, pumpkin. Remind them whose daughter you are...*

"You little...*fucking...cunt.*"

The words were cruel. So...fucking cruel. I flinched with the sound. Then, around shuddered gasps, I whispered. *"What...what did you call me?"*

"You heard me," he shoved upwards and took a step toward me. "*Little...fucking...cunt.*"

My fist clenched around the knife. But he was a beast now, his rage gaining momentum right in front of me. I'd known he was dangerous, knew he had a cruel streak...but not like this...*never like this*. Agony carved through me, plunging deep, the blade poisoned with his love.

But had he ever loved me?

"I loved you," I gasped. "Gave you everything..."

The cruel curl of his lips was instant as a low chuckle slipped free. "Of course you did, 'cause that's what broken little bitches like you do. I fuck you once and you come panting like a dog in heat, all delusional and frenzied, starving for attention since daddy fucking died. So easily manipulated."

I flinched hard, and tried to swallow. "D-don't you d-dare say that."

"Psychotic, delusional, and neurotic. They fed you so many fucking drugs in that place it was easy to draw you to me, like a moth to the fucking flame. All I had to do was show you a little attention. A whisper here, a touch there, and you were mine. All I had to do was hand you the Valachi bitch's photo and whisper about payback and it was a done fucking deal. You unraveled, and kept unraveling. But it's over for you now, Sophie. I'd like to say it was fun while it lasted but honestly, not even the sex was that good. It was more like fucking a corpse."

Fucking...a...corpse...

A cold shiver moved through me as the savage gusts of wind suddenly died.

He was a stranger now. A disgusting, heartless, crude, *piece of shit.* He scanned the trees, drawn by the sudden absence of the cyclonic gusts, then looked up.

I took a step backwards, slow, careful, my boots making little sound. Then another, and another, putting as much distance between us as I could.

"The eye," he murmured.

I didn't care about what he said, until he lowered his gaze to me. "The eye of the storm."

But the way he said it and the way he looked, dark, dangerous, *unhinged,* made me turn and lunge.

Twigs snapped under my steps as I raced for the trees.

"*Sophie!*" he roared behind me.

But I didn't stop. My heart raced...and my body went with it, slamming through the trees.

Crack!

Agony ripped through my thigh, sending me flying sideways through the air. I slammed into a palm tree and screamed as I fell. The pain ripped through my thigh and reached up into my hip. *Get up...GET UP!* I shoved against the ground, but my hand slipped, sending me crashing back down.

The snap of twigs came from behind me. I gripped my thigh and twisted, turning to face him as he came closer, the gun in his hand pointed at me. "I tried to warn you, Sophie, but did you listen?

Did you give a fuck about what I wanted? You only *ever* think about yourself. But that doesn't matter...not anymore."

He lifted the gun, the muzzle aimed at me. "Just one loose fucking thread to burn away," he muttered.

Boom! The thick palm leaf next to his head jerked as a bullet tore through.

He flinched, then dove to the ground and took cover.

Boom!

Boom!

Gunfire exploded, the shots hitting the tree where his head had been.

"*What the fuck!*" he roared, and scurried forward, heading toward me.

Hell NO! I lifted my left leg and gripped my thigh. The pain was blinding, tearing up through my side. I lashed out, driving the heel of my boot into his shoulder. The movement was weak, but still it knocked him sideways. He hit the ground with a *thump*, then under the *thud...thud...thud* of oncoming footsteps, he pushed up and plunged deeper into the island brush.

Then he was gone...

My breaths were ragged and fierce, tearing from my chest as I pushed to stand. A crash came through the trees before a... "*Sonofabitch!*" followed.

I tried to shove upwards, but the pain turned blinding, sending me crashing back down. I cried out, rolling and thrashing, gripping my thigh as the pain gnawed and savaged, like fangs in my flesh. I didn't need to look through the bloody hole in my pants to know there was a bullet lodged somewhere in there.

A scream lodged in the back of my throat, tearing free with a guttural moan. Footsteps stopped on the other side of the palm. Hard breaths followed. He was close...*so very close.*

The knife...

I searched the ground around me as a scream bubbled up to the top of my throat. *No.* I bit down on my lip, pinning the sound in place. Blood bloomed. The tang filling my mouth as I caught the glint of steel in the distance, just out of reach. *If I could just...*I pushed, twisting on the ground, and reached.

Snap!

The sudden sound made me freeze. But the blade of the knife was almost within reach. I bit down harder as panic rose. A shadow moved in the corner of my eye. I turned my head, catching movement as he stepped toward me...*and I froze.*

Long blonde hair, black coat. Bruno Bernardi turned his head, scanning the trees as he lifted his gun, taking aim.

Kill him NOW! my father screamed inside my head.

I shifted my focus back to the blade, my heart hammering hard. It was now or never...now, *or die trying...*

I shoved forward, swallowing the scream that punched into my mouth and closed my fingers around the handle of the sharpened steel.

FORTY-EIGHT

Evan

I took a step and scanned the trees as Bruno took off running, looking every bit as dangerous as the damn assassin. The attacker was just here...*somewhere*. But in that second before Bruno fired his gun, I thought it sounded like...

A woman's scream.

Movement came from the corner of my eye, drawing my gaze toward the thick leaves of a palm. Someone rose from the darkness. Someone who wobbled and swayed on her feet, her blonde hair matted with sticks and leaves. Fresh blood smeared down the side of her cheek, growing brighter in the sun as she turned her head and those cold, empty eyes found me.

"Bruno..." I whispered and took a step backwards.

"*You?*" she cried, confusion creasing her brow. "You're dead... dead...dead...dead...I killed you."

RUN! that voice screamed inside me. *FOR FUCK'S SAKE, EVAN, RUN!*

"Killed...killed...killed you," she mumbled.

And I was in that bunker all over again, staring into the eyes of madness, madness that stepped toward me, that lifted a blade coated in blood. *"Killed her, Daddy."* Madness insisted. *"We killed this bitch already."*

I froze for a second, until rage detonated like an inferno in my chest. "The fuck you did!" I snarled, and clenched my grip around the gun.

Thanks for making it so goddamn easy. Her words echoed back to me.

*What...*I stuttered in my head. *What's easy?*

Your death.

Her lips curled, the smile sickening as it grew. My hand trembled at the sight, and seconds hovered in suspense like time itself had forgotten about us. Until, with a savage *roar,* she hurled herself toward me.

I raised the gun, my hand shaking, my finger squeezing the trigger. But it was all too soon...*all too soon!*

Boom!

The weapon kicked in my grip. But the shot went wide, slamming into the trunk of a tree beside her. With a bestial scream, she hit me hard, head down, shoulders slamming into my middle. Agony tore through my side, making me scream as we went down and hit the ground hard.

The gun flew from my hand. Fists and nails were all I had as she unleashed above me, hitting, punching, shrieking with sheer unbridled sickness.

Her nails raked down my face and slaps stung my cheeks. I fought with all I had, trading blow after blow, driving my fists into the sides of her face. *"Get the fuck off me!"*

Until she drove her fist into my side.

Agony exploded, detonating behind my eyes in blinding sparks of white. My blows stopped as my breath was trapped in my lungs.

"You're *dead!*" she howled, and drove her fingers into the wound. *"Dead. DEAD. DEAD!"*

White bled to gray, and black moved in at the edges.

I was going to die.

Die here in the middle of nowhere.

"*EVAN!*" Bruno's roar punched through the haze.

As I came back to reality, the blinding pain slammed into me. Bruno was a blur behind us, his gun trained on the back of her head, until she jerked her gaze over her shoulder and lunged to the side, dragging me with her. I punched and slapped, the momentum throwing me forward, to slam my elbow into the bridge of her nose.

Her eyes widened as a scream of terror and pain wrenched free.

It was all I needed. My thighs clenched, the muscles rock hard, driving against hers. She bucked and howled, desperation like stars in her eyes. I saw her now. Saw her for the pathetic, unhinged beast she was. She was nothing...*no one*. Just a girl hidden behind the disguise.

A disguise that looked like me.

The radiating pain in my side was nauseating. Still, I clenched my thighs around her, fisted her shirt, and rolled. She wobbled for a second as she rose, until her head snapped upwards and that emptiness moved in her eyes once more.

But it didn't matter. I was right where I needed to be. I dropped my hand to the ground and my fingers wrapped around the cold steel as I lifted my hand.

Boom!

She stiffened above me.

Boom!

BOOM!

She slowly sank and hit the ground at my side like she was made of nothing but water. The gun in my hand was tilted upwards. Bruno's muzzle was trained on the space where she'd been, his finger easing off the trigger as a splutter came from beside me.

"Thought...he...loved...me..."

I turned to her. Her words were faint, punctuated by jerky, shallow breaths, before her chest sank...and didn't rise anymore.

Death moved into her eyes.

Like life had taken a step backwards and slipped away.

"What the fuck did she say?"

I slowly lifted my gaze, my hand still clenched around the grip of my gun. "She said *'I thought he loved me'*."

Bruno just searched my gaze, confusion moving in. "He who?"

"I don't know." I lowered my gaze to her once more.

Bruno moved close, grasped my hand, and lifted me to my feet. The pain stabbed deep and a cry ripped free, making me press my hand against the wound.

She wasn't so terrifying anymore. She was small and pathetic... wearing *my* fucking face.

"Christ, she looks like—"

I lifted my hand. "Don't say it. Just, *please* don't say it."

He didn't, just took a step toward me, giving her a kick in the side as he went. But she never flinched, never moved. She was as dead as dead could get. And in some sick way, I kind of felt sorry for her. There was another piece of the puzzle here.

Something I wasn't quite grasping.

I thought he loved me.

The words were haunting, making it hard for me to hate her. If she'd done this for fucking love, then we had bigger problems to worry about. "Bruno."

"Yeah?" He met my gaze.

"I don't think this is over somehow."

He rubbed the back of his neck, his gaze fixed on the bitch who'd tried to kill us. "Me neither."

FORTY-NINE

Bruno

I didn't want to look at the crazy bitch. Still, I watched for movement from the edge of my vision and reached for Evan's hand. "Let's keep moving, figure out a way to get the fuck off this island."

She just looked at me, looked right through me. *Did she hate me now?* The terror seemed to hit me from nowhere. *Did she see me as the monster I was?*

My hand trembled, the recoil of the shot still flowing through me. I swallowed hard, my gaze moving to the bitch.

"Yes," Evan murmured, her fingers sliding between mine as she took my hand. "And we're never coming back."

"You got that right," I agreed, and tore my focus away. My heart was hammering as I took a step backwards, but no matter how hard I tried to look away from that face, I couldn't.

Christ, she looked like Evan...the resemblance shook me. Tremors tore free from the inside as I stared into the bitch's wide, unblinking eyes, then moved to her parted lips, lips I'd kissed, not knowing they weren't the real thing.

Kiss me. The memory of that night pushed into my mind. My hand grasped Evan's. "Come on."

I pulled her backwards, dragging her away from the crazy bitch who'd tried to kill us. There was resistance, until she gave into me and followed as I moved back through the trees and headed toward the trail once more.

But I didn't ease my grip on the gun, didn't stop scanning the trees for movement all around us. *He was still out there...*

I pulled Evan closer, that need to protect roaring like the fucking wind inside me.

"Come on," I urged, pulling her back the way we'd come.

But as we hurried toward the Institute, no more screams came from the trees. The trail was deserted. The hairs rose on the nape of my neck. I didn't like it. Not the absence of the wind...and not the desertion. There were more of them out there, more who'd come to kill or kidnap, and I sure as hell wasn't waiting around to find out.

I needed to get Evan to safety, then go back for D. Fuck if I was leaving the stubborn asshole out here. A pang of agony tore through my chest and made me feel panicked...made me hate myself a little more. *He's not dead...not dead.*

A branch shifted at my right, making me freeze and whip the gun upwards. But then another branch moved, and another. In an instant, the wind arrived once more, slamming into me from the other direction. Evan stumbled backwards with the sudden force. I gripped her tighter, lowering my head as I pulled her behind me and we hurried, charging back along the track.

Every fucking movement had me on edge. But there were no more men in black lunging from the trees at me, no more howls of rage. There was just the wind, the neverending fucking wind. I slowed as the trees fell away, leaving us to stumble out into the clearing.

"Bruno," Evan murmured. "I don't like this."

"I know." I pulled her with me. I didn't like it either, not one fucking bit.

But we didn't have a choice. Then, as we raced toward the rise, I caught movement in the distance. My heart leaped and the gun rose in my hand as a team of three men burst from the grounds, heading toward us.

Only, one of them caught my eye first. I recognized him instantly.

"Evan!" The Commander roared, and lifted his hand, motioning the two at his sides forward.

"Mateo!" she called desperately.

We raced forward, meeting them. But he didn't move to her side, just scanned the island behind us. "Are you both okay?"

Evan just gave a nod, her grip tightening around mine. "Yeah."

"What the fuck happened?" I barked, rage burning inside me at the sight of him.

"We were attacked, eight, ten. Six of them are dead, the others have disappeared." He scanned the trees behind me. "Your bodyguard?"

"Shot," I stated. "Back there," I jerked my head toward the trial. "The last cabin up on the peak."

The Commander just turned toward his men and nodded. "If he's out there, we'll find him."

Both his men left, heading toward the trail. They moved fast and with chilling purpose, guns up and trained on the trees on either side. I'd forgotten just how well-trained these men really were.

"We found her," Evan declared. "The other Evan."

Mateo flinched and searched her gaze before shifting to me. "Dead?"

I nodded. "She is now."

A nod, and he motioned us forward. "Come on, let's get you two to safety. There's still more of those bastards out there."

I hated the wave of fucking relief that descended with the Commander at our side, but it wasn't about my goddamn pride... only survival, and we had better chances with him than on our own.

We hurried back toward the buildings, though part of me wanted to turn around, to help his men find my damn pain-in-the-ass bodyguard.

Don't make this all for nothing.

His last words haunted me. "You better be fucking alive," I muttered under my breath. "Or I'll come for you my own damn self."

Evan's hand squeezed mine as we hurried back toward the buildings that rose in the distance. More men headed toward us... two teams of three fanned out around us, semi-automatic guns aimed at the trees behind us.

"Get them to safety," Mateo commanded one team. "The bodyguard's still unaccounted for. I'm going back to the cabins. You three are with me."

He just nodded to Evan as one of his team moved, sweeping around us. "Go, stay down until we know it's safe," he called, his voice fighting the wind.

"Let's go." The leader of the team motioned us forward.

We left the Commander and his guys behind, hurrying toward the buildings once more. "Where are we headed?"

"Building one," the team leader called over his shoulder. "We have it secured."

I nodded, gripping Evan's hand.

"Is anyone else...you know, dead?" she asked.

The leader glanced my way, then met her gaze. "Yeah, but don't worry about that now. Let's just concentrate on getting you safe."

Exhaustion moved in as the burn of adrenaline started to die away. We'd been running for hours, hours searching, hours fighting. Evan started to slow, pulling on my hand.

"Easy," I called to the guards. "She's exhausted."

They eased their punishing pace, scanning for movement.

"I'm okay," Evan denied.

She ground her teeth and pushed on. But I didn't miss her hand as she pressed it to her side. She was still injured and in pain. Her face was pale. *Jesus*, she'd run and fought, but not once had she complained. An ache bloomed in my chest, moving deeper than anything I'd ever felt before.

What I felt for this woman scared me.

A lot.

The memory of her standing there as the bitch lunged at her with a knife slammed into me. I'd reacted on instinct, like protecting her at all costs wasn't something I had to think about, just something I had to do. I could still feel my finger clenching around the trigger as the gun kicked in my hand.

Protect her...

The same need raged in me now as she slowed, hard, coming to a stop.

Her eyes widened and her breaths were fast and panicked. "Bruno," she mumbled my name as her knees trembled, and she collapsed to the ground.

I lunged, catching her around the hips and yanked her hard against me. "Easy, I've got you."

Fuck, she was pale...growing white as a damn ghost. I lifted her in my arms as she yanked her shirt high.

The once white bandage was a bloody mess. "What the fuck!"

I didn't think, just swung her knees up, gripped her against my chest, and ran like hell. *"She needs the damn doctor NOW!"*

"Hold on," I growled as I ran. "Hold the fuck on, Evan. Don't you goddamn die on me...don't you fucking die."

FIFTY

Evan

Three months later...

"THIS IS ALL TOO FAST," Dad muttered as he paced back and forth, adjusting his tie for the tenth time. "Why don't we think about this for a minute? I mean, you just got out of the damn hospital."

"What's there to think about?" I muttered, and leaned closer to the mirror, adjusting my makeup. "A Valachi is marrying a Bernardi."

He turned, meeting my gaze in the mirror.

It was the truth. But what he didn't realize was that I wanted this. *Mrs. Bruno Bernardi.* A cold shiver raced through me. Bruno wasn't an enemy anymore. Nor was he just an ally. He was my lover, even if he did still skirt around the one act that'd change things between us. He was a friend, a protector, the one person I found myself excited to see every day.

My pulse raced at the thought of him just a few feet away. I swallowed hard and glanced toward the closed door. He'd be nervous, running his fingers through his hair as he paced the floor. I knew him, probably better than I knew myself.

I rose and straightened my dress. "So, unless you plan on making Adrian Bernardi your wife, then this is it." I took a step closer, lowering my voice. "This is, after all, what you wanted, right, Daddy?"

The muscles of his jaw bulged as he clenched. "Eight years ago, maybe."

I gripped the lapels of his jacket and stared into those clear blue eyes. "Nothing's changed." I met his stare and something unspoken passed between us. I knew the reason for the pact. Knew only too well how spilled blood from our enemies had a way of coming back to us. I knew the Bernardis wouldn't turn on us...this just sealed the deal.

A vow for a vow.

A blood pact joined with rings.

He glanced down at my side without saying a word. He didn't have to, the look said it all. He was scared for me, his only heir. But he didn't need to worry.

A knock came at the door before it cracked open and Jessie peeked her head in. "We're all ready for you out here."

I gave Jessie a nod and dropped my hands, smoothing his jacket as I went. "Okay."

But Dad wasn't done. "Are you sure you want to do this?"

I'm immensely proud of you, never forget that. But we need a line for this family. A male line. Dad's own words came back to me now. They were the same words he'd said to me moments before I met Jannick Bernardi. I wasn't marrying that piece of shit...but I was still holding up my side of the bargain...

I need you to be my girl now, can you do that? Can you be my girl and make this Irish bastard love you?

Make him love me...

I exhaled hard and held out my hand. "Ready, Daddy?"

Make him love me...

Dad took my hand as we went to the door. The music started as I walked along the hallway and slipped my hand around his arm. He straightened his spine and quietly cleared his throat. I didn't need to look to know the great Michele Valachi was crying.

The off-the-shoulder cream dress hugged my hips and flared out, accentuating my curves. Deep purple roses in one hand, my eyes fixed on the prize as we rounded the end of the hallway and caught sight of the filled pews.

The soft harp music seemed to swell inside the church. My gaze went to the end of the aisle, to where Bruno stood facing the priest. My heart stuttered as he turned. I watched as his gaze swept past the faces I couldn't see...*because all I saw was him.*

His eyes widened and his lips parted. Panic surged inside me. It was like meeting him all over again, the surge of desire, that burn inside me that surged upwards. I was a walking inferno when I was around him, desperate to feel the quench of his touch.

Everything else faded away. I didn't see those around me turning to stare, didn't hear the music, didn't even feel my father's hand as it curled protectively around mine. All I saw was Bruno as he took a step, his long strides consuming the distance between us.

"Bruno," my father growled, giving him a deadly stare. "Take good care of her."

There was a hint of a smile on my future husband's face before it was gone and a steely gaze settled in. The priest started talking, reciting vows I'd read a hundred times in the lead-up to this day, vows I'd changed in my head., vows that meant more than just to obey.

I was a Valachi, after all. Our own vows were different, ones of strength, ones of unity. Ones where I might take his name, but he didn't take my legacy. But we'd make it work. A Bernardi and a Valachi. Bruno squeezed my hand as I stared into his eyes.

For a second, I was back on that island, frozen with fear and rage as that crazy bitch who'd stolen my identity lunged at me with a knife. *Boom! Boom! Boom!* I flinched, standing here with the memory of the gunshots. But Bruno was here, taking a step closer, sliding his hands around my waist to draw me close.

The priest stopped mid-recitation, clearing his throat with displeasure. One savage glare from Bruno and the old guy kept going, slowly at first. Murmurs came from the front pews. I glanced toward them, finding Dad and Jessie on one side, then the cutting glares of the Bernardis.

Adrian Bernardi watched me carefully, his dark eyes fixed on mine, pinning me to the spot. My pulse stuttered and an ache swelled in my chest as I glanced from him to the savage glare from Cillian.

They didn't move, didn't smile.

Not even a hint.

It was all savagery with them.

All blood pacts and whispers of revenge.

"Hey," Bruno whispered, drawing my gaze.

But before I met his gaze, I swept mine through the others, searching for the one Bernardi I didn't want to see at my wedding...*or ever again*. But Jannick wasn't here, not sitting in the front pews or hiding in the back where it was standing room only.

Bruno gently gripped my hand, his lips moving as he recited his vows and slipped the rose gold band onto my finger. I licked arid lips, my breaths stopped.

I met his gaze and found peace as the priest finally muttered the words. "I pronounce you..."

"Kiss the bride," Bruno murmured, preempting the words.

There was a cockiness in his eyes, a whisper of something brewing in his head. I closed my eyes as his hand cupped my cheek, and gave myself up to the moment.

The moment I never thought I'd want.

Or have...

I wasn't supposed to be here, not standing in front of him...not having crawled out of that bunker. His kiss moved deeper, drawing a moan from the back of my throat. A murmur echoed from somewhere at the edges of my world. But in the center, there was just this...just Bruno's body pressing against mine...just his fingers sliding through my hair, holding me still, until he broke the kiss.

My lips throbbed from the assault, my breath stolen as my husband pulled away.

"Mrs. Bernardi," Bruno murmured.

"Mr. Bernardi," I finished.

"We did it." His smile grew wider.

It was infectious. The corners of my mouth tugged as the heady feeling wrapped itself around me tight. "We did it."

He leaned closer as the church erupted in a thunderous round of clapping and whoops and hollers, his lips moved to my ear. "You know what this means, right?"

A surge of excitement rose in me as he pulled back. The answer to his question sparkled in his eyes. I couldn't catch my breath when he eased away, turned to the packed church, and punched our clasped hands into the air.

What this means...

A tremor coursed through my body, because I knew what this meant.

...finally.

FIFTY-ONE

Bruno

I closed the door behind me, watching her as she made her way through the living room of my three-bedroom penthouse apartment, lowering her gaze to the floor to sneak a peek at me behind her. She was nervous, her hands fluttering to her hair, pulling out pin after pin, until the soft brown locks cascaded down her back.

She'd changed her hair since we'd come back from the island, changed a lot of things, but one thing remained between us. That *hunger*. I didn't think it'd ever be sated. It was a beast of its own, growing stronger between us in the days and the weeks, and finally the months, since we'd escaped that goddamn hell and come back home.

It was Hell, there was no doubt about that.

Hell when I'd raced for the doctor with her bleeding out in my arms.

Hell as the doctor pushed me from the room and worked on her for three hours straight, fixing the damage that bitch had caused, what they'd *all* caused. Panic tried to push in, but I wouldn't let it.

Not tonight...tonight I had something special planned.

I pushed off the door and strode toward her.

She reached around her back for the zipper. "Want to undo me?"

"No," I answered, watching her turn with a look of annoyance.

"Why not?"

"Because we're leaving." Behind me, a knock came at the door. I turned and strode toward it, flicked the locks, and yanked the handle.

"Boss," Deviouz muttered, striding into the apartment.

A pang tore through my chest at the sight of his slight limp. I'd wanted him to take more time off, Christ knows he needed it. The stubborn pain-in-the-ass just shook his head at the first words, then turned, giving me his back, threw an *"I'll be there,"* over his shoulder, and left the goddamn room.

The bodyguard was getting a little too possessive...

A quick scan of the apartment and he settled his focus on Evan as she met his gaze.

"D?" she questioned, glancing my way with a confused frown.

"You look beautiful," he said, and smiled. "But there was never any doubt. I'll grab the bags."

"Bags?" Her brow creased. I could see that annoyance moving in once more, stealing that sexy, seductive glint in her eyes.

"Yes, bags." I strode to her and reached out my hand. "You ready for the rest of your life, Mrs. Bernardi?"

"What are you doing, Bruno?"

I just gave a sly shrug as Deviouz strode from the bedroom with the two suitcases in his hands.

It was the important things, some clothes. Toiletries already waited for us in the car. The rest would wait until tomorrow.

"Come on," I murmured, giving her hand a tug. "We don't want to be late, do we?"

"Late...*late for what?*"

I just chuckled. "You'll see."

Begrudgingly, she gave a sigh and slapped my hand away. The woman was goddamn feisty...and I fucking loved it.

"Better be worth it," she muttered, and followed D back out of the apartment and headed for the elevator once more.

I sighed, and followed her with my gaze as she slipped from view. The thud of her heels echoed on the slate tiles all the way to the elevator. I glanced around the apartment and turned. What she didn't know was this wasn't our place anymore. The sale had gone through yesterday for a cool three million. *A bachelor's pad...*the brochure said, and that's exactly what it was.

A place for those who liked the freedom of the complex and the stunning view over the city. But that wasn't me, not anymore. I had another future in mind. A future where I could not only protect those I loved, but where I could build a goddamn army. One that would be fucking vicious.

I'd *never* let what had happened to Evan ever happen again.

Not to *any one* I loved.

I followed the echo of her heels, pulling the door closed behind me, and headed for the elevator as the doors opened. Evan stepped in, her gaze moving to mine as Deviouz stepped in front, carrying the two suitcases. He'd been dubbed 'The Miracle'. Found as close to dead as anyone this side of it could be, he'd been brought back twice before they reached the infirmary.

Thank God for the nurses who'd kept him alive until the doctor finished with Evan.

He'd tried to push them away when they told him Evan was unconscious, tried to reach for his damn gun and growled, 'Evan comes first'. I stepped inside the elevator and met the bodyguard's gaze. He was her head of security, the one man I trusted more than anyone to stand at her side.

And mine.

"You missed a good service," I grumbled.

"Did I?" he responded quietly, and shifted his gaze to the doors as they closed. "Your kiss was a little weak, Bruno," he complained. "Better work on that, brother."

I fought a smile as the elevator moved. *Asshole.*

But the moment he stepped free, striding toward the two other guards now under his command, a switch flipped inside him. He became commanding, cold...he became the protector. He handed the two suitcases over, and gave orders to the two others, who moved in an instant, one striding from the complex to scan for movement on the street, while the other moved to our backs.

But there was no attack as we strode through the doorway and headed to the waiting limousine. Evan flinched at the blare of a car horn, but I lengthened my side, coming up beside her. One hand on the back of her arm was all she needed as Deviouz opened the back door and ushered her inside.

"You going to at least give me a hint?" she urged, leaving me to slide in beside her as she took her seat.

"Nope," I answered, earning a stabbing glare.

She didn't like surprises.

Didn't like the thrill.

She liked solid, *safe.*

She liked knowing where she was headed, all while trying to forget where she'd been.

Her hand went to her side on instinct, and a flare of pain cut across her face. The surgeon had said it was a miracle she'd survived, and it wasn't just the wound itself and the torn stitches. It was the infection that almost took her from me, the kind of infection that had scarred her insides. There'd been talk of possible infertility. She was still wrestling with that.

I gripped her hand, sliding my fingers between hers. "Trust me."

She gave me a hint of a smile as the limousine's engine started and we pulled out into the traffic. We didn't have too far to go, just through the heart of the city and out the other side. By the time the traffic had died down and stars glinted in our view instead of high-rises, Evan breathed a little easier.

"You like it out here, huh?" I murmured, unable to take my eyes from her.

She smiled. "Yeah."

I settled back as pride moved through me. The towering twelve-foot wrought iron fence up ahead glinted in the headlights. The place was big, and secure, *very secure*. D pulled the limousine up at the intercom, lowered the window and pressed a button.

"Bruno," Evan started, leaning forward to peer through the windows. "Whose house is this?"

I watched her expression as I answered. "Ours."

Her eyes widened as the heavy steel gate in front of us rolled backwards. The state-of-the-art security was handled by a well-trained team of guards, all under Deviouz's command.

"Holy shit," she whispered as we pulled forward, rolling along the driveway toward the looming three-story mansion in the distance.

"Can we afford this?" she whispered.

"Yes," I answered, smiling.

Five million dollars, the place had cost us. Bernardi and Valachi money.

Our money.

She jerked a surprised and elated glance my way. Not much made her smile lately and as the corners of her mouth curled, growing wider, I knew I'd found the one thing that'd made her feel like a kid all over again.

"How did you know?"

"About the house?" I gave a shrug. "Your father mentioned it in passing, said you fell in love with it after an article in some architecture magazine."

"You've got to be kidding me..." she muttered, reaching for the door handle before the limousine even came to a stop.

"Evan." I lunged for her hand, but it was too late, she'd shoved the door open, making D brake hard, coming to a stop with a curse just in front of the garage.

"Jesus, E!" Deviouz barked.

He was the only one who'd dare talk to her like that, the only one she'd let. I scooted my ass across the seat, chasing her through her open door. One glance behind us and I caught sight of the dark Explorer as it pulled into the driveway and the gate closed behind it. Headlights blinded me for a second before the lights were dimmed and the four-wheel drive turned off the main driveway, disappearing around the back of the house to the guards' quarters.

D had already made himself at home, moving in a week ago to oversee the security upgrade that cost us a small fortune. But the look on her face was worth it.

CCTV cameras shifted above us as Evan raced toward the entrance of the house.

Concrete rose in front of us in a lopsided rectangle. Black steel shimmered and sparkled against the entrance lights.

"Bruno...*it's magnificent*," she whispered, and turned toward me. "I want to see it all...*every bit of it.*"

"You will," I assured her as I strode toward her, that burning hunger moving in. "Tomorrow."

She stilled as I lifted my hand and pressed the buttons, and unlocked the front door. "Tonight, you're otherwise engaged, Mrs. Bernardi."

She smiled at the name, a slow, seductive smile that wasn't one she'd worn before. She'd changed a lot since we came back from the island. Gone was the girl…here was the woman, a woman healing…a woman *changing*.

"My little phoenix," I whispered.

"What?" she smiled, confused, as I bent low and lifted her in her wedding dress into my arms. "What did you call me?"

I stepped up the wide concrete steps to the entrance of our home. *Our home.* It felt like forever that I'd dreamed of this moment, of sharing this with her. "My beautiful, entrancing, *powerful phoenix*."

She slid her hands around the back of my neck as the front door clicked open and I carried her through.

"I like that," she whispered, her gaze snapping into focus. "I *am* a phoenix."

"Damm right you are," I growled and strode toward the staircase.

My body warmed and my muscles flexed. Desire burned through me as I stared into her eyes and slowly climbed. "My goddamn gorgeous phoenix. I'm going to fuck you tonight, over and over and over again. I hope you're ready for that?"

A shiver passed through her body, quickening my stride.

She just smiled and bit her lip. "Yeah, I'm ready for that."

Fuck me…

I carried her up to the top floor and along the hall to the massive master bedroom that took up the entire space. "Lights," I commanded. "Dimmed."

Soft amber lights splashed against the black, coated glass. Outside, the stars sparkled in the night. But I didn't turn my head to look, all I saw was her. I strode toward the king-sized bed in the middle of the room and gently lowered her to her feet beside it. "Now, you were saying something about this zipper?"

Her chuckle did things to me I never knew could be done. My cock hardened as that hunger burned in the pit of my groin. She tipped her head to the side, the long line of her neck exposed.

I wound my arms around her, careful of her side, and pulled her back against me. My lips found her warmth, kissing that spot at the back of her ear that she fucking loved. She let out a moan and dropped her head against me, leading me to slide my hand up her body and cup her breast. "I'm gonna fuck you nice and slow...*at first,*" I whispered.

Her breath caught with the words before a moan slipped free. I dragged my hand upwards, cupping her neck. Her pulse spiked against my fingers. The panicked throb in her veins made me stiffen.

"Easy," I whispered. "It's just me here, just me..."

"Bruno." She fought the panic as I closed my hand gently around her throat and kissed her neck.

"Just me, Evan. Just me," I urged.

She battled her demons and fought that panic with all she had. Just like she was fighting that bitch on the island all over again. I kissed her neck, then slid my hand up under her jaw and turned her mouth toward me.

I could still feel the kick of the gun in my hand. Still see the bloom of blood as my shot found the target. Still see the fear in Evan's eyes.

"I'll never let anyone hurt you," I promised, gripping her jaw and kissing her hard.

And I wouldn't...not some crazy bitch with a vendetta, or some fucking assassin determined to take what was mine. I broke away, leaving her gasping and trying to catch her breath as I reached around her, finding the zipper. "No walls between us," I murmured. "When you're here, in our bedroom, I want you to trust me. Can you do that? Can you...let yourself go?"

I slid the zipper down and let her wedding dress fall into a heap on the floor. My breath caught in my chest at the sight of the cream-colored sheer bra she wore, her dusky pink nipples puckered against the fabric. "Jesus fucking Christ, Evan."

"Yes," she answered, and lifted her hand. "I can do that."

I lowered my head, taking her tight, little nub into my mouth and sucked through the fabric. A moan rumbled in the back of her throat, the sound driving all the way to my cock. Fuck, I wanted that sound from her, *craved that sound from her*. I lifted her, letting her wind her legs around my waist as I lifted my knee onto the side of the bed and laid her gently down in the middle.

I pulled her heels free as she rose up onto her elbows, watching me as I worked the buttons of my jacket and tossed it to the side. My tie was next, then my vest as I kicked off my shoes and slid my shirt over my head. She reached around for the clasp of her bra.

"No," I commanded. "That's my job now. Only I get to undress you like this. I get to reveal every goddamn, delicious inch of you."

We'd danced around the act, touching, kissing. I'd brought her to orgasm with my mouth. But I wanted to wait for this...for it to *mean something*. And as I unbuttoned my pants and pushed them to the floor, I knew we'd made the right decision.

Her gaze traveled down my body. I surge of pride ignited more heat inside me. I slowed my movements, letting her savor the moment, because I would. "Like what you see?"

She jerked her gaze to mine as I lowered my pants and boxers, letting them crumple at my feet. "Very much so."

I stepped forward, climbed onto the bed, and prowled toward her. She flinched at my touch as I grasped the back of her ankle and kissed the inside of her leg. But it was okay, soon my hands and lips and cock wouldn't feel so alien to her. Soon, one brush of my lips and she'd melt in my arms. The mighty Evan Valachi would purr like a kitten when I touched her and that's just how I wanted it to be.

I worked my way along the inside of her ankle, then slowly up along her leg with feathered kisses that made her tremble.

"Bruno." She reached for me, but I pulled away.

"Not yet," I insisted, slowing against the inside of her thigh. "Relax, let me take care of you."

She had a lot to learn about me...one very important rule I had. *I ruled the bedroom.* I reached up and grabbed the sides of her panties, sliding them down her thighs. "Not until I tell you to." She looked at me with those big doe eyes, and leaned back down.

"Good girl," I murmured.

Her breath caught and her lips parted. "W-what did you just say?"

"I said...*good girl.*"

Excitement widened her eyes as I dragged her panties down and cast them aside. "You want to be my good girl, don't you?"

"Yes," she whispered breathlessly.

"Because you know what happens to good girls." I pushed her thighs apart and looked down at her perfect fucking slit. "They get rewarded."

I lowered my head and pushed my tongue into the top of her cunt, driving in deeper to find that part of her that made her buck and moan. She did, unable to help herself. Her fingers slid through my hair as I pushed my arms under her thighs and shifted her on the bed, tilting her hips to meet my mouth.

"Oh, Jesus..." she moaned. "Bruno, I'm going to...

"No, you're not," I commanded. "You will not come until I tell you to. Do you hear me?" I growled, sliding my tongue deeper, finding the center of her. She was slick and ready. Christ, she was ready...*and I was done waiting.*

I pulled away and rose up on the bed over her. She opened her eyes and looked up at me. Against the fan of her beautiful brown hair, she looked like a goddamn angel. *My angel.* "You ready for this?" I shifted my body, my knees sliding between her thighs.

"Yes," she whispered as pain moved through her eyes and she looked away. "Even if I can't have children..."

"Hey." I cupped her chin and forced her gaze to mine. "We don't know that for sure...your body will do whatever it needs to do. Until then..." I surged upwards, pressing my cock against her core. "Your body is mine, just like it was mine on that island."

Her eyes shone with knowing, a secret for us. She gripped my waist, her gaze pinned by mine as I pushed harder, sliding the tip inside.

One thrust and I pushed deeper, driving all the way.

There was a flare of agony across her gaze before the stony stare of determination moved in.

I drew out slowly, easing her this time, turning the pain into fire that moved between us. So slow...so fucking slow, I worked my cock inside her. She lifted her knees, her body moving under mine. She was all I'd dreamed of. *All I wanted.*

Just this...she let out a guttural sound and slid her hands over my ass, cupping tight as I thrust.

"This," I groaned. "Is mine...you got me?"

She dropped her head to the side and closed her eyes. Her lips parted, her breaths hard and fast. A tiny crease carved down her forehead. I reached up, grasped her neck gently, and fucked her harder, the thrusts brutal. "Mine..."

There was no holding back now. No hiding who we truly were... not to each other.

Her eyes opened, that almost detached stare filled with hunger as she curled her lips and bared her teeth. "Mine," she growled, and arched her back. "Mine..."

She came in a lather of sweat, bucking and moaning as I came hard and fast, filling her with my seed. She moaned, writhing under me, and finally stilled, watching as I rolled to the side of her body. My breaths were savage as we held each other's gaze. There were no words, just a knowing between us...this was how it was supposed to be.

It had been more brutal than I'd wanted...more fueled by need.

I pushed upwards, sliding the strap of her bra lower, then reached underneath, twisting the clasp to pull her bra free. Her chest rose and fell with panting breaths and for a second, I didn't see my wife...

I saw *her,* the woman with no name.

The woman with no past and no future.

The woman who'd whispered her dying words for a man who'd never hear them.

A man I was desperate to find.

I rolled over, making sure to take my weight on my hands, and lowered my head, kissing the top of her breast, before taking her nipple in my hand. In the corner of my eye, I caught the smear of blood on the inside of her thigh, shining bright as I pulled down, moving over her ribs and lower.

I took my time on the raised red scar on her side, and trailed my hands down her body. I was already growing harder, my balls tightening, my body humming with need. "On your knees, Evan," I directed. "I want to fuck my wife from behind."

I took her twice more that night, driving my body inside hers until she collapsed face down on the pillows and raised her hand in defeat. "Enough...can't take anymore. You win."

I just smiled at her, lowering myself to kiss her shoulder. "How easily you admit defeat. We're going to have to work on that, Mrs. Bernardi."

"Sure." She sucked in deep breaths. "Tomorrow."

I just chuckled and pulled back. "I need to run into the city for a minute. D's here, all you have to do is lift the handset beside your bed and dial nine. You okay with that?"

"You're leaving me along to do business on my damn wedding night?" she grumbled.

"I can stay if you want." I leaned closer. "I'm sure there's ways I can entertain myself." I slid my hand under her body and cupped her breast.

She moaned, but this time with annoyance, rolling to the side to slap my hand away. "Go," she ordered. "Bring back something chocolatey."

My grin grew wider as I pulled away. "Chocolatey it is."

FIFTY-TWO

Bruno

BRUNO

I GRIPPED THE STEERING WHEEL AND PUNCHED THE accelerator, hurtling along the dark, quiet road toward the city. I hated leaving Evan behind, especially tonight of all nights. But one glance toward my cell phone and I knew I had to.

Ten goddamn minutes before the wedding started and I was sent a text. Jannick was the last person I wanted to hear from on a day like today. I clenched my grip around the steering wheel. But the text was one I'd been waiting for.

I pushed the Suburban harder, the headlights carving through the dark on the lonely stretch of road before I turned off toward the city. Fear gripped me at the thought of leaving her alone. But D was there, patrolling the grounds, ready if she needed him.

By the time I'd left, she was fast asleep, her breaths deep and steady. There'd be no nightmares tonight. My body had made sure of that. Twenty minutes later, and I was turning off the freeway, heading home once more. One car was parked outside on the street, the sleek, black limousine as familiar as the license plate, *Valachi*.

There were no lights on in my family's home.

But I knew they were up anyway.

They were waiting for me.

I parked the Suburban and climbed out, locked the door behind me and headed for the rear entrance of the house. Shadows moved instantly, heading toward me.

"It's me," I muttered as a flashlight clicked on, the bright beam aimed in my eyes.

"Sorry," Emmaruth growled, and switched off the beam.

"They inside?" I checked.

"Yeah." The towering bodyguard stepped to the side. "They're waiting on you."

A nod, and I moved to the door, turned the handle, and pushed. The faint scent of cologne hit me, mingled with the stench of cigar. They'd been smoking...all of them, by the smell of it. Christ, I hoped Evan didn't smell it on me.

I clenched my jaw and made for the study, set off to the side and sunken at the rear of the house. As I neared and the voices of Michele Valachi and my father grew louder, a tremor of apprehension carved through me.

I pushed the door to the study open, watching each of them turn their heads toward me. My father was first, rising from behind the desk. "Bruno."

Evan's father was second, staying seated in the chair at the edge of the room. His piercing blue eyes were cold, cutting, dragging me back to the kid I was in that alley all those years ago, haunting me still to this day.

"Here he is." Cillian strode forward, a cigar still alight between his fingers.

"You wanted me here," I growled. "So I'm here."

"On your wedding night of all nights." The deep snarl came from the shadows, and that's where they should've stayed.

But they didn't. The guttural snarl spilled out into the light as the darkness gave birth to a beast.

Jannick was even bigger than the last time I'd seen him. Powerful muscles, arms that strained his shirt. He moved with the kind of grace that belonged in the animal kingdom. Fluid, *predatory*. Long limbs consumed the space between us as the eyes of a killer fixed on mine. "How was she?"

My lips curled into a sneer. "What the fuck did you say?"

"I said..." the sonofabitch had the nerve to fucking smile. "How is she?"

It was a test.

A fucking test and he knew it.

I'd been summoned here, just like I was nothing more than a kid.

I took a step forward, meeting my cousin eye to eye. "Watch your fucking mouth when you speak about her. Blood or no blood, you do not talk about my wife."

"Jannick," Cillian warned. "Show a little damn respect."

Still the shit-eating grin remained. "I am...trust me."

"You want to tell me what this is all about?" I held his stare. "Or are you going to piss me off a little more?"

"Yeah," Jannick answered, taking a breath.

The tension died in his eyes as he shifted his gaze around the room. "You want me to hunt, so I hunted."

Hunted...there wasn't a better term for what Jannick did. I hated to think about what he did in his free time.

"The woman was Sophie Harrison, that much we knew. But there wasn't a helluva lot to work with about her. Mom's remarried and removed from her life. She suffered a mental breakdown at the age of twelve and spent the next eight years in and out of mental institutions until she escaped the last one and never went back. But here's where it starts to get interesting. You see, I did a little digging on those who stayed in crazy town, and those who worked there. Led me to a guy named Barron Santiago. A male nurse who was in charge of her care." He pulled a Bowie knife from his waistband, twirling it on his palm like it was a damn quarter. "It was a false name. False credentials. False everything."

My breath caught in my chest. There was no movement in the room, not even a whisper.

"I didn't find him," Jannick said as he met my gaze. "But I found his fucking lair. I found not just him...but all his little fucking friends."

"The attack on the island...the attacks here in the US." My dad rounded the desk and headed toward me. "They're all connected, every single one of them, and it goes deep...deeper than we thought."

"All the way to the very top," Cillian murmured.

"But we don't give a fuck about that." Michele Valachi pushed up from his chair. "They tried to kill my daughter."

"Tried to kill my son," my father snarled.

"Who are they?" I took a step closer, my gaze riveted on Jannick. "I want names, details...I want fucking blood for what they did to her."

Jannick smiled, his lips sliding over his teeth as he took a step, stopping right in front of me. "I'll give it to you, too...let me be your fucking weapon and I'll bring them all to their knees... every...single...one...of...them."

"All the way to the top," I repeated.

My cousin was never going to be the heir.

He was always going to be the animal.

The beast which slipped its leash.

"All the way," he whispered.

"Then go..." I stepped to the side. "Bring them to me."

FIFTY-THREE

Evan

"This is new," Bruno murmured and fingered the long russet-colored strands of the wig I wore.

"Yes." I looked up at him. "Do you like it?"

His gaze bore into mine. The intensity made my breath catch. It's always the same with Bruno...intense, demanding...*compelling*. Especially when it comes to me.

"If you're wearing it, then I like it," he answered, his brows furrowed for a second. "But do you need it this time?"

This time...

I look past him to the boarded-up derelict warehouse and pull the coat tighter around me.

My pulse was already scattered, frantic, racing. I could almost smell it in there. The cold concrete choking. Panic fluttered inside me. "Yes." I met his stare once more. "I think it might help."

He gave me a slow nod. "Whatever you need, you know that." He reached up and brushed a strand of hair from my face. The sweet before the savage, right? Because once we walked through those doors, everything would change...like it always did.

I couldn't help but find the door now. Couldn't help but see the rusted chains on the locks and the boarded-up windows over smashed glass. That same terror clawed its way up my throat and clenched tight. I'm almost back there, to that day...that *fucking day*.

"We don't have to do this, you know," Bruno said quietly, but he knows the truth as well as I do.

We do...

It's therapy.

Our own special kind of therapy. I opened my eyes and he saw this, my desperation and need. Then he lowered his hand and gave a careful nod.

He leaned closer, but he didn't kiss me. Instead, he growled in my ear. "Pain and pleasure, right?"

The words make a lair of the flutter in my belly. I thought it was panic, but maybe it's him. Maybe it's always him. *God, I hope so.*

Because I'd rather by tormented by a desire for my husband than by that *bitch*. My hand went to my side, to the dull throb that still haunted me, all these months later. "Yes." I breathed. "Pain is pleasure."

Bruno's hand moved to mine, his fingers clasping tight. "Then let's get started."

He turned, pulling me gently toward the chained front door, only letting my hand go in order to work the single key he had in his pocket into the lock. Chains fell, hitting against the door frame with a *thud*. Then we're inside, in that stifling, dank darkness. It wasn't quite the same as the bunker where she held me prisoner... but it was close.

Close enough to resurrect the demons.

And banish them for a little while at least.

My husband bought it for demolition. But he kept it for me.

For this purpose alone.

The steel links gnashed as Bruno secured the door from the inside. I stood in the dark, staring into that black pit that waited for me, until Bruno flicked on the light from his cell, and I was bathed in the iridescent white.

I didn't move while he came closer and stood at my back. He didn't touch me, not yet. He knew what I needed.

"Get inside, Evan," he commanded.

There's no tremor in his voice, just a hardness. And as always, I couldn't move. I was frozen.

As always, he gave me a way out, making sure I knew who was really in charge here. "You know the word to say if you want out."

That cold, wet air was a rag down my throat.

"Evan?"

I couldn't think. Couldn't move.

"Evan." The concern in his voice snapped me out of the panic.

I flinched and jerked my gaze over my shoulder. "I know."

"You still want to do this?"

No...yes. I don't know. I didn't know which Hell was better. The nightmares that plagued me...or this. I winced, remembering the nightmares. The gripping, overwhelming terror where I woke screaming, feeling that blade as it plunged into my body once more. Not that...*not fucking that.*

"Yes," I whispered. "Yes, I want to do this."

"That's my phoenix," Bruno murmured, his voice growing darker, more intense...more controlling. He reached around and brushed the back of his curled fingers over the peak of my breast. I hardened with the sensation, unable to stop that charge tearing through my body all the way to my pussy. "Now get in-fucking-side, Evan."

I moved, triggered by that savagery in his tone, and took a step. My heels crunched on debris and shards of glass. The place was filthy and hollow, nothing more than concrete and steel. Half-finished and soulless, containing nothing more than my moans and my screams.

I dropped my hand and unbuttoned my coat. The frigid air reached in, finding its way between the buttons of my blouse. I made my way to the heart of this shell of a building. To where there's a room with a bed in the middle. One just for us. Bruno's steps were heavy behind me, drawing my focus to him.

"You're back there, aren't you?" he murmured behind me. "That day...that bunker. You opened your eyes. Tell me what you see, Evan."

"Her," I answered as that bitch raged inside my head. "I see her."

She looked like me...

That's the first thing I remembered. Her hair, her clothes. They were my clothes and my hair. They were all mine. In my head she took a step toward me, and it's only then I see the knife in her hand. The silver shine glistening.

She's going to cut me...

She's going to...

I unleashed a moan. The sound wounded and feral. But then Bruno's voice invaded. "I'm right here. You can feel me, right?" He took a step closer until his body pressed against mine. Heat pressed against my back. "You can feel I'm right here."

I nodded. "Yes."

"Good," he murmured and reached around.

He worked the buttons one by one until he pushed the opening apart. His hand moved to my breast. His big hands kneading, mauling. I'm not there, not yet. I'm still trapped in that Hell. Still seeing the shine of steel as the knife plunged inside me.

"So goddamn beautiful," Bruno murmured, sliding his fingers under the edge of my bra. "I want to fuck you all day, every goddamn day. Your body is mine. You understand me?"

He gave a soft pinch of my nipple, somehow still hard enough to make me flinch, but there was no pain. Just that same fierce flare that hit me between my thighs. He knew just where to go.

"Tell me you understand, Evan."

"I understand," I answered.

"Tell me what you see now. In that bunker where she stabbed you."

I closed my eyes again. The knife. The blood. "I'm falling." I can almost feel the thud as I hit the ground. "And she's leaving."

"To die." His words are brutal, and my heart lunged against my chest. But his fingers. Oh, God. His fingers, rolling, pulsing, grazing across the peak. Then he slipped lower down my stomach, staying away from the scar, and reached for the zipper of my slacks against my hip. "She left you to die, helpless, bleeding."

My slacks fell, landing at my feet with a *thump*. They were dirty now and ruined. But I didn't care. Bruno pressed harder, lowering his head to kiss the top of my shoulder. "You're bleeding out, watching her leave. Tell me what you feel, Evan."

His breath was warm on my skin; his fingers careful, sliding under the elastic of my panties as he reached for my clit.

"Talk to me, Evan," he growled out. "Keep talking to me."

My voice trembled, still I forced the words. "I see nothing. Nothing but emptiness and I just know that this is the end." Because here was the truth of the matter. Here was the core of my nightmares. If I was honest, it wasn't really about her. It was all about this moment, this desperation, and knowing I couldn't do a damn thing about it. My heart thundered now, just as it did then. And I can't help but feel that same nothingness reaching for me now, just like before.

Bruno slid his fingers all the way along my crease and pushed inside. I stiffened, dropping my hand to grasp his thigh. Still, he never stopped fucking me, sliding back out before he danced around my clit.

"Death," the murmur came against my ear. "That's what you see, isn't it?"

"Yes." Heat built inside me at the circling of his finger, making me shift against him, aching for more.

"Get on the bed, Evan," my husband demanded, his fingers slipping from my body.

I made my way to the bed in the middle of the room. Trembling fingers worked the buttons of my blouse and dropped it at the foot of the bed before I reached for the clasp of my bra. Then Bruno was there, sliding the straps from my shoulders, letting the garment drop. I stood there before him in nothing but my panties.

"So goddamn beautiful." He slid his hands down my body, catching the edges on my G-string. "So alive."

He kneeled, sinking to the filthy floor in his Armani slacks before he dragged my panties down with him. His lips were warm as they kissed my hips and the curve of my ass. I lifted my foot on instinct, stepping out of the panties until I was naked in front of him.

"Bend over the bed, Evan."

I did, hands splayed on the comforter as I sank into the plush warmth. It was beautiful, mink, white. Something so beautiful shouldn't be in a place like this. The idea of that hit me. Beauty, warmth, perfection mingled with the darkness and the dank stench.

"Talk to me," he urged. "Tell me what you're feeling."

"I feel helpless," I answered as the heat of his breath warmed my body.

"Helpless." He kept going, pushing inside my pussy. "So goddamn helpless."

I unleashed a moan at the sensation as he fucked me with his fingers. There was no hesitation with us anymore. Not like it was on our first night. He pushed his face in hard against my ass, licking and searching. "Fuck, you taste so good."

His breath. His words. The sensation of his fingers drove me deeper into that desire. I closed my eyes and pushed back against him.

"Good girl," he murmured. "So goddamn good."

The praise made me whimper. I fisted the comforter and rocked, driving myself toward that moment where desperation turned to desire. That moment where all I thought about was him. Where all I *felt* was him. His big fingers slid inside me, that warm tongue giving me exactly what I needed.

"Jesus..." I moaned. "Bruno, I'm going to..."

He slid his finger out, gave me one lick, and pulled away. "No, you're not. Because we're not anywhere near done, Evan."

I trembled as he rose from the filthy floor. The rattle of a buckle followed slide of leather. I stayed like that, bent over the bed, the sheets buckling in my grasp. I knew that this night was for me, that this was more about driving away the darkness than sex.

"Not anywhere near done, Phoenix." The warmth of his cock pressed against my ass.

Fuck. This is what I needed. Bruno was an ass man, and he claimed mine every opportunity he had. The head of his cock pushed against the hard ring of my ass. I exhaled slowly and forced all my attention to this feeling. To the push against me... the force of his hunger.

I unleashed a moan and dropped my head forward. "More... please, Bruno, more."

He slipped his cock along my crease, pushing into my pussy just enough to wet the head. I closed my eyes, unleashing a moan at the sensation of him stretching me before it slipped away, leaving me wanting. "Bruno."

"Yes, baby?"

I needed more. More desperation, more drive. I needed him to take from me. To take until there was nothing left. I ached to be empty. To feel nothing but his body taking what it wanted from mine. He thrust slower, pushing against the tight ring of muscle of my ass until that burn rose as he made me stretch.

"Breathe, Evan."

I loved it when he spoke to me like this, when he called my name and made his demands.

"Fuck me." He groaned, pushing the head of his cock inside before he pulled back out.

"Turn around and lay back."

I shifted, sliding my ass along the bed until I arched my back against the bed.

"Knees up, legs spread." He looked down at me, his dark eyes glittering in the murky gloom as he watched me slowly open.

I was vulnerable to him, exposed and trembling. He looked down at me, his gaze sliding down my body until it lingered between my thighs. "Touch yourself, spread yourself for me."

I reached down, my body quivering with a touch of my own hands as I cupped my pussy, slid two fingers on either side and opened.

"That's the way, baby." He leaned closer, watching me before he left a hand and dragged his finger along my slit, and pushed inside, working me until I moan.

Heat rushed through me and lingered in my belly, blending warmth with desire and anguish all in one. I shifted my ass on the bed, widening my legs, watching him as he stared down at me.

My breaths became heavy. That need to come moved closer and closer. "Bruno..."

"Let go for me, Evan," he urged.

And I did, letting that inferno unleash inside me until it was all I could think of, and all I could feel. I wanted to come, come so fucking hard.

Then, in an instant, he pulled away.

I lifted my head. "I'm not..."

He lowered his body, his hands pressed on the inside of my thighs, opening me as he leaned forward and licked. I closed my eyes, pressed my head back against the building and unleashed a moan. "Oh god. Oh god, Bruno."

Each lap of his tongue stoked the flames. In the wake of his fingers, the desire had ebbed. Now it rushed back to the surface, more desperate than it was before.

I thrust against his mouth, reaching down, sliding my fingers through his hair, pressing his head against me. "Harder, more. I need more."

He speared his tongue inside, curling the tip until he dragged along my crease and circled my clit. I cried out with the sensation, bucking my hips as he sucked that tiny nub. Electricity hummed, tearing through my body until all I could think about was being fucked. "I'm going to come... I'm going to—"

He pulled away again, lifting his head, his lips glistening with my desire.

"What the fuck are you doing?" I snarled, pushing his head back down, needing to ride his face.

He rose in front of me, gripped his cock, and aimed it at my entrance before thrusting in hard. The sensation was overwhelming. He rammed into me, punching his hips forward until the invasion was so brutal it was all I could feel.

"Do you want to come, baby? Then come."

The ebb and flow.

Ebb and flow.

Come, don't come.

Frustration and overwhelming need flooded me. It was cruel and beautiful all at the same time, a perfect torment balanced on the edge of a blade. I unleashed a moan, and that turned into a cry. I could feel the scream building in my chest, clawing its way up my throat until it ripped free.

The guttural sound bounced against the walls of this filthy warehouse. I clamped my mouth down, still in the sound.

"No." Bruno smiled. He was savage. A beast. Thrusting his hips as he fucked me with all of his strength. "Do you want to scream, baby? Then scream."

That sound came once more, tearing from me as I clawed his back, pulling him against me. "*Harder!*" I howled. "Bruno! For fuck's sake, fuck me harder!"

And he did, leaning over me, caging me in until the brutal thrusting of his hips bounced me against the bed.

My orgasm barrelled into me until I was a shuddering, weeping mess.

"That's it, baby." Bruno growled. "Scream it all out."

White sparks danced in the back of my eyes. The end came rushing over me, sweeping me away with an unmerciful roar. I trembled, shaking and shuddering. I couldn't feel my body, I couldn't feel my mind. There was nothing but him as I floated in nothingness.

Bruno grunted. He lowered his body, gripping hold of me, his breaths were heavy and hot against my ear. "I love you." He groaned and came in a rush.

FIFTY-FOUR

Bruno

"Evan?" I looked down.

She was curled against me. Knees drawn up, arms wrapped around her shins. The sight hit me like a sledgehammer to the chest. I swallowed, tried to calm myself. The last thing she needed was for me to unravel. "Baby, can you hear me?"

She let out a moan. The sound was wounded and low, straining something in my chest. I winced, knowing there was nothing I could do to help her. I wanted to hold her, wanted to kiss her, wanted to feel something else but like a bastard.

What we did on these nights wasn't just sex. It was savage and raw. It was a damn battle against the demons that plagued her. I'd fulfil any role she needed: husband, protector, hitman as well. It didn't matter. *Whatever she needed.*

When I composed myself, I reached out, wanting to touch her. But I didn't, just clenched my fingers and pulled away. I know I can't reach her right now. She was all the way in the dark now, trying her best to crawl back to me.

I needed her back.

Because I can't go through this world alone.

I rolled over and climbed from the bed, then gathered my clothes from the ground where I left them. The air was pungent and heavy. Cold concrete over the scent of sex and hunger. My hunger. I know that I'm too much for her. But I can't help myself. She's all I think about. All I want, every second of every day.

I want her smiling. I want her free. Most of all, I want her safe. I pulled on my clothes and gathered my things before I started the slow process of dressing her. "Evan, baby. I'm going to get you home, okay?"

She's unresponsive, and I do the best that I can; talking to her as I slide her G-string over her feet and along her legs, working the garment back into place, before I start with her slacks. Her bra was next, and I couldn't help but linger at the warmth of her body. I leaned down, closed my eyes, and dragged in the scent of her before lightly pressing my lips to her shoulder.

Her eyes were closed, but I knew she wasn't asleep. Because when you're sleeping you're not gripped in panic. And Evan was panicked. Her chest rose and fell with shallow breaths. Her pulse a flutter under my touch as I gripped her wrist and fed her limbs through the arms of the blouse.

"It's okay if you can't come back." I try to keep talking to her. "It's okay if you need to stay there. I get it. Believe me, I do. But there must be a better way to get through this, baby. There had to be a better way to get past what happened on that goddamn island."

I worked the buttons of her top with shaking fingers, then rose. I didn't pull on her coat or slide on her heels. She doesn't need them, not when I'm here. Still, I grab them and slide one hand under her knees before I lift her from the bed, leaving the sweat-stained sheets behind. I'd return later, strip the bed, and take the soaked bedding to the cleaner until next time.

The fact that there was a next time made me sick to my stomach. I didn't know what else to do. And I tried everything. But tonight was the worst it'd ever been. The nightmares that plagued her since the island had been slowly growing worse, growing in intensity.

She'd been in and out of so many damn psychologists' offices, I'd lost count. Five of them in the space of a month for her to spiral back here...

Me fucking her, blending pleasure with her own personal version of Hell.

The police listed her abduction and the attempt on her life because of the powerful connections her father had. But those on the Commission knew the truth, and the real events that happened on the island.

"Sleep, baby." I cradled her against me and carried her out of the warehouse to the car. "I've got you."

I hit the button, starting the engine as I strode toward the car and yanked open the door, sliding her into the passenger's seat. She shivered and drew her knees up to her body, shifting so her back faced me. I reached out and adjusted the heat for her, then I closed the door and headed back to the warehouse. I locked and chained the warehouse door as the night she first came to me resurfaced in my mind. It'd been three weeks since I closed the deal on this place. I'd already made plans to tear the place down. But she asked me to stop them. She said she had better use for the place. A way to help her fight back against the darkness.

Christ, that was six months ago. I didn't want to think about how many times we'd done this.

Six months of fucking her in the filth and the dark.

Anyone else would think we were fucking crazy.

Fuck what they thought.

All I cared about was her.

She was just a shadow when I turned and made for the driver's side, yanked open the door, and slid behind the wheel. I found her as I shoved the four-wheel drive into gear and backed out. But she never opened her eyes. She was asleep, or close to it. Spent; body, mind, and soul. She'd sleep all night now. And tomorrow…

Tomorrow I prayed she'd be better. Happier. Filled with hope instead of torment.

Until next time.

I drove her home, slowing to pull into the driveway, until the sensor triggered the gate to open. Movement came from the dark. I glanced to one of Devious' men as he patrolled the grounds and gave a wave, pulling the four-wheel drive around the back of the house and climbed out.

Her breaths had slowed by the time I killed the engine. I climbed out, rounded the front of the car, and pulled her into my arms to get her into the house. My steps hit heavy as I carried her through the house and upstairs to our bedroom. Still, she looked so goddamn perfect as I yanked back the sheets of our bed and laid her down.

"You can sleep now," I murmured and worked on removing her clothes. "I'm right here. No one is going to get to you."

I removed her blouse, her slacks, then her bra and soiled panties, leaving her naked under the sheets until I tugged the comforter high. She reached out and grasped my fingers before I pulled away. "Bruno."

"Yeah?"

"Thank you for taking care of me."

My heart throbbed, aching with the words. "Always, baby. Always."

"I love you." She slid her hand away and rolled over.

"I love you too," I answered, but her breathing was already deepening as she slid back into sleep.

I stood there, watching her for a moment before I worked the buttons of my shirt, kicked off my shoes, and made for the bathroom.

The shower filled the room with steam. I didn't need to leave the door cracked open. I know she'll sleep, and I pray that in the morning, she's better. Heat stung as I stepped into the spray and braced my hands on the wall. That ache in my body lingered, stopping my hands from drawing her close to the edge before leaving her to slide away.

It's a good ache.

A powerful ache.

I could still feel the moment I slid into her. Still see the desperation in her eyes...when all she saw was me.

All she felt was me.

My body.

My love.

I washed and dried my body, then tugged on boxers before I made my way to bed. She never moved when I climbed in. I watched her, desperate to pull her into my arms. But she needed sleep more than she needed me to touch her. So, I slid my hand under my head and watched her, my mind shifting to tomorrow.

Tomorrow I'll kill her demons...one by one.

"MORNING."

I cracked open my eyes to find her close to me. Her perfect blue eyes were fixed on mine. *She's back, thank fucking God.* I gave a weak smile. "Morning," I said, and exhaled with relief. I took in every second of this. Her. Me. *Us.* I steeled myself and tried to keep concern from my tone. "Are you heading into the office today?"

She gave a nod. "For a while. I need to do some bookwork, anyway. Catch up on all of the interstate runs that we have coming up for the next few months. There's a lot of shipments to move. My father thinks we might be able to push into new territory. You?"

What? Michele never spoke to me about any new goddamn territory.

I licked my lips. "Pushing into unfamiliar territory is dangerous." I can't help my gut clenching. I didn't want her involved in anything that could bring any more attention to her, especially now.

Her smile widened. "Bruno, everything we do is dangerous." She rolled, leaving the comforter and sheet to slide away, giving me a glimpse of her breasts.

I let out a soft snarl. "You can always stay in bed with me. I could make it worth your while." The scent of her made my cock harden.

But she gave me a chuckle, sliding out of reach. "I thought you were busy today?"

I was busy...hunting down the men who came to kill us. "Never too busy for you." I lunged playfully, grabbing hold of her as she slid from the bed.

The crack of laughter she gave made everything worthwhile. She stumbled backward, then turned and headed for the bathroom. "You're just insatiable, aren't you?"

I flopped back down against the pillow, smiling. "You have no idea."

I listened to her hum under the hiss of the shower and tried to swallow the pissed off flare of anger as my cell gave a *beep*.

Deviouz: It's all ready to go.

I WINCED and punched out a reply.

Me: Did you know Michele wants Evan in the office today?

I WAITED...

> D: *No. The plan was*

I DIDN'T NEED to wait for an explanation.

> Me: *He fucked us.*
> Me: *There's no way I'm having this go down without her under guard at the house.*
> D: *It's too late for that. Far too late. Talk when you get in.*

THERE WAS NO ANSWER. I'd already said too much over text. But there was no way out of this. Michele Valachi fucked us. "Asshole," I muttered.

"You say something?"

I jerked my head up at the sound of her voice. I forced a smile, watching her step out of the bathroom and towel dry her hair. "Nothing. Just wish you'd say at home today."

She stilled, lowered her hands. "Why?"

I just gave a shrug. *Because shit is going down and I need you... safe.* I wanted to say the words, but I couldn't. I couldn't tell her how dangerous today really was...I just couldn't. "I thought we might make plans. Maybe even take off tonight. I can have the jet on standby, go anywhere you want. Jamaica, Belize...hell, Paris for that matter."

"Oh?" One brow rose. "Paris...that sounds...*nice*."

There was a smile on her lips, an actual smile and after the haunted look in her eyes last night it looked almost like the sun had come out across her face. I shoved upward. I wanted that sun to stay, to feel the warmth and let it dance across my skin, for just a little while longer. "Then, Paris it is."

"I thought you were busy today," she said carefully. "You've been cagey, weird."

I winced at the words. She didn't seem to notice. I prayed like Hell she didn't notice. "I am." I rose from the bed and padded around to her as she stood in the doorway of the bathroom. "But as soon as today is over, I'm all yours."

"All mine," she repeated, her smile growing wider as I pulled her into my arms. "I like the sounds of that."

I grinned. "I figured you would."

Beep.

I winced and internally cursed the sound of the interruption and, just like that— the spell was broken. Evan's smile faltered, and she took a step backward, glancing across the bed to the dresser where my cell gave a *beep* again. "You'd better get that."

And if it was any other day, I would've ignored the damn calls. But I couldn't...*not today*.

"Paris." I started stepping away and turned toward the gating sound.

"Maybe."

I winced and hurried, snatching my mobile from the dresser. I glanced at the caller ID. *Fuck. Of all damn people.* I hit the button before answering. "Yeah?"

I turned, shielding the screen from Evan, but I didn't need to. She just glanced my way with a look of disappointment, and then she stepped into the bathroom and closed the door.

"What?" I said a little louder.

"What's the hold up?" Jannick snapped. "I didn't come all this way and do the things I did to stand here with my dick in my goddamn hands, Bruno. So quit blue-balling me and give the fucking command."

Give the command.

Do it.

That's what he wanted to hear. It's what he *deserved* to hear. Six months ago, I unleashed a hunter. Now I had him tethered and bound, right before his chance to kill. "I'm coming in."

"Then get your fucking cock out of Valachi pussy, and get your goddamn ass in the goddamn car."

I winced, opened my mouth to snap right back, but the call was over...and the line was dead.

By the time I opened the door to the bathroom Evan was done with her hair and makeup. She gave me a hint of a smile as she pushed past and stepped through the door.

"Evan," I called.

Bur she was gone, moving into the walk-in closet. There was nothing I could do but get today over with and move on with the rest of our lives. I showered and dried. Evan was gone by the time

I stepped out. I glanced out of the bedroom window as I fitted my holster over my chest and slipped on my jacket.

Ten minutes later I was headed for the city. I reached out, pressed the button on my cell, and Jannick answered on the third ring. "Yeah?"

Only two words were needed. "Take them."

FIFTY-FIVE

Evan

Something didn't feel right. I sat behind the desk in my father's study, trying to focus on the list of interstate runs in front of me. The map was flat out on the desk at my right, pinned with all the markers that corresponded with the list of trucks and inventory numbers on the screen. But I couldn't focus on them. The numbers blurred, the details were just not sinking in.

As hard as I tried, I couldn't concentrate, and I *had* to. There were a lot of runs happening next month. A lot of escorts needed for not two borders, but five. We were moving everything from guns, drugs, to fucking diamonds cut straight out of a mine in South Africa. Their value made me sweat just thinking about it.

There were a lot of wealthy men who required a lot of dangerous goods and my father was desperate to corner the market. But the pinpricks that race along my arms had nothing to do with money and everything to do with that panicked feeling in my stomach. One that wouldn't go away.

I lifted my gaze to James, who stood in the corner of the office glancing out of the window. "You need to hover so damn close? What's going on with you today?"

It wasn't just the breathing down my damn neck, either. It was the twenty-minutes added to the goddamn trip into the city this morning that were supposedly due to "precautions."

Precautions, my ass. The guy was starting to freak me out.

First Bruno was not happy about me coming into the office and now this.

"Nothing." James answered. "Just doing my job."

I gave him the wave of my hand. "Can you at least do your job in the next room?"

He never moved, just gave a shrug. "Don't tell me you're sick of my face already." He gave a chuckle.

Sick of his face? I barely saw him. He was a master at blending into the background, even with a six-foot-four muscled frame. I didn't see him really, just knew he was *there*. Until today.

Today he bugged me, drawing my focus to the bulge of his gun under his jacket and my own husband's cagey questions. There was something going on. Something Bruno wasn't telling me. I glanced at my cell and picked it up, punching out a message:

Me: Hey, what's going on?

I HIT send and waited for a reply. It was never long before Bruno texted me back. It didn't matter what he was doing, he always made time for me. I sat my cell back down and tried to narrow in on the details in front of me, making sure we paid who needed to be paid. It all came down to money and connections, and my father knew them all. Over three hundred thousand had been spent greasing palms and aligning times to get the guys across the border. We had each shipment tracked down to the minute.

And it all needed to go smoothly.

Still, I couldn't help but glance at my silent cell. I picked it up, checked the signal, and made sure it was working. There was no reply, not for me at least. James turned, grabbed his own from his pocket, and glanced at the screen. It was lit with a message on the screen. Was it Bruno?

Jealousy flared deep inside me.

I couldn't *not* be drawn to the way James slipped his phone back into his pocket and turned, glancing at me before focusing on something else.

The fact he was in here at all said how much trust we were putting in the bodyguard. No one other than family was privy to the details of Valachi business…and here he was. Former Navy SEAL who stood there watching me from the corner of his eye. I glanced at the outline of his cell under his jacket and fought the need to ask him who was messaging him.

You're being paranoid…

The voice rose inside my head. But was I? I'd learned the hard way a little suspicion was a good thing. The wound at my side gave a twinge, reminding me why. I'd ignored that nagging voice inside my head once before, and I almost paid for it with my life.

I wasn't about to make the same mistake again. A grating feeling grew into my heart when I looked at my silent cell. I wasn't a nagging wife, wasn't clingy, but Bruno was turning me into someone I wasn't. I snatched my cell from the desk and rose. "I'm taking a break."

"Good," James muttered. "I could do with a walk myself."

I shot him a glare. "Unless you plan on accompanying me into the bathroom, you can take a walk somewhere else."

He scowled for a second, and I could see he actually thought about it. Anger flared, burning inside. *Just try it.* I inhaled hard and turned, leaving him behind. Bruno's lack of messaging was starting to get to me. This wasn't like him. Not like him at all.

I strode out of the office at the back of the building and made for the private area. It was dark, all shadows and sullen lights. The place was black leather and chrome; it was a man's place designed for seedy deals and hookers. It wasn't what I wanted. But this was my father's game...for now.

Things would change when I took over.

And I *was* taking over. With or without a damn Bernardi at my side.

I made for the ladies bathroom and stepped inside, locking the door behind me. Unable to wait any longer, I punched out a text to Deviouz.

Me: Hey, is Bruno with you?

I WAITED A SECOND LATER.

D: *Yeah.*

YEAH?

That yeah didn't ring true. I pulled up the map loaded on my cell and checked D's location. He was west. Way out west. Then I shifted, checking the tracking on Bruno. He wasn't with him. His cell wasn't, at least.

So, either Bruno was without his cell...or his bodyguard was lying.

Me: *Okay, just checking.*

I DECIDED to message Bruno again, this time under the guise of dinner plans as to not appear as the needy wife.

Me: *Thai for dinner?*

A SECOND WAS ALL it took for the bubble and those three tiny dots to appear. *Thank God.* Relief washed through me as I waited for his reply...and waited...and waited. Then the dots stopped flashing...and the bubble disappeared.

What the Hell?

I swallowed my anger until it was an ache. "Just answer. Give me anything...anything to signal you're okay."

But he never responded, and in the quiet, that nagging voice came out to play. *It's you...you're too much. Last night...last night pushed him over the edge.* I winced as flashes of what we did last night returned. *That's it baby, that's it, scream it out. Scream it all out.*

"Oh, God." I braced my hands on the sink and dropped my head. "It was too much, too dark...too *everything*."

I pushed him away. I'd *been* pushing him away, forcing him to do things he didn't want to—*for me*.

"No," I moaned out, shaking my head. "I did this...I did this...I—"

He was having an affair.

I clenched my eyes closed. He was seeing someone else, at least. It was the only thing that made sense. The only reason he'd avoid me, the only reason Deviouz would lie for him. Because the bodyguard did lie...

It was another woman.

It had to be.

It was the only thing Bruno would ever hide from me.

The only thing that made sense.

Agony carved through my chest. I shuddered, buckled, and hit the floor. "No...no...*no*." Not Bruno. I couldn't lose Bruno. I couldn't...*lose...the only thing I had left.*

Cold from the tiles bled through my slacks. I curled my knees up, the act just like I'd done before—*just like last night*—but there were no tears, just an emptiness. A cruel bitterness that swallowed me whole.

A soft knock came on the door. "Evan?" James called.

He was checking on me, making sure I was still here. Making sure I didn't ruin whatever Bruno had planned.

"Mrs. Bernardi?"

I winced at the name as pain crushed my chest. "Mrs. Bernardi," I repeated. Was I? Was I, really? I lifted my hand and stared at the simple gold band etched with diamonds. I wore the ring, but I was losing the man.

I was losing Bruno.

"I'm here." My words were hollow and strange when I answered. "I'm here."

"Okay," The bodyguard on the other side of the door answered. I guess he didn't know what else to say. There was nothing to say. That bitch...*that fucking bitch finally won.*

I stayed like that, sitting on the ground with my knees against my chest until I couldn't stand the sight of that bathroom wall any longer. Then I rose, smoothed down my blouse and swallowed my pain.

Bruno wanted me to stay home today. He said so last week, making sure I was resting and getting plenty of sleep. If he wanted me at home, then that's where I needed to be...at home.

I yanked open the bathroom door, drawing James's focus from the end of the hall. "Take me home," I demanded.

"Already? Didn't you want to—"

I didn't wait for him to finish, just turned down the hall and headed out of the building to my car. By the time I yanked open the rear door, he'd followed me out, reaching for the handle just as I yanked it closed out of his reach.

They all worked for him.

All worked for Bruno or my father.

No one was loyal to me.

Not me alone.

I tugged the seatbelt closed and wrapped my arms around myself as James climbed in behind the wheel. "Cold?" he asked.

I met his gaze in the rear-view mirror. "Does it matter?"

He scowled for a second, then adjusted the temperature of the car and backed out of the garage before heading out. Security gates of my family's compound opened then closed. I sat back, losing myself in my head. No matter how hard I tried, I couldn't tear myself away from the anguish in Bruno's eyes last night, and that growing fear he betrayed me rose like a storm in my head.

By the time we turned into the drive away of my home, all I could feel was the darkness, and all I could hear was the thunder. He was leaving me...*no, he couldn't*. He needed my name, needed my business. So, he was just going to ignore my calls when he was with someone else? Was that it?

Was that it?

James pulled the vehicle into the garage at the back of the house. I was already climbing out before he killed the engine. He knew better than to follow me inside the house. That was my only boundary. No protection inside, unless in an emergency.

This might be an emergency for me...

But not for them.

I left him behind, all but running for the rear door of my house. A house that Bruno bought me. A house where we were supposed to be happy...but what now?

I waited...

And steeled myself for the end of my life as I knew it.

FIFTY-SIX

Bruno

"Don't tell me you're going home already?" Deviouz strode toward me from deeper in the warehouse, moving out of the shadows like wrath himself.

"I have to." I sucked in a hard breath, answering. "Evan will be done by now, and I want to make sure I'm home before dark."

D glanced at his gold watch, staring at the time while all I saw were the flecks of blood on the wristband as he muttered. "Then you better get going."

Evan...

Shit.

I winced as fear punched through me. I forget about the text messages...

I grabbed my cell with shaking fingers.

"She doesn't know, right?" I jerked a glare at him.

My bodyguard just shook his head. "Not a damn thing." There was blood on his face and his hands were a goddamn mess.

I gave a jerk of my head. "You might want to get that cleaned up before you go anywhere."

Deviouz glanced at his fingers, clenching them into a fist. "Who said I was going anywhere?"

An icy shiver of fear moved through me. I was already breathless, shaking and trembling from what we're done. Adrenaline was a goddamn bitch, but Christ, this felt almost righteous. "We're really doing this, aren't we?"

"Yes, we're really doing this," D answered.

This was an end to the darkness and the monstrous events that haunted us from the island. This was the only thing I could do to protect the only one that mattered to me...Evan. I'd go to the ends of the earth to make sure she was safe, killing her nightmares one after another.

There were four men at the back of our building. For men bound, beaten, and bloody. Four men who begged for their lives, promising anything in return. Money. Power. As if they had anything we wanted...maybe they had something...their goddamn lives.

Believe me, I was going to take those, too. Snuff them out one by one. Right after they confessed.

I needed that confession. I wanted to hear from their lying, cheating, filthy goddamn mouths what they did and why. They'd tell us the truth—I glanced at the blood on Deviouz's hands—*eventually*.

I slid my thumb across the screen and punched out a message in reply to the ones she'd sent me hours ago.

Me: Sorry baby, got caught up. I'm on my way.

I MET my bodyguard's stare. No words were needed. He'd keep going after I was done, I was sure of that. There was just as much rage in him then there was in me. We wanted to know the depth of how deep this shit ran for them. We wanted to understand, no...*I* needed to understand because then I could hate.

And fuck me, I did hate.

I hated them for what they did to us.

I hated for what they did to *her*.

I could still see Evan's haunted eyes, still hear her tormented screams, and feel the trembling of her body, night after night, when she woke, terrified for her life.

We all carried scars. None more than Deviouz, who almost didn't make it. Six gunshots and a knife to the side almost took the man down. How the man was still standing in front of me was a miracle. A savage, ruthless miracle. And I was thankful for every goddamn second I had with him.

"Go." He gave a jerk of his head. "I'll take care of everything here."

"You'll call if anything changes?"

He gave a low, threatening chuckle, then turned, giving me his back. "No. Now go be with your goddamn wife."

Asshole...

I hurried from the warehouse, nodding at Oliver and Paul as they stood sentry. We had the entire place on lockdown. But it wouldn't be forever. By tomorrow, this would all be over. I pressed the button and climbed into the Explorer, staring at the dark satin on my hands. I wiped them on my slacks before shoving the four-wheel drive into gear.

Deviouz wanted to drive, especially after today. But I needed him here...working.

I backed out of the parking space, glancing at Jannick's black Mercedes before I turned my focus toward home. What the hell would I tell her? *Hey, by the way, we abducted and tortured the men who funded the attack on the island today...how was your day?*

I winced, concentrated on the road as I drove out of the city and headed for the quiet back road that'd take me home. By the time I got home it was almost dark. I pulled in, waited for the gate, and then pulled around the rear of the house, parking next to the Range Rover.

An icy northern wind picked up as I climbed out and glanced at Evan's car before making my way to the house. The torchlight clicked on as I neared. I flinched and jerked my gaze to James as he stepped out.

"Mr. Bernardi."

"James," I answered. "She inside?"

"Yeah."

But the way he said it sent a flare of concern ripped through me. Was she sick? Was she...*bad?* I lengthened my stride and pushed through the rear door and into the house. But there were no lights on, no dinner cooking, no sounds at all. "Evan?"

And no answer...

I climbed the stairs, making my way up to the bedroom. "Evan?" My voice echoed in the silence. That cold wind plunged deeper, chilling me to the bone as I stepped inside the bedroom. But the place was in darkness...

I craned my head, listening.

"I texted you today."

My heart hammered, making me jump at the sound of her voice. "Jesus Christ, E." I barked, inhaling hard. "You scared the shit out of me." I searched for her, finding a silhouette in the darkness. "What the hell are you doing in the dark?"

"Where have you been, Bruno?"

The way she spoke made me cautious. I caught the faint gloom against her body. "I'm sorry I didn't get back to you."

She stepped toward me. "Where have you been?"

Panicked, I gave her a half truth. But even that was dangerous. "Jannick...we had a meeting."

She inhaled sharply at the sound of his name. "Jannik knows where you were?"

It was dangerous saying his name. For the both of us. Her father had matched her with my cousin, forced her to court him until the fucking bastard raped her...right in front of me. I hated him for that moment. I wanted to kill him for that moment…I would if he wasn't fucking blood. And a goddamn savage.

Jannick was merciless. The kind of beast you unleashed on your enemies and for the past six months, I'd done just that, and led us here today.

"Yes, baby. He knew where I was today."

"When you were with another woman?"

What? Her words were a punch in the gut. "Another woman?" I took a step closer, pulling her into my arms, but she was rigid and unforgiving. "Why the hell would you think I was with another woman?"

"Then where were you?" She tilted her head up to me. There was fear in her voice, real fear, and I was the cause of it.

"Evan…"

"Where were you!" she screamed and shoved away, stumbling backward. "You don't answer my questions. You don't text me back, and I know damn well Deviouz was lying when he said you were with him. You're keeping secrets from me, Bruno, and that was the *one* thing we swore we'd never do. I know something is going on, and I know you're lying because of it. So, I'm going to ask you one last time and, I swear to God, you'd better tell me the truth. Where were you?"

My senses were screaming, caught between the pain I'd caused her with the truth and the demons of her past. If I could just get her to wait. "The meeting…" I started.

She just turned and left with barely more than a sound. The light flicked on inside the walk-in closet, flooding the bedroom. The thud of something hitting the floor drew me closer. "Evan...*Evan*, what the fuck are you doing?"

Her hands shook as she shoved clothes into an open overnight bag. "What the hell do you think I'm doing, Bruno? I'm leaving."

"Leaving?"

Fear drove me forward until I grabbed her. "No, no, this isn't happening. Baby, please."

She wrenched out of my hold. "Don't. Don't bother to try to evade the truth, Bruno. I'm done."

"Done?" I shook my head, unable to understand what was happening.

Tears glistened in her eyes and rolled down her cheeks as she yanked a jacket from a hanger and turned for the door. I couldn't stop myself from stepping in her way. "No. No, you're not going anywhere."

She lashed out, punching my shoulder. "Get the fuck out of my way, Bruno!"

I couldn't do it. Couldn't just stand aside and let her leave. I wasn't that kind of man. I looked down as I grasped her arms, still seeing the dried blood. "Don't..."

"*Don't what?*" she screamed. "Don't leave? Don't lie? Don't hold things back from me? Tell me what do you want from me, Bruno? *What do you goddamn want!*"

You...

That's all I wanted to say. I want you. "I'm not having an affair, Evan."

Her lips curled back from her teeth, her eyes were wide and wild. Still, I'd never seen anyone more beautiful. "I keep nothing from you, Bruno. I give you everything. My nightmares, my love, my goddamn honesty, and you give me secrets and lies. I told you once before I can't live like that. I *refuse* to live like that. So, I'm asking you to move out of the doorway, don't make this any harder than it already is."

"We found them…" The words slipped free before I knew. And the ugly truth was there.

She flinched, her brows pinching as she gripped her overnight bag with one hand and her jacket with the other. "You found them?"

I nodded. "Yes, baby. We found them."

Her chest rose hard, and then fell. "The men you've been hunting?"

"Yes."

A look of torture cut across her face. "When?"

"Three months ago, and we've been gathering evidence every day. We needed to make sure before we"—I licked my lips—"Before we made contact."

"Made contact," she whispered, repeating the words.

I gave a slow nod, watching as it hit home. She knew we were after the men who helped orchestrate the attack on the island, but that was all. She didn't know who…or why. She didn't know anything until now.

"Today…" she whispered. "Today you made contact?"

I swallowed hard and brushed her arm, then winced as I looked at my hand. I pulled away, curling my fingers, and she knew. God help me, she knew. She grabbed my hand and stared at my fingers. Anyone who was in our line of work knew what it was. We'd seen more than our fair share.

I expected her to break down. I expected her to lock herself in this walk-in closet. Fuck, I would if I were her. She'd been through more than any one person should.

She lifted her gaze to mine, and those blue eyes that reminded me so much of her father glinted like ice. "Take me to them."

"What?" I hissed. "No, Evan."

Those lips curled tighter as she took a step closer and growled. "Take. Me. To. Them."

In this moment, she wasn't my wife. She was Evan Valachi, the daughter of Michele Valachi, heiress to the Valachi family. She was dangerous; she was deadly in this moment, a force to be reckoned and someone you didn't want in your way.

I fell in love with her power and her strength and, for my own selfish reasons, I used it to my advantage. Now I stood before as a husband...and an equal. She demanded no less. She *deserved* no less. I gave a nod. "Okay, if that's what you want. I'll take you."

I expected her to drop the bag, leaving her things where they should be—in our home.

But she didn't. When I stepped out of the doorway, she carried them with her.

"Aren't you going to leave your clothes here?" I followed her into the bedroom.

"Why?"

"I'm doing what you asked, taking you where you want to go."

She spun on me and closed the distance. "Oh, don't you worry. I'm still leaving, Bruno. I'm going to take some time to think about this night. Because you didn't just lie, you treated me like a fucking idiot. I sat in my father's office today and planned the next month's inventory of guns and bombs and fucking smuggled diamonds," she forced through clenched teeth. "And you treat me like I needed wrapping in cotton wool. Have you forgotten the woman you married? Have you forgotten *who I am?*"

I swallowed and swallowed again, trying like hell to find the right words. "I guess I did." My honesty stunned her. I rubbed my temples. "I just wanted to protect you."

"You protect me by standing with me. *You* protect me by including me. How the fuck did you think this was going to go any other way?"

"You're so fucking tormented," I whispered. "So fucking sad, and I wanted to do this."

"You don't get it, do you?" she whispered. "You just don't see."

"I guess I don't," I answered. "You want to see them...you want to see the kind of things I've done to protect you, then go ahead. Get in the car, Evan. I'll show you who I really am."

FIFTY-SEVEN

Evan

He was really taking me. I glanced across the car to find his scowl deepening. Bright lights from oncoming cars blinded me as we headed for the city. Bruno hadn't spoken a word since climbing into the car, just stared straight ahead. His jaw clenched, hands fisting the wheel. I glanced over my shoulder to my overnight bag I'd thrown in the backseat, along with my coat.

He thought I wasn't serious. Then he found out just how serious I was.

Fear trembled through me. I wasn't going to stay if there were secrets. I've seen enough of the way my father treated my mother to know what was in store if I let this continue.

I wasn't my mother.

I wouldn't take the lying and the cheating.

I wouldn't take the secrets and the rage.

I wouldn't take anything less than pure, brutal honesty.

The drive back into the city was awful and quiet. I sat there, trying to keep hold of the rage I felt inside. But I just felt scared, I just felt anxious...and the darker Bruno became, the more afraid I became as well.

We pulled into the warehouse, waiting for the gate to roll open. We had three men working in the yard, under the guise of labor. But there was no mistaking the bulge under their jackets and the way their focus drifted along the street, watching the cars that passed behind us. We were under lockdown. There was no mistaking that. We drove in and parked around the rear. There were five more men who stood in the open; they carried guns as they watched the rear of the warehouse.

I glanced toward the bunker we had at the back of the warehouse. The one locked and secured and was off-limits to anyone who wasn't cleared by the Bernardis' or the Valachis'.

And in this case, those people were few.

Bruno pulled the Explorer into the garage and killed the engine. But he didn't climb out, just turned to me with fear in his eyes. "I really wish you wouldn't do this."

"Because you don't want me to find out the truth?"

Sadness cut across his face. He scowled deeper. "No. Because I don't want you to see what I really am."

It took all of my strength not to touch his cheek. "Bruno, I've always known who you really were. Why do you think I married you?" My voice was soft and somber. The truth was always much crueller than a lie.

He gave a nod, then climbed out of the car. I followed and, after I left my bag and coat in the back, we headed toward the bunker. His fingers moved across the keypad, punching in the numbers as he lifted his gaze to the camera poised above the door. I didn't need an explanation to know who was inside. Deviouz would be watching, maybe even Jannik, too.

The thought of seeing him again after all these months made me feel panicked. He was just as much in entwined with my nightmares as the bitch who stabbed me. My husband's cousin had been the one that drove me away from my father and the rest of my family. He'd been the one that made me fear the Bernardi name.

Until the island...

Bruno yanked open the door and held it open for me. He was the one who bought me back from that place alive, and the who made me realize that a name was just a name. That we control who we become, and that's why I fell in love with him.

The door closed with a *bang* behind us. I couldn't help but jump, and clamp down on the inside of my mouth, stifling a scream. Steps lead down into the darkness. The murky glow of light spilled across the bottom of the stairs, barely lighting the way.

"Grab hold of the railing, Evan." Bruno's hand brushed my arm, then closed around my wrist, guiding my hand to the railing. "I don't want you to fall."

I stepped, my ankle buckling until I found my feet.

"Careful, baby."

I licked my lips and kept going until I reached the bottom. The moment I did, my steps faltered. The stench of blood and fear hit me like a slap, one that reached around and gripped tight before dragging me back to that filthy bunker in my nightmares. My knees locked, and my feet refused to move...

"Evan," Deviouz murmured.

I flinched, my breath caught as my eyes adjusted to the gloom until I was able to spot four men kneeling in the middle of the bunker; their hands bound behind their backs and a black shroud over their heads.

I glanced at Deviouz. To those brown eyes that always seemed so warm and comforting but were now cold as stone. His jaw was hard, his scowl deepening as he cut Bruno a glare behind me. Still, my bodyguard said nothing, just watched as I stepped closer, dragging my gaze from the men in front of me to the wall of information behind them.

Six months.

Six months of watching. Six months of waiting, gathering every piece of evidence they needed to find the truth. These were the men...*these were the men who funded the attack on the island.*

This is what Bruno had been working on in the background as well as running the family business. I had no idea...

"Who are they?" My voice was hoarse. I licked my lips, cleared my throat, and tried again. "I said, who are they?"

In an instant, the sight of the blood and the bunker hit me. I couldn't breathe. Couldn't catch my breath and the pounding inside my head was deafening. The walls closed in, and it was too much like that hell where she left me to die. It was too much, too sudden, too real...

A sickening sound wrenched from my throat. I shook my head, trying to dislodge the image in front of me. But I couldn't do anything but stare at those men as they kneeled on the floor, with their hands clasped behind their backs and those black cloths over their heads. I wanted to see their faces. I *needed* to see their faces. But I couldn't. I couldn't do anything but turn around and run.

I shoved past Bruno and grasped the railing before I all but threw myself up the stairs and slammed against the door. But it wouldn't open. The lock held tight, closing me in. I shoved and shoved, driving my shoulder into the door.

"Evan!" Bruno roared. "Evan, for God's sake, *stop!*"

"I have to get out of here..." desperation was a shrill scream inside my head. *"Bruno, I have to get out!"*

Then he was there, shoving the door wide for me to stumble out into the cold, night air outside. I sucked in lungfuls. The world was spinning because I couldn't get enough air. I stumbled, dropped hard, and hit the ground. Agony tore through my knees. Bruno grabbed me with powerful hands, pulling me from the ground until I was against him. "Evan, baby. Talk to me."

I shoved against him. "Don't." I shook my head and moved backward before I turned and lunged toward the warehouse.

My hands were shaking. My fingers barely hit the buttons as I stabbed in the code for the lock and then yanked on the handle. I was inside before I knew, still I couldn't shake the image of that bunker, or the smell and knowing that this was it, this was the end...the end to the monsters who tried to kill us. Bruno's steps were heavy behind me. *"Evan, talk to me!"*

Talk to him?

Talk to...him.

"Bruno, don't."

"I told you," his voice was a growl behind me as I raced into the office and slammed my hands against his desk. The thud of boots muffled the pounding of my heart. It was all I could hear until the click of the lock came behind him. "I told you, Evan. I warned you it was too much."

I squeezed my eyes closed and shook my head. My hands braced on the edge of the desk. "I can't."

He slid his hands around my waist and pulled me against him. "Turn around, look at me." His voice was etched with fear.

I did as he demanded, opening my eyes before I turned to meet his stare. "Do you think I'm a monster?" he asked.

Was he a *monster?* The words hurt me to hear.

"Yes," I answered, slowly. "But aren't we all?" That was the truth of it. We were all monsters, each one worse than the other. Until there was no "other" left. Just beasts...killing, brutal beasts.

His body was so warm pressed against mine. "I tried to warn you." He lowered his head to murmur, "I tried to make you understand. There's no stopping this, Evan. No undoing what we've already done. No, what *they've* done." His hand slid along my back, and with my head pressed against his chest, I could hear the pounding of his heart.

"They're the ones who started this..." His words vibrated against my ear. "But I have to be the one who finishes it. To protect you."

Those last words hit home. *To protect you.* That's what drove Bruno. Me.

It was *always* me.

I couldn't do anything but hold on to him, sliding my hands along his back. He was so real in this moment so blindingly real and raw. Through the horror and the torment, something else rose to the surface. The kind of hunger that didn't deserve a place in what I'd just seen. Still, it was here and howling.

I clenched my fingers, fisting his shirt until I pulled him closer. Bruno looked down at me. That savage glare in his eyes sparkled with excitement. "Evan—"

I rose and wound my hand around the back of his neck, pulled him close until I kissed him. That heat turned to something alive. That's how he felt to me...*alive*.

Fierce yarning filled me. He kissed me back. His tongue pushing into my mouth as his hands slid over my body and cupped my ass. A moan tore free. That sound was all he needed, tearing him away for a second. His lips were red from the force of my mouth. "Evan, I—"

"Shut up, Bruno," I demanded, pulling him back down. "And fuck me."

I fumbled with the buttons of my blouse and kicked off my heels as my husband yanked at his belt. We were savage in that moment, desperate and aching. I shoved my slacks and panties down, stepping out before Bruno was on top of me, driving me back against the desk.

We scattered papers to the floor. I sent a coffee cup and pens and something else he was working on flying.

But I didn't care, and neither did he.

The room was filled with the dark, sultry scent of him. In my head, all those dark, tortured days where he spent hating and hunting slammed into me. Where he gave the order to take them...and set unmerciful events into motion.

"Jesus, woman," he growled the words out as he palmed my breast and drove me back onto his desk. His calloused thumb brushed my nipple, sending a shudder tearing straight to my clit. "Can't you see?" he murmured and licked his lips, dragging his hand from my breast to my side until he caressed the scar at my side. "Everything I do is for you."

I saw it now.

Saw just how deep I was under his skin.

And just how hard I drove him…giving him my love.

I reached up, slid my hands under his arms, and pulled him down. "I love you," I whispered. "Christ, I love you"

He reached between us, grabbed his cock, and aimed it against my core. "You drive me to madness," he gritted out, then bucked his hips.

Desire flooded me with the invasion. I dropped backward, leaning flat on his desk, leaving him to grab my hips and drive himself deeper. He was all I could feel, all I could see. All I wanted. His big hand splayed against my stomach as he thrust hard.

"You're…not…leaving…*me*," he growled out, bucking his hips. His eyes were dark and savage. "You got that? There is no *out*, Evan."

Desire slammed into me with his words. I gasped hold of the edge of the desk, widening my legs. "Deeper," I demanded. "Fuck me deeper, Bruno."

He leaned over, slid his hand around my throat, and squeezed. It wasn't hard enough to cut off my air, but it was forceful enough to make me realize just how serious he was.

"Till...death...do...we...part." His lips curled. His words savage as he thrust his cock into me.

Only I knew it wasn't a threat to my life...

No. I knew Bruno too well for that.

It wasn't a promise of taking care of me in sickness or weakness.

It was a promise of violence, of the kind of bloodthirsty ferocity that would terrify even the leaders of the Commission. My orgasm slammed into me, dragging a moan that rumbled in my chest. This was the making of Bruno. This was his play for power...only he didn't realize it.

With an unmerciful growl, he closed his eyes and gave one last thrust before stilling.

Hard breaths punctured the air.

Reality was slowly creeping in...

This was his making, and he didn't understand at all.

But I did...*I did.*

I pushed up on shaking limbs to slide my hands around his body. "No leaving." I forced the words around my gasps. "On the condition there are no lies, Bruno. No secrets. Not between us."

He pulled away, staring into my eyes and slowly gave a nod. "No secrets, not anymore."

I searched his gaze for a flicker of deceit. But there was none.

Some part of me knew there never would be again.

Because he knew what would happen if there was.

FIFTY-EIGHT

Bruno

Jesus Christ...

My breaths were savage, my pulse raced. I still buried my cock inside her. She'd think I was even more of a monster now. I pushed against the desk and glanced at the floor that was littered with the contracts of the three warehouses we were buying, as well as pens I'd signed them with. My office now looked like a goddamn bomb hit it.

Still I didn't care. I eased backward, looking down as my cock slid from her pussy. Her desire glistening on my shaft, I lifted my gaze as she turned to look at me over her shoulder.

"No more secrets," I whispered.

She turned, grabbed her panties and slacks, and pulled them up to cover herself. "Everything else can go to hell, Bruno. But we need to be honest with each other. If this marriage is going to work, it needs brutal honesty, and nothing less."

I gave a nod.

She adjusted her clothes, worked her blouse into place and smoothed down her hair before she leveled me with a stare. "I want to go back in there."

I flinched with the words. "What? No."

That flare of anger sparked in her eyes once more. That fierce determination to be what she was meant to be. And that was an unmerciful force. I tried to control my fear and my tone. "Are you sure about this?"

There was that steel steadfast look in her blue eyes. That plunging artic cold that forced her to keep going. This was the beast that saved her in that bunker that day. This was the determination that made her get up from that floor and keep moving, even as she bled out.

I'd seen glimpses of this Evan on the island when she fought not just for her life, but for mine as well.

"Yes," she answered. "I need to do this for myself."

I thought of her back in that place, staring at those men as they knelt on the concrete floor. She didn't understand what she was saying. She didn't understand who they were. But I knew. I knew how dark this went, and the loyalties that were ruined. Maybe I needed to trust that she was stronger than I thought.

If this moment gave me any kind of reflection, it was that.

"Are you prepared for what you will find?" I worked the buttons on my shirt, watching her.

"No, but that won't stop me anyway."

I knew at this moment it wouldn't.

"Okay." I met her gaze. "If you really need to do this, then let's do this. I'll be right there with you."

She straightened herself, inhaled hard and nodded. "Okay, I'm ready."

I opened the door, letting her walk through first as we headed back out of the warehouse. I didn't like the idea of her going back down in that bunker, but I wouldn't stop her. Not if it meant keeping things from her. I'd let her decide what she could handle. But she could be damn sure bet I was going to be right here for every damn second of it.

She pushed out of the warehouse, and I followed, making sure it locked behind me before we headed back to the bunker. Her fingers shook as she punched in the code, yet still, she never slowed. She yanked the door open and stepped into the darkness.

I followed her back down. This time she grabbed the railing, taking the steps slower until she reached the bottom. Deviouz was standing there, waiting as the moans and the whimpering from the four bound men continued. D glanced my way, one brow rising with a question: *Everything okay here?*

I gave a nod and turned my attention back to Evan, watching as her gaze moved to Jannick as my cousin stepped out of the darkness, followed by her father, Michele Valachi.

She reacted at the sight of my cousin, her breath caught, and her hands clenched at her side. But Jannick never spoke to her, just glanced my way.

"Evan." Her father glared, not impressed that his daughter was here in this blood and filth.

But she never answered, just turned her focus to the men kneeling in the middle of the room. Her focus shifted to the board against the wall at the end of the bunker, one filled with the information we needed to take these bastards down. But her attention didn't linger, instead she moved into the middle of the room, until she stopped in front of them.

My pulse thundered. She was too close, far too fucking close, making me break out in a damn sweat. Deviouz shifted beside me, his hand dropping to his gun. Neither of us wanted her here.

"Remove the coverings," she demanded.

I winced as Deviouz stepped forward. "I don't think that's a good idea—"

She never looked his way, just stared down at prisoners. "Remove. The. Coverings."

The bodyguard cut a glare my way. Still, he did as she demanded and stepped closer to Garland Cantrall and ripped off his hood.

Evan flinched, taking a step backward. I wanted to stand at her side, but I knew she had to do this on her own. Reese Mantrel was next. The tape across his mouth stretched tight as he jerked his gaze up to her and unleashed a muffled, savage roar. The bastard could howl all he wanted. I wasn't about to let her stand here and listen to the lying filth.

I stepped closer as Deviouz neared to the third man, and I steeled myself for my wife's reaction. D lifted the covering from Liam Petrov's head. There was a second before he glared up at her. There was blood crusted around his nose. The bastard put up a good fight, for a while at least. But he was no match for the brutality of Jannick.

"Liam?" Evan whispered. Her blue eyes grew wide as she met my stare.

I just gave a slow, careful nod. She wanted to know…now she did.

She took a step forward until Deviouz barked. "No!" His gaze tracked her movement. "Don't get too close, E."

One slow nod and she stepped backward. And the son of a bitch in front of her howled, his words indistinguishable.

"Dad?" Evan looked at her father. "He's your best friend. My uncle." Her words were a murmur as she wrapped her arms around her body.

"He's also a liar," I answered, as his muffled cries only grew louder. I took a step until I stood beside her, but I fixed my attention on him. "We have all the evidence we need."

"You funded the attack on the island?" she whispered.

The bowed man in front of her was silent. And for a second, I thought she was going to crumble… I thought she was going to break…until she took a step forward, whipped her hand through the air, and unleashed a slap across his face with a *crack!*

Liam's head rocked to the side. He fell, hitting the concrete hard.

"You tried to kill us!" she screamed, and the room rocked with the sound of her fury. "*You son of a bitch!* You son of a goddamn fucking bitch!"

She lunged, slamming into him with her fist, repeatedly. His eyes were wide, knees drawn to his chest. He tried to protect himself, but it was useless with his hands bound behind his back.

A blur of movement came from the only one still with his head draped in cloth. Harland Quinn lunged forward, tracking her by sound alone, and unleashed his fury as he slammed into my wife.

"No!" I roared, driving myself toward them.

And in the blur of an instant, the room erupted into chaos.

FIFTY-NINE

Bruno

"EVAN!" I SCREAMED AS THE FOUR MEN KNEELING IN FRONT of me lunged.

Screams erupted, coming from Deviouz, Jannick...and her father.

But all I could see was her. All I could feel was her. Adrenaline pumped through me, and in an instant, I was ripped from this bunker and thrown back into that island once more. All I could see was Evan as she was grabbed from behind by that bitch who tried to kill her on the island.

"No!" The three betraying bastards lunged in front of me, dragging me back to the bunker. One of them rushed me while the other two made for the stairs.

Bang!

The gunshot boomed inside the bunker. Liam Petroff fumbled, dropping to the ground. He was so quick, slipping his hands underneath him before he shoved upward and lunged; he grabbed Evan and slid his cuffed hands around her throat.

"No!" I roared as he yanked her with a savage jerk. Her hands flew backward and, for a second, her feet left the floor with the force. I made for him, driving toward him until his eyes widened and that tether around her throat grew tight.

One panicked yank and he tore the tape free from his mouth and sucked in hard breaths. "Come closer and I'll snap her goddamn neck." He yanked, making her eyes widen and her breath catch.

I froze and glanced at Evan as she gasped, shaking her head as Liam dragged her backward.

"There's no getting out of here," I forced the words through clenched teeth. "You're a dead man either way, Petrov."

"Then if I'm dead, I'll take Evan with me."

The sound of those words was a knife in my heart. My lips curled as I glanced at his hand. "You won't make it."

The words weren't a threat, but a promise.

Boom! Boom!

The crack of the gunshots boomed inside the bunker. But Petrov jerked, yanking the cuffs tighter around her neck.

Screams erupted behind me as Petrov stumbled backward, using my wife as a shield.

I turned my head, leveling at Jannick as he took aim at Petrov's head. "*No!*" I roared.

Evan unleashed a gasp as Petrov stumbled backward, skirting Deviouz. "Let me go, Bernardi." He yanked her harder against him. "Let me go or I will fucking kill her now."

She shook her head. "*No.*" Her word was a hiss.

"There's no getting out of this." I shook my head. "You're dead either way." I took a step closer, my gaze fixed on his as though I could somehow draw his focus to me and only me. "So let her go."

His eyes were wild, cutting to Jannick behind me before he leveled his glare at me. "The bitch didn't die before, but she will now if you take one more fucking step, Bernardi."

I saw that connection in her eyes, saw the moment reality hit home. Her blue eyes darkened until they were almost steel. Her lips curled, baring her teeth, and there was that fighter I knew.

There was the Evan who wasn't just my wife, but who was a Valachi.

She yanked her arm backward, then drove her elbow into Petroff's side.

The bastard doubled over. The air was nothing more than a hiss as it left his lungs.

She spun, still clutched in his hands. "You tried to fucking kill me!" She unleashed her blow, slamming into his shoulder. "I loved you!"

She tried to wrestle out of his hold, but Petroff held tight, clinging to her.

There was no stopping her now. No holding back her pain and her fury. Her blows were wild, slapping and punching as she unleashed a tirade of blows. Petrov stumbled backward, his hold easing around her neck. Then she stopped, grabbed a hold of his shirt with both hands, and drove her knee into his balls.

He doubled over, his hold slipping over her head as she ducked and kept on hitting him, driving her fist into his nose. *"You fucking bastard! You fucking, goddamn bastard!"*

Petrov's head snapped backward, and I rushed forward, pushing her out of the way. My hands were around his throat in an instant as I yanked him close. "You will *never* touch my fucking wife again." I stilled. "You understand me?" I drove my fist into the bastard's face, watching his head snap backward.

But Evan wasn't done. Unleashing a scream, she lunged, pummeling him as she screamed. *"You fucking bastard!"*

"You should've died on that island!" he howled, blood spurting from his nose.

Smack.

My fist hit his nose. Blood gushed out, splashing against my arm.

His screams were nothing more than whimpers. "You should've died, all of you should've died!"

Smack!

Crunch!

I drove my knuckles into his face. Through the pummeling and smacks of fists on flesh, Petrov hissed. "You should've all died."

That was the last straw. The last words I wanted to hear from his mouth. I clenched my fist around his throat and squeezed, driving all my strength into that pressure. His face turned white. Eyes bugged out of his head. I squeezed and squeezed, unleashing my rage until it was all I could think of.

Protect her!

Save her!

There was no breath for him, no air...

His hands slapped my arms. His feet flailed, kicking desperately against the ground. But there was no getting out of this. They wanted us dead, yet he was the one who was dying now...

Minutes were all it took. Still, it felt like a lifetime as I waited for his movements to come to a stop. When I released my hold, a single slow breath released with a hiss, and he dropped to the floor.

"Bruno..." Evan choked words were all I heard

I jerked my gaze to her, then lunged, pulling her against me. My words were hoarse and husky as I ran my bloody hands over her body and cupped her face, staring into her eyes. "Are you okay?"

She nodded "Yes. I'm okay."

Thank God...

SIXTY

Bruno

"EVAN."

Her breaths were hard and heavy as she turned to me. There was a spark of fear. I lifted my hand and brushed her cheek. "Are you okay?"

She froze, her chest stilling for a second before she lowered her gaze to the dead man at my feet. My hands ached, fingers burned, still curled with the memory of being wrapped around Petrov's neck. Then she gave a slow nod.

"You scared the fuck out of me." I slid my murdering hands around her, drawing her against my chest. "When he grabbed you like that I thought…"

She clung to me, fisting my shirt in her hands. Hands that were flecked with blood. "I'm okay," she whispered, repeating the words to herself. "I'm okay."

"What the fuck happened?" Deviouz strode toward us, his gun still in his hand.

I looked down at my curled fingers, still feeling the blows on Petrov's face. "Everything is okay now."

My bodyguard moved closer to Petrov, giving him a kick to make sure he was dead. But it was Jannik who drew my wife's focus. The gun was still in his hand, still aimed at the two dead men at the bottom of the stairs.

We bought four men in alive, and now they were all leaving in body bags.

"Evan." Deviouz moved to her side. "Are you okay?"

She gave a nod. "Yeah, thanks to Bruno," she said as she lifted her gaze to me. Christ, my heart felt like it was gonna come out of my chest. I stepped closer, pulling her against me once more.

My hand slipped over her body, I could feel the pounding of her heart against my chest, and it took all my strength not to carry her from this place back into the quiet of my office, to undress her, to search her body for every goddamn bruise and scrape. I needed to feel her warmth, feel her heartbeat, feel the life throbbing in her veins.

I just needed to feel *her*...

"This is a goddamn mess," Michelle Valachi muttered.

It took all my strength not to lunge across the room and grab the bastard by the throat. Instead, I pinned him to his spot with a glare. "It wouldn't have been had we just stuck with the plan in the first place."

The plan that had my wife safe at fucking home, not in the middle of the goddamn city.

There was a flinch in his eyes before he glanced at his daughter. The bastard knew damn well what he'd done. Deviouz moved to each body, then set to work, dragging them into the center of the room.

"So, what the Hell do we do now?" Michele Valachi looked at me like I had all the goddamn answers.

"We do what we've always done," I answered, holding his daughter against me as I turned to Deviouz. "We clean house and then we protect what's ours."

I grabbed my cell out of my pocket and pressed the button. A curt and careful tone answered me on the second ring. An address was all I gave before I gave Deviouz a nod. My bodyguard straightened, dropping Petrov's feet to the floor, then grabbed his cell and punched out a message.

Jannick set to work, removing any identification on the bodies, rings, wallets. Their cells had already been destroyed and left behind before they even came near the place.

"Evan, baby. You might want to go home for this." I glanced her way, hating the thought of her leaving. She looked shellshocked. Not a good time to leave her on her own, especially after what it just happened.

"No." She rolled up her sleeves, and started helping D, rifling through the dead man's pockets, pulling out anything that could lead back to us.

"It seems as though you have this handled, Evan," Michele muttered, giving a nod to his daughter.

But my wife barely gave him so much as a glance, just rose from one body and moved to the next as her father turned and left, disappearing into the gloom of the stairs, leaving behind only the thud of his boots.

Only then did Evan look his way.

I caught the twitch in the corner of her cheek as he disappeared. Her father was a cold, ruthless man...and the only one standing in her way of taking over the seat on the Commission.

I glanced at the pile of bodies at her feet. The bastards were the last connection to the events that happened on the island. The last fucking tether that held us trapped in that place. They came to kill all of us one by one, and yet we survived.

That trapped *her* in that place. We were the ones who severed the connection.

Not the Salvatores. Not the Rossi's. The Bernardi's...and the Valachi's.

Me...

And Evan.

We were the ones making a play for lead chair on the Commission.

Deviouz straightened and grabbed his cell as the screen brightened. "The cleaners are here." He glanced my way.

"Go." He looked from Evan to me. "We'll take care of this."

"Will we?" Jannick snapped.

Deviouz glared at my cousin. The man had all but raised the both of us over the years. "Yes," he answered, earning a glare. "We will."

"Fine," Jannick mumbled. "Whatever."

The door above buzzed, drawing Deviouz's attention. He looked at the cameras.

"The cleaners are here." Then turned his focus to me. "Go, both of you."

"Okay." I crossed the room and reached out, giving her my land.

She took it, then jerked away when she saw the blood on the tips of her fingers.

"Here." I grabbed a handkerchief from my pocket and wiped the blood from her fingers before tossing it on top of the bodies.

I led her to the stairs, pushing open the door as the clean-up crew waited.

They didn't need instruction, just for us to be out of their way. I gladly left them, pulling Evan with me as we made for the Explorer. I unlocked the vehicle and wiped the handle of the door and opened it for her.

We were inside in a heartbeat, and we'd backed out of our parking space and drove through the gates of the warehouse before I finally gave in and exhaled.

"It's really over?" she asked.

I glanced at her and gave a smile. "Yes, it's really over."

And it was...finally.

I OPENED the rear door of our home and waited for her to step in. Three men patrolled the grounds. But inside this house, it was just us. No bodies, no impending attacks. Just a quietness. Just her.

I grabbed her hand, leading her along the hallway, through the kitchen, then up the stairs to our bedroom before I turned.

"You scared the hell out of me today." I work the buttons on her blouse and let the clothes fall at her feet.

I'd burn them by morning, and the cleaners would come and clean the car and everything else we'd touched.

She held my stare. "You scared me."

I leaned down, capturing the point of her chin until I took her mouth. Her body pressed against mine, the warmth comforting. I worked the buttons of my own shirt, shedding my clothes before I led her into the shower, making sure the water was hot.

She shuddered against me, her teeth chattering. She wasn't cold, but in shock. We both were. We showered in silence, then stepped out, dried ourselves, and went to bed, sliding under the sheets naked.

But there was no sex tonight, just warmth and comfort. I held her in my arms and closed my eyes. Still, sleep was a long way from us. I held her against me until the silence of the night became comforting. By the time the sun rose and peeked through the curtains, we were calm.

"Bruno?"

"Mmm."

She lifted her gaze to mine. "I think I'd like that trip to Paris now."

I leaned down, brushed her lips with mine, and whispered. "Your wish is my command."

Epilogue

EVAN

The sounds of the smell of the city hit me the moment we pulled up outside The Four Seasons Hotel in Paris, and the rear door of the limousine opened. The scent of freshly baked bread and coffee wafted over me as the greeter opened the door and held out his hand.

"Madame." He smiled. "Welcome to Paris."

We touched down at night time, before climbing into the hire car and headed for the city. The tour through the bright lights of Paris was spectacular to say the least. My breath still raced, that excitement building like the flutters in my chest. It took me a long time to realize that we're finally here.

The wheels of our jet skid against the tarmac, and we were out, breathing in freedom.

Freedom...

In Paris. The city I'd dreamed of seeing.

Bruno rounded the rear of the car. The concierge just smiled and gave a slow nod as he made for the rear of the car and hauled out our luggage. I took my husband's hand, giddy with promise. Because that's what it felt like now. A fresh start and finally hope of the future, no longer filled with the ghosts of our past.

"We are finally here," I whispered as Bruno close the door behind me.

He smiled, grabbing my hand tighter. "We are finally here."

It was our dream to come here. A dream that hadn't eventuated until now. Before this we couldn't escape the fear of what happened to the island happening again.

So, we closed ourselves off, barricaded behind fences and guards with assault rifles while we waited for change.

This was change...

We had changed.

Doors of the hired car closed with a thud. The concierge grabbed our bags as we made our way into the lobby. The moment the glass doors closed behind us we became swallowed by a vacuum of silence.

Bruno headed to the reception desk and slid his card across the counter. The check-in attendant gave me a warm, bright smile. Although she spoke in French, Bruno knew enough to fumble his way through the conversation, gaining keys to our room after he finished checking us in.

I couldn't help but chuckle at him as he glanced my way and grimaced. Seconds later, he was striding toward me, and he motioned for the elevator. We rode all the way up to one of the executive suites, then waited as the bellhop ushered our luggage inside.

Warm caramel sheer chiffon curtains fluttered, catching a breeze from outside the moment we stepped in. It was beautiful, brown and black, mirrored with warm beige tiles and soft, plush carpets. We waited while our bags were unpacked, and they stored away our clothes. Bruno's focus never shifted from me, waiting until the bellhop was finished. Bruno tipped him, walking to the front door, and closing it behind him.

The faint sound of the city drifted in. Horns blared under the drone of the traffic. Still, I pushed the sounds aside and watched my husband as he strode along the hallway toward me. And this moment felt far too perfect...

As though we didn't deserve it.

A smile trembled at the corners of my mouth as Bruno spoke. "God I've never seen anything so beautiful as you are right now."

My smile faltered as fear pushed in. Then, in an instant, he closed the rest of the distance between us and slid his powerful hands around my waist. "I want it all when it comes to you, Evan. I want it all."

He leaned down, brushed his lips across mine, and I couldn't stop the flutter in my chest. My hands went around him, pulling him close. I wanted it all when it came to him as well. Every single thing...

The good.

And the bad.

He broke the kiss to whisper against my ear. "Smile, baby. We're in Paris."

And that made me smile. "We are in Paris," I repeated. "We're... in...Paris."

His hands slid over my ass, cupping me hard against him. "And I'm about to fuck you in the most beautiful, consuming way."

I let out a chuckle as he worked the buttons of my blouse and I followed, tugging off his jacket and his shirt.

He lifted me up and carried me across the bedroom until we fell, hitting the mattress before we sank into the soft comforter.

"Christ, you are so beautiful," he whispered. "I'm so damn lucky to call you my wife."

"Bruno?"

He left his head. "Yeah?"

I held his gaze, the words stuck in my head. Still, they couldn't come out. I knew what the doctors said; after the attack and the knife wound there was a strong chance I'd never carry a child. Would marriage without children be enough for him? Would *I* be enough for him? I didn't know.

"Nothing touches us here," he whispered as he dragged his finger along the edge of my jaw, lifting my gaze. "Okay?"

I gave a slow nod. "Okay."

He lowered his head, kissing my mouth, then my neck, and worked his way lower until he found the swell of my breasts. Warmth closed around my nipple as he took me into his mouth. I unleashed a moan as he kissed all the way down my stomach until he met the crease of my pussy. Lips, tongue. He slid his finger along my center and gently pushed in deep. "So goddamn beautiful."

I lowered my gaze, watching him as he tasted me. My hand went to the back of his head, fingers sliding through his hair. Bruno was right. This was perfect. This was enough. I didn't need to think about the future because I was sure the future was thinking about me.

It was planning, scheming. I didn't know what it had installed.

But I knew one thing. That whatever happened, Bruno would be by my side, and I'd be beside him.

I unleashed a moan as desire flooded my body. The stroke of his tongue stoked the flames before he rose upward, leaving me to reach down, clenching my hand around his cock.

God, I loved how he loved me. All-consuming. Strengthening.

And always protective...

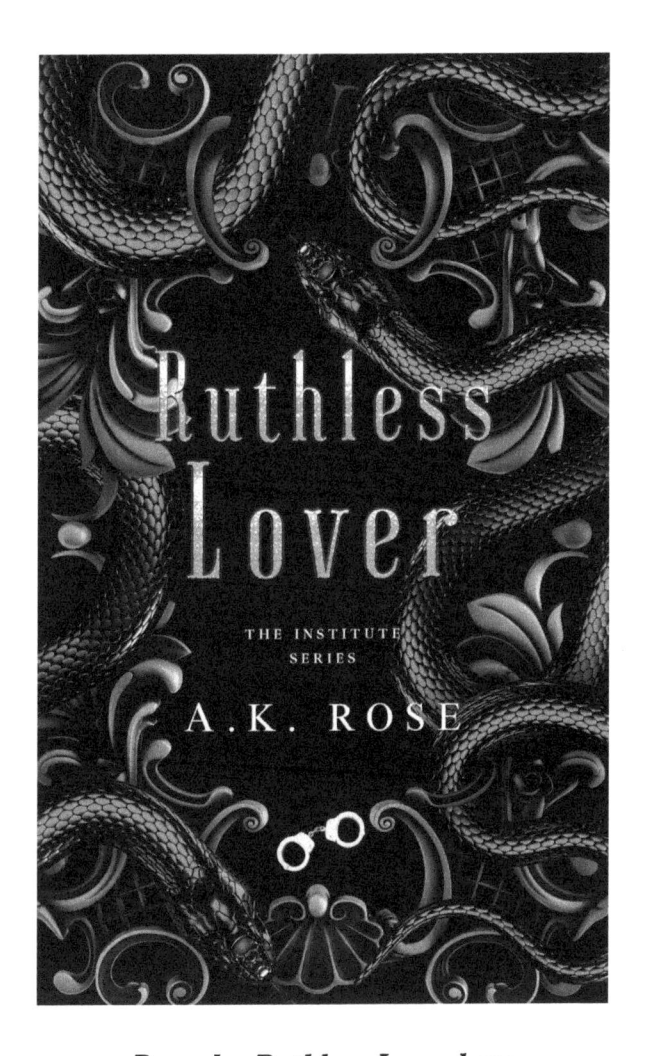

Preorder Ruthless Lover here

She hated me…in the most savage, violent way. I deserved it all.

Her fists. Her rage.

But I didn't deserve her love.

Leila Ivanov, daughter to a dangerous Russian Czar is the perfect woman.

Smart, resourceful, stunningly beautiful with piercing blue eyes and a wicked smile.

But that's not why I wanted her.

I needed to find a way out of the mess I created.

A mess where the CIA came knocking on my door armed with information.

Information that was dangerous...*and could get me killed.*

And I'd use the wrath of her family to escape it.

But amongst the deceit I found myself falling for her quiet perfection and her deep, throaty laughter.

I found myself falling for her.

Until it was too late...

Those I'd been running from came for me...but they found her instead.

Now I'm staring at the bruises on her face and the betrayal in her eyes.

and I'm on my knees begging her to stay.

I'll do anything. Pay any price. *Kill any man I had to*...even if it means my end.

Because a life without her...is no life at all

.

Milton Keynes UK
Ingram Content Group UK Ltd.
UKHW020721290923
429627UK00015B/753